# THE DEVIL AT HOME

Also by Oliver Lange

*Defiance—An American Novel* (formerly titled
   *Vandenberg*)
*Incident at La Junta*
*Red Snow*
*The Land of the Long Shadow*
*Next of Kin*
*Pas de Deux*

# THE DEVIL AT HOME

## OLIVER LANGE

STEIN AND DAY / *Publishers* / New York

First published in 1986
Copyright © 1986 by Oliver Lange
All rights reserved, Stein and Day, Incorporated
Designed by Louis A. Ditizio
Printed in the United States of America
STEIN AND DAY/*Publishers*
Scarborough House
Briarcliff Manor, N.Y. 10510

**Library of Congress Cataloging in Publication Data**

Lange, Oliver.
  The devil at home.

  I. Title.
PS3562.A485D48   1986      813'.54      85-40256
ISBN 0-8128-3041-5

For Nancy

# THE DEVIL AT HOME

# part one

It is taught: if one dies laughing, it is a
good sign for him.
                    —*The Talmud (Kethuboth)*


I will leap laughing into my grave because
the feeling that I have five million people
on my conscience will be for me a source
of extraordinary satisfaction.
                    —*Eichmann*

THE VIEW, OR vista, that the squinting eye now beheld at leisure was, if one cared for that sort of thing, rather spectacular.

To the uninitiated the topography might have seemed strange, the terrain alien, but the colors, well, they were enough to challenge the palette of a Tintoretto. Sublime pinks and subtle reds in all their infinite shadings—corals, raspberries, fuchsias—and, caught here and there in the folds of crenellated valleys, streaks of brown that ranged from burnt umber to raw sienna, even ocher.

Beneath the bright illumination the colors of this landscape shone glossily, wetly—traceries of cerulean blue and, at one side, a fungating mass whose base was a somber carmine that abruptly shaded to violet and then, toward the crest, turned into an engorged angry purple, like a sunset Vesuvius.

"Done yet?" Carl Mast inquired patiently, but not too patiently, or timidly either. The voice, a roupy baritone reminiscent of shoreside surf or gravel tumbling down a tin roof, did not belong to a man whose emotional baggage was encumbered by patience or timidity.

"A little longer," Meyer replied in his kindly fashion.

"Longer? How much is longer?"

"Not much."

"Figured you'd left for lunch," Mast said. He sighed and then, as though addressing Mecca, bowed his head onto his crossed arms.

"Have a peek," Meyer said to White, his colleague. The two switched places and it was White's turn to peer into the Zeiss eyepiece. Meyer murmured, "See? Right upper quadrant?"

White, by far the less committal of the two, observed at length and finally nodded. "Indeed."

The two stared at each other. So much can be said in a glance. In the lifted eyebrow: a world of opinion. In the slightly pursed lips: a fund of knowledge. Mutually shared, agreed upon.

With a faint sucking sound the colonoscope was gently withdrawn. Carl Mast, emitting an exasperated groan at one end and a stray bit of flatulence at the other, raised his head: "A regular quick-draw McGraw, that's you, Meyer."

"You may get up now, Carl," Meyer said.

Carl Mast did, frowning. He disliked the quasiavuncular use of his given name. *You may get up now, Carl.* Doctor to patient, and the patient himself a physician. Meyer, a friendly sort. Well, that was okay. Anyone who earned his daily bread by looking up *arschlochs* had a right to be as friendly as Mister Rogers if he wanted.

Mast regarded the proctologist. Meyer, in his middle fifties, white-smocked, bespectacled, and of serious mien, was young enough to be a son. White, the colleague, also of the proctological persuasion, even younger.

Both men were intently scrutinizing the instrument that had recently been unplugged from him.

An impressive device, over two and a half feet long, resembling a black, neoprene-sheathed electrical cable, with a kind of pistol grip to which were attached various levers and knobs, as well as suction and $CO_2$ triggers. The flexible tip of this snaky monster contained a port for the fiber-optic and lens system, an aspiration port, a biopsy port for the long forceps-snare, and a $CO_2$ vent that enabled portions of the sigmoid, as well as the descending, transverse, and ascending colon to be inflated. Via the up-down and left-right knobs, this state-of-the-art instrument was capable of threading itself through the colon, following every twist and curve, pausing here and there for a peek at a polyp or to suction or snip a sample, searching, with the help of lubricating jelly, ever deeper, until the patient might, with some justification, wonder which end of him was being examined.

Carl Mast, gazing at the colonoscope without affection, said, "Must be fun driving that thing. You guys need a license to operate the brakes and turn indicators?"

Meyer and White: as intent in their examination of this utensil as two small beach-roaming boys who have stumbled upon a rare and mysterious treasure suddenly cast up at their feet by the sea.

Mast peered too, leaning closer. "See anything? Gold dust? Precious metals?"

12

"You should be so lucky, Carl," Meyer said.

"That," frowned Mast, pointing accusingly, "unless I'm greatly mistaken, is shit. I'm virtually certain of it. Am I right boys, or am I right?"

White nodded. "No blood, though."

"Sorry about that," Mast said. "Want to poke some more?"

"No. When was the last discharge?"

"Yesterday," Mast told them. "Dark, perhaps two or three cc's."

Meyer placed the colonoscope in a sink and then handed Mast a towelette and a gauze pad moistened with liquid soap. The old man used the latter to scrub vigorously between his buttocks and then wiped himself with the towelette. His expression was austere, even grim, but not without a certain dour amusement.

He was famous—many said infamous—for his humor. Meyer and White knew this. In fact, Carl Mast was famous period. Nodding toward the instrument, he remarked, "In med school we called that a silver bullet."

Meyer permitted himself a slight smile.

"I suppose the jokes about proctologists haven't changed much," Mast said.

"Probably not," Meyer said respectfully. Fame, after all, was fame.

"The proctologist who begins his examination by placing a hand on your shoulder is a caring person," Mast said. He finished with the towel. "The one who begins by placing both hands on your shoulders is up to no good."

Meyer and White smiled thinly. They'd heard that one a thousand times. "Get dressed, Carl," Meyer said.

Still naked except for Supp-Hose stockings, Mast seemed in no hurry. "So? Now you know my innermost secrets?" He cocked his head at them quizzically. "All right, what gives?"

His speech, White mused, was intriguing. It captured the attention. The English—or rather American—was idiomatically flawless, at times erudite, cultured (White had once heard the old man speak on TV, on behalf of UNICEF), but just as often Mast showed a penchant for the bite of colloquial slang, nor was he above occasionally indulging in dialects that would have been corny, if not actually offensive, in a person of lesser renown. But, there it was. Genius was apparently not bound by noblesse oblige, and Dr. Carl Mast, it would seem, was equally at ease addressing the United Nations on a pressing matter concerning the World Health Organization (senior members of which he and his late wife had been for many years) and haggling over the price of lox in any Manhattan deli. Mast's familiarity with the language in all its shadings was marred only by an accent that announced to even the deafest ear that he was foreign-born. The accent was German. Actually, Swiss-German. Mast hailed from Zurich.

Swiss-German, Dr. White thought now: or, more than likely, Swiss-Jew. For whatever reasons—and weren't there always reasons?—White mused, the old man had somewhere along the line cast off the Star of David. Had not he himself, born Weisenstein, become White, for the "euphony" of it?

IN RESPONSE TO his patient's "What gives?" Meyer said, "Let's talk in the office."

"Fine," Mast said, tossing the towelette into a bin. "Do you moochers have any of my ouzo left, or have you been schlupping it on the side?"

"No, we have it," White said diffidently. "It's one reason we look forward to seeing you as much as we do." He glanced at his watch. "Five to five. Right on time."

That was a demand of Mast's, to be the last patient of the day. After the examination—this was his fourth visit in as many weeks—they would sit down over snifters for a low-pressure chat ... about him. He'd brought the liter of ouzo to alleviate and make more palatable any discussion of his symptoms: the bloody stools, the sensation of lower abdominal "fullness," the vague pains where no pains should be.

Naturally, Meyer had straight-off forbidden all alcohol. "It'll be impossible to judge the results of the lab tests. As for the medications ..." And so on and so forth.

To which Carl Mast, in that powerful German accent, had replied, "Please! Forget the reforming, can't we?"

So the liquor was tolerated not only as a concession to an important and obviously ill patient but as a way by which three mature men, a trio of professionals in the best sense of the term, might relax for a few minutes while they discussed certain matters that, at best, could only be described as depressing.

At that moment the door to the examining room swung open and Mrs. Farquahr, Meyer's and White's office nurse, stepped through it.

Mast held in one hand his shorts, preparatory to donning them. They were of the boxer variety, white cotton, loose, airy in the legs and bottom, comfortably baggy, with an elastic waistband.

Standing easily beside the examining table on which only minutes earlier he had crouched froglike on cocked elbows and knees,

14

his rump raised to Doctors Meyer's and White's flexible invader, Mast was . . . the only word is: ancient.

In appearance he resembled a kind of humanized caricature, though far less hairy, of one of those elderly orangutans that are on view in various zoos, those sad, grieving old fellows who, slumped and seated in an attitude of total defeat, always look as though they are waiting for a city transit bus to drive up and whisk them away, patient, resigned, unaware that no bus stops in front of their cage. Or perhaps, more precisely, Mast resembled a caricature of a human that might have been drawn by an orangutan, which is a dubious proposition, since orangs, among all primates, are notably bad drawers. But if an orang *had* an artistic flair and if he had an urge to create an impression of an extremely old and decrepit human, the end result on paper might very well come close to what Mast was in the flesh.

In itself, the face was no mystery. It had been seen often on television and in periodicals: long-jawed, quite fleshless, seamed and wrinkled, the simian eyes deeply set, alert, always moving, on guard, eternally suspicious, crafty. The nose a hooked blade, like that of a blunt tomahawk. The brows bushy, and the mouth . . . but that was a little difficult to tell. All of it was hidden under an impressive handlebar of a mustache, white, untidy, indifferently trimmed, and stained at its walrus fringes by the chemical reactions of Turkish coffee, tea, bourbon, vodka, ouzo, and the Gauloises that Mast was so fond of and that he virtually chain-smoked, not such a small feat for a fellow his age. The ears were literally outstanding, protruding from a domed skull that was devoid of hair except for a snow-white fringe which, as though to make up for that which had vanished elsewhere, Mast wore collar-length. A dignified turkey dewlap wobbled beneath the chin, and the dome of the skull and the wrinkled face were colored Bermuda brown, indicating that Mast either visited that island's sunny shores or used an ultraviolet lamp. As a matter of fact, he did both.

Certain women seeing that face were prone to conjecture that as a younger man Mast must have been "rather interesting," "interesting" being a euphemism for "sexually attractive." Mast had never been what might be called handsome, but interesting? Well, why not? The old fellow had undoubtedly had his adventures, although to date he had refused to dictate his memoirs on the grounds that his personal life was "scarcely worth recording," a sure sign of a too-reluctant virgin or else a shrewd old whore with plenty to keep hidden. Or perhaps Mast was merely waiting for the right bid from one

15

of the larger book clubs, not that he needed the money. In addition to being famous—his career had, once or twice, but of late with increasing regularity, been likened to Albert Schweitzer's—he was financially well off. Not exactly wealthy. Not really wealthy, anyway. Just well off. Well *enough* off, that is.

Though the naked shoulders sagged, the chest was strong, starkly ribbed, the flesh of the breasts wrinkled and drooping, covered with a shag of wiry white hair. The stomach: a comfortable kettle, a friendly Falstaffian protuberance dimpled by a navel and ornamented with a cicatrix salute—a diagonal appendicitis scar from long ago. Below, more hair, and the genitalia: Mast's precious jewels, slung low in their rugose sack, and the penis. Circumsized, White noted, as did Nurse Farquahr, a narrow, veined, slender shaft, which, though tumescence was not the problem (and probably had not been for some time), was of an eye-stopping length, easily six-plus inches. Some thumper, thought White. Had the younger Mast been "interesting?" Indisputably.

The thighs were skinny, the knees gnarled protrusions that would have looked more at home on hallowed oaks and, here and there, were bits and tufts of lank snowy hair, like the shredded remnants of spun glass dangling from the naked branches of abandoned Christmas trees. The calves, encased in their Supp-Hose, were, oddly, marvelously well-shaped. Mast the Younger had perhaps been athletic. The entire epidermis, ruined by age, so scarred and blasted by time that it resembled an ill-used elephant hide, was crisscrossed by an unsightly tracery, the surface network of an antique circulatory system: blue veins and red arteries everywhere, some—no, many—varicose, so that the skin was mottled and splotched. All this, along with an assortment of wens, warts, freckles, keratoses, lumpy cysts and minor keloids, proved beyond any arguable doubt that Mast the Elder was not merely old, but *very* old.

He stood there calmly eyeing Mrs. Farquahr as she, just as calmly, eyed him. Mast was not in the least modest or shy. Finally she, who had been a nurse for thirty years and seen it all, said easily, "Oh, I'm sorry, Doctor Mast. I thought you'd dressed already."

The old eyes glinted—with amusement or malice, White could not tell. There was something about those eyes that he did not like. They were too watchful, too knowing, at the same time revealing nothing. Who knew what lay behind such eyes? They could almost be the eyes of a madman, White decided. But then, wasn't it true—some madmen were saints? And, *mutatis mutandis,* some saints madmen?

16

The eyes judiciously regarded Mrs. Farquahr. And then Mast spoke. Or rather the words were suddenly audible, since the mouth that formed them was hidden by the drooping mustache. The words simply popped into existence, the way eggs leave a hen's ovipositor: "You were expecting maybe Arnold Schwarzenegger?"

The vaudeville-Jew dialect again. So needless in one so great, thought White. Swiss, my foot. I'll bet he wears his yarmulke in the shower!

"SO NOW WE talk?" Carl Mast said. He lifted his ouzo in a toast to Meyer and White: *"Zum wohl!"* and downed the glass's contents neat.

Both men raised their own glasses, White murmuring the proctological salute: "Here's looking at you."

They were seated in the interviewing office the two specialists shared. Walnut-veneer paneling. Shelved against one wall: medical books, a number of which dealt with the endless problems encountered by the human digestive tract, lower latitudes. Also numerous weighty tomes on genito-urinary diseases. This, in addition to proctology, was White's forte. He and Meyer made a swell team. As far as renal and ano-genital disorders were concerned, the pair had the east side of Manhattan sewed up.

On Meyer's desk: a large framed Kodachrome of his wife and children—all frowns, squints, and smiles. Behind them loomed the Meyer manse, American-colonial, red brick and split shingle: behind that, a tasteful array of trees of the sort indigenous to Scarsdale, Dobbs Ferry, or Great Neck. The foreground was bisected by the terrifically elongated shadow of a hulking figure, presumably Meyer Pere, shooting with the late-afternoon sun at his back. In the curved driveway: a freshly waxed silver-gray Bentley sedan, poised as though ready to leap into fray against Merritt Parkway traffic. Meyer adored that Bentley as much, in fact more (though he did not admit to this) than he did his wife, an admirable woman and mother, nifty Norma, who spent an enormous amount of her time and their money on needy distant relatives of hers, including some great-aunts and great-uncles she had never even met. Norma was a family girl.

White's desk displayed a black-and-white professionally posed studio portrait of his cherished only issue, Melody by name, profile shot, the better to display the classy retroussé nosejob he'd bought her last summer. She was at Vassar, studying something. No one knew quite what. Least of all White.

Carl Mast reached for the bottle on Meyer's desk, poured himself another two fingers, then inserted a fresh Gauloise into the center of the opening that presumably existed somewhere beneath the hirsute cowcatcher of a mustache and fired up. Twin streams of gray smoke jetted from his nostrils. There was a brief fit of coughs, wheezes, gasps, and barks, after which Mast settled back into the comfortable leather armchair, suddenly all business. No more comic dialect stuff. That aspect of him seemed to have been voided along with the first thick cloud of Gauloise smoke.

Cigarette in one hand, drink in the other, Mast said, "Have you anything of interest to tell me about this excrementitious carcass of mine?"

Meyer eyed the cigarette with open disapproval. Gauloises are to a "light" cigarette what a glue factory is to a rose and Meyer, a nonsmoker, felt his eyes watering. "I hope you've at least cut down," he said, opting to let slide the ouzo business. Mast certainly had something to drink about.

"A mere pack a day," Mast replied, obviously fibbing. The insides of his fore- and middle fingers were stained dark brown. Seeing the doubtful look on Meyer's face Mast went on peevishly, "Meyer, for God's sake, what the hell do you want? There's a point beyond which worry and concern become unconstructive and, quite frankly, a ridiculous waste of your time and mine."

Meyer and White, both decent, caring men, stared at their patient who, imbued with an aloof grandeur, was clearly less perturbed than they.

Dressed, Mast presented a somewhat more attractive overall image than the stripped version Mrs. Farquahr's mildly startled gaze had encountered not many minutes earlier. Quite the grandfatherly type—if, that is, one was prepared to accept as grandfatherly an authoritarian old curmudgeon who obviously was used to having his own way. The present Mast exuded confidence, a studied calm, and an air of sophistication, even imperiousness. Had he grandchildren (he did not, he thanked God), Mast would never have dreamed of dandling them on an heirloom knee. He looked entirely capable of striking or kicking out at any chirping prepubescent who might test his patience or loose his anger. In fact he disliked children, in the flesh anyway, although there was incontestable evidence that via his decades of work with the World Health Organization and other international organizations several millions of children around the world were alive and flourishing who might otherwise have perished of famine and disease; and, in particular, he loathed American children, whom Mast had once described (on "Meet the Press," no less) as "a revolting gaggle of pampered brats and pimpled young neurotics, devoted to Punk and Pac-Man, both of which interests are bound to insure their future intellectual and moral bankruptcy."

In the following two weeks NBC received over three thousand letters from indignant moms and pops. By then Mast was in Paraguay. Amnesty International had begged him to lend his good name and influence to an investigation of alleged military brutality against a faction of rampaging machete-wielding mountain peasantry. That was very much Mast's style. He did not seem to seek the limelight. In fact, most of his life's work had been performed behind the scenes. Occasionally, however, the public's attention was drawn to him, as was that of certain committees in Stockholm and Oslo. He had, as Meyer and White knew, won this year's Nobel Peace Prize. It was rumored that his name had been submitted in three previous years. Age and failing health, it was said, had played a significant part in earning him this eleventh-hour accolade.

As for his outer appearance, it was less formidable than the personality, though in excellent taste. Dark-blue pin-striped suit of superior woolen material, tailored in the European style, single-breasted, conservative, a shade old-fashioned. A vest of the same material successfully encapsulated the chest and paunch. Black English oxfords. The tie a striped gray-and-maroon: Windsor knot. On a rack in a corner hung a gray overcoat, more specifically a chesterfield, with a sheared beaver collar. Draped over it, a practical wool muffler, for this December day's inclement weather. Lastly: a Borcelino fedora of soft black felt, with an extraordinarily wide brim, the right corner of which was turned up, Anzac style. A folded English umbrella leaned against the wall. Mast was seldom seen without it, especially in Manhattan. In addition to providing portable shelter from rain or snow, it had a ferrule of almost lethal length and sharpness, very handy for poking at Negro muggers—"all those over-indulged, smart-assed african *schwartzers* who think they own the place" Mast said of them—and other hoody street types with a

21

penchant for molesting senior citizens. The umbrella also made walking pleasanter (chronic meniscus problem, left knee).

Not that Carl Mast gallivanted about New York that much. Manhattan interested him little, except for such business as he might have there . . . he had done the theaters, museums, and other cultural attractions, but that was years ago.

He was known to be a rather solitary old fellow when left to his own devices, with no close friends or family, and he never entertained, which was perhaps understandable since his time and presence were much in demand by those involved with various international functions, banquets, *fetes d'affaires,* and government caucuses.

For his private comfort when in New York, his parent organization maintained a small apartment in the Sutton Place area. In Geneva, he owned a pleasant cottage with a view of the lake. When vacations came his way, which was not often, Mast was fond of Bermuda, Antibes, Portugal's Algarve district, famous for its groves of carobs, and the Caribbean's Leeward islands. With advancing years a man finds that a warm spot in the sun has increasing appeal.

DR. MEYER NOW considered how best to go forward with their talk. He put aside any further chidings about tobacco or alcohol. Mast, himself a medical man, knew the statistics. Further, he represented a very special patient toward whom Meyer, and White, too, felt considerable respect and regard which, had they been willing to admit it, was more than a little tinged by awe. After all, it wasn't every day that a couple of garden-variety proctologists had a chance to sit around over ouzo with a Nobel laureate.

Meyer, outwardly calm, donned the mask of professionalism. With a faint sigh and then a glance at White, who nodded almost imperceptibly, he went straight to the point. Bad news is never improved by beating around the bush. "My . . . our . . . advice, Carl, is—well, it won't come as any surprise—immediate hospitalization."

There it was.

"The sooner the better," White interjected. *Immediate* apparently had not satisfied him. If a fellow was paying for the opinion of two specialists he deserved hearing from both of them.

Carl Mast considered their statements, then sipped at his liqueur. He said, finally, "You're right. I'm not surprised." He paused. "Surgery?"

Meyer nodded. "Complete lower exploratory."

Mast looked gloomy. "So it goes, eh? A man comes into the office for a checkup and ends up under the knife."

There had been the barium enemas with contrast studies and an expensive assortment of prescription drugs, not to mention regular invasions by the colonoscope. And now: the scalpel. Interestingly, Meyer had discovered early on that the prostate—that classic walnut-sized troublemaker—was in great shape and would have been more appropriate to a man of thirty-five than to one who was eighty. The trouble, as all three knew, lay elsewhere. So far there had been no impaction or constipation. Mast's stools, of which he brought weekly samples in tightly capped stuffed-olive jars, were quite hard but otherwise reasonably normal; in fact, as Mast had observed, the round brown pellets he had obediently fished out of his toilet bowl were not very different looking from the olives the jars had originally contained: "We can't think of anything else, we can always play marbles."

He said now, "An exploratory of the sort you recommend is no simple operation."

"Indeed not," Meyer agreed.

"And if you find nothing?"

"We close you up, one, two, three. You'll be out of Sloan-Kettering in no time."

"But if you do find something?" Mast inquired.

"We repair what we can."

"And if you can't repair?"

Meyer regarded the old man. "We do what's necessary."

Mast nodded. "Ah, right there on the table. Get it over with. Why make two trips? A colostomy, I suppose?"

"It's a distinct possibility."

Mast nodded again. "The old rubber bag." He looked at Meyer. "And if there's metastasis? As there very likely may be?"

Meyer frowned. "Carl, we don't know that. We won't until we go in." Then he shrugged. "Once we have you open, we can evaluate."

Carl Mast tasted his ouzo again. The strong tang of licorice was wonderful. "Then again, you might do nothing, right? Just sew me up and turn me loose."

That last surgical decision, Mast knew, would be tantamount to a death warrant. Only so much can be excised from the abdominal cavity. Beyond a point, a carcinoma's metastasis would make mockery of the word "repair."

There were, as White had pointed out two weeks earlier, a number of points in Mast's favor. So far the bleeding was confined to the lower bowel. It had apparently not spread to the bladder, ureter, or upper renal system, nor to the prostate either. The abdomen was firm, though somewhat tender, yet there was no palpable mass or observable diffuse enlargement.

Further, Carl Mast was in reasonable, in fact excellent, shape for a man his age. Chemistry profile, blood pressure, and heart—all were good. There was the liver problem, due to excessive alcohol intake, and the lungs were in terrible condition, thanks to half a century's addiction to Gauloises. But all in all, the old fellow was a far better specimen than he probably deserved to be.

Meyer, as though this had just occurred to him, said, "Your general profile is quite good, you know."

Mast poured himself another two fingers. He said broodingly, "Who're you kidding? My body's a shambles. We all know it. But my mind. That's what interests me." He regarded them. "Want to know something? In my opinion—and I ought to know—my mental faculties are better today than they were forty years ago."

"I believe it," White said, and Meyer nodded.

Mast said, half to himself. "Most of us fade after sixty . . . arteriosclerosis, a stroke, Alzheimer's, gradual deterioration, wow, you name it. Personally, I regard a failed mind as worse than a failed body. But occasionally, you know, there's that admirable rara avis, the man or woman whose mental processes remain undiminished into the eighties, even the nineties. Believe me, boys, it's a real pleasure to encounter such a person, wouldn't you agree?"

"You, Carl, are an outstanding example, if you'll pardon my saying," White agreed.

"Truë," Mast replied, smiling. "The trouble is that this mind of mine, with which I am entirely satisfied, is residing in a corpus that's ready for the trash heap."

"I wouldn't go that far," Meyer said cautiously.

Mast ignored this. "I'm delighted about the prostate. That means I could ejaculate into a young woman. If I felt like it, that is. Very nice to know. Would you believe it, I still get nocturnal erections? Pretty good, eh?"

Meyer chuckled. "Men your age—not often, but often enough—have engendered children, you know."

"I certainly wouldn't want to go *that* far." Mast withdrew a silver cigarette case from the inner pocket of his jacket and extracted a fresh Gauloise. He said drily, "But I'll keep it in mind." Then, serious again: "How long?"

"Difficult to say, Carl," Meyer replied. He had never liked this

24

part of it. After almost thirty years of practice it was still unpleasant. "First the exploratory . . ."

"And if I refuse the exploratory?"

Meyer, introspectively drumming a middle finger on his desk blotter: "Umn. That's another story." He paused. "From what we've found so far . . . a month? Three? Hard to say. That, as you know, is the reason for the exploratory. The sooner the better."

"Immediately, I'd say," White put in.

"However, the damned prognosis, as *you* know, may be the same after you've gone in," Mast pointed out.

"Entirely possible."

"Or I could die right there on the table."

"It has happened," Meyer admitted.

"Perhaps my past has caught up with me." Mast sighed enigmatically. Then he said, "Excuse me. My mind was wandering." He stared at the two of them, almost as if seeing them for the first time. "Yes, of course. By the way, I appreciate the forthrightness both of you have shown. The problem must be identified, right?"

"Carl, we don't want to give you the impression that the situation is hopeless," Meyer pointed out.

Mast chuckled. "Not hopeless? Perhaps not. On the other hand, I see no reason for blithe optimism."

Striving for objectivity, Meyer said, "You're a seriously ill man."

"Quite serious," White said.

"And there's no way to calculate the odds," Carl Mast added. Neither of his listeners responded to this. He went on, mildly cheerful again: "However! On to other matters. Which some might deem of more importance than the little cut-and-sew job you two want to perform. You know of what I speak?"

Meyer sat back in his chair, folding his arms across his chest. Stared at his patient, then nodded. "The Award?"

"Precisely. They expect me in Oslo in eight days," Mast said.

"Of course."

"The schedule's all arranged. The hotel reservations, the airline tickets, all that. Scandinavian Air, a most pleasant line." Mast stopped and then said, "Am I to disappoint the Nobel Committee? The entire Norwegian Störting, not to mention all those Stockholm bigshots?"

"We still urge you to admit yourself into Sloan-Kettering as quickly as possible," White insisted.

"Sure. Were I in your shoes I'd advise precisely the same," Mast said with a smile. "However, it stands to reason that I cannot be in two places at the same time. I could accept in absentia, via a representative." Mast's smile broadened. "But then, if I did that *I'd* miss all the fun!"

"We understand," Meyer said. "A difficult decision, yes."

"Oh, it's quite a shindig," Mast explained. "Full dress. The other medal winners have to lump it together in Stockholm. But the Peace Medal is a solo shot in Oslo, on the same day the others are being paid off in Sweden. An international event of signal importance. A great honor. To think it all started when old Al got the idea to mix nitroglycerin with kieselguhr, *voilà*, dynamite, a relatively unfractious material. Managed to make himself a few shekels, didn't he?"

Meyer and White remained silent.

"Al thought dynamite would be a boon to mankind," Mast continued, again half to himself. "But, of course, it's also good for blowing people up. War, quite simply, is wonderful business. Ask the Krupp crowd." He sighed. "And so now the name of Nobel is synonymous with just and good causes, all guaranteed to advance humanity. Out of evil, it would seem, much good can come." Frowning, the old man mused, "But aren't things supposed to reproduce according to their kind? From trees, more trees, from dogs, more dogs? So how from evil, good? A paradox, wouldn't you say?"

"Perhaps," Meyer said. "Right now, however, our concern is with you."

Mast's next remark was more puzzling still. "Physician, heal thyself. And, if possible, have fun while you're at it."

"I don't follow," White said.

"No need for you to," Mast replied. "It's something that concerns nobody but myself. A private matter." He recollected himself, puffed at the cigarette, drank. "Well! As you noted, the decision is mine."

Meyer and White, all ears.

"I'm going to attend," Mast announced. "If I listen to you guys, a week from now I'll be in a hospital bed, feeling like a carved turkey. I'll be sick and miserable. Neither is good for my temper. Further, the prognosis or condition may not be in the least improved, as you yourselves admit, and it could even, let's face it, be worsened."

He paused. "I will, naturally, want to bring with me any Rx's you care to prescribe. Especially morphia, in case this stupid tummyache becomes any severer. I promise to take your medications. However, I intend to eat and drink and smoke. In short, I am predisposed toward having the best possible time. *Warum nicht?*"

"You really intend to go?" Meyer asked.

"I wouldn't miss it for the world."

"You know the danger? The possible consequences of delaying even a week or two?" White asked.

26

Mast turned to him. "Let's be honest, okay? Put yourself in my shoes. You're in your eighties. At best you're not far from the end of your life-journey. Moreover, you have a carcinoma, or at least every indication of one, in a very bad place. Probably your situation is already terminal. You've been awarded an important honor, and you have already notified the committee of your humble acceptance. They await you next week, arms outspread, red carpet unrolled, eh? By going, how much have you to lose? A shortening of your life, which is for all practical purposes almost over? White, my boy, listen to me! To attend would probably represent the last fling you'll ever have! The big bash, as they say. Conversely, if you stay, what is accomplished? At best a palliative prolongation, a stretching out—a week, a month, oh, what the hell, let's say six—of an existence that has long since lost most of its charm? Of keeping alive a moribund carcass? White, tell me! What would you do?"

White looked thoughtful for a long moment. Then, quietly, shyly: "Personally, I'd crawl out to Kennedy on my stomach if I had to and get on that plane." He hastened to add, "I speak off the record, of course, not as your physician."

Carl Mast considered this. Then he nodded. "Well said, Horatio."

"My name's Bob," White replied.

The old man continued, "Of course, a lot of the pomp and ceremony is boring brouhaha, a very nice word, by the way, that comes from the Hebraic *barukh haba*: 'blessed be he who enters.' You have to listen to lots of speeches before you get a chance to give your own. One shakes hands with all sorts of smiling strangers, none of whose names one remembers for more than two seconds. And sitting for a long evening in tails and a collar can be agony. Everybody is cheerful, but nobody, *Grüss Gott,* will dare crack a joke. Very serious, you know. At such a solemn gathering levity is conspicuous by its absence. What a shame." Mast thought this over and then chuckled. "I wonder if I could do something about that."

"Jokes?" White inquired. "At the presentation of your award, you want to tell jokes, Carl?"

Mast shrugged. "I suppose it depends on one's sense of humor. That's why I admire you Jews. At least your religion, along with the Zen Buddhist's, has a chuckle or two in it, although admittedly the latter is of a harsher variety. Yes, the Jewish view of life is estimable, for its rich tradition and its ability to smile."

White gently cleared his throat. "I've noticed that you seem to have a certain familiarity with Judaism."

Mast apparently divined what was on White's mind. He said, again with that smile that wasn't a smile: "So? I look Jewish?"

Pure Mosholu Parkway.

White looked thoughtful. "Well, as a matter of fact ... now that you mention it. A forebear perhaps?"

"Sorry to disappoint," Mast said. "I was baptized Catholic. To my knowledge the blood of the sons of Abraham is absent from my veins. In some ways that saddens me."

White looked a bit disappointed but said, "Even so, it's wonderful to see a gentile with such a scholarly ..."

"If I could be a Jew," Carl Mast interrupted, "I would like to be a *tsaddik*, yes? One of your wise and just men, who possess all the virtues. I would explore my *yetzer ha'ra*—my own inclination toward evil. I'd spend my last years studying the Haggadah and maybe even contributing a few humble parables of my own. No, my boy. Perhaps unfortunately, my only connection with Judaism is academic. I am a student, an observer, nothing more. The same goes for Catholicism and, for that matter, all other formal religions. I do not practice the art of religion. Or the art of nonreligion, either. No atheism, no agnosticism—who has time for that dreck? Merely an interested kibitzer, that's me."

"I find that difficult to imagine," White said.

Meyer said unswervingly, "Carl, will you agree to hospitalization the moment you return from Oslo?"

Mast said, "I'll give the matter full consideration. That's as far as I intend committing myself at present. In the meantime, I intend to enjoy."

Meyer said stubbornly, "The point is, Carl, you could—may—have years ahead of you yet."

Mast frowned. "With a *tohchus* like mine? You trying to kid me?" He considered this and then, half to himself, added, "Lillies that fester smell ranker than weeds."

He rose, reached for his chesterfield and Borcalino, donned them, wrapped the muffler about his neck, then shook hands with the doctors.

Meyer, meanwhile, had written a handful of Rx's, which Mast tucked into a pocket. "Carl, if there's any significant change. Increased bleeding, obstructive symptoms. Well, we'd have to act quickly. I don't have to tell you."

"No, you don't," Mast said agreeably. "I'll keep it in mind. And thank you again."

"It's been our pleasure," White said.

Carl Mast turned to leave, paused in the doorway, affixing the two of them with a droll look. "Do you really think I could?"

"Could what?" Meyer asked.

"Impregnate a young woman?"

"Possible," Meyer said, smiling. "Entirely possible, Carl."
"What a perfectly splendid idea," Mast said.

AS THEY WENT about closing up shop for the day Meyer and White chatted. The latter said, "How long do you think he really has? I mean, even with the surgery?"

Meyer shrugged. "He's dying. You know that as well as I. So does he." The proctologist considered this. "What really counts is the quality of life still available to him. That's what he's thinking of. If we open him up, what'll he have? Maybe six months? Of lying in a hospital bed, sinking slowly? No fun. He's in a I-don't-give-a-damn mood. Can't blame him for that. So, then, let him have his medal and be fussed over."

*The quality of life.* An expression Meyer and White often resorted to, especially with terminal cases. How much sense was there in fighting to keep alive a body like the one Mast was saddled with? Mightn't it be better to let the vital-support systems collapse and so make an end of it? A vexing question.

"He's already operating largely on will power," White noted. "Most men his age would be in bed weeping. He's got chutzpah." The physician corrected himself. "No, it's more than chutzpah. He's tough, and he's brave. I admire that."

Meyer nodded and then sighed. "Will power . . . toughness . . . bravery. All very nice, but, beyond a point, of no real help." Both men had at times seen demonstrations of will power in a dying patient. The mind, fiercely strong, refusing to give up the fight, battling against the inevitable.

"He's certainly lived an interesting and rewarding life, hasn't he?" Meyer said.

White nodded and then chuckled. "And now he wants to be a *tsaddik?*" He considered this. "He passes for gentile but somewhere along the line a Jew was in the woodpile. Well, to each his own."

"You know, I looked again while I was palpating," Meyer said. "I'd swear they're scars."

As part of Mast's regular weekly examination the lymph glands and other parts of the body were felt. Many carcinomas display a jack-in-the-box talent for popping up here and there, so the groin, the armpits, the base of the neck, and the mastoidal region were carefully checked for any sudden enlargement.

It was behind the ears and under the chin that Meyer earlier had discovered what he believed to be faint hairline scars, perhaps the remnants of old incisions. It was really impossible to know for sure, considering the condition of the epidermis, and moreover Meyer was no dermatologist.

But even so he thought they were scars. He had not asked Mast about them since they were not germane to the current problem, although he had made note of them in the written case history. He said now, "I'll bet you anything that at some time in the past our *tsaddik*'s had himself a face-lift."

"So? That's not uncommon these days," White said. "As a matter of fact, I've been thinking about having a couple of tucks taken in the jowls and chin." The proctologist did indeed possess a double chin that clearly would not disappear with dieting. He mused aloud, "After all, doesn't everybody like to show the world his best side? It wouldn't surprise me if the old man's as vain as he's brave. No one wants to look at an ugly face. Take my daughter. Because of a new nose, she swears her whole life has changed. For the better." Then White frowned. "Last month somebody thought she was Irish. That's better?"

"SOMETHING NICE, SOMETHING pleasant but, above all, not too big," Carl Mast said into the mouthpiece of the telephone two days after his office visit to Doctors Meyer and White. "I'm definitely not in the market for dirigibles."

In such fashion spoke the man of whom *Time* magazine had recently written in its Religion section: "... Mast's charisma has multidenominational appeal—Jews, Catholics, Muslims and Hindus have pointed to him as an exemplar of their tenets. Dedicated to justice, self-sacrificing and unflagging in his efforts on behalf of the world's underprivileged, he has avoided rather than sought the public eye, and the religious press has speculated whether his Nobel acceptance speech will champion some new view of mankind's plight."

"I understand perfectly, Doctor," the man at the other end said.

This was Constantine Phraxeteles, born and raised in a West-Side slum but in recent years risen to the enviable post of "administrative coordinator" at the United Nations. A far cry from Hell's Kitchen.

Constantine, in his late thirties, with a happy round face and expensively manicured hands, liked to dress well, and in addition to being fluent in five languages was a born hustler. He was one of the various lesser functionaries of that high-minded international organization and his job was to insure that life in New York went smoothly for visitors from abroad and that various assignments, some minor, some pretty important, were expedited without troubling these foreign VIPs whose minds presumably had no time for the trivia lesser mortals are heir to.

If a homesick Senegalese dignitary, par example, expressed a passionate craving for fried cockroaches dipped in chocolate, he turned to Constantine, who could immediately pinpoint which Manhattan gourmet shop stocked Afric delicacies. If an Iron Curtain delegate had an item or two that he wanted to get back to his country, and which exceeded the weight and dimensional allowances of his portfolio—say, a satellite dish—it might not hurt for him to talk to Constantine. Invariably friendly, attentive, and absorbed by the problem at hand, multilingual Constantine was a mellow fellow to have around. He knew how to get things done. Best of all, he was the absolute soul of discretion. He said now, "About five-feet-five, Doctor?"

"Sure, okay," Mast said, "but slender, see?" He made of his free hand a smallish cup. "Nice tits, understand? No mushmelons."

"Willowy?" Constantine ventured.

"You got the idea," Mast replied. "But no toothpick, either. A looker. Knockout legs, that's a must."

"Any age preference?"

"No geriatrics, Constantine. A young one."

"How young is young?"

"Are you kidding?" Carl Mast responded. "For someone like me, everyone is young!"

"Thirteen? Twelve? Younger?"

"*Liebes Mensch!* What am I, a monster? No! Young is under thirty. Over twenty. That, for a normal man, is young. A person with some knowledge of the world, understand? But at the same time not some worn-out retread with a cuntful of callus. Anybody drawing social security needn't apply."

"Of course."

Mast reflected. "Beautiful, if possible. D'you think that's possible, Constantine?"

"Entirely possible, Doctor," Constantine replied. "Racial or ethnic preference?"

"Caucasian. Maybe, but not necessarily, Nordic, a blondie, a brunette, who cares? A little surprise isn't the worst thing," Mast said. "One other request, Constantine. Is it too much to ask for a girl with intelligence?"

"How intelligent?"

"A *Mensa* I don't need," Mast said. "It would, however, be uplifting to have someone capable of maintaining a rudimentary conversation without stopping every minute to pick her nose. Charm, a bit of chic. A touch of flair, that is to say, style. You follow me?"

"*A quelle heure?*" Constantine inquired.

"*A sept heure, d'accord?*"

"*Chez vous?*"

"You want I should meet her outside the World Trade Center?" Mast thought. "She must be discreet. And presentable. The residents of this building regard themselves as dignified, beyond reproach. God only knows where they ever got such an idea." He thought again. "You have someone?"

"I believe I do, Doctor."

"She's good?"

"Incredible." Constantine added, "So I've heard, anyway. Literally *fantastique*. Young. Very beautiful. She should be in movies."

"How much?" Mast asked, not much impressed.

"Five hundred, Doctor."

"Eh?" Mast growled. "Oh, boy, she must have one made of mother-of-pearl! Are you kidding? That's a lot of money."

"That's her fee," Constantine said with sympathy. "Cash."

"What's wrong with MasterCard?"

"Doctor Mast, you're too much," Constantine chuckled.

Mast said, "What's your *mordida*, Constantine?"

"Not a cent, Doctor," Constantine said. "My absolute word of honor. It's merely part of my job."

"Tell me another," Mast said, frowning. "Listen, what's so hot about this éclair that she has to pluck an eye out of my head? The last I heard, you could get a first-rate call girl in Manhattan for the entire night for two bills, tops."

"Times have changed, Doctor."

"Yes, but I *haven't*!"

"Five years ago I might have been able to arrange something in that price category. But not today."

"Whoever said the dollar's strong is crazy," Mast observed. "How long's she been in the life?"

"She's not exactly in it," Constantine said guardedly.

"An amateur? For five hundred you want to send me a beginner?"

"By no means an amateur, Doctor," Constantine said agreeably. "I've known her now for several years. She sees only two or three people a month. She is...discriminating." He paused and then went on: "I've never heard a single complaint from any client she's visited. Quite the opposite. Certain gentlemen will go so far as to telephone me from abroad, weeks ahead, to make sure of her availability. That in itself is something of a compliment, *n'est pas*?"

33

"She's really that special?"

"I'd say so, Doctor. Definitely for a gentleman with impeccable taste. An exceedingly refined young lady."

"Okay, Constantine, trot her out of the woodwork at seven and I'll look her over," Mast said. "But if she isn't everything you say, it's strictly hello-goodbye, I'll slam the door in her face. For five bills I can hire a harem off the Minnesota Strip for a week."

"She's a remarkably nice young woman. I think you'll like her."

"Nice?" Mast grumbled. "Niceness has nothing to do with it." He hung up the phone.

MAST HOPED SHE would be clean. At his age and with his position, not to mention the troubles already plaguing him, it would be absurd to show up at the offices of Meyer and White with a case of galloping herpes.

He also had some misgivings about the outcome of the evening he had in mind. What he had revealed to the proctologists was true: he did achieve nocturnal erections frequently, but these were a country mile removed from the libidinous vigor that had troubled his youth.

It had been more than two years since he'd had intercourse, and that had taken place in Burma at the end of a tour that country had hosted to show off the impressive progress it had made in recent years.

The "progress," so Mast had concluded, was questionable. In the towns and villages there were lots of pastel-colored concrete tract homes, and even electricity, but in the Irrawaddy Delta there were food shortages, and in the mountain highlands, where the great teak forests grew, domesticated elephants were still used to move and stack huge logs. Elephants, Mast had opined, were picturesque, not progressive.

The girl had been exquisite, scarcely out of her teens. Her name was Mai and she had been lined up by the Minister of Natural Resources. Although she spoke no English and they had sex only once, Mai was delightful to have around during the final three days of the tour. She was petite, almost dolllike, cheerful, caramel-colored, with a dazzling smile and straight black hair. Her skin had smelled of jasmine and she had loved the Beatles. As the minister himself had remarked, "If a guest visits, one sees to it that he is fed, given drink, made comfortable. It is a matter of courtesy."

So too with Constantine, with his plump pleasant face and olive complexion, always ready to break a leg to further the cause of international relations: "By all means, doctor, if I can place myself at your service, please don't hesitate. To be alone in a foreign

34

country is not always pleasant, between men certain matters are understood, so if there is anything I can do, *any*thing . . ." He had slipped Mast his calling card, which was imprinted with the name "C. Phraxeteles," the number of his UN office, and his unlisted home phone.

Mast got the message. Smiling noncomittally he had accepted the card and later tucked it away in the lid-flap of his attaché case along with a collection of others. That had been over a year ago, and the card had remained unused until this frigid December day.

Not that Mast had anything against the sort of girls a dating service such as Constantine's could provide. It was merely that age had tempered the appetite, and at eighty Mast's hunger pangs were those of a dainty nibbler.

Now, having hung up the phone, Mast sat for a minute at his escritoire, still questioning the wisdom of involving himself in an endeavor perhaps better left to younger and fitter men. Above the desk hung an oval mirror framed in carved walnut. Regarding his image he finally said aloud, "It will probably come to nothing."

Even so. Not many minutes later he made another call, to a nearby Gristede's, where he had an account, placed an order; and then still another, to a liquor store on First. No matter how the evening went, he and, presumably, his guest would require sustenance.

He worked at the escritoire on various papers until the orders were delivered. Then, after unpacking the sacks, Mast poured himself a small ouzo, undressed, showered, shaved, talced and lotioned himself, and chose suitable garb from his wardrobe for the evening ahead.

THE WHORE, GRISELDA Nadelmann by name, five-feet four, weight 108, twenty-seven years old, I.Q. 148, currently a Ph.D. candidate in Columbia University's Department of History, also taking a few side seminars in business and economics, touched the gloved forefinger of her right hand to the button that triggered an electronic chime somewhere inside the apartment. She looked, if further description is necessary, very pretty, in fact lovely, that is, beautiful, even stunning. Or, as Constantine sometimes described her, but, wisely, never to her face: strictly USDA Choice.

Decked out smartly: a soft camel's hair coat, raglan-sleeved, belted at the waist. Beneath that: a beige cashmere dress, slit up one side to just above the knee, with a long ribbonlike belt that ran beneath her breasts, crossed in back, and was tied at the waistline in front. At her throat: a small teardrop diamond on a delicate chain of white gold—concealed for the present by a silken scarf in shades of brown accented by subtle blacks. Boots, gloves, purse: all matching, of black Italian leather. Hat: mink—elegant, expensive-looking, burnt umber blending at the tips to a softer sienna, and delicately bejeweled with a scintillation of sparkling water droplets, for it was snowing again outside. Very fetching. Beneath the hat her hair, simply—which is not to say cheaply—coiffed, was jet black, glossier than polished obsidian. Eyes like a doe's: a glinty emerald green, their natural largeness enhanced by eyeshadow in beige and bronze, grading to deep green and italicized above and beneath by eyeliner and mascara. The lipstick: Burgundy, not rosé.

Having heard no response from within, Miss Nadelmann again depressed the button that activated the muted chime. She knew very little about the person she was preparing to address.

Her acquaintance, Constantine, had been of only limited use. On the phone he'd said, "A *very* distinguished gentleman, Gritch. Quite the pooh-bah, in fact."

"How distinguished?" Miss Nadelmann had asked with interest.

"The Nobel, sugar. Your first laureate. Impressed?"

"Intrigued," she said. "Tell me more."

"Mast. Carl. Doctor. Top-drawer credentials."

"I've heard the name," she said. "What time, and where?"

Constantine supplied this information.

She said, "Anything special I should know?"

"I don't think he's kinky," Constantine replied. "Probably old-fashioned." He added, "Of course, one never knows, does one?"

"Overnight?"

"I'd say so. Let him decide. He wants someone with real class."

"I see."

"And brainy," Constantine went on. "Right away I thought: Gritch, the original whiz kid!"

"Now I remember—there was an article in some magazine last week about the Prizes," she said and then paused, frowning, recollecting. "You're sure there's nothing special, Connie?"

"Umn, in a way there's one little thing," Constantine said, pausing too as he sought the right words. "He's sort of getting along in years."

"How far along, Connie?"

"Well, honey, I wouldn't exactly call him a spring chicken."

"Connie, how *far* along?"

"A bit elderly, Gritch," Constantine said.

She was silent, listening.

He added, "Definitely elderly, in fact."

She was still silent."

He said, "Old, baby."

"Sixties? Seventies?" she said.

"Older, I'd say, though I don't know exactly," Constantine replied. "Let's say eighty. Ball-park figure, Gritch."

"Christ," Gritch said. "I better bring along a heart pacer."

"You can handle it, Gritch."

"I'm no magician."

"You've got talent."

"Are you sure he really *wants* a date?" Gritch asked. "I mean . . . holy Toledo, that's getting on up there!"

"Who knows? He may only want you to sit on his lap and whisper filthy stories into a senile ear. It could turn out to be a fascinating evening. Use your imagination."

"I have a hunch I'll need it," she said. "Eighty!"

"You'll do it then?"

"I'll do my best, Connie—but I can't provide divine intervention."

"He'll be enchanted. Toodleloo, and don't forget to drop my hundred in the mail." Constantine hung up.

The commission was reasonable. It was their standard agreement. Of talent Gritch had plenty, along with a satisfactory inventory of work skills that had been honed by her three-year-long involvement with Constantine's dating service.

They had met one evening at Columbia's International House, on 123rd, where a couple of exiled Russian poets were giving readings. Afterward, over coffee in the cafeteria, they had talked and become friendly.

Out of this chance encounter a business relationship had developed that had been mutually profitable. How many other young men and women Constantine represented was not known to her nor did she care. She got by quite adequately seeing from four to six tricks a month. The at-times unsavoriness of her labors was mitigated by two unarguable factors. Short hours and excellent pay. Neither of which would have been her lot had she accepted the teaching assistanceship that had been the department's standing offer to her since she'd begun graduate studies. The clients she visited were almost always, in one way or another, important. Gritch discovered that the conversations she had with these men were far more interesting than attempting to teach a roomful of fuzzyminded nineteen-year-olds.

After she had hung up the phone, Gritch—the nickname had been acquired around the age of fifteen back in Passaic, New Jersey— went to the *Who's Who* that was part of her apartment's library and, donning a pair of black-framed eyeglasses, read the entry on Mast.

It was a fairly long bio, what with the listing of all the honorary degrees he had been awarded: doctorates from Cambridge, Edinburgh, Bonn, Paris, Geneva. In one capacity or another he was or had been a member of or advisor to an astonishing number of philanthropic organizations, including WHO, UNICEF, the ILO, Amnesty International, UNITAR, the UN Economic and Social Council, the International Red Cross, the African-American Institute, and a host of other associations, many of them Jewish, devoted to war relief, refugee relocation, and aiding children in need. Of particular interest was Mast's years of work in emergent Third World countries. He was, it seemed, a true internationalist.

"Quite a track record," Gritch mused.

BUT OF MORE importance than Constantine's or *Who's Who's* remarks were her own impressions as she waited at Mast's door.

The Sutton Place address was an excellent one. The uniformed doorman downstairs, polite but all eyes, had announced her arrival via a house phone, and when permission had been given, discreetly ushered her into the terrazzo-floored lobby. She was, by now, familiar enough with wealth not to be abashed by it, but what was significant, at least to her, was that the gentleman she was about to meet cared little about the possibility of a compromising situation. Occasionally her clients worried about such things, but this man apparently felt safe from such dangers or else simply did not give a damn. More often than not Gritch visited her people in some of Manhattan's finest hotels. The idea of coming to Mast's home appealed.

She very much liked the door before which she now stood. It was of heavy wood, painted satin black, with raised decals in gold leaf, and it had a large curved doorhandle of polished brass.

Suddenly, and without noise, the door swung open, and the man who had apparently been standing behind it said, "Yes?"

From his age and mode of dress she surmised that this was her host and not a manservant.

The tone of his "yes" was one of mild surprise, almost wonderment, despite the fact that not much more than two minutes ago the doorman, a boozy-looking Slav with a grenadier mustache, had announced that she was on the way up.

Mast's quizzical expression struck Gritch as being suitable to someone greeting an Avon representative or the local canvassperson for Muscular Dystrophy. She was aware that this was merely a small delaying tactic on his part, a minor male device by which the prospective buyer could gain a few added seconds during which he would be able, so to speak, to inspect the goods being peddled. In that

38

now-open door was an eye-level peephole, but such instruments made any visitor look like a freak.

What she saw was a distinguished-looking elderly gentleman dressed for an evening "at home," in neatly pressed gray flannel slacks, black polished loafers, and a dark green velvet, frogged smoker's jacket, belted about the waist. Arranged about the open collar and neck of the jacket was a handsome paisley ascot. The white fringe of hair that curled over the collar had been carefully brushed and arranged, as had the mustache. In one hand: a Gauloise.

"Doctor Mast is expecting me," Gritch Nadelmann said, with a beautiful smile. "Have I come to the right place?"

Her voice, as she was perfectly aware, was one of her best tools. A remarkably pure, lilting soprano, musical without being adolescent, adult but not matronly. In the avian world it would have been associated with the nightingale or thrush. Better, the sheer musicality of it carried a faint undertone of latent sensuality. That voice had struck straight through to more than one man's heart, and now she was pleased to see that it had once again found a target.

The old man's shoulders straightened almost imperceptibly. The bald but, nonetheless, leonine head came up alertly. He looked like an ancient tom sniffing the air for the presence of a female. Indeed, in the cab on the way downtown, Gritch had applied a touch of fragrance to her wrists, and behind the earlobes, something not in the least strong but merely faintly, irrefutably *there*.

Still smiling she observed the effect she had made on him: her appearance, the fragrance hanging in the air between them, and the voice, that young-girl's silvery-sweet "Have I come to the right place?"

He said in a rather courtly fashion, "Yes, I believe you have."

"You're sure?" Gritch Nadelmann said, wanting to be sure. So far he had made no move to stand aside.

He weighed this second question, and then with a smile and a slight dip of the head—it wasn't really a bow but there was an elegance to the movement that she found attractive—he said in a heavy German accent, "But you must forgive me. To keep you here like this. Won't you come in? Please do."

"Thank you," she said, and did.

IN THE HALLWAY she unfastened the camel's hair coat and let him help her out of it. As he hung it in a closet she caught him checking out the cashmere dress. She loved that dress and had paid a lot for it, and now she thought: just what the doctor ordered.

The gloves were removed next and were placed along with her purse on a small hallway table. On the table was a sterling-silver salver of the sort ordinarily reserved for incoming mail but which now contained a single unaddressed white envelope. It would, she surmised, contain money. Her host, as if reading her mind, inclined his head again and murmured, "For you."

"Thank you," Miss Nadelmann said. She slipped the envelope into her purse, at the same time removing her cigarette case and silver lighter. Later she would, on a trip to the bathroom, inspect the contents of that envelope to confirm that it contained currency of the realm.

"May I ask your name?" the old man said as they walked together into the living room. Outwardly serene, Gritch was inwardly alert as her mind judiciously weighed various impressions.

"Griselda Nadelmann," she replied. "But everyone calls me Gritch."

"Gritch?"

"Yes."

"It sounds abrasive."

"Perhaps onomatopoetically, but, believe me, I'm not," she said. "And you're Doctor Mast?"

"Please . . . Carl." Again he dipped his head slightly and she wondered if despite his maturity there was in him a touch of the shy boy. She said, "I've been reading about you." He was silent. She shot him that smile again. "I'd like to offer my congratulations."

"Ah," he murmured. "Oslo."

"What a splendid honor," she said sincerely but at the same time gauging his susceptibility to flattery. "I mean, to have your efforts recognized, after so many years."

Mast did his utmost to look patriarchal, but only succeeded in looking like he'd swallowed a mouse. "Thank you."

Gritch glanced about, inspecting her surroundings. She said admiringly, "You have excellent taste."

Mast made a vague gesture. "Small, but for a man like myself, adequate."

The apartment was, in fact, no larger than her own. Living room, kitchen, hallway, bath, and, visible through one open door, a bedroom.

The living room, though expensively furnished, was somehow Spartan, comfortable without being touched by intimacy. A long low couch, upholstered in muted blue shot silk, equally handsome armchairs, end- and cocktail tables and, against one wall, shelves of what appeared to be technical and research books, as well as stereo

40

turntable, tape deck, and speakers. Though no expert on floor coverings, she thought the rug was an Aubusson: motif of roses, vines, and ferns. On the other walls several oils and small prints were hung. There was nothing in the way of personal memorabilia, nor had any woman left her influence here. No vases of flowers, no sign of anything feminine.

It was perhaps a place suited to the tastes of a fastidious old man who liked his independence and privacy. And his comfort too. Someone who demanded the best but who felt no need for ostentation.

In a side alcove she noted a table laid for two. Had he arranged this? Nice, she thought. White linen tablecloth, five candles in a vaguely menorahlike candelabra. Did anyone else ever dine there with him? Or when he was in this city was he in the habit of eating alone at that table? Whatever, the elegance of the dining alcove (the candles were as yet unlit) bespoke an old-fashioned courtliness, and she liked this.

She began to understand that the evening would pass in accordance with his own concept of how the thing should be done. Whatever Mast had in mind, it was definitely not a hit-and-run job.

A record played on the stereo; Gritch recognized Vivaldi. She said, "'The Seasons'?"

"'The D-minor flute concerto,'" he replied casually but with a flicker of interest. Her question had not been without effect. This was a girl who knew music. Mast's expression seemed to say: "Well! The evening may not be a disaster."

Aloud he remarked, "I have 'The Seasons' too, if you would prefer that. Also some excellent Palestrina, early Handel, Haydn, Mozart, Mendelssohn."

"Mozart. But later," Miss Nadelmann said pleasantly. Beautiful background music wasn't always easy to come by. She adored dancing, but only to certain tunes.

Mast said, "Would you care for something to drink?"

"Please. A Gibson. Very dry. Three onions," Gritch replied, seating herself on a couch. She had a fondness for Gibsons. Nevertheless, for the sake of her host, who might feel obliged to match her drink for drink, she warned herself to go easy. A tipsy date meant trouble: anything stronger than Serutan could have a debilitating effect on someone this man's age. In which case Mast might turn petulant, though probably not belligerent. The boiled-noodle syndrome was not that uncommon, even among far younger males. And yet, bitterly, they insisted on their money's worth. Which for her might involve hours of jawcracking work.

41

Mast made drinks, brought them over, and sat beside her. They touched glasses, his bearing ouzo, hers the Gibson, in an almost ceremonial toast, and drank. Lit cigarettes—she had the long mentholated brand. Exhaled calmly and regarded each other. Mast said, "Concerning dinner, not knowing your preferences, I thought of lobster and steak. The latter is a reasonably good filet. A choice seemed sensible. Some, you know, have an allergy to seafood, especially crustaceans."

"I have no allergies, and may I have both?" Gritch replied, tasting her drink again. "I love good food."

"My tastes, and culinary skills, are simple," he said. "Whenever I'm in this country I find myself dining out more than I care to. Formal dinners are mostly a combination of bad food and business talk—the former gives me indigestion and the latter is tedious. An evening such as this is most pleasant."

She glanced at him. "Are you in New York often?"

"Perhaps two months out of the year—five or six trips," Mast said. He shrugged. "I come and go. As I'm needed."

Beneath the self-deprecation he obviously liked talking about himself, and she tried to draw him out, falling back on what she'd gleaned from the *Who's Who* entry: "My impression is that there's precious little time when you aren't needed."

Though his expression was guarded he did not seem to be in disagreement. He said, "It's mostly a question of money, you know. Here, and in Europe, too, there are important people whose cooperation facilitates programs in other parts of the globe. They must be endlessly reassured that they are not being taken advantage of. Usually they are too busy to check out a situation personally. So I go in their stead, and when I return, if they like what I have to tell them, there is the potential for further cooperation."

"You make yourself sound like some kind of high-echelon salesman," she protested.

"Not a bad comparison," Mast replied. "Except that I earn no commission."

She looked around again. "But you live quite comfortably."

He smiled. That dry smile, she thought, lessened the harshness of his face. There was something about him that she liked. He made a small gesture with one hand and said, "Wherever I go my expenses are, how shall we say, absorbed? By this or that government, or bank, or cartel. It goes with the territory."

Gritch would have liked to ask whether this evening's entertainment would be absorbed, too, but the question was inappropriate. She said simply, "Very nice for you."

42

"Yes, it does make my work more enjoyable," Mast replied. He too looked around, though with less interest. "It's pleasant here, true. But there's another side. Try sleeping at night in a Cambodian hotel room in the middle of August under a mosquito canopy when the temperature is over a hundred and the air conditioner is kaput. Out there everything breaks down! And the humidity. Don't ask. The walls of such rooms are so covered with a growth of spongy mold that they feel alive to the touch. The toilet may or may not flush, and for a shower you have a trickle more suitable to a leaky faucet. In the morning you shake centipedes out of your shoes, and of course the shoes themselves have, during the night, sprouted their own growth of fungus, as have the armpits of the shirt you removed before retiring." He chuckled. "In a week you smell like a decaying mushroom. And *that* is exactly when you must don suit and tie in order to attend a banquet at which, I need not remark, photographers are invariably present. So, although miserable, you must display a happy smile. Everybody in Asia smiles constantly. All Asians are *born* saying cheese. Tell one of them he's got terminal leprosy, and he bows and smiles delightedly."

Mast tasted his drink. "So, my dear, it's not all peaches and cream."

BY THE START of the third round of drinks, she saw that they were becoming friendly.

He said, "It would be good if you could tell me something about yourself. However much you want, however little. I don't wish to give the impression that I'm prying into your personal life. However, for me, Gritch, a stranger is a stranger, and a face in the crowd, even one as unforgettable as yours, means nothing. Strangers are people I tend to be wary of. Personalities, on the other hand, can be interesting."

"I agree," she said, lighting a fresh cigarette. "What would you like to know?"

He cocked an eyebrow. "Look at it from my point of view. I have arranged to have a companion. I needn't add that such an event represents a drastic departure for me. At precisely two minutes past seven my doorbell rings. My guest is punctual. I am impressed, all the more so because of the terrible weather tonight. I open my door and what do I see? A ravishingly beautiful black-haired vision. Without exaggeration this is one of the loveliest young women I have ever encountered. She is dressed exquisitely and when she speaks, the sound of her voice is . . . well, words fail me!"

Gritch smiled.

He continued: "She has culture, sophistication, great charm. She even, *ach wunderbar*, knows of Vivaldi. She is intelligent. I can't help but think that I'm pretty lucky to have such company. My dear

Miss Nadelmann, you are, if you don't mind my saying, something else." He paused. "Old Mast is absolutely tickled, take it from him. She gives every indication of being interested in his work. This, of course, is a form of flattery. Flattery is not always a bad thing, eh? With merely a few well-directed questions she's got him gabbling away. Well, why not? He's by no means immune to attention, especially from a young goddess."

He paused again and lit a Gauloise, puffed, exhaled leisurely: "This goddess, however, is a mystery to him. Who knows? Perhaps all goddesses are mysteries. Obviously Mast is thinking, 'Oh boy, this is one goddess a guy could have a lot of fun with!' But he's also aware that he has on his hands an unusual young woman. I'm not talking about beauty or poise but, more specifically, about *her*. His invitation for her to tell him a little about herself is, despite the odd fashion in which they have made each other's acquaintance, sincerely meant."

He stared at her. "The entire evening lies before us, my dear. If humanly possible I would prefer that we spend it in the manner of good friends capable of finding some enjoyment in what each has to offer the other, rather than as two strangers solely bent on consummating a business transaction."

She was surprised. Her mind had been busy computing what sort of man he was and what he might be after. But his own mind had not been idle either.

When he'd said "tell me about yourself," Gritch thought he was hinting about sex talk. Occasionally she'd been with clients who were aroused by detailed descriptions of what she'd done with other men. The sucking, the fucking—all of it. Some johns practically got off just hearing her tell about it. At times her descriptions were accurate but at other times she'd just make up a lot of wild stuff, the zanier the better—holy Toledo!

But this wasn't what Mast wanted. He sounded interested in her. Which wasn't to say he wasn't seriously interested in sex, too. She was sure of that now. Off and on since first entering the apartment she'd wondered if all he really needed was company. At his age anything like a real erection would have to count as a blessing. And seeing that perfectly laid dining table and hearing the talk of food, it had occurred to her that what she had to contend with was not a horny old goat but an amateur chef.

She intuited now that his sexual interest would be heightened, perhaps enormously, if she sketched a picture for him of *who* she was. This, she thought, is a man who is intrigued by minds as well as behinds.

Ordinarily she would have been cautious about discussing herself. It wasn't just that she was a basically private person. Most men weren't that interested in knowing anything about a woman. But Mast was not most men.

She thought: Well, all right. Ask and ye shall receive.

Even as she spoke she realized that he fascinated her.

"IF I HAD to describe myself in one sentence it would go like this," Gritch said. "I want to achieve something worthwhile with my life. Something of significance. I don't want to be forgotten or disappear without a trace."

"You are competitive?"

"Only in the areas that matter to me."

"Ah. But you strive to be a high achiever?"

"Definitely."

"And how do you intend achieving significance?"

"I'm afraid I don't have a clear idea as yet," she replied. "Did I mention that I'm a grad student?" Briefly she told him of the academic side of her life. "I'll have all my course requirements out of the way this spring. Then I can get on with my thesis—I think writing that will give me the insights I'm after. I've already had the topic approved: *The Phenomenology of Distinction.*" She glanced at him. "What causes certain men to stand out above the masses? Why certain individuals and none of the billions of others? That's what I want to understand. Some lead, most are led."

"You are not the first to ponder such questions," Mast observed drily. "Tell me, these courses you're taking, they are demanding?"

"Yes. I study a great deal."

"This part-time work of yours, it provides the income you need?"

"For the moment." She paused. "It *is* part-time, you know."

"Yes," Mast said, still more drily. "So I was given to understand. You are . . . I imagine the word is selective."

"Extremely."

"Very wise of you." He glanced at her. "Has the work created any psychological stress or trauma?"

"Stress, yes," she said as she tasted her drink. "Look at it this way. I'm attractive, and intelligent. But there are thousands of women in universities around the country who fit that description: beautiful and brainy. Yet they don't do what I do. Why me, then?"

"I'm asking you." The simian eyes regarded her.

She smiled. "All right, then, I'll tell you. Plenty of these bright, gorgeous types happen to end up with a guy who just incidentally underwrites the tab for their life-styles, hmn? But, of course, the idea is that these women aren't doing what *I* do." Her voice was amused. "Actually, various men have offered to sponsor my education. Very convenient for me, and for them, too. Their thought was that such an arrangement would change my situation, make it ... respectable. What a *nice* word. Except that I don't like that kind of contract. Does that make me more honest? Or am I just falling back on a rationale that's been used plenty of times before by women like me?"

"I can't answer that," he said.

She shot him an oblique look. Something in her wanted to take a risk she'd never before taken with a client. Finally, her mind made up, she said, "You, Carl, lease out your mind, knowledge, expertise, whatever you want to call it. In exchange you get this—" she gestured toward the room, "—and now, finally, a gold medal. You lease your mind, and I happen, occasionally, to lease my body. Is one so much different from the other?"

"I agree," Mast said with evident enjoyment. Then he became serious. "For you it's a matter of integrity?"

"Let's call it independence," she replied. "An evening like this isn't always easy. But no one has a string on me. Nobody owns me." She smiled. "On the other hand, I've had some delightful evenings, I'm having one now." She let the last statement hang for a beat. "That's not flattery."

"But there is, as you said, stress."

She shrugged. "Society doesn't approve of someone like me."

"You care what society thinks?"

"No, I don't—not when it's wrong," she said. "Of course, in actual practice it's not that simple. I have to exercise prudence. The way it works out is that I'm one person at school, the conscientious student, but in a different setting ... here, for example ... I'm another."

"A psychiatrist, I am sure, would be interested in the stress factors caused by acting out two such conflicting—polarized—personas."

"Psychiatry should be taken with a large grain of salt, in my opinion," she said. "You know, I saw a shrink once. I was having some depression."

"We all suffer depression at times," Mast remarked. "It's the commonest ailment. What did he tell you?"

"A lot of claptrap." Gritch flashed that grin at him. "I was neurotic, he said. Also a man hater. I told him that on the contrary, I'm uncommonly fond of men. He said I hated myself. I explained to him that I hold myself in quite high esteem. Then he decided I had a father complex. I said my relationship with my father was far too

**48**

complex for simplistic labels. So he climbed back on the neurosis hobbyhorse: I was obsessed by a need to control and manipulate men, engage in power plays. I admitted that I was indeed fascinated by power, but not the sort a call girl exercises."

"It sounds like his therapy was a waste of time. How did it terminate?"

Her smile broadened. "He hinted, and not subtly, that he could cure me with a 'special' couch technique. He was very persuasive. I pointed out to him that a person like myself would never pay seventy-five dollars an hour for such treatment, and that it was he who should be paying me. 'But I'm not the one who's sick,' he argued. I told him he should let me be the judge of that."

"Physician, heal thyself!" Mast said delightedly. "I said that just the other day to someone. 'Heal thyself and, if possible, have a little fun while you're doing it!' Speaking of healing, Gritch, I wonder if you'd consider doing something for me?"

"What?"

"Would you mind kissing me?"

She turned toward him happily. "I thought you'd never ask." Moved closer, leaned against him, and kissed him on the mouth. The mustache tickled, felt bristly, smelled of Gauloises and ouzo.

As they parted she felt his breathing quicken. He said, looking at her, "Was that unpleasant?"

"Certainly not," she said. "I do like you. Please believe that."

"Miss Nadelmann. Gritch. You're too kind."

For a minute they sat there like that, kissing. He was very gentle. Finally, she murmured, "Is there anything I can do to help?"

"Do whatever it is you enjoy doing, Gritch," Mast advised.

She was silent for a moment as she considered this. Then she said, "Would you like me to dance for you?"

"Dance?"

"I'm quite good."

"Modern?"

"Ballet."

"Heavens! You're a ballerina too?"

"I study. Not seriously. It's just something I love."

He glanced toward the hallway table on which lay her purse and gloves. "Have you your costume?"

With calm forthrightness Gritch said, "There is no costume."

"Really?" the shaggy brows rose with pleasure.

"Would you like to see me dance, Carl?"

"Now?"

"Why not? It's early."

"Gritch, I believe I'd like that very much," Mast said. "We can have dinner later. It won't take long to cook."

"Is the lobster thawed?"

"I certainly hope so."

"I thought the idea might please you," she chuckled. "You never know, it might give you a new lease on life."

Mast frowned. "I wouldn't want to go that far."

RISING, SHE ASKED where the bathroom was, excused herself and left, pausing to pick up her shoulder bag, which contained among other things cosmetics, lip gloss, toothbrush, a small tube of fluoridated dentifrice, both neatly wrapped in plastic, a pillbox containing Quaaludes and Midol but nothing stronger, a thin wallet that held ID, twenty dollars (tucked into her right boot was another twenty), and a card indicating that in the event of sudden death all salvageable organs were to be deposited in the nearest organ bank, a ring holding four keys, and a spare pack of the menthol-flavored cigarettes she had recently taken a fancy to. There was also a two-dollar utility knife with a triangular razor blade that could be withdrawn into the handle for safety's sake, ideal for cutting linoleum or flesh. The knife was her protection. It had never been used. In her commercial peregrinations—some girls have all the luck—Gritch had liaisoned with inordinately decent males.

While urinating in the bathroom she checked the contents of the envelope. Five one-hundreds. Finished, she patted herself dry, considered using a drop of fragrance there but then elected not to. She rose, pulled up her panty hose, tugged down the cashmere dress neatly, and then removed the high-heeled, Italian-leather boots. They were just a touch tight at the instep.

Before her was an ordinary medicine chest with a mirror. She examined the interior quickly, noting that in addition to the usual bachelor necessities there was a large assortment of prescription drugs.

His health, then, was not that good. No digitalis or nitro pills, though, so it wasn't a heart problem. Gritch had a ghastly fear of having a client die, literally, on her.

Closing the chest she examined her face in the mirror. A bit of sheen at the sides of the nostril wings. Take care of that. She touched up her lips with gloss.

Done at last, she opened the door and snapped off the light. She had been gone less than three minutes. No man, especially one as old as Mast, for whom time might understandably be important, liked to be kept waiting. As she walked into the living room she said,

"Sorry to be so long." In her right hand she held the boots.

"You weren't long at all," Carl Mast said happily.

WITHOUT HEELS SHE had that sensual walk peculiar to dancers . . . oddly graceful, hip-undulating, slightly duckfooted. Mast, seated on the couch, stared delightedly. Her legs, which he had been wondering about, were superb: the ankles slim, the feet narrow, the calves finely modeled. Like a neat child, she carefully placed the boots against the wall beside an armchair, toes pointing out.

Leisurely she began undressing, reaching behind her neck to unfasten and start the zipper, and then behind her back to open it to the small of her back. The soft cashmere dress slid smoothly from her shoulders, and she carefully stepped out of it, shook it briefly, and then draped it over the back of the chair. Her slip was of silk, tea-colored. She drew this over her head, revealing a flimsy frothy bit of a bra, the cups trimmed in lace, and sheer panty hose.

Carl Mast, the absorbed spectator now. Her breasts were small, obviously firm—the bra was decorative rather than supportive. "Enchanting."

She flashed an affectionate grin at him. At the base of her throat the teardrop diamond sparkled. "There's something about a woman undressing in front of a man that always excites her," she said. "Transference. Her body is familiar to her, but it's the knowledge of what it's doing to the person looking on."

Ambling over to the stereo she began flipping through albums. Mast's collection was good. Leaning forward he poured more liqueur into his glass, at the same time more or less keeping an eye on her. "My dear, dear girl! I don't know if anyone has ever mentioned this to you, but you have a magnificent derriere. Simply superb. Well developed without being in the least steatopygous. And despite the straight posture and proper set of your shoulders, you have a slight curve at the small of the back. I'd be on guard about that. Now you're young, so it's nothing to worry about, but at forty it could develop into lordosis." He paused, admiring that delicious curve. "In French, we say that such a curve is *ensellure*. The pelvis slightly tilted rearward. Many men find it irresistible."

"Do you?"

He tasted his drink. "Oh indeed! To say the least."

She paused and gave him a bemused glance. "Do you think I'm beautiful?"

"I most certainly do, Gritch."

"How beautiful?" She removed the bra, turned half toward him and idly touched the tips of her breasts.

51

Carl Mast, utterly sincere: "Miss Nadelmann—Gritch—you are, I must say, an extraordinarily attractive young woman."

"Tell me I'm beautiful." She stood there calmly, waiting. "I like to hear it."

"You're beautiful. Truly."

"Would you like to make love to me?" Their voices were subdued, composed. They might have been speaking of the weather, or of the balance in a checking account. They might have been discussing anything except what they actually were discussing. She continued caressing the tips of her breasts. "Do you want me?"

"Yes."

"Would you like to do things to me?"

"Yes."

"You can do anything you like, you know."

"I'll certainly keep that in mind, Gritch."

"Would you like me to do things to you?"

"I surely would."

"What sorts of things?"

"I'll come up with something, Gritch."

Now she paused to tug the panty hose down over her hips, which were wide, somewhat bony, the stomach wonderfully flat, smoothly muscled. When she had gotten the hose off, she placed them on the chair with the dress. Turning she gave him that tender smile again. Her expression so loving, so vulnerable. "Has it been long, Carl? Since you've been with anyone?"

"Couple of years, Gritch, give or take a century or two," Mast said. "My age, you know."

"Age has absolutely nothing to do with it," she said. "I'll guarantee you that, darling."

"I think you may be right, my dear."

"Two years?" She clucked her tongue. "That's much too long for a man like you."

"Oh, I agree. Categorically," Mast murmured. Again she shot him that loving smile. It warmed him to the core of his being. "Getting a bit warm in here," Mast observed. He lit a Gauloise with fingers that were trembling slightly.

Gritch regarded him. "I suspect, Carl, that we are going to have an incredible evening."

"I shouldn't be a bit surprised."

She turned back to the albums and found an old favorite, "Les Sylphides." A wonderfully romantic piece, with some excellent solos for the female.

The music played and she spent a minute or two doing limbering-

52

up exercises while Carl Mast, quite dazzled by now with her beauty, observed.

Touching her toes and then, going farther, she placed the palms of her hands on the floor while straight-legged. Grasped one ankle in both hands, bent farther until her forehead grazed her shin. Then the other ankle. Placed a foot on the back of an armchair and used the latter as a makeshift barre. Flexing, twisting from the waist, one arm delicately outstretched.

And then, ready at last, while Mast calmly, but not so calmly, sipped his drink, she danced for him.

GRITCH WAS NOT a professional ballerina and never would be, not that it mattered a particle.

To the nympholeptic eye there are few things lovelier than a lovely girl who is naked and who, moreover, is not the least self-conscious about her nudity.

For a woman to achieve such a carefree state of mind she must be unshakably convinced of her desirability. Enter Gritch: pirouetting and high-stepping about on that handsome Aubusson rug.

Before five minutes had passed Carl Mast was actively, irrefutably aroused. Setting down his drink—a bit spilled over the rim of the glass—he said, "Would you like to see my bedroom?"

Gritch completed a jeté and ended with a deep curtsy, arms arched in a butterfly pose, head bowed, obeisant, submissive. "Yes. You want to? Now?"

"I believe I do," Mast said reflectively.

"BE GENTLE WITH me, won't you?"

This was Mast talking, not Gritch.

"Oh, darling, yes."

"I'm not exactly a candidate for the decathlon."

"You're fine, you're fine."

The lights were out, the room was dark except for a faint glimmer that came from the windows. Gently they kissed and played and eventually Gritch's right hand wandered on an exploration of its own. "Holy Toledo!" she said.

"Yes," Carl Mast responded. In the dark his deep voice seemed louder, younger. "An oldie but a goodie. I'm rather proud of it."

Bending to her task she said, "You certainly have every right to be."

"Quite a soft-on, eh? Surprised?"

"Impressed," she murmured, surfacing for air. "A prizewinner in more ways than one, that's you, darling."

Carl Mast proved a leisurely but competent lover. She sat atop, riding his member in slow time, like a kid on a carousel steed. Then broke into a jog. Attained a brisk canter, and finally, to her considerable astonishment, managed to orgasm at full gallop. Mere moments later he did too, although his own climax was a minor flurry, an excited tweak and twitch.

For a moment Gritch was puzzled. In her private life she was perfectly capable, on certain occasions, of sequential orgasms, much in the manner of a roman candle going off, but with a paying client the spasms that racked her were almost always counterfeit: she was clever at feigning passion.

But Mast had aroused her.

How odd, she wondered. It had to be because she'd revealed something of her personal self, she decided. That and the fact that she liked this old man. The trouble with liking someone was that sooner or later you wanted to do something for him.

At the same time his performance had been more than satisfactory. Gritch told him so. Mast, almost purring in the dark, said, "Thank you. Thank you, my dear."

She nestled in his arms. They lay on their sides, resting for a while, and then she went to the bathroom to clean up. When she returned Mast said, "I wouldn't mind dinner now."

"That lovely steak and lobster? Umn!"

"Sex sharpens the appetite, doesn't it? I could eat a horse."

In the dark she threw him the compliment he sought, chuckling softly, "I practically just did."

A LATE DINNER, say after nine, can be a pleasant interlude, especially when one of the participants has worked up a hearty appetite, while, for the other, it is even more agreeable when his companion is naked, garbed, so to speak, only in youthful beauty and natural charm. Gritch, though a veritable fashion plate when the eye of the world was upon her, cared little for encumbering or binding garments in private. She ate in the style of the young, with a zest that impressed her host, who, a cautious octogenarian at the table if not in bed, picked slowly at his steak, the lobster, the dry, toasted French bread, the simple endive salad.

Their mood was one of mutual relaxation and affection. Carl Mast's reasons for feeling so fine were obvious. Dressed again in gray slacks, velvet jacket and ascot, and revivified by the astringency of a generous application of bay rum vigorously patted onto forehead, cheeks, and neck, Mast was urbane and at ease. Rather patriarchal. Except for Gritch's eye-catching lack of costume, he might have been entertaining a seldom-seen but deeply cherished granddaughter.

Gritch felt fine too. The steak and lobster were excellent. She suspected that except perhaps for a little kidding around their business with sex was done. He was not apt to rise to the occasion again.

Apparently he expected her to spend the night. That was all right. Outside in the dark the wind howled, sending blizzardy sheets of snow whirling through Manhattan's skyscraper canyons, but in here it was warm and comfy. Mast seemed to be enjoying her company over dinner as much as he had under her, earlier. Though obviously an independent cuss, he was apparently not immune to loneliness.

In Gritch's realization of this, he suddenly became more human, more comprehensible. A big shot. A lonely old bird. Living a bachelor existence at a classy address.

He was an attentive host. Refilled her glass with a light Colombard he'd opened. She tasted it. "From '71 to '73, those are this vineyard's best years," he remarked.

The dining alcove was lit only by the candles in their menorahlike holder. The soft light they cast played on her shoulders, neck, the diamond pendant, the small, perfect breasts. Mast eyed these various assets. Though satiated, he clearly appreciated her femininity.

"How are you feeling?" she asked, dipping a piece of lobster into melted garlic butter.

Carl Mast wiped his mustache with is napkin and smiled. "If it weren't for the weather I'd say it was spring."

LATER THEY ADJOURNED to the living room for dessert and liqueur. "You are," Mast said as she arranged herself on the couch, "quite the alluring Jewish princess."

He was referring to an observable trait peculiar to her ethnic background, that is a definite tendency toward hirsuteness, evident in Gritch not on her perfectly modeled thighs and calves (those sculpted surfaces had been treated from bikini line to ankle with an expensive depilatory) but here and there—and elsewhere as well. A delicate dusky down, an adorable flue, on the forearms especially, reappearing again at the small of the back, which Mast, the enchanted anatomist, had already noted as being of *ensellure* camber, then disappearing southward where it developed into a luxurious jungle, as indeed often happens to fragile plants exposed to a hothouse atmosphere, so that at the core of her there grew a truly splendid dark thatch, which now led Mast to observe, with unconcealed admiration, "That's a great bush you have, Gritch."

"Thank you," she said. "I'm glad you like it."

At that moment the object of his attention happened to be a scant six inches from his right cheek. He was seated on the floor while she, on the couch, sat with right leg drawn almost to her chin, leaving the other relaxed and akimbo, its foot resting on the floor. In one hand she held a dessert dish containing a compote Mast had concocted of cherries, sliced mandarin oranges, bananas, and pears, drowned in clear syrup. With the fingers of her free hand she leisurely picked at this assortment while Mast, seated as he was, rested his head against the inner part of her left thigh, and admired the labial treasures half hidden by that curly jungle.

Feeling playful, Gritch selected a plump bing from the compote and daintily placed it between her lips. Nibbling, Mast acquired it, and they both fell to laughing. Looking down at him, she stroked his white locks and said, "I'm glad you didn't use thistles in this dessert."

"Or tuna fish, either," Mast smiled. "May I have another?"

He got one.

"Feel like fooling around some more?" she inquired, watching him as he chewed.

Mast removed the pit and deposited it in a nearby ashtray. "I certainly do. But another part of me says, 'Forget it.' The mind always has big ideas but a penis is honest."

He moved up onto the couch beside her. "Maybe tomorrow morning, but even then I'm not counting on it. I can enjoy your company in other ways." He lit a cigarette, poured Courvoisier for them, and said, "You have already provided me with all I expected, and more. I'm grateful." He thought about this. "For me, that's unusual. I don't *have* to feel grateful to anyone anymore."

She eyed him. "Not even the Nobel committee?"

He smiled. "Because they made the obvious choice?"

"That's arrogant."

"It is." He tested the cognac. "It's irritating, you know, to compose a speech and then wait year after year to deliver it." He chuckled. "I suppose I haven't done badly."

"Oh, cut it out," Gritch said. "Next week you'll be standing up on that podium in formal dress, ready, actually goddamned *eager,* to grab that medal."

Mast shrugged. "I never sought it, you understand. That's the truth."

"Carl, I doubt that." She lit a cigarette of her own, tucked both feet under her, and shifted her hips so that she was facing him. The look she gave him was direct, level. "Tell me, when did you realize you were special? What was your early life like?"

THERE WAS MORE to this question than mere curiosity. Mast was not the first VIP she'd liaisoned with who, before the evening's work was done, had found himself engaged in a serious exploration of his career. And after sex had been attended to, what better subject was there than a review of one's own exploits, achievements, and triumphs? It was a subject a man never tired of talking about, especially when his listener was a lovely and bright young woman whose attention was not feigned.

As Gritch had happily discovered, in searching for information about power—the kind that tangibly changes the course of human destiny—one was not necessarily confined to library shelves. The true scholar looked to the contemporary world.

In a sense the time spent on dates arranged by Constantine represented an investment in bona fide research. She looked at Mast and wondered what was so unusual about him.

"I WAS BORN," Mast said, "in Zurich in 1905, an only child. Father a pharmaceutical salesman. Mother, oh, just a mom of the Swiss variety, buxom, beefy, lace-aproned, although she did have some musical talent, zither. Childhood uneventful, very ordinary, which is to say there were no neuroses or psychoses of the sort that even then commanded the attention of Freud, some of whose lectures, by the way, I attended later while studying medicine in Vienna. Lower school, *gymnasium,* the university years—nothing unusual, I'm afraid."

As she listened Gritch sensed there was something wrong about this recitation. In her experience men did not talk in this way about themselves.

The tone of his delivery was oddly flat. It was as though he had memorized his own biography. He was not so much describing himself as ticking off items from a precis that long ago had been committed to memory.

She thought it best not to ask about this and instead remarked, "From such a prosaic beginning to *Who's Who?* Do you really have twenty-two honorary doctorates?"

"Haven't counted 'em lately." Mast smiled. "Let's see. What else can I tell you?" He went on. "At nineteen young Carl decided upon a career in medicine. That same year his father died, to be followed, two years later, by the musical mom. Money had been set aside for a decent education. I studied in Vienna and, later, Berlin, and graduated in '29, the same year, incidentally, that a hothead named Hitler began causing trouble."

Mast lit a cigarette, puffed. "I spent most of the thirties in Germany, France, Austria, and Italy. I was interested in what this country calls public health. Young Carl's career, you see, had taken a strange turn. In medical school he had, to his embarrassment, discovered an aversion to treating patients on a vis-à-vis basis." Mast grinned. "That's the worst kind of aversion a physician can have, eh? Medicine had appeal, but not the actual practice of it. So,

58

although the title 'doctor' precedes my name, I have never actually healed anyone. The humblest GP is more of a doctor than I ever was."

Nicely put, Gritch thought. But it still sounded wrong. In addition to his pleasanter sides, Mast, she was sure, was arrogant, conceited, disdainful. Capable of crushing anyone who got in his way.

He went on: "I eventually got into ecology—acid rain, air quality control, damage to the environment. Believe me, fifty years ago it was worse. I helped clean up the Rhine. That was in Essen. Today people fish in the Rhine, the water is potable. Back then the river was a trickle of sludge; the factories used it as a garbage pit. I was good at talking to people. An arbitrator. Governments everywhere need such men. They are as necessary to the machinery of civilization as water to a thirsty man."

"Most of your early work was in Germany?"

"Yes. Occasionally I returned to Switzerland," Mast said, "but I had no ties there, no family, not even friends. In Germany I had fun. The Swiss, you know, are not given to wine, women, and song. They have an exceedingly *nice* country," he observed. "Small, neat, highly respectable. And stultifyingly boring. Yes, Switzerland is such a nice place that people from all over the world beg for the privilege of keeping their money in her banks. It's a country with an absolutely impeccable reputation. If you doubt this, get a Swiss passport. Infinitely better than one of your American jobs. Far more doors—and borders—are open to a Swiss citizen than to an American."

Gritch returned to what interested her. "But there was still no recognition for you?"

"Ah. That came later," he said. "After I married. I was in my forties by then."

"Behind every man, a woman?"

"Nonsense," Mast said. "Hélène looked out for me and herself as well. Four years older. Also a physician. We met in 1946, after the war. We made a good team. Public health again. In Germany there was suffering. Disease, a general collapse of health standards, bad sanitation." He paused, frowning. "I'm getting ahead of myself. Early in 1944 I became ill—pneumonia, followed by pulmonary complications. A lengthy convalescence was prescribed. I spent the remainder of the war in Zurich, recuperating. It was there that we met. An ambitious woman, she was already involved with WHO, which was then in its infancy. Gradually I became involved too. I had no wish to return to a war-ravaged Germany, so different from the country I'd loved. Eventually, with Hélène, I was made aware of problems outside Europe, especially in India and Africa. We traveled a good deal. By then we were fairly well-known, in international public-health circles. We were married fourteen years. She died of cancer. No children. Look in the *E.B.,* if you like. There's an entry on her. Dr. Hélène Fischer-Mast."

Mast stared at the young woman beside him. "Gritch, I meant it when I said I never sought notoriety. I have no formula for success. It's something one somehow encounters. That's all. A gradual thing." He nodded. "Of course, now that it's here I find I enjoy it very much."

She had a sudden image of Mast as the rest of the world saw and treated him. At an age when most people had long since retired, he traveled. How many miles a year did he fly? One hundred thousand? Two hundred thousand? He thought no more of packing a few bags and going off to the Congo or Nepal than most Americans thought of taking a weekend drive. His mind was wonderfully alert, and she didn't doubt that he kept to a schedule that would have worn out men twenty years younger. How did he manage it?

She thought: He'll probably go on like this until he burns out or keels over. It's his career that keeps him going. Aloud she said, "Okay. Obviously you're a workaholic, but you still haven't told me what you actually *do.*"

He shrugged. "Suppose you happen to know, for example, that in England there's a surplus of Aureomycin worth several million pounds. And let's suppose that in Cameroon there's an epidemic of a particular disease that responds to treatment with this drug, which is sitting around in refrigerated storage. So? What happens? You get some people together and talk. Men and women, whether European or African, will respond to judicious treatment, especially when they're acting on behalf of their governments, and most especially when the eyes of the world press are upon them." Mast smiled. "It's like a big swap shop or flea market, where you trade one thing for another. That's what world health is."

She persisted. "What was your greatest achievement?"

"My involvement with Norman Borlaug," Mast said unhesitatingly. "That was via the Rockefeller Foundation. Norman got the Peace Prize himself, you know, back in '70. He was the plant geneticist and architect of the so-called Green Revolution. Developed a high-yield, short-strawed, disease-resistant wheat, suited for use in the developing nations of the Third World. Yes, a simple stalk of wheat, but it changed the way the world eats. By going over to Norman's dwarf wheat Mexico became agriculturally self-supporting in the middle fifties. I assisted in developing it in Pakistan." He shook his head. "We had an awful time overcoming local prejudice. Those dumb Pakistanis swore the new wheat caused

60

sterility. A highly questionable disadvantage in Pakistan, wouldn't you say? By the end of the sixties the Green Revolution had spread to India, Turkey, Morocco, Lebanon, and dozens of other countries." Mast considered this. "Yes, I never felt bad about being involved in such programs."

"*Who's Who* said you've done a lot in Africa, too."

"God, Africa! There's always something happening there," Mast said. "That place is a goddamned oversized petri dish! Sure, I was involved with the tsetse fly for almost six years. Typhus, smallpox, beriberi, yaws, syphillis, malaria, filariasis, which you know as elephantiasis. In Africa, it's either starvation or disease. And not only Africa. There are always disease 'explosions' detonating around the world, Gritch. In the past year I've been an advisor right here in this country, on AIDS, the gift you can't live with."

"So now you're a big shot," she said, eyeing him. "And y'know what? I have a feeling you get your jollies by throwing your weight around."

Mast laughed. "It sure beats working for a living."

"AND WHAT OF you?" he said now. "What else are you besides a graduate student? Friends? Family?"

"Friends, yes," she said. "Nobody terribly close, though."

"No boyfriend?"

She hesitated. "I don't want to become involved with a long-term thing."

"No family?"

"Mother died when I was ten. My dad when I was twenty-two." She paused. "He raised me. He was a wonderful man."

"A scholar?" Mast asked. "Was it he who introduced you to the pleasures of learning?"

"No scholar." She laughed. "Steve Nadelmann ran a forklift out at the Passaic Sanitary Landfill for most of his life. He used to say, 'They swear all us Jews are filthy rich, here's one they should take a look at, Nadelmann, shoveling goycrap around five days a week.'"

"A religious man?"

"Not especially. And I'm not at all. I'm quite aware of being Jewish, though."

"You loved him?"

"Yes," she said simply. "He was gentle and sweet, and lots of fun. 'I'm betting my bucks on you, Gritch,' he'd say. 'You're going to knock the damned world flat on its ass." She grinned. "I believed it, too!"

"He knew you were bright?"

She nodded. "He used to say, 'Go ahead! Ask her something. Ask her *any*thing.' He died the month before I finished college. He'd have been taking pictures at graduation and nudging everybody with his elbow, and saying, 'Hey. That's my kid, y'know! Go ahead . . . ask her *any*thing.'" For just a moment there was a shininess in her eyes. "He was some guy."

"What do you think would happen if he were alive and knew of this part-time work of yours?"

"Are you serious?" She stared at him, astonished. "He'd have a stroke! What a dumb thought."

"He never achieved any distinction of his own?"

She smiled. "Oh, he got his name and picture in the *Passaic Herald* once. At the landfill he found a wallet. It had twenty-nine hundred dollars in it. He turned it in. He said, 'We could use it, but maybe the owner has greater need.'"

"What happened?"

"They ran the picture and the story. The wallet was claimed by some fat Italian chick. She'd gotten in a fight with her husband and withdrawn everything in their joint account, and then she got drunk and lost the wallet. When she sobered up she went boohooing to her old man, and then she spotted the picture of Steve Nadelmann, the most honest dingdong the Passaic Department of Sanitation ever had." Gritch shook her head. "She tipped my dad five bucks, for turning in almost three grand! Can you beat that?"

"What'd he do with the five dollars?"

"Oh, he bought a gallon of wine and got stinko. When I put him to bed he was still laughing to himself, 'Five? I don't understand the significance. Why not ten? Or two bits? Why five?'"

"Money was always a problem?"

"Yes. Even with his insurance. Columbia gives me a partial fellowship but it doesn't cover everything."

"No thoughts of marriage?"

"God, no."

"Children?"

"They take too much out of a person's life."

Mast considered all this. Finally he nodded. "I think you'll have a fascinating life, Gritch. I'll be interested in following your progress, if I can stay around that long."

She thought of the medicine chest in the bathroom, with its assortment of Rx's, and said, "You seem in great shape. What we did in the bedroom was fine."

He patted her bare knee. "Thank you. As I said, I'm grateful. At this stage of the game, I'm not exactly stud material. Also, in addition to being old, I'm sick."

"Very?"

"You want me to qualify?" He frowned. "Sick is sick . . . the opposite of being well, okay? Nothing of what ails me, by the way, is contagious. I swallow so many damned pills during the day that there's no room in my stomach for real food." He paused and then said more calmly, "And speaking of the proper care that I so richly deserve, I'm fatigued." He looked at a clock on the wall. It was past eleven. "You'll stay?"

"I'd love to."

"At twenty-seven I could make love four times in one night, get up the next morning, and put in a solid workday," Mast observed. "But now? The old need their rest. They're said to be poor sleepers, the elderly, grabbing forty winks whenever they can. Not me. I hit the sack, it's all over. No dreams, only snores."

"I'm afraid I snore too," she said.

"Then let's snore together," he said. "I'd very much enjoy waking tomorrow morning to find you beside me, Gritch." He stood up, scratching his stomach. "It's been a swell evening."

"It certainly has," Gritch said, and she meant it.

THE NIGHT PASSED without incident. He rose at four, as was his custom, went quietly out to the kitchen, put on the Silex coffee maker for her but made a pot of Ceylon tea for himself and then, seated at the kitchen table, worked for several hours on various documents. On one trip to the bathroom he discovered a heavy discharge of blood mixed with his stool. At seven he brought her coffee, gently patting her shoulder until she wakened. She smoked two cigarettes, drank three cups of coffee, and went to the bathroom twice.

Later they had a leisurely breakfast, during the course of which Mast took seven pills. "What're they for?" she asked.

"I have to keep my doctors happy."

She munched a piece of toast. "I'll have to be going soon."

"I myself have an appointment at ten."

She glanced at him. "With people who must be reassured that their money isn't being wasted?"

Mast smiled. "I have, by the way, greatly enjoyed our time together, Gritch."

"So have I."

He beamed. "What a lovely thing to say. Even if it isn't exactly one-hundred percent true."

They lit cigarettes—she was on her second pack of menthols—and sat for a few minutes. "Will I see you again, Carl?"

"That's difficult to say."

"I'll leave you my number, if you like. It's unlisted." She was surprised by her offer. The phone number was private. A link between her two worlds. She'd never given it to a client.

"Excellent idea."

"Will you return here after the Award?"

"That too is difficult to say."

"You must be quite excited by it all."

"I suppose I am."

"I'd love to see that medal," she said. "I'll watch for you on TV. Have you written your speech?"

"Oh, I most assuredly have," he said genially. "It's designed to be provocative. Very brief."

Puzzled by his tone, she glanced at him. "What are you going to talk about?"

"By next week you and everyone else will know," he said.

SHE LEFT AT nine, as exquisitely dressed as she'd been fourteen hours earlier. In the hallway they kissed goodbye.

Mast showered, and well before ten was ready to face the world. His first appointment was with three Chase Manhattan officers. He would ask them for money, and get it. After that there was another meeting at the Wenner-Gren Foundation, on Seventieth, off Fifth, that would deal with the education and upgrading of certain groups of Australian aboriginals who had first come to the attention of the civilized world via years of work by a late associate of Mast's, Geza Roheim, a pioneer in the field of anthropological psychoanalysis. Then he had to meet with a group about a geological expedition into northern Manchuria, for many years locked up by Mao, but recently there had been improvements in Sino-European cooperation. Like Ping-Pong diplomacy, cultural and scientific intercourse often acted as a prelude to the real game: commerce, trade, business. It was all a part of progress.

As he donned his chesterfield a vicious pain—Mast knew it wasn't gas—surged through his lower abdominal area. He had to pause for several minutes, doubled over, panting, one hand braced on the kitchen countertop, until the attack passed.

In the bathroom he took two more pills, washing them down with a glass of water. The face in the mirror was yellowish-gray, sheened with sweat. The pain had been the strongest yet.

Perhaps, Mast thought, he had pushed himself a little too far with the delightful Miss Nadelmann.

But he knew better.

IT WAS SAID later by some, including the liveried waiters who had served the formal banquet that preceded the ceremony, that the old man had drunk far too much.

Certainly he had not done badly by the champagne and brandy, and there was even an anecdote to the effect that when a waiter, at the commencement of the banquet, leaned over his right shoulder to offer a goblet of a famous Norwegian mineral water, Mast had snapped a churlish, "Get that dinosaur piss out of here!"

Whether he'd been drunk or merely overwhelmed by emotion remained in doubt; what incontestably happened was this:

After the chairman of the Peace Prize Committee gave the introduction, Carl Mast rose and slowly made his way forward. He was seen to weave slightly, though most in the audience assumed that the natural infirmities of age were the reason for his listing to starboard as he steered a course for the central dais and podium where, after being shaken by the hand, he would accept what he had come to receive.

TV cameras were trained on him. Strobe flashes on press cameras winked. In the past day-and-a-half he had been photographed hundreds of times.

The filmed footage showed Carl Mast in close-up, as members of the Norwegian Parliament—the Störting—applauded. Dressed in white tie and tails, chest stuck out, a shade belligerently it seemed to a few, he mounted the dais, shook hands with Günther Hölving, the

Committee chairman, and after the latter had made a few additional remarks, accepted the check, gold medal, and document.

Mast bowed rather formally, again teetering slightly, to the right, to the left, and to the Störting. Then, at the podium, without referring to written notes, he spoke, hands gripping each side of the lectern, as if perhaps to steady himself. Head thrown back. The bald dome of his skull glinted beneath the massive crystal chandeliers. His expression was grave, composed, and yet there seemed to be a hint of joviality about him, a twinkle in those eyes that constantly glanced about, perhaps even the start of a smile beneath the handlebar mustache:

"YOUR HIGHNESSES [FOR the king and queen were present], members of the Störting, and of the Committee, I thank you for this honor you have seen fit to bestow upon me.

"I accept it not for myself but for my work, for whatever I have done, good or bad. As a man I count myself as not mattering much. As for the work, I can debate its worth too, either admiring or devaluing it, as I please.

"The achievements of any one man during his short span on earth—though mine, I fear, has been anything but short [here there were murmurs of laughter and a brief outburst of applause]—very often amount to little. Under a microscope and illuminated by the glare of day-to-day life they may seem considerable. But all the chronicler has to do is wait. Usually not even a century's waiting is required, often a few decades will suffice. Soon enough time confirms that great works, whether for good or evil, are not really so earthshaking.

"If there are those who would argue this, so be it. That is their concern, not mine—at best I would take their well-intended suasions in the spirit of Paul's message to the Corinthians: *'I will destroy the wisdom of the wise.'*"

Here the old man's mind momentarily seemed to wander. He frowned, looked almost confused. Holding out his right hand, as though searching, he muttered, "Whatever Carl Mast is, he is no cicerone to the monuments of peace or the museums of progress."

Then, more loudly, he went on: "I do, however, feel compelled to set the record straight. I may have occasion to speak at greater length about my motivation but I charge you now to remember that free choice is involved. I am a strong believer in both the capacity and the duty of human beings to choose. But I make this particular choice without any sense of moral or ethical urgency."

His voice was acerb. "My scientific side has always had a fondness for seeing the proper thing in its proper intellectual place, and more than once this has gotten me into trouble."

Again he paused. "Be that as it may. It is with this attitude that I must amend your citation to include another person." Again he paused for a beat, his expression composed. "The other person who deserves an equal share in this award is Kasper Heislinger."

Those present, including members of the press corps, exchanged puzzled glances. The name was meaningless.

Mast continued: "As Kasper Heislinger I existed for the first thirty-nine years of my life. That is all. The name, I see, carries no great significance. That is as it should be. Why should you, who are dedicated to the betterment of mankind, be expected to know such a man as this Heislinger who, for all practical purposes, vanished from the face of the earth decades ago? No matter. Your informational deficit will not continue for long.

"I am sure that somewhere there is an historian, an archivist, for whom the name will ring a certain bell, evoke a memory, a recollection of other times and places. I would invite him, and the rest of the world, to be the judges of me, and of Homo sapiens, surely one of evolution's more risky experiments."

Mast paused once more. Then, as if suddenly grown weary, even bored, he concluded, "Thank you."

As he stepped down from the dais there was a perfunctory round of applause. Walking back to his seat the old man was seen to smile at all those who were smiling at him.

In one hand he held the parchment diploma. In the other the flat black case containing the coveted medal. A heavy gold disc, three inches across. On one side, a bas-relief of Alfred Nobel. On the other, three nude male figures representing peace and fraternity among nations, and the inscription: *Pro Pace Et Fraternita Centum.* At current gold prices the metal alone was worth over a thousand dollars.

THE SPEECH HAD not been long, but given its bizarreness newspersons at media centers around the world paid attention to it. The Heislinger name was handed over to the centers' research departments and within hours information began surfacing. In some far-off cities the data discovered on microfiche or in computer memory banks contained only a line or so. Elsewhere, in places like Tel Aviv, there were dossiers.

The first person to target in on the name was a night researcher on the *Frankfurter Tageblatt.* He sat for several minutes staring at the information displayed on the screen of the computer on which

67

he had punched in a query program. The dates of the entries concerning Heislinger ranged from 1937 to 1946.

His eyes widened and finally he said aloud, though there was no one to hear, "Christ! They've given the Prize to a war criminal!"

The most significant entries in which Heislinger's name was mentioned dealt with verdicts handed down at the "Doctors' Trial," which convened in Nuremberg in 1946 for the purpose of examining inhumane and medically unethical practices by more than two hundred and fifty German and Austrian physicians under the Nazi regime. Heislinger had been charged, convicted in absentia, and sentenced to life imprisonment.

EARLY THE FOLLOWING morning a meeting was held in the Tel Aviv offices of the Central Bureau of Intelligence and Security that, in addition to internal affairs, handled certain operations outside Israel's territorial borders. The CBI & S was known as *Mossad*.

Colonel Yosef Armon presided. Also present were a Bureau lawyer, Schmuel Lubinsky, and an intelligence officer, Ezra Vered. For almost an hour the three men had been going over material that had been pulled from *Mossad* files.

The biographical profile in the Heislinger dossier was damning enough. This was the communique that years ago had been distributed to worldwide agencies including Interpol, London's CID, and the FBI:

HEISLINGER, KASPER W. (Dr.) Born, April 22, 1905, Regensburg, Ger. Father: Gustav (Chemical salesman, I. G. Farben), Mother: Ingebord, née Steidlitz. No siblings.

EDUCATION: Unterschulen, Regensburg. Un. Heidelburg, 1925. Un. Berlin, Un. Vienna: medical doctorate 1928–29. Postdoctoral: (Psychology), Vienna, Munich.

OCCUPATIONAL SPECIALTIES: Active in government programs in the '30s, public health: sanitation, infectious-disease control. From 1939 onward served as special psychological advisor to *Einsatzgrüppen* task force units; was instrumental in formulating basic operational policies at camps, including Auschwitz.

POLITICAL: Joined NSDAP, 1935. In '37 assigned to SS under Himmler.

From '39 onward subject's duties included those of medical consultant to R. Heydrich and A. Eichmann. Principal activities involved psychological indoctrination and morale maintenance of *Einsatzgrüppen* and *Konzentrationslager* personnel. Formally commended twice, '40 and '41 by Himmler. Awarded Reich Order of Distinguished Service, '42. Personally commended several times by Himmler in correspondence, who cited efficiency and zeal in matters pertaining to Final Solution.

PHYSICAL: (SS Records): Height: 173 cms, wt.: 75 kgs. Circumference of head: 57 cms. Shoe size: 8½. Eyes: Brown. Hair: Brown. Dental: gold crowns R-19, L-8, L-10. Amalgams: R-13, L-29, 30. 3-cm scar, left deltoid. 8-cm scar, inside left ankle. Appendectomy. Note: *Subject lacks blood-type and ID tattoo under left arm, customary to SS personnel.* Fingerprints: NA. Dental X-ray: NA.

LEGAL: Found guilty, Nuremberg, '46, on following counts: 1) Crimes against peace 2) Crimes against humanity, specifically genocide 3) War crimes—violations of the laws of war.

DISPOSITION: Although statutes of limitations in some countries have expired, France, Germany, and Israel carry subject on their lists of most-wanted war criminals. Unquestionably the Nazi Collaborators (*Punishment Act*) of '50 could still be exhumed.

INCIDENTAL: Early in '44, following an alleged illness, subject vanished from Germany. Postwar investigations by Allied powers were ineffectual in locating subject.

For some time it was believed he had made his escape from Germany via connections in Switzerland, Milan, and Rome, i.e., the faction of Roman-Catholic clergy known as "the Vatican Express," who were instrumental in aiding many Third Reich offenders to escape prosecution and to relocate, especially to South America.

In '65 a report that he was alive in Montreal proved groundless. In '68 another report placed him in Palo Alto, California. The general consensus at present is that if Heislinger is still alive he is in Central or South America or the Middle East.

Information on this subject should be relayed to *Mossad* offices, Tel Aviv, so that appropriate formal procedures concerning arrest and extradition may be initiated.

"BUT WHAT THE hell does it *mean?*" Colonel Armon asked. "To just blurt it out like that? At a formal ceremony?"

"He's obviously gone off the deep end," Ezra Vered said.

"Do you mean he's gone mad with guilt?" Lubinsky asked. "Or mad in the sense that he no longer knows who he is and for some weird reason has identified himself with a criminal? Carl Mast, yes—him we know. The Lebanese mess—he helped with refugee relocation. But if he's Heislinger . . ." The lawyer shook his head. "Yosef, you better move carefully on this one."

"I intend to," Colonel Armon said sourly. He was a short man in his late sixties, one of the last old-time professional Nazi-hunters, a career soldier and intelligence officer who'd come up through the ranks of the *Shin Bet,* and before that he'd made his reputation as a militant hawk in the *Hagana,* back during the days of the British Mandate. As a youngster he'd survived a year at Dachau and a second at Auschwitz.

"No fingerprints, no dental X-rays, no tattoo," Lubinsky pointed out. "There's not much to go on."

"I'm still filing an international arrest warrant," Colonel Armon said.

"But suppose he isn't Heislinger?" Lubinsky demanded. "I mean, Yosef, this is a damned important man! Keep in mind that if it comes to a trial there can't be any question about identity. So he says he's Heislinger. And I say, so what? The photographs alone raise strong doubts."

"Cosmetic surgery," Armon said.

"A possibility," Lubinsky agreed. "Still, the difference is remarkable."

Once again they looked at an assortment of photographs that the research department had pulled. Those of the contemporary Mast were excellent: they showed the bald skull, the mustache, the strong jaw. There were even shots of him taken two days earlier, in Oslo, being greeted at the airport.

But those of Heislinger, taken as far back as 1937, were not nearly as good. Colonel Armon, inspecting them with a magnifier, mused, "Ever notice what lousy photographers the Nazis were? Not with the big boys, of course. Goering, Goebbels, Schacht—no, *their* pictures are fine. But the underlings? They show up blurred, grainy, half hidden. It's as though, even then, they didn't want to attract attention." Armon peered closer. "But an expert could analyze and compare—things like ear shapes, eyes, posture."

Certainly the Heislinger in the pictures bore no resemblance to Carl Mast, even taking into consideration the more than forty-year age gap.

The best photograph showed Heislinger in the black SS uniform, a slender man, hatless—the shot must have been taken indoors— the dark hair brushed neatly back from a high forehead. The nose was quite short, a stub, very different from the curved beak Carl Mast sported. Heislinger's mouth had been on the prim side, a thin line, the lips pressed together. What lay beneath or behind that mustache of Mast's was anybody's guess.

70

Lubinsky frowned. "Too much time has passed. All we really have to work with are a few scars, a couple of crowns, some amalgam fillings. And the fact that he says he's Heislinger. Not enough, not enough."

Armon was still looking at the photographs. "Do you think it's possible Heislinger managed to change his appearance so that people might notice him more instead of less?"

"That would take incredible nerve," Ezra Vered said.

Armon ignored this. "Let's suppose Heislinger made it to Switzerland and elected to settle there instead of choosing the Middle East or South America. How far is Zurich from Munich? A couple of hundred kilometers?" Armon paused. "Remarkable. To vanish from wartime Germany and then assume a new ID, start a new life. How could he have made the switch from Heislinger, a participant in the Final Solution, to Mast, a respectable Swiss physician? How'd he transfer money or securities? He'd have needed a flawless set of papers, an entire history, mind you, of someone named Carl Mast." Colonel Armon shook his head. "I'd say it was impossible, Lubinsky, except for one thing. What the hell happened to Heislinger? His disappearance confounded even the Nazis—we know that they conducted a search for him that lasted over a year. Officially he's never been declared dead. So? Where'd he go?"

Neither Lubinsky nor Vered could answer this. Colonel Armon went on, "By '44 there was no doubt about how it would end. Everybody knew. The Nazis, please remember, were never stupid. Sure, they carried on with the war and attended the big rallies, but even so, they *knew.* Goering and Himmler and von Ribbentrop were already sniffing around for ways to save their skins. Heislinger, too. He vanishes. In '46 he's convicted in absentia, but nobody's really thought about him for decades. And now suddenly, out of a clear sky, an old man up in Oslo makes a stunning declaration that he's our man. *Why?*"

"I can't tell you that," Lubinsky said. "All I know is that if I were his counsel I'd file for a psychiatric evaluation. Yosef, what you don't understand is that if he is Heislinger, any defense lawyer could prove him incompetent."

"He's not going to get off that easily," Armon said testily. "Start preparing that international arrest warrant—get it out immediately. Vered, contact Norwegian Security. Ask them to place this Carl Mast under protective custody for the time being."

Lubinsky said, "Technically, you know, the old man hasn't committed a crime. Simply saying that you were a Nazi, even a wanted one, doesn't constitute grounds for arrest or detainment. They may not feel justified in holding him, Yosef. And to be honest, I could

**71**

understand any reluctance they might have. After all, the man's just gotten the Nobel."

"That's why I'm going to the prime minister," Colonel Armon said. "I'm putting the same request through diplomatic channels, as a double check. Norway's reasonably friendly. Maybe someday we'll be able to do them a favor in return."

BUT THEY HAD waited too long. By the time Ezra Vered made contact with Norwegian Intelligence and they had checked Mast's hotel, the old man was gone. The mechanics of police and intelligence surveillance being what they are, several more hours passed before the name was discovered on a Swissair passenger manifest. Mast had returned to his home base, Geneva.

Oslo CID was relieved to learn this. One officer said to his colleague, "Lucky for us he's left the country. Somebody else can worry about him. Personally, if I had him here, I'd put him under wraps with half a dozen bodyguards. Somebody'll go after him quickly. The man's as good as dead. That is, if he's really Heislinger." He thought for a moment. "He's marked, even if he isn't."

"The Swiss probably have him in custody already," the other officer said.

THEY DIDN'T, ALTHOUGH Ezra Vered found them highly cooperative. By then it was late afternoon.

Mast was not at his Geneva home but a manservant said that the doctor had been there earlier that day. He had gotten some papers from the wall safe in his study and then departed, saying he had business at his bank.

The investigating team thought it odd that a man on the run would behave in so unevasive a fashion, but then again there was already a good deal about Mast, or Heislinger, that was odd. The manservant knew the name of the bank. After leaving a plainclothes officer on duty in the house in the unlikely event of Mast's return, the team located the bank's manager—he had just sat down to supper—and after some argument, which not even a government subpoena totally quelled, they eventually got a look at Mast's safe-deposit box. Not surprisingly, it was empty.

At this stage, Swiss government opinion was ambivalent. Certain officials wanted very much to talk to Mast, but, like the Tel Aviv lawyer, Lubinsky, they felt a need to proceed with caution. In Switzerland, Mast was a national hero. That weekend the Geneva City Council planned to celebrate "Carl Mast Day," during which a small plaza was to be renamed in his honor. Still, the Oslo speech had been a shocker.

Quietly, internal-affairs operatives began the tedious business of checking Mast's background prior to 1945. This would take time but eventually the truth would out: the Swiss are painstaking and accurate recordkeepers. WHO officials, meanwhile, were refusing to comment on any aspect of the old man's involvement with that organization beyond steadfastly and paranoically maintaining that "Doctor Mast's longtime devotion to philanthropic causes is above reproach."

Again, hours passed. Eventually, outgoing flights from Geneva International were checked. One of them listed Mast as a passenger to Rome. At Rome, Alitalia confirmed that he'd flown to Frankfurt. Lufthansa verified that he had gone to London.

From there it was learned that he had booked a one-way flight to New York's Kennedy. But by then another day had passed.

Still later it would be said that Mast had fled Switzerland, leap-frogging around Europe in order to confuse his pursuers, but Mast was to scoff at this. "With the holidays at hand, air reservations are always difficult. At times one cannot take the shortest distance between two points," he maintained afterward. "In any event there was absolutely no question of my 'fleeing.' I merely returned to Geneva from Oslo, attended to some personal affairs, and then left. No one detained me."

No one had. It turned out that U.S. Customs and Immigration had not been alerted. Two mornings after the Oslo speech Mast's flight landed at 9:15. By 10:00 he had been processed through customs and had apparently walked straight out to the taxi area with a porter wheeling his bags, hailed a cab, and, as mysteriously as Kasper Heislinger had exited from Hitler's Third Reich, vanished into New York City, a metropolis that was as familiar to him as Geneva.

U.S. Immigration declared, and rightly so, that it had acted properly, since Mast at the moment he landed was to their knowledge a legal international traveler with bona fide credentials. Even so, at least one Jewish agency bitterly took the department to task for letting Mast "prance through, as though they'd laid out a welcome mat for a mass murderer."

Among France, Germany, Switzerland, Israel, and the U.S., a great deal of telephone and teletype correspondence was set into motion concerning what came to be known unofficially as "the Heislinger dilemma."

Researchers went back to source material, some of it forgotten for years, and so more information was brought to light. In the complicated and somewhat loony chocolate-soldier world of the Nazi military juggernaut, Heislinger had been only one echelon down from Eichmann.

That made him, if he still lived, big game.

Certainly he had been more important than the infamous Dr. Josef Mengele, Auschwitz's *Weisse Engel*—the White Angel.

MOSSAD'S ORIGINAL DOSSIER had been so expanded that a file cabinet was now required to contain it. By Armon's order the cabinet was moved to a vacant room down the corridor from his office, along with tables and chairs for the researchers.

Late in the afternoon of the third day following the Oslo speech, the Colonel visited this room, letting himself in with his key. The staff had already gone, and it was almost dark outside. Stacked in neat piles on the work tables was Heislinger evidence, to be read through, cross-indexed, and then filed. Armon pulled out a chair and sat down. He did not turn on the overhead worklights. There was no need. Outside, the twilight deepened. He took out a cigarette and lit it. In the near darkness of the room, the match flared brightly.

In this room was Heislinger. Or at least his history, a summation of his career.

The researchers—five men and women—were dedicated, and often they were horrified, too, as more and more material was unearthed. But they were, after all, young. This was ancient history they were working with. Something that had happened generations ago.

BUT FOR ARMON all of it could have occurred yesterday.

He knew, in a way that his young assistants would never know. An elderly man, sitting alone in a darkened office, smoking.

Turning it over in his mind. Thinking.

Trying to grasp how it had happened. The enormity of it.

Heislinger, it seemed, had managed to get about during those wartime years.

His name turned up not only in the extermination camps and Einsatzgrüppen strike-force records.

At the Krakow ghetto they knew of him. And at Warsaw too.

He had been associated—to what extent was still not known—with certain medical experiments on human subjects that were so macabre that they literally beggared description. Decompression rooms where high-altitude "tests" were conducted for the Luftwaffe—the air was evacuated until the subjects' eardrums and lungs exploded.

Mass sterilization with X-rays, of both men and women, without their knowledge. Victims immersed in freezing ice water for hours, to test survival techniques for the German Navy: tied securely,

**74**

naked, with wires leading to their rectums, which contained thermometers that could be electrically monitored, they lay in the tanks. When the body temperature reached 85 degrees, they were removed, and attempts were made to revive them.

Other, darker deeds.

And always, genocide. The word itself was really too much for the human imagination to encompass.

No matter how minor an actor he might later claim to be, Heislinger had been there.

He had participated in the tragic progress of those nameless myriads who had been uprooted by the mass deportations of the early forties, all those who had been flung to the winds by the disasters of war, those poor millions who were swallowed up by the crematoria ovens of one stinking death camp or another . . . the old, the young, the rich, the poor . . . genius, and ignorant peasant . . . and all the children, too.

Step right along, ladies and gentlemen. Come along, children. Don't be afraid.

*Macht schnell! Links für die Badenzimmern, rechts für Arbeitgruppen.*

*Rechts.* Right.

*Links.* Left.

*Rechts . . .*

*Links . . .*

That was *der Weisse Engel's* main task as camp physician, to sit at an ordinary wooden table in Auschwitz's unloading yards when the death-trains came in, long lines of boxcars, using a riding crop as a baton, flicking it left or right, *links, rechts,* as each terrified Jew or Pole or Serb or Hungarian stepped up and snapped to respectful attention. Mengele had also been guilty of illegal medical experiments, but he was best known as a sort of one-man welcoming committee.

Those fit enough were assigned to the work gangs: *rechts.*

All the others, grandparents, children, infants nursing, women, the halt and the lame, received the flick that meant death: *links, zum Badenzimmern.* The "bathing-rooms," in which overhead jets released the Zyklon-B. For a while the screams could be heard. But not for long.

*Der Weisse Engel,* it was said, could "examine" five hundred newcomers an hour, using this technique.

How to eradicate a culture, destroy an entire people?

One at a time, apparently. *Links. Rechts.*

Later, after the bathing-rooms had been ventilated so that the *sonderkommandos* and *kapos* could go in, the dead bodies were still upright, they had been packed in that tightly, the corpses blue-skinned, their legs covered with feces, some of the females streaked with menstrual blood. With the pregnant ones, there were often miscarriages—voided fetuses and placentas.

The *kapos* worked among the adult cadavers. Broke loose the gold and silver fillings and dental prostheses, using sturdy pliers.

From time to time the ovens could not handle the press of corpses. Too many trains were coming in.

Then the newcomers were taken outside the wire compounds to be "processed" by rifle and pistol fire, at the edges of long, shallow pits that were later bulldozed. It was said that for years afterward the grasses and weeds indigenous to the Auschwitz and Buchenwald areas bloomed in a riot of splendid profusion because of the peculiarly enriched soil—attendants could not cut the stuff fast enough!

The old camps, once so busy, were government-owned monuments nowadays. There were conducted tours, films, and photographic exhibits, but that all this could have actually taken place was somehow unbelievable.

Had it really happened? Armon knew it had.

How could the country that gave the world Goethe, Schiller, and Beethoven erect that immensely ironical sign of greeting that still looms above Auschwitz's main gate: *Arbeit Macht Frei.*

*Freedom Through Work.*

Whoever said that Germans didn't have a sense of humor?

*Arbeit Macht Frei.*

A stern admonition? Yes.

But, all in all, sensible advice.

"Cooperate with the Germans."

"Yes, it's the intelligent thing to do."

"Our situation will get better."

So must they have counseled one another, the nearly two million who obediently entered that wide gate.

Whether they knew it or not, they had come home. They would wander no more.

# part two

The greater the man, the more powerful his evil impulse.

— *The Talmud*

Among ourselves it should be mentioned quite frankly, but we will never speak of it publicly . . . I mean the cleaning out of the Jews. It's one of those things that are easy to talk about: "The Jewish race is being exterminated, it's our program, and we're doing it." And then they come, eighty million worthy Germans, and each one of them has his decent Jew. Of course the others are vermin, but *this* particular Jew is a first-rate man!

— *Heinrich Himmler, Speech to senior SS officers, Posen, October 4, 1943*

"HELLO?"

"My dear girl!"

"Who is this?"

"How enchanting to hear your voice again."

"Who *is* this?" But even as she spoke she felt an awful rush of fear. That cultured voice, the heavy accent.

If an expression could have been put into dialogue hers would have said: *"!"*

"Have you forgotten the compote we shared?" The voice coming over the phone was avuncular, affectionate: "How *are* you, Gritch?"

Astonished, she managed a pointed: "You!"

TALKING BLITHELY, MAST sailed on: "Thought I'd give you a jingle. I'm back. Obviously. Miserable weather, isn't it? You busy?"

"My God! What do you want?"

"Wondered if you happen to be free this evening, Gritch," Mast said. He seemed to be speaking loudly. In the background she heard the noise of traffic and the honking of car horns.

"Where are you?" The question was not as inane as it sounded. Her mind was floundering. She felt a great need to fix that gutteral voice in space somewhere—*what if he's calling from a block away!* It was like a nightmare in which an invisible menace was present, threatening, hanging in the air.

"Fifty-fourth and Fifth, a mere stone's throw from my bank, why do these newfangled booths offer no protection from the elements?" Mast said. "A quiet evening? Is that possible, Gritch? The weary traveler has returned."

He paused, waiting for her response. There was none. He said, "Want to see my medal? I brought it. Swell medal, Gritch."

"Listen, do me a favor—*go away!*" she said truculently. Then her voice rose indignantly, "Your picture's everywhere. *God!*"

At a loss for words, she stopped. Mast said earnestly, "Don't hang up, Gritch—please?" He, too, paused. Then: "I'm exactly the same person I was when we last saw each other. Damn, it's cold!"

"Listen, you've had a mental breakdown. Go to a hospital. That speech! Why'd you do such an insane thing?"

"Fascinating story, Gritch, wouldn't you like to hear it?"

"No," she said. "I mean, not from you personally. Thanks, but no thanks."

GRITCH HAD THOUGHT a great deal about Carl Mast since the news broke. In fact, he was all she'd thought about. Yesterday she'd even turned down a date Constantine had rung up about, using the time-tested excuse that she wasn't feeling well and would be out of action for a while.

As a matter of fact, Gritch not only felt unwell and upset, she was terrified. So frightened that for the first time ever she seriously contemplated abandoning the life of part-time prostitution.

It was one thing to make expense money by rendezvousing with this or that VIP.

But Mast was different. She had spent a night with a man who was now being accused of crimes against humanity. The charges leveled against him by Israel and other countries, if true, were enough to sear the mind.

She'd slept with a putative war criminal. Not only that, she'd *enjoyed* it. He'd made her laugh. They'd touched each other with unfeigned affection. She'd really liked this man. Had even given him her number, an unprecedented gesture.

It was too much.

For the first time since she'd started working for Constantine she felt debased. If Mast was who he'd claimed to be in that speech. God, he'd used her body, and her mind, too. The thought appalled her.

Fame, she understood, came in many forms. For some women, touching Robert Redford would be like touching fame. But Gritch had touched Mast, and now there was the feeling that she'd been in intimate contact with millions of deaths—it was of course an utterly irrational idea; but it persisted.

80

When the first news stories broke on TV and in the papers she'd been horror stricken. But then, gradually, she'd calmed down.

She was safe. Absolutely no one knew. Except Constantine, who, when they'd chatted, had been curious as to whether she'd heard what they were saying about, as he put it, "your distinguished laureate." In a calm tone of voice—which she hoped concealed her real feelings—she told him that in her opinion Mast was a spacy old freak who'd gone 'round the bend, or maybe he was acting out some whim or fantasy, who the hell knew? "He was charming and decent to me, so why don't we just leave it at that, okay?" And that's how it had been left, at least as far as Connie Phraxeteles was concerned.

But her mind kept working.

War criminal or not, they'd arrest him. Maybe they'd already picked him up somewhere. She'd never hear from him again. She was sure of that.

And in imagining this, she suddenly was aware of having missed out on a momentous opportunity. The reaction was so typical that she almost smiled. She knew—or thought she knew—herself very well. If confronted by real danger, she'd run. But, once safe, there was that flicker of curiosity to know what the danger had been like, a sense akin to disappointment in herself for not risking, exploring.

Very possibly—who could tell?—she'd been the last person Mast had been intimate with prior to Oslo. He had relaxed with her, "been himself," whatever that meant.

What an opportunity.

Gritch thought to herself: If only I'd paid more attention! Damn, if I could have made him talk about himself more. I might have been able to make him open up and tell me what he was going to do. And *why*.

Aloud she said, "Jesus!" They were describing him as an avatar of the twentieth century's best qualities. And now maybe of its worst ones, too!

Would she ever meet a human being of such tremendous implications again? It had been a once-in-a-lifetime shot.

She admitted, finally, that the moment had escaped her. It was past, done with. In a way she was glad, in another, sorry.

But now, suddenly, out of nowhere, that gruff voice, at once charming and unctuous: *"My dear girl. How enchanting to hear..."*

It was no exaggeration to say she was stunned.

AT THE SOUND of Mast's voice most people would have clapped the receiver onto its cradle and refused to answer incoming calls for the

81

rest of the day. Or perhaps, like good citizens, they would have dialed the FBI: "Yes, good afternoon, I'd like to report a war criminal down on Fifth . . ."

But Gritch, as she was so fond of pointing out, was not most people, and now her mind told her: It's not true! Opportunity sometimes *does* knock more than once!

The rational side of her mind screamed: Tell him to fuck off and then hang up.

But the emotional side of her whispered: Don't blow it! He wants or needs something special. That's why he's calling.

There wasn't time to analyze. She had to choose.

Perhaps a minute had passed since his initial "My dear girl." In that time Gritch, though she was not aware of it, had already reached a decision, in a sense encoding her fate forever.

She said pleasantly, "When did you get in, Carl?"

"THIS VERY MORNING, Christ, it's freezing out here. So, having attended to several business matters, I thought that perhaps we might get together this evening . . . or much better, this afternoon. Come on, Gritch, what d'you say? Have a heart. My feet are ice. It's snowing again." Mast paused. She listened to more sounds of traffic. "The usual fee? A little sociable companionship? That's all I'm asking for. And a place to warm my toes." There was silence. "Gritch. You still there?"

For a moment her resolve was shaky. "I'd planned on going to the library."

"Ah, the compulsive schoolgirl. You'll ruin your eyes. The studies can wait."

She thought: He's not really Heislinger.

But her curiosity was growing. She said in a more friendly voice, "Your calling like this surprised me."

"Full of 'em, aren't I?" he said agreeably.

"Now that you mention it, yes," Gritch said. "And yes, I'd really love to see you. The library can wait. What time shall I come down? I'm dying to hear about the ceremony." She hesitated. "I can be ready in about an hour. All right?"

"I'm as free as a bird from here on out," Mast said. "But a small favor, if you don't mind. Your place, not mine?"

SO THAT WAS why he'd called. The fear returned. She said bluntly, "They're after you, aren't they?"

"Please. Let's not be melodramatic."

She said, "Clients don't come to my place, Carl. Ever."

"My dear. An exception? Just this once?"

"Why can't I meet you at a hotel?"

"Manhattan hotels appeal largely to funeral directors and suicides with a penchant for high places. I'm a homebody. As a favor?" She was silent. Then: "You're on the run."

"Gritch, stop imitating a Mafia moll. It's beneath you."

"You want a place to hide. That's why you called."

"Nonsense," Mast said irritably. "I'm cold and tired after too many hours in the air. Crossing the Atlantic was abysmal. A largish female seated next to me had too obviously neglected to use deodorant. Her attempt to compensate for this social misdemeanor by applying generous dollops of K-Mart cologne caused an olfactory insult that can only be described as overwhelming. A massive matron, as I said, from, so she informed me—as if *I* cared—a rustic hamlet, Gary, Indiana. Her effluvium was such that I was quite unable to catch my customary nap. Really, you know, the only thing to do in mid-Atlantic is snooze. No, Gritch. What I want right now is warmth and comfort. A hot tub. A passably decent meal. A night's sleep."

"I don't believe you," she said. "Haven't you any friends you could go to?"

"None whom I would judge completely dependable or even trustworthy."

"What in hell makes you think you can trust me?"

"What in hell makes you think I do?" Mast replied. "Circumstances, however, dictate that I must place a degree of confidence in someone."

"Why me?"

"There are reasons."

She knew what that meant. Except for Connie Phraxeteles, the "soul of discretion" as he said of himself, there was no link, no connection.

"What's wrong with your apartment?" she demanded, knowing what the answer would be.

"It's being surveilled," Mast said simply. "I learned of this only a short while ago."

"By whom?"

"It seemed best not to tell my cab driver to stop so that I could inquire," Mast said, obviously still attempting agreeability. "Listen. I won't cause you trouble. I promise. A private get-together, okay? The sacred Nadelmann name will be protected. Five hundred. Like before." The irritability flashed again. "This is turning into a blizzard!"

In the background she heard a ringing, as of a bell being listlessly swung to and fro. "What's that noise?"

Mast said sotto voce, "There's an ersatz Kris Krinkle, all red suit and white whiskers, standing guard jollily over a trivet from which is suspended a black iron kettle into which gullible passersby are flinging coins. Unless I'm greatly mistaken, his forebears were rescued from Tanganyika. He looks colder than I feel. Gritch, damn it, have a heart."

"You have money?"

"Yes." The relief in his voice was evident.

She gave him the address. On 101st, off West End.

He said, "See you in an hour. I have to pick up my suitcases. Listen, dash out and get me some Gauloises and a few bottles of decent wine, like a good girl."

The operator broke in: "Please deposit another twenty-five cents . . ."

Mast, waspish: "Hey, why must you interrupt? You know something—the goddamned trouble with AT&T is that it's got no *heart*."

But he was addressing an automated tape. "Your three minutes are up. Please deposit . . ."

Just before the phone went dead he yelled at Gritch, "Run a tub!"

THE INTELLIGENCE AGENT, Gerber, first name Mordecai, was experiencing the discomforts of winter too, of the sort the English can sometimes offer the international traveler at London's Heathrow in December, where the morose Gerber was sweating out a seven-hour-long interval between flights. Heathrow's central heating facility had, in the inexplicably British way of things, malfunctioned, gone on the fritz, to the acute inconvenience of several thousand holiday travelers who, like Gerber, sat bundled to the ears in the vast terminal's cavernous glass-walled lobbies.

Gerber, a protégé of Colonel Armon, shivered miserably—he was coming down with a head cold—aware that certain journeys seem fated to go wrong from the start.

In Frankfurt am Main a storm had delayed all flights including the one that eventually got him as far as Heathrow, and the air terminal there, though a tribute to modern German design, lacked insofar as Gerber could ascertain anything resembling a kosher snack bar. His Alitalia flight from Rome had carried a group of anthem-singing *Wehrmacht* vets who were returning to their homeland after a North African tour of some of the less-disastrous of Rommel's *Panzerkorps'* battlefields. There was loud talk of great

84

desert adventures the men had undergone back in the good old days, and the stewardess had served snacks of such suspect appearance that Gerber had not even tasted. In Rome itself there had been an argument at customs concerning his expensive collection of photographic gear, for such was Gerber's ostensible occupation, or so his Israeli passport said: free-lance photographer.

The front was one that he had used before and one that appealed. He loved photography.

As for his actual profession Mordecai loved it too and, moreover, was even better at it than he was with a Hasselblad, Nikon, or Canon. Though he resembled an ascetic scholar, he possessed an admirable trait: in any assignment, no matter what the risk, he had an absolutely unflappable calmness that had earned him the unqualified respect of his associates.

Born in Yonkers a decade after the Third Reich's extermination camps had reached peak efficiency, Mordecai had immigrated with his parents and younger sister to Israel at the age of ten.

There, as sometimes happens with certain personalities, he had developed a strong sense of patriotism along with an exaggerated concept of what was right and what was wrong. He was, in the words of the philosopher Eric Hoffer, a true believer; that is, an incomplete human who is incapable of realizing self-fulfillment except as the follower of some mighty cause. He also felt that in any healthy social system rules had to be enforced. An innocuous-sounding conviction perhaps, but one capable of backfiring.

After college he had entered civil police work and eventually switched to government security and intelligence. His superiors in the latter branch knew of his work. There he was considered by many, including Colonel Armon, an outstanding example of contemporary Jewry, one of the finest of the "new generation" who, whether reformed or conservative or orthodox, were as up-to-date as an Atari video game while still maintaining strong links with the Pentateuch.

Mordecai in his way was as devout as any nineteenth-century shtetl-dweller who lived and died within the Pale. Whenever possible he followed tradition and observed the rituals. He was also, however, a formidable young man. As such he had found a special niche among the Chosen, who had finally come into their own, stepping out of the ghetto and into the brightness of the sun. And what a pleasant warmth it provided! In short he was an appealing, intelligent, and civilized young Israeli who could carry out an execution as ruthlessly and with as much freedom from guilt, shame, or remorse, as the most rabid Shiite terrorist.

At thirty, unmarried, six-feet-four, slender of build, bespectacled, pale-skinned, reserved, with wavy black hair and wearing a neatly barbered beard and mustache, Mordecai looked more like a Talmudic student than a photographer, let alone an intelligence agent or, perish the thought, a man capable of violence. All he lacked was earlocks and, as if to compensate for this omission, his garb was almost Old World—dark suit and tie, a sensible black homburg worn squarely atop the head, and an overcoat of heavy broadcloth material which, though neatly buttoned, somehow gave the impression of a kaftan.

His features were modeled along classic lines of the sort that down through the centuries have caused the hearts of sensitive Jewish maidens to miss a beat.

The face was narrow. The expression solemn, grave, almost bemused or stunned, as though its owner were too lost in philosophical conundrums ever to take heed that some young women looked on with longing and admiration. Behind the spectacles the eyes were gentle, warm, brown, with thick curling lashes. A girl who gazed into those eyes too long ran the risk of losing her senses. The mouth, clearly visible beneath the short mustache, was a pink and perfect Cupid's bow.

Handsome Mordecai Gerber. Apparently oblivious—but not really—to his natural charm, he seemed to live mainly for his work. Women in Tel Aviv, some goaded by the hot fires of youth, some old enough to have had better sense but nonetheless still goaded, took note of him.

Such a curious fellow. So quiet and reserved, so polite. Although sexually a dozen women removed from virginity, Mordecai was still capable of reddening when a pretty girl's eyes locked with his. Why, he wondered, should this be? The shyness lessened once the actual mechanics of a conquest were underway. As soon as the bedroom was gained, the blush vanished, to be replaced by a well-nigh unquenchable horniness and staying power, as those who were conquered could happily attest.

Mordecai had honed his amatory skills with the same dedication he brought to intelligence work, but even after he got very good at the business of leaving women weak with pleasure there was still that innate bashfulness, that tendency to blush when a blush was the last thing in the world he wanted. Mordecai berated himself for this too-human failing but was quite unable to do anything about it. Furthermore, he noticed that certain women were vulnerable to such masculine modesty; some in fact seemed quite unable to contain themselves.

So while the shyness was genuine it was also a trait not without value, and when the mood was upon him Mordecai worked it for all it was worth. He had never been in love. Not yet anyway. The work he did was so important that anything resembling a normal private life was secondary. Besides, he was a little leery of women, not because they were what they were but because his body needed them. No human being, he decided, ought to be able to exercise that kind of hold over another. It was almost enough to make one shudder!

He never discussed his feelings with the female friends who were interested in enriching his life, but instead adapted a counterfeit posture that closely paralleled the spurious free-lance photographer facade he used in his professional work. The line he used, while forthright enough, was also as old as the hills: he was not ready to "get serious," his work "must come first," but, who knows, maybe later . . .

It was a pretty good act and he had it down pat. The expression grave, rather melancholy. A pensive sigh. Sad, ah very sad. Duty prevails. Regrettable, but what's one to do?

A good dinner in an expensive restaurant was not the worst balm to wounded feminine pride.

Even so a few young Tel Aviv belles, excruciatingly aware of their own beauty and virtually consumed by the smoldering embers that scorched their vitals—such a divine conflagration and, damn, he was so *eligible*—were literally, in private that is, reduced to frustrated viragos after hearing such words. Not ready? Not ready! So when was ready? The agonies of the youthful, though frequently ecstatic, are more often merely miserable.

Colonel Armon, who knew about his protégé's personal life, approved. He assessed Mordecai for what he was: bright, dedicated, highly trained, and capable of carrying out any assignment. True, some of the young agent's peers regarded him as odd. "A prude," and "too stuffy," it was said of him. This did not trouble the Colonel. Armon was perfectly aware that far weirder types were attracted to intelligence and espionage work. One simply had to acknowledge their limitations. Once a person knew those, he knew how to use their owners.

So, then, Mordecai: apparently as ingenuous as a lamb, except that those who worked with him regarded him as a cool and sometimes scary colleague. He went about his job. Spent a good deal of time out of the country, but in Tel Aviv lived comfortably; in fact, quite well. This was as it should be: the True Believer must be rewarded. He read, studied, went to temple, took pictures, and tooled about the city in a burgundy-colored Datsun sports car. Made of his kitchen alcove an excellent darkroom, producing prints that sometimes won prizes in contests. Life in Israel was not all that bad, though like everyone else he complained about the out-of-control inflation that beset the country, and the worthlessness of the shekel.

MORDECAI'S PRIMARY ROLE in the Heislinger dilemma, as outlined to him by Colonel Armon, was to act as a backup whose services might be called upon only in the event that something went awry with the official steps already being undertaken.

Mordecai, with his grave expression, pointed out that in his opinion too many things had already gone wrong: "Somebody ought to have grabbed him immediately. If you ask me, sir, he's made us all look stupid."

"These things happen," Colonel Armon admitted. "By the time we got through to Washington, he'd left Kennedy."

"Into New York," Mordecai noted.

"His apartment is being watched. Also all contacts and organizations he's had dealings with."

"Have you ever tried to find somebody in New York?" Mordecai's expression grew gloomy. "There are a lot of people in that place."

"He can't hide."

"For someone who can't hide he's doing an awfully good job of it," Mordecai said. Then, displeased by his dourness, he attempted lightness and got flippancy instead: "Well, certain things are in our favor. Whenever we see a *schwartzer* or Puerto Rican in Manhattan, we can be sure he's not Heislinger." He paused. "What've we got there?"

"A full team," Armon said. "Fourteen men."

"Who's in charge?"

"Sy Abarbanel. You've worked together before."

"Sy? Oh, yes." He and Mordecai were friends.

Armon stared at Mordecai. "Heislinger won't escape. Don't worry about that."

"I'm not," Mordecai said. "Find him for me. That's all."

"Under no circumstances are you to attempt an arrest," Armon cautioned. "That procedure's within the province of international law. You are merely to be at hand."

"What about extra ID, in case it's needed?" Mordecai asked. "Special equipment?"

"All taken care of," the colonel told him. The special equipment, which ranged from conventional handarms to *cartouche* gas pens capable of releasing a deadly spray that would take effect in fewer than ten seconds, to equally silent $CO_2$ operated devices that fired a projectile the size of a phonograph needle, would be provided Mordecai in New York, or for that matter in any other city around the world, when Mast was located, and if it was definitely established that Mordecai's talents were required.

"Of course, it's highly unlikely that we'll need you," Armon concluded. "You'll be able to take all the pictures you want."

"FOR SOMEONE WHO'S supposed to be on the run you're in a pretty fine mood," she said.

This was true. Mast seemed too satisfied, too pleased with himself, and his obvious high spirits annoyed her. The wheedling and cajolery with which he had pleaded his case on the phone had been replaced by a brusque bossiness and an all too transparent conviction that his needs were to be served.

He had not been in the apartment five minutes before Gritch thought: Why, the son of a bitch acts like he *owns* the place!

"WHY SHOULDN'T I be happy?" Mast said. "The odds were a hundred to one in favor of my sitting in a cell this minute, but . . . here I am!" He went on ruminatively, "There's really a lot to be said for acting on the spur of the moment. Extemporaneous behavior bewilders the logical mind. I must remind myself to indulge in it more often." He sighed with pleasure. "There I was, twiddling my thumbs in the ticket line at Geneva International, wondering in what fashion I ought to spend my last hours of unadulterated freedom. Lo and behold, I thought of you, and the splendid evening we had."

"Stop being a wise-ass," Gritch said. "Why *did* you come back to New York?"

"There's something wrong with New York?" he asked.

At that moment Mast was buried almost to his mustache in a

91

tubful of hot water, all but his face and bald dome hidden by the billowy froth of a bubble bath. Now and then he made small groaning noises of what might have been pain but were actually contentment.

Standing beside the soap dish was a large steam-frosted goblet of champagne. Another bit of extemporaneous behavior. Spotting a seroboam in Gritch's fridge—she had been saving it for the holidays—Mast had decided that its contents were a more suitable accompaniment to a bubble bath than the wine he'd sent her trudging out into the snow to buy. Alongside the goblet lay a sodden, inadvertently splashed Gauloise.

His vexed hostess sat on the lowered lid of the toilet, blue-jeaned, legs crossed, the left tube-soxed foot tapping an angry midair cadence. The jeans, socks, and comfortable baggy gray sweatshirt were part of her student-at-home costume, as were the heavy black-framed spectacles she wore to correct a longstanding myopic problem.

Dressed thus, frowning with concentration and devoid of make-up, she was nonetheless very nearly as lovely as she'd been when they last met. Moments earlier Carl Mast had said as much: "Don't know if anyone's told you this, Gritch, but you've an incredibly lovely face."

His own rather resembled a happy terrapin's, wrinkled, suntanned, bobbing in a lathery sea of cumulo-foam. He said now, "In New York I've got a chance. Shoot me a little more hot, will you? As I said on the phone, I need a breather."

He paused to enjoy the jet of steaming water that spurted downward into the tub. "I asked myself, what country in all the world has the time and leisure to play host properly to an old rogue like me, to give him the audience he deserves? Yessir, the land of the free, where entertainment has as much value as the dollar, where there are 'round-the-clock news channels, where the appetite for novelty, for something different, is virtually insatiable. Of course in *das Heimatland* I've got an even better chance. I could walk out of any courtroom there a free man, exonerated, but world opinion would scream: *rigged trial!* Enough, enough, what the hell are you trying to do, turn me into a blanched onion?"

She shut off the water, feeling irritation: Had he completely forgotten words like please and thank you? He sank a little lower, propping both feet on the faucets, the soapy toes doing an anemone dance. The inside of her mind was a stew of nerves and conflicting emotions. Who did he think he was? Who did he think *she* was, a goddamned chambermaid?

Gritch hated being used but she liked even less being as scared as she was now. She was beginning to wonder if something very bad for her might come out of all this. The hot water Mast was presently lolling in was delightful enough for him, but she was likely to find herself up to her ears in another, metaphorical kind. "They'll get you sooner or later," she pointed out. "You must know that."

"Not necessarily," Mast replied. "Because I'm going to turn myself in. When I'm ready, that is. At my age a man is entitled to respect, and part of that respect involves not being rushed."

WHAT IN GOD'S name was he babbling about? She didn't know. What upset her was not being in control of the situation. Gritch didn't care for that at all.

Mast, she was beginning to understand, insisted on running his own show.

Far worse, though, was the risk she was taking. Like most good citizens she was paranoid about the law and went out of her way to avoid anything that might lead to a confrontation with its representatives. Now, all of a sudden, she had a wanted man on her hands, not merely in her home but in her tub.

He was certainly adept at having his own way. There was a lot of the con man about him: the smooth surface charm—it had taken no time on the phone to get her to relax her heretofore inflexible rule about keeping the two sides of her life separate—and, behind that, self-centered toughness.

It occurred to her that with Mast's being so old he might not give a damn about his future. But hers? Why, her whole life could get royally fucked up if she didn't watch her step.

He seemed so oblivious to *her* side of the situation.

She'd done him an enormous favor, after all.

Having gone this far she'd made up her mind to find out what made him tick.

He was gaming her. But two could play at that.

MAST SUDDENLY GLANCED up at her as though intuiting that certain feathers, now ruffled, might need smoothing. His voice became attentive, almost self-reproachful: "Really, my dear, I can't begin to express how grateful I am for your immensely kind invitation. To let me invade the privacy of your home like this. Out of the blue, so to speak. Even though it was overcast when I flew in. A chance to pull myself together. Most kind of you."

"Don't mention it," she said coolly.

"I detest a churlish guest, don't you?" Mast continued, turning on the graciousness for all it was worth, as she had, not many moments earlier, turned the spigot on the hot tap: "I've interrupted your schedule. You are sacrificing valuable time to attend my wants. Also, let me say that I am not insensitive to the uniqueness of your having me here. I understand your caution. It's wiser not to mix personal and business affairs. I shan't forget it. Am I really the first guest you've permitted?"

"Yes."

"Smart girl."

"Smart that you're the first or smart that I've never had anyone here?" she asked.

"Both, my dear girl, both," Mast said, beaming up at her from the suds. "I'll make it worth your while."

"If you really want to do that, start by telling me about Oslo," Gritch said bluntly. "I think it's fair that I know, Carl."

Mast chuckled. "Yes, I can see that you're curious." He picked up a loofah and leisurely began working on a knobby knee. "However, you can't expect me to articulate in five minutes what I've thought about for decades." Adroitly, he switched subjects. "Homey nest you have here, Gritch. It reflects your tastes perfectly. It's *you*."

"Oh, cut the crap," she said disgustedly. She thought: *It's me.* Shows how the hell much *he* knows!

THE GROUND-FLOOR rear apartment at 417 West 101st Street, though pleasant, was by no means spectacular. Three rooms, with a small walled-in garden out back, at present unusable due to recent snows. A large and airy back bedroom containing a bureau, dressing table, armchair, TV, stereo, and a queen-sized bed covered with a throw of Malay batik. Mast, upon inspecting this room, immediately sat on the bed, bouncing tentatively, then thumped with one fist: "Excellent, excellent."

In the living room: a long low couch, tables, lamps, shelves of books, another TV, and her desk, actually a heavy door to which had been mounted fold-down legs. On it were her IBM typewriter, calculator, electric pencil sharpener, a fluorescent lamp, office supplies, dictionaries, a thesaurus, and a framed photograph of her late father, Steve, looking big, burly, gray-haired, handsome. He stared seriously at the camera and had his arm around a skinny dark-haired moppet who seemed to be all elbows, knees, and glittery orthodontic grin: Gritch at eleven or twelve.

The kitchen, though tiny, was clean and freshly painted. A pleasant work area with a hand-over counter facing onto the living room. Expensive French copperware hung from a pegboard over the stove and there was a microwave, which was mainly used to heat the endless cups of coffee she sipped during the course of a day's studying.

Here and there about the place were potted plants: Australian orchid, ferns, ivy. Large, framed prints hung from the walls: a Degas, a Wyeth barn in autumn, two Klees, three Manets. A cast-stone Giacometti reproduction rose skeletally from the walnut cocktail table. In Gritch's opinion her residence was tolerable. She had no intention of living like this forever, but until she acquired her doctorate it would suffice.

The bathroom where they were now talking was not unusual except for the tub, which was definitely superior, an immoderately large receptacle fully five feet long, with old-fashioned, nickel-plated faucets and iron legs cast into lion's-feet claws. Gritch, when she was not at the books, often loved to lie and soak in it, neither thinking nor planning nor scarcely even breathing but simply *being*. She had fallen in love with that tub the moment she set eyes on it ... such a tub was a kind of retreat. Floating lazily in it, as content as a fishlette in an aquarium, she was able at times, especially after a bit of grass and Cinzano, to attain a degree of relaxation that did wonders for her moody temperament. And now, someone else was taking his ease in it: a very smooth and fast-talking shark.

"AH! HOW DELIGHTFUL it is to do nothing and then rest afterward," Mast said. It was an hour later. They were having dinner.

The bath had revived him. Dressed now in dark slacks and a white silk shirt that was open at the collar, with a fresh scarf folded about his neck, he was relaxed and at the same time ebullient.

She thought uneasily: It's harder kowtowing to him than it is turning a trick.

What she hadn't realized was that the apartment, until this evening, had been a sanctuary for her, too, a refuge similar to what he had so earnestly argued for over the phone earlier: a very private place. It was her secret hideaway. Once inside it she had no need to play the part of a date for the evening, nor the proper grad student, either. It might not be the Waldorf but when the front door's triple deadbolts were locked, she could let her hair down.

Mast tilted his goblet, swirling champagne at the bottom. "Gritch I have a proposition I'd like to make you."

"Oh?" Perhaps that bath had revived him in more ways than one.

He caught her expression. "No, this is serious. I'll write it in real ink, if you like."

He was, she judged, mildly tipsy. Understandable. The jeroboam was half gone, not to mention that for the past forty or fifty hours he'd been flying. He *did* hold his liquor well. Gritch herself had drunk sparingly, so as to be alert to his least remark. Not that it had done her much good. Thus far she had not succeeded in getting one candid statement out of him. Desultorily, she picked at the food on her plate.

Mast himself attacked dinner—a filet of sole, salad, breadsticks, and a hefty wedge of Emmenthaler—with more gusto than might be expected in someone who ought to be, at the very least, in the throes of jet lag, chewing, sipping, swallowing and, from time to time, gesticulating with knife or fork. Those deep-sunk eyes were blood-shot and the bags under them dark with fatigue but even so his mood was convivial, in fact, jolly. She wondered when he'd crash and burn. What he needed was twelve hours of uninterrupted sleep. She was beginning to think she did too. His presence irked her and now she decided: He's too damned pushy, if you ask me!

As if reading her mind he smiled amiably and said, "Gritch, a little birdie is telling me that you're feeling *kvetch* tonight. Eh? Patience, my dear, patience."

HOW IN THE world did he *do* that, she wondered. Several times now he'd been able to guess what she was thinking. Gritch liked to imagine that her face impenetrably masked her thoughts, but at times—and when she least expected it—he seemed able to pierce that mask effortlessly. And why the phony Jewish accent? Was he taunting her? She asked, "What's the proposition?"

"How would you like to work for me?" he said. "A temporary job."

She shook her head. "Not interested."

"Hear me out."

"Talk your head off, if you like," she said. "Having you here tonight is chancy enough. If I'd had any brains, I'd never have let you inside the door."

"The salary would be three thousand a week," Mast went on. "That's cash. No checks. No IRS."

"Carl, what the hell d'you want from me?" Her anger was beginning to get the best of her. "I don't need your money. Shove it! Let's have a pleasant evening. But tomorrow, goodbye."

He said, "Of course, I'd have to live here. For the time being, I mean."

She was appalled. Why the fucker actually wanted to move in on her. "No way. You want protection? Go to the State Department. Ask for political asylum."

"That may come later," he said. "They might or might not offer it."

"Carl, that's your problem. Right now you're sitting here putting on your chairman-of-the-board act, but the truth is that there are an awful lot of people out there who're hot after your ass! I won't be involved." She shook her head. "Holy Toledo!"

"We're talking about real money, Gritch."

"You've come sniffing at the wrong door."

And she meant it. The five hundred he'd handed over minutes after arriving was an absurd amount to pay for a place to sack out. And now this new offer. No one talked that much money unless there was danger.

BUT THERE WAS still something that gnawed at her—she had to *know*—and with that she got a grip on herself.

Ask straight out. Get it settled once and for all.

She tasted her champagne and then gave him a serious look. Quite businesslike. No coyness. "I want to ask you something, Carl, and it's important. I mean, what you tell the world is your affair. But here . . . I want total honesty."

He sat across the table from her, listening, serious too. Reaching across, she laid her hand on his.

"What I must know, for my own peace of mind, is this: are you really Heislinger?"

Mast paused, then said calmly, "Well, as a matter of fact, Gritch, I am."

He might almost have said, "I'm in extermination," the way Jewish merchants used to say "I'm in ladies' garments," or "I'm in wholesale kitchenware."

She heard the words. Tried to swallow but achieved only a gulp and then, hurriedly, let go of the hand she had been holding. As though its owner were an AIDS victim or a moribund leper. Whispered, "You *can't* be!"

"I have incontestable proof," Mast replied. "That's why I went to a bank today, to rent a safe-deposit box. Everything's in it. Money, too."

As she sat there staring at him she felt a sudden warmth at her bottom. Realized she was wetting her pants. The sensation spread.

"Excuse me," she said, rising quickly. "Be right back." With that she dashed for the bathroom. There she voided what was left in her bladder. Then removed jeans and underpants, washed herself, dropped the wet garments into the hamper, and strode barebottomed into the bedroom where she put on dry clothing. She returned to the dining table, wiped her chair with several paper towels, threw the wad into the garbage, rinsed her hands, sat down.

Mast looked at her, aware of what had happened. Flaking off a morsel of sole, he placed it in his mouth and said, "The shock of recognition?"

"You took me by surprise," she said. "I'm sorry."

"Don't apologize," Mast remarked. "Involuntary micturition's by no means a rare phenomenon."

"It is for me," Gritch said. "The last time that happened I was maybe nine. My dad took me for a ride on a roller coaster."

"An automatic defense mechanism," Mast explained. "Animals, and men, too, when suddenly confronted by danger, often void water and defecate simultaneously. A way of lightening the body so that its owner can flee more quickly. On the battlefield it happens all the time."

She lit a cigarette, one of her long brown mentholated kind, realizing how adroitly he'd led her into a change of subject. It was Heislinger she wanted to know about, not animal responses.

He was staring at her. That simian look again, the brooding eyes unblinking. Finally he said, "Some of the commentators are suggesting senility has laid waste to my mind. No, Gritch. It's nothing like that."

"A game," she ventured. "It's some weird joke you've dreamed up."

"At my age, life per se is a joke . . . and a game." He forked another flake of sole, chewed, nodding. "Heislinger, though, was—is—no joke. Of course, much of what's been said about him—the facts—are mixed up. I myself saw an article in the London *Times,* they call that a paper? Full of half truths, distortions, sloppy reportage. Not that I offer that as an alibi. Heislinger was guilty enough."

"But how do you live with the memories?" she insisted.

"I manage. Quite comfortably, in fact."

"But the guilt!"

"*Ach, scheiss!*" Mast scowled. "Guilt is for idiots. Who in hell has time for guilt! Next you'll be sniveling at me about morality. You miserable Jews are as bad as Christians. You're all breast-beaters."

"Then why did you confess?"

"It was time to."

"Because you're old? You wanted to set your soul at peace?"

"The soul doesn't exist," Mast said. "Or if it does, mine is so untroubled that I've never even noticed it. Speaking of soul, this sole is splendid. How'd you do it?"

She mumbled distractedly, "Five minutes, oven preheated to 375°. Dash of marjoram and lemon."

Mast said, "Heislinger never killed anyone personally, you understand. But as an accessory, he was without doubt involved in the deaths of many." He paused. "It would be wonderfully convenient if there were extenuating circumstances. In my own admittedly redundant view, however, murder is murder."

MAST REFILLED THEIR goblets from the jeroboam. "Of course, in this era-gone-mad all we hear is 'extenuating circumstances.' 'Justifiable homicide.' Nowadays you can assassinate a world leader and get off the hook by pleading temporary insanity." He drank some of his champagne. "After the war, at Nuremberg, the defendants had alibis too. They were following orders. They were only a cog in a big machine. They didn't know. *Dreck!* You terminate five or six million kikes, somebody knows. Everybody knows! Whom did they think they were kidding?" His voice grew hard. "Is that why you don't want me on your hands? Because you're *Jewish?*"

"Very astute of you to hook that up," she said coldly.

"I don't see what that has to do with it. It didn't stop you from taking my money that first evening. And earning it, too, I should add."

"That was different," she snapped. "I'd never heard the name Heislinger."

"But today you had, and you still invited me for the night. And once again you took my money."

"You practically invited yourself. As for the five hundred, take it back if you like—and get out."

"So listen to the high-class princess all of a sudden!" Mast exclaimed delightedly, again falling into that execrable dialect. "Such high principles you never saw."

"Jews and ex-Nazis—or crazy old men who claim they're ex-Nazis—don't hang out together," Gritch said. She hated that accent.

"What? Is this prejudice rearing its ugly head?" Mast demanded. "Gritch, I'm surprised. And at that, you're wrong. Himmler had a dreadful time keeping his SS boys from dropping pebbles into Jewish girls' wells. Back then it was like an interracial thing, *ganz verboten.* Quite similar, in fact, to attitudes prevalent in your revoltingly provincial American South—where, even today, a white woman who enjoys the comforts provided by a *schwartzer* inamorato is, how shall we say, looked upon with disfavor? For Heinrich the roles were reversed. No clean-cut Aryan lad was allowed to poke his wienie up a *yiddische* mousehole. Such a no-no, but of course it happened. The sweetest thing about forbidden sex is that it's wonderful fun." Mast drank. "No, there's too much evidence that Jews and Nazis were in many ways bound more closely than either cared

99

to admit. Economically, socially, psychologically. There is, after all, no better marriage than one in which each party is indissoluably wed to the other by ties that, though symbiotic, are nonetheless stronger than blood." He eyed her. "Three thousand. That ain't hay, girlie. Stick with me for a while. Maybe you'll learn a few things. And I don't mean that soporific shit they force-feed you in grad school."

"I can't work for you," she cried loudly. "Can't you *see?*"

"Why in hell not?" he yelled back. "In the camps who d'you think did the down-and-dirty for us? Who d'you think were in the *Sonderkommandos* and *Kapos*? Jews! Yiddles!"

She glared at him. "You motherfucker! You're trying to make a *Kapo* out of me!"

His voice overrode hers. "*They* operated the ovens. *They* yanked the teeth. *They* sorted the clothing and clipped the hair. So much women's hair you never saw, mountains of it, along with truckloads of gold watches, earrings, bracelets, rings—chop the goddamned finger right off if the ring's a tight fit! It was Jews who herded Jews into the gassing rooms. Not the SS. *They* stood around taking it easy, having a smoke and a chat while the *Kapos* did their thing. Ah, they were merciless, those workgangs of happy-go-lucky *Kapos*." He stared at her. "Upward of six thousand a day, Gritch. And that was just Auschwitz."

"I've read as much about the Holocaust as the next person."

Mast gave a Mephistophelian chuckle. "The smoke from the crematoria chimneys was visible for thirty kilometers. Very distinctive aroma, y'know. Kentucky-fried Jew. Extra-crisp, no charge!"

For a moment she stared at him, mouth agape. Then, furiously: "For the *Kapos* it was a matter of survival. They had to!"

"What am I hearing, extenuating circumstances again?" Mast shook his head and laughed. "Back then we needed the *Kapos,* and now I need you. A worker, an assistant of sorts, someone intelligent."

"Quit handing me a line of crap," she hissed. "You want a place to hide. Someone to front for you. You think that because I peddle my body I'll sell anything. . . . You're wrong! Oh, you rotten bastard! Who're you kidding, you fucker? The reason you want me is because no one would think of the two of us. I'm perfect for you."

"Precisely," Mast said. "I'm acquainted with a lot of people in this town, kid, and I know enough to stay away from them right now. So then who? Enter Nadelmann, girl student, strictly legitimate—pardon me while I laugh!—lives the life of a bookworm all by her lonesome, way up on the West Side, so busy she ain't even got time for a steady boyfriend, you don't watch out you'll end up with frown wrinkles before you're thirty, reading all that junk! Yessir, a bona fide university lollipop!"

She groped for words, in a rage now.

Puffing at his cigarette he said, icily, "What I like about you is that you...don't...move...in...my...world. You're a nonentity. That can be useful." He considered this and then threw his next words in her face: "At best, whom do you know? Who knows you? A hundred, perhaps two hundred—I'm being generous—students, teachers, storekeepers? You have no family. You live a solitary life, except for part-time whoring...and *that,* my dear, is a hobby I may or may not elect to discuss with you later. Yes . . . your cover is damned near flawless. The point is," Mast sneered, "nobody has ever heard of Griselda Nadelmann. You're an utter *nobody!*"


SHE FELT LIKE she'd been slapped. Wished with all her heart that she'd never told him anything about herself.

Mast drank more, and continued, this time in tones that were diffident, "Ah, come on, Gritch. After all, what does an old has-been like me need? I'm no trouble. I require food, shelter, liquor, tobacco—also someone who can put together a few documents I'm interested in preparing. I'll need research material—the campus library can provide that—also photocopying. Oh yes, also someone to get my Rx's refilled. I have prescriptions. You'll have to go to different pharmacies, not in this neighborhood. There will be other minor errands. Okay. Three thousand a week. For however long I engage your services. Plus incidental expenses, naturally." That's less than the five hundred per night you customarily ask for spreading your legs, but I feel it's fair to set a lower fee on a weekly basis, don't you agree?"

She shook her head. "You're not going to turn my entire life upside down."

He shrugged. "It would be for a month. Certainly not much longer than that. You'll have to drop school, an important consideration, but the remuneration'll make it worthwhile. Sex, by the way, would definitely be a secondary item. What d'you say? I'm not stingy, girl. You could, with a bonus, end up with twenty or thirty grand, perhaps more. Hmn? In for a penny, in for a pound?"

Again, stubbornly, she shook her head. She was troubled, still uncertain if she was listening to Heislinger—or Mast, a loony old Swiss with a Holocaust fixation.

He claimed to be both men, but what did that signify? In Califor-

101

nia Jesus-freak cults turned up three or four Christs every year. There were people who categorically believed that the world was flat... for that matter, there were raving anti-Semitic organizations dedicated to the proposition that the Holocaust and the death camps were merely an enormous Wailing-Wall propaganda story concocted by scheming Jews and Jew-lovers. Some people still swore by the prophecies of Nostradamus, others were convinced that the unicorn existed along with the Sasquatch and the yeti. This world was chock full of nuts, so why not Mast?

Something else bothered her.

This man was dying. She sensed it. She said, "What's wrong with you? I mean medically?"

"Cancer."

The dreaded word. She was silent for a moment. Finally: "Terminal?"

"Oh, shit, life itself is terminal," Mast growled irritably. "Like the mortician's motto, eh? 'When doctors fail, call on us.'" He paused. "I visited my doctors today. Just before I phoned you. They give me two to six months. Probably less. It's best to under- rather than overestimate this sort of thing."

"Then?"

"I'll get sick. And then sicker."

"What you need, Carl, is a nurse, cook, maid, and secretary, not me," Gritch said. "I'm sorry, but the answer is still no."

HE SAT THERE staring at her. When he looked at her that way he was scary. The glittering eyes, assessing, weighing, the mind busily at work. Searching where to probe next. She felt cornered. He *could* be cruel. She knew that now. Again she felt anger.

"Okay," he said. "Let's set the question of salary aside for the present. Suppose we regard you—and me—from a different perspective."

"Nothing will change my mind."

"What I'm thinking of—my recall is exceptional, by the way—is that conversation we had on our first evening. That *was* a lovely evening, wasn't it? You told me you were interested in power. In those who exercise it, and how they acquire it. Correct? So much so that this doctoral thesis of yours will be entitled, what, *The Phenomenology of . . .*" He hesitated.

*"Distinction."*

Mast nodded. "Real egghead, for sure. What I remember clearly is your saying you want power for yourself but that you don't know

102

how to get it—and you thought writing the thesis would provide insights."

She sat there listening. Amazing that his memory was so on track! Most men would have forgotten.

"Suppose we do this?" Mast continued. "In return for your, shall we say, reluctant hospitality, I'll give you an opportunity for an in-depth investigation of what you, with your tiresome academic stodginess, term the phenomenology of distinction. Not a representative cross section of men of importance but a detailed profile of Heislinger-Mast! Perhaps a biography based on actual interviews."

That got to her.

"Do you have any real understanding of what a book like that would be worth in terms of today's market?" Mast asked. "I mean, how many asshole grad students can put together a thesis with a two-hundred-thousand hardcover sales potential? Don't ask! I *know* what theses are. Ostensibly a 'contribution to knowledge,' pardon me while I belch, all they do is end up gathering dust on library shelves. But a definitive account of *me* . . . Why, you'd knock Columbia University's history department flat on its moldy ass. Don't you realize? A coup, Gritch! In the palm of your hand!"

"Fuck *off,*" she said, but even as she spoke she saw a glimmer of salvation. She thought: Scholarly research . . . that's not aiding or abetting a criminal. It's not the best excuse, but it's *something.*

Suddenly Mast was weaseling and groveling, as he'd been on the phone that afternoon, leaning closer across the table, "You're not stupid, Gritch! D'you know what a publisher would pay for the rights to such a manuscript? D'you know what any TV network would give to have access to such material?" His eyes flashed. "Do you know what it would mean to your future, your career? You want to be important? So okay!"

She made an effort to regain coolness. "The only thing you're forgetting is that I could also end up in jail."

His fist smacked the top of the table, rattling glasses: "You once asked me how it happens . . . that first, vital step that takes a person from anonymity to center-stage-front. It doesn't take much, don't you see? A bit of a push, that's all one needs, a little luck, fate, who the hell cares what you call it? A leg up. God, who ever heard of Salinger or that wimpy-looking Bill Moyers guy before they hitched their wagons to far more powerful men? Look at 'em today! Can you do it, Gritch? Are you a *doer*? Or are you like so many of the rest, an idle dreamer?"

She said nothing.

He drew a word picture for her, his eyes staring into the future, hands weaving above the table, "'*Kasper Heislinger-Carl Mast, THE JANUS.*' A knockout title! By Griselda Nadelmann, Ph.D. Right up there, *Schatzi, numero uno* on *The New York Times* best-seller list!"

"Any reader would guess in a second it was an exposé written by a whore who'd harbored you. I won't have the world think of me that way."

The insinuating slyness in his voice made her goose-pimple: "In the long run, Gritch, who the fuck really cares? Twenty years from now, eight or ten books down the line, d'you think it'll matter to any of your adoring readers if Griselda Nadelmann was once a world-class cocksucker? Certainly not! Because by then you'll be a person of consequence, right up there with the best of them. All you require is a start." He paused. "None of us, you must realize, gets to be important in precisely the way we'd choose. If *real* distinction is offered, you damned well grab at it. For a good reason. It may never be offered again."

They argued back and forth for most of another hour. When reason and logic—Mast's reason and logic—did not persuade, he finally turned brutal, while she in turn grew hysterically defiant. "I won't do it. You can't make me!"

"But you will," he insisted.

"Filthy old bastard, who d'you think you *are?*" Gritch in a rage now. Catlike, all abristle, claws unsheathed. "What am I, crazy or something . . . listening to this *shit?*" She got up, walked deliberately to the closet by the front door, muttering, grabbed at his topcoat, scarf, and hat. Turned and flung them on the floor by his chair. "Get out!"

"You don't mean that."

"I don't? Think again, baby!" Her voice had risen into a dangerous soprano register, close to siren shrillness. "Stop with the bluffing," he said, but his voice lacked conviction—she had turned to the door and was struggling furiously with the deadbolts. A fingernail broke and she swore, then glanced over her shoulder at him: the true virago look. "Out of here! Now!"

"You'd throw me into the street?"

"Fucking-A!"

"You won't." He was shaking his head emphatically.

"Says you."

"No! You won't, because it's already too late," he snapped. "I'm *here.* If you make me leave and I'm caught, the first thing they'll demand to know is where I've been!" He snickered and then mimicked himself, the German accent ludicrous: *"Ach, lieber Mensch, I vus visiding dis liddle goopcake. Fräulein Nadelmann, such a sveetsie . . ."*

"YOU WOULDN'T DO that."

"Of course not, providing you do what I require of you," Mast said. "What matters is that it's safe. No one will know! Money . . . and enough material for a book, if you want that." He stared at her. "Stupid ungrateful bitch! Why do I waste my time on you? Can't you see . . . this is a matter of importance?" Muttering, he lit another Gauloise, drank more champagne: "I was wrong in my estimation of you, I see that now. You have no *real* potential. Your dreams are just that: fantasies. At base you are what you'll continue to be for the rest of your life . . . a petty whore, a miserable slut whose cleverness is all surface glitter. Your problem is that you can't give anything of your *self*. Who can respect a woman programmed to give nothing? It would be like falling in love with a computer. A computer can do many things for a person, but it can't give love. You are a shell, a mere husk!"

"Who the hell are you to talk about love—fucking murderous butcher!" she shouted. But the words came out wrong, like chaff driven before a gale. She sat down across from him again, a sudden bleakness appearing in her eyes.

And Mast, divining that he'd touched a raw spot, dug further, his voice increasingly confident: "Is that it, Gritch? You can tell me." He peered at her. "That's what it is, no? In this crazy life each of us has something he or she fears. I understand. Yes. Tell me! Do you believe you are unloved? That you have never been loved—and will never be loved?"

He regarded her, his expression somber. She stared down at her hands in her lap, incapable of speaking.

Mast nodded, sighed, puffed at the Gauloise, then removed its ash by touching the glowing tip to the side of his ashtray, rotating the cigarette slowly until the coal at its end was a fiery point. "So. At last it comes out." He looked at her in a not-unkindly fashion. "That's why you elected to become a prostitute. You're like a goddess of love who cannot be touched by love. This apartment is more than a comfortable nook poised between the two worlds you inhabit—the world of the mind and the world of the body: it's a shrine, Gritch, your personal sanctum where, until now, no man has been allowed to worship! Yes, you are beyond love. And that deeply troubles your more feminine side. After all, who but a blind fool loves a whore?"

She said almost in a whisper, "You're wrong. My dad loved me."

Mast said gently, "Gritch, your father *used* you. As a surrogate for what he himself could never become: a person of consequence, of intelligence, perhaps even brilliance. He wanted to demonstrate that a rare rose could flourish and bloom amid the humble ambience of a stinking garbage dump somewhere out in Jersey! Surely you must see that. And I haven't the slightest doubt that even as a child you could sense—differentiate—between being an object of pride and an object of love!" He waited for a moment and then struck: "What was his name...Steve, yes. *'That's my girl! Go ahead...ask her something...ask her anything!' 'Gritch, you're going to knock the world right on its ass.'* That photograph on your desk there...a little girl and her immensely proud daddy. His expression says, *'Look at this kid I made. Pretty good for a dumb Yid who shovels goycrap around all day, eh?'*" Mast smiled. "Parents *are* proud, aren't they? Be that as it may, he's gone from your life now. You were alone then—and you're alone now."

She bowed her head and began to weep.

"You don't even have anyone to whom you can bring home a wonderful report card, full of A's, gold stars."

She tried to speak but couldn't.

The kindness in his voice was genuine; a victor can afford generosity. "Gritch—my dear, dear girl—you must realize that this is exactly why you are attracted to me. No, don't interrupt! This evening we've argued. But it's really yourself you are fighting. What, after all, do I actually represent?"

"I hate you."

"That will pass," he said. "You may despise me but you like me too. Try to maintain objectivity. You've already related to me in a way no whore would permit. You've also said—and I take your word for this—that there is no intimate relationship available to you in the academic side of your life...because you are too busy with your studies." Mast sighed again, reached out across the table and touched her on the shoulder, almost a patting: "The reason you will never reject me or turn me out into the night is because I really care about you. In your heart you know that. There's no point in arguing further. It's over, Gritch. You say you hate me now. That may be. But you won't let me go." He nodded. "The truth is, my dear, I'm all you really have."

FINALLY, DONE WITH her, he retired to the bedroom. Though he was, as he'd once told her, a sound sleeper, he wakened sometime after eleven that night and found himself alone.

106

He discovered her asleep at the table, with her head pillowed on her arms, her face swollen and tear-streaked. Gently he roused her and led her to the bedroom, where he helped her undress. Swaying, eyes closed, half in a stupor, she tried to brush away his hands, then gave up. Lying beside him in the bed she fell asleep again immediately, like a traumatized but restless child. Then he slept too.

GRITCH WAS NOT the only one whose sleep was troubled that night because Mast was free to prowl about the city. He had not lied to her about his activities that afternoon, which had included visiting the offices of Doctors Meyer and White:

DR. MEYER WAS in surgery until 3:00 P.M. and since there were no afternoon office visits scheduled his colleague, White, had told Mrs. Farquahr to take a long lunch—he was, in fact, seated at the nurse's desk filling out part of the monthly accumulation of Medicaid forms when the door opened and in stalked Carl Mast.

The proctologist's jaw dropped.

There had been considerable argument between him and his partner since Mast's Oslo revelation. In his way, each man stood for one side of two schools of thought among contemporary American Jews. White, a reasonable man, strongly believed that far too much attention had already been devoted to the Holocaust. Enough already, let's be done with it, can't we get on to the present and the future? Meyer's position was antipodal: he felt the story could never be told in sufficient detail and that the world must not be permitted to forget so ghastly a crime lest it be repeated.

White looked mildly distressed when one more film or novel or analysis dealing with Nazi atrocities was brought to his attention, and seemed ready to throw up his hands in despair before this endless inundation: "There have been so many lately. What else is new?"

Meyer, on the other hand, was not much inclined toward for-givingness. And he was not alone.

Had not the historian Dawidowicz's chin practically trembled with wrath when she outlined her three fundamental questions concerning the Holocaust? They were as much indictment as inquiry:

> How could a modern state carry out the systematic murder of a whole people for no other reason than that they were Jews? How could a whole people allow itself to be destroyed? How could the world stand by without halting this destruction?

Had not the philosopher Karl Jaspers, a Christian whose wife happened to be Jewish, attempted a more serene observation? And once again failed to maintain glacial calmness:

> "Anyone who . . . plans the organized slaughter of a people and participates in it, does something that is fundamentally different from all crimes that have existed in the past."

Perhaps what mattered most was that Doctor White, sitting there with his mouth open, did not perceive himself to be an espe-cially brave man. He was not a coward, but he was not heroic, either. And it certainly would have required someone with immense self-possession not to flinch before the person who now stepped up to Nurse Farquahr's desk:

"HOW'S BUSINESS, WHITE?"

White, trying for professional decorum, achieved no more than consternation: "You're back!"

"As you can see."

The two men did not shake hands. White blurted, "What do you want?"

"I need refills," Mast told him. "I have only enough for a few more days. I want you to write me out a new set. For two months."

"I can't do that," White said. He had turned pale. "Those Rx's are controlled . . . the morphia. No pharmacist would fill such large prescriptions without questions."

"Write 'em in batches, two-week intervals," Mast ordered. "I'll fill 'em as I need them. Come on, man, damn it, I don't have all day."

There was a coldness in the old man's voice. White, cowed, felt as though he were being told to do something at gunpoint. Well, a sort of conversational gunpoint but, still, this was highly unpleasant. He dearly wished Meyer were present.

"I'll get your case folder," he said.

"Do that."

White said. "Really . . . I don't know what to say . . ."

Mast stood there, checking each prescription before slipping it into his wallet. When he was satisfied that he had enough, and enough of the right kind, he said, "Thanks. And *Mazel tov*. For your first good deed of the day."

White was spared framing a response—it would have been lame: Mast had turned and marched out the door.

MAST HAD ALSO been truthful about the bank business. He rented the box, year lease, at a financial institution a half-block from his regular bank, under the name Wilhelm K. Breitmeister—so the master-signature book read. He was presented with two keys. The woman in charge of vault admissions cautioned him in mother-hen tones: "If you lose them, we have to drill out the entire lock and box . . . very expensive. Keep them in separate places."

"I'll carry one under my tongue," Mast said. "Any idea where I ought to hide the other?"

That afternoon he put two hundred thousand dollars in hundreds in the box. Earlier, at Kennedy, the customs agents' eyes had widened in admiration but there had been no difficulty beyond his filling out a Form 4790, a declaration of international transfer of funds in excess of five thousand dollars, a routine formality, the record of which not even the IRS had access to. It was really wonderfully simple to move large sums around. "My personal fortune, such as it is," Mast told the agents. "Think it'll snow?"

How long such a sum might be expected to last someone like Mast, now that he was a wanted men, was uncertain. Considering his waning health he was probably correct in remarking to Gritch, when she later queried him about how much he had, "Plenty."

In his wallet he carried the Nobel Committee's check; he had not attempted to cash it and never would since it was not unrealistic to assume that a stop-payment order had been issued. The check went into the safety box along with a conformed copy of his will leaving the Geneva house and all his personal belongings to WHO. In the box there were also documents, photographs, and various papers in German, by now foxed and faded with age.

To the casual glance they looked innocuous enough. A bundle of family memorabilia perhaps, brought to the States by a tired but cheerful old gentleman who had just stepped off British Airways Flight 130.

When asked by customs what they were, Mast had quipped. "The history of my wild and woolly youth. There are even a couple of love letters, from ladies who by now have probably passed on to a better life. I will be happy to translate, if you like."

The customs officials smiled, poked about a bit and then, after making their log entry, turned toward the next passenger waiting in line.

"YOU CAN'T IMAGINE my shock. Just walked in!" White told Meyer when the latter returned from Sloan-Kettering. "Without an appointment."

"I'm phoning the FBI," Meyer said. "And the Israeli consulate."

"No. Listen, I'm serious. We don't want any part of this," White said vehemently. "Believe me, we don't need the treatment the press will give us. The nerve of him! Why attract attention?" And at this point he echoed a sentiment of Gritch's: "I'd rather not get involved."

"I'm calling."

"It'll hurt the practice."

"You never know. A little notoriety isn't the worst thing," Meyer said. "Remember McCluskey?"

McCluskey, a gynecologist, was something of a myth to the Manhattan medical community. In the process of performing a routine hysterectomy this surgeon had inadvertently left a pair of Kelly forceps in a patient's abdominal cavity. Five years later, after chronic discomfort, the lady was X-rayed and the offending instrument revealed. "Hey, Brian, I think you got a malpractice suit on your hands that's outa sight," the physician who read the 14 x 17's informed McCluskey. This turned out to be true. The woman in question collected three hundred thousand, the press went after McCluskey's hide, and his malpractice insurance went, well, out of sight. The g-y-n man prepared to embark on a fresh career in South America, Madagascar, anywhere. Then for no fathomable reason his appointment book began filling up. Half the women in New York City wanted to consult with him. Why should this be? There was no explanation. But to this day Brian McCluskey was considered one of the top ladies' problem docs in Manhattan, a celebrity.

"Bob, this is too important," Meyer insisted now. "He's got to be stopped. You saw the article in the *Times*. Heislinger set up the euthanasia program over there. More than eighty thousand Germans got the needle. Mentally retarded, geriatrics, the insane. Helpless people. Hitler claimed that keeping them institutionalized was

112

too *expensive.* Just put to sleep … *zap!*" He snapped his fingers. "Bob, that was Heislinger!"

"I'm going to have a Tranzene," White said.

Scowling, Meyer sat at his desk and reached for a directory, talking half to himself as he flipped pages. "He was in the middle of it, with Heydrich, Eichmann, Himmler, Hoess. That whole crowd!"

Suddenly White calmed. Not a great deal, but enough. If this was the way it had to be, all right.

In an odd—and certainly not brave—fashion Bob White possessed an objectivity his angrier colleague lacked. He said now, frowning, "Be sure to tell them that he may be passing himself off as a Jew. I'd bet on it."

"Why do you say that?"

"Because I have a hunch that in his warped way he knows more about Jews and being a Jew than you or I ever will," White replied. "Mention those scars too."

TWO DAYS AFTER Mast had joked with the agents about his wild youth, Mordecai Gerber arrived at Kennedy and was processed as routinely as had been the man he now referred to simply as his "assignment."

His cold had worsened. He looked wan and fatigued. Mordecai did not care for air travel. Aloft, his sinuses had a tendency to block up and, with the cold, his head felt as though it were stuffed with cotton.

His mood improved later, at the team's apartment, on East Eightieth off Lexington. There was hot tea mixed with vodka, and at long last edible food, and conversation too, with his friend the team chief, Sy Abarbanel who, noting Mordecai's condition, immediately dispatched an agent to buy Contrex spansules.

Abarbanel in his late forties, short, rotund, with thinning hair and a graying mustache that he imagined made him look distinguished but which did not, had been born and raised in Manhattan, between Avenues C and D, in former years a ghetto for Jews of Russian and Polish heritage but more recently home turf for a more polyglot ethnic group of Puerto Ricans, blacks, and Middle Eastern types. Abarbanel was not in the habit of visiting the old neighborhood much; like Mordecai he now called Israel home.

Abarbanel was one of the few in *Mossad* who did not think Gerber a strange duck. Perhaps this was because each possessed a natural air of dignity and quiet reservation. If there was a joke or something to be laughed at, neither broke up, but an alert observer might detect an exchange between the two, a brief flicker, a lightninglike meeting of glances. Though their expressions remained sober, they understood and were sensitive to each other's style. The relationship was by no means a father-son thing but more that of older brother-younger brother.

Their friendship had grown out of the admiration and respect each developed for the other's work, and it now extended to their off-duty time. In Tel Aviv Abarbanel had a wife and three daughters, ten, twelve, and sixteen years old, and during the summer months he and his family and Mordecai often went to the beaches, to picnic, swim, eat, sip wine, laze about. Like intelligence men around the world, Mordecai and Abarbanel found it difficult to trust anyone outside their profession.

The girls, of course, had developed a mad crush on Mordecai.

Sarah, Sonya, and Tanya, his suntanned and nubile worshipers, all three with dark mops of wavy hair. Sarah's knees were knobby and she had astonishingly large feet. Sonya was determined to be a film actress and already had the face and nymphet figure to back up her ambition. But Tanya, at sixteen, speculated suicide; the sad fact is that she was overweight, which, though she did not know it, made her all the more lovable. Abarbanel's wife, whom for reasons known only to himself he called Pootsie, was a happy-go-lucky matron who tried to conceal her satisfaction with life by complaints no one really believed: "Three girls are two too many, a son would have been okay, they say boys aren't so demanding." The girls ignored this but were enchanted to discover that Mordecai, in addition to being a dreamboat, was ticklish.

He took their teasing and adulation with style, and after a few glasses of wine even teased back, though he still blushed with marvelous ease. He was used to female attention. His sister, Becky, who was in pre-med and who sometimes joined the beach outings, was a tease too—"Mister Eagle Scout, his work's so important he can't even let out a *hint*"—but like the Abarbanel children, she too was adoring. Abarbanel happened to know that Mordecai was helping her financially, just as he knew that some of his younger friend's paycheck was set aside for his widowed mother, who was not partial to life in Israel. She had once been to Santa Monica and was unshakable in her belief that that crowded, palm-fringed strand was the only romantic cul-de-sac left for a retired Tel Aviv matron, "formerly Yonkers," who still had a few good years left in her.

IT TOOK LESS than an hour for Abarbanel to brief Mordecai on the progress of their search. Most of the team's fourteen members were

114

out developing secondary and tertiary informants. Heislinger's apartment was being watched; his phone had been tapped; hotels were being checked; employees at air, bus, train terminals—in short, all exits from the city—were in the process of being contacted; and there was a cooperative captain at police headquarters down on Centre Street who had been useful before; several thousand photographs of the contemporary Mast had been printed for distribution. All of this was routine and necessary, and all of it was terribly tedious and time-consuming.

Actually there was no way of knowing if Heislinger was still in the city. But Abarbanel said, "I have a gut feeling he's here ... don't ask me why. I also think somebody's protecting him." The team chief thought about this. "Who in their right mind would want to do that?" He sighed. "This town's full of crazies."

Mordecai was rereading for the second time the only real tip they had so far. It had come from the Israeli consulate. Two doctors had been treating Mast for over a month prior to the Oslo trip. Cancer. The old man was dying, they said. He'd seen one of them two days earlier and had demanded prescription refills, which had reluctantly been provided. Mordecai mused aloud: "He's sick. He's gone underground. Somebody may or may not be helping him. All very iffy, if you ask me. We could tag him in a few days ... or it could drag on for months." He paused. "Not too many months, though, if he's as ill as these pillrollers claim."

Sy Abarbanel nodded, and then looked at his friend. "Mordecai, how do you evaluate this Heislinger? I mean, what category would you place him in? On a par with Eichmann, or Hoess?"

Mordecai blew his nose. He was feeling better but the Comtrex was making him sleepy. The hot tea, vodka, and food were a boon. He said, "Interesting that you ask. It's what I asked Armon. When he first called me in to review the material, my impression was that Heislinger was a minor functionary."

"Armon doesn't agree?"

"He certainly doesn't," Mordecai said. Both men knew the Colonel well enough—knew that he verged on the fanatical, and that any of the old Third Reich gang who still lived would be brought to bay, if he had his way. Mordecai went on, "He changed my mind, Sy. He's old. Set in his ways, but give him credit. The researchers dug out plenty, and they're still digging, but it was Armon who spotted the first clue."

Abarbanel sat watching as Mordecai searched through the *Mossad* material on Heislinger, and underlined something. "Here," he said, handing over the stapled sheets, "see for yourself."

Abarbanel read aloud, "The SS instigated a confidential nation-wide search for Heislinger."

Mordecai smiled. "Armon was intrigued by that. He told the research staff to poke around more, and they did. Sy, the SS had a manhunt going. Why would they be so frantic to find him? An ordinary colonel?"

"They wanted him as badly as we do now?"

Mordecai said, "Apparently they wanted him so much that with the war going against them, with their whole world coming apart, they searched for almost sixteen months. Armon isn't sure, but he believes he knows the reason." Mordecai stared at his associate. "He thinks Heislinger may have in his possession documentation authorizing the Final Solution."

"I DON'T FOLLOW you," Abarbanel said. Like Mordecai, he had done his share of Holocaust studying, had lost relatives. But so had many in Israel. "Except as historical curiosities—and God knows, we have enough of them still *walking* around Tel Aviv—of what use would such documents be?"

"Sy, they'd be priceless. Think a minute. An actual instrument, stating explicitly what was to be done, perhaps signed by Himmler himself. Or even someone higher up."

The team chief understood then. The archive material concerning the Third Reich, including documents drawn up by the Nazis themselves, filled nobody knew how many warehouses. There were literally mountains of the stuff: orders, reports, analyses, files, films ... more than enough "junk" or "history" (depending upon how one viewed such material) to reconstruct down to the smallest detail the labyrinthine bureaucratic and military machine that had ruled Germany during those years.

But nowhere was there a formal instrument authorizing the Final Solution. No one had wanted to put his signature to such an executive order—not even Hitler. The Solution was known about, talked about, referred to in writing thousands of times, but an actual *order* specifically authorizing the extermination of millions had never come to light.

Of euphemisms there were plenty. The Nazis were unsurpassingly creative when it came to dressing up Death in bright springtime colors.

Was not the expression "final solution" in itself the ultimate euphemism?

The human cargoes carried by the long death trains were referred to as deportees, or refugees being processed for relocation, or volunteer expatriates, or undesirable aliens. No matter that these trains spilled their half-starved contents out into the bleak unloading yards of Auschwitz or Bergen-Belsen. The Nazi mentality, it seemed, had an endless variety of ways in which not to call a spade a spade.

A "disciplinary action" could mean arrest and incarceration but it might also signify the lining-up and machine-gunning of an entire Polish village before an open pit. "Rigorous measures" were to be employed in dealing with "racially inferior types," and a district under occupational rule had to be "cleansed of ethnic impurities."

Of every three Jews alive in Europe in 1939 two never made it to 1945, and nowhere was there a piece of paper deliberately condoning this singular decrease in population.

"ARMON'S WHISTLING IN the wind," Abarbanel told Mordecai. "I've studied all this. . . ." He motioned toward the pile of folders. "What would a small-timer like Heislinger be doing with such a damning piece of paper? It doesn't add up."

Mordecai said, "The specialization in public health was mostly a cover-up. Sure, Heislinger helped design camp facilities—dorms, kitchen, water, and waste systems—but that phase of his career was over by '37 or '38 . . . for that matter, his work with the *Anherbst* and the Reich Research Council was done with, and neither of these outfits cared about how the camps were built. We know that Heislinger traveled a great deal more than would be warranted by any lower-echelon public-health expert. France, the low countries, Scandinavia, Poland, Russia, or at least as far into Russia as the Wehrmacht was able to penetrate. His official orders described him as 'medical consultant.' This ties in with what was later revealed about him during the Trials. 'Morale maintainance,' of *Einsatzgrüppen* and concentration-camp personnel, psychological indoctrination, that sort of thing. Quite a switch from public health."

"What interests me is how close was he to Himmler," Abarbanel broke in. "Okay, he was a colonel, but so was Eichmann. And in my opinion Himmler scarcely knew—or gave a good rat's ass—that Eichmann existed."

"He was apparently close enough," Mordecai replied. "According to Armon's weasels he was a sort of ear to Himmler. A flunky, yes, but also a flunky who was trusted enough to travel from one end of Europe to the other."

"A roving hatchet man?"

"More than that. Heislinger had a reputation for obstinacy and, worse, speaking his mind. He got himself in trouble plenty of times.

Can you imagine? Telling Himmler where to get off? That would take nerve."

"Himmler wasn't the type to put up with shit from a subordinate. Do you have any proof?"

"The Doctors' Trial, in '46," Mordecai said. "Some of the statements made by the defendants conflict, but even if we take their depositions with a grain of salt, Heislinger was never a brown noser. He was tough. A gadfly. The impression we have is that Himmler was shrewd enough to see that a man who wasn't afraid to speak his mind could be of value."

"Come off it. The top Nazis surrounded themselves with ass-kissers."

Mordecai ignored this. "What Armon and the research bunch think is that one of Heislinger's main jobs was to justify mass executions to the officers commanding the rank and file."

"They didn't need convincing," Abarbanel objected. "All they required was an authority **figure** to tell 'em it was okay."

"Not everyone, Sy," Mordecai said. "When you're involved in large-scale extermination there are always a few who'll put on the brakes. And that can be touchy. You get one officer saying 'no way!' pretty soon you may have hundreds. Himmler'd worry about that."

"Heislinger was a sweet-talker as well as a troublemaker?"

"More than sweet talk," Mordecai said. "Okay, you're in the SS, right? Say, a captain or a major. And an order comes down to get rid of a thousand, ten thousand Jews or 'undesirables.' The order is verbal, or if it's written it relies on the usual nonsense—'X number will be processed.' If you're a fanatic, fine, you start handing out the ammo. But supposing you're not quite a fanatic . . . maybe you start thinking about things like the Geneva Convention and the rules of warfare. So you say, 'Listen, this is murder we're dealing with. We're miles from the front lines, so it's not the enemy—it's civilians—there's no way in the world we can call it combat. Sorry, but I want to see a written order or authorization before I have my boys start. And I don't mean some mimeographed piece of nonsense full of obtuse phrases. Please understand, I'll do this if I have to. All I'm asking for is an explicit order saying that I am directed to kill every Jew, Pole, or Serb I can lay my hands on. In short, I want it in writing.'"

"Armon thinks Heislinger had such an order to dangle under the noses of the fainthearted? Impossible! Himmler would never have trusted such evidence to any subordinate."

"Well . . . a fellow like Himmler could always have claimed it was counterfeit," Mordecai said. "Or he could have disclaimed any knowledge of it. That argument was pulled by plenty of those who stood trial in Nuremberg. But if Heislinger *did* have something like an explicit order . . ."

"Speculation," Abarbanel argued. "Guesswork."

"Sure it's guesswork," Mordecai agreed. "But don't forget that the SS, by Himmler's own order, carried on that intensive manhunt. They wanted him. Why?" The younger agent paused and then said, "Sy, if nothing else, Heislinger must have observed an awful lot of what went on. Do you know what Armon said to me? This man Heislinger may be the Nazi equivalent of what Solzhenitsyn has been to the Gulag Archipelago. Solzhenitsyn of course was a victim, Heislinger an oppressor. But, you know something? I agree with Armon. If we can get Heislinger and make him talk! Priceless material. That's how Armon feels. He's dead serious."

"A Nazi Solzhenitsyn?" Abarbanel smiled. "When we nab him, maybe I ought to ask for his autograph."

THE MORNING AFTER they had fought, Gritch listened with swollen, reddened eyes as he expounded over coffee: "You are a confidante now. I'm at your mercy. I admit this. My life is in your hands. What would it take, after all? A phone call? You wouldn't even have to leave this apartment. You could wait until I was asleep. Or you could try to kill or disable me. Eh? Would you like to do that?"

She stared at him, unable to speak. Mast smiled. "No. You're not the type. You see, I have faith in you, Gritch. I haven't the time to worry, understand? If you like you can flee, abandon me, turn me in, betray me in a dozen ways, but I'll tell you now that I shan't fret about any of these possibilities."

Her head ached fiercely. She went and got three aspirin, washed them down with black coffee. She felt exhausted, though she'd slept for hours. Mast continued cheerfully, "Look at the bright side. We'll have fun working together. It'll be mind-opening for you. Does that appeal?" He gave her a sharp look. "You shake your head but that means nothing. You want to *know*. And to find out you must trust me."

"What is it you'd like me to do?"

"We need a photocopier, also a cassette recorder—get the best— and tapes, say, a hundred hours' worth to start. We must tape everything. Use your credit cards and I'll reimburse. I want food, liquor, tobacco, anything else that's necessary. Get enough for at least a week or two. I can't have you running out to shop every two minutes. Later, books. For the research. I'll make up a list."

As Gritch listened her mind went back to their first meeting. He'd paid, had called the shots, but to a degree she'd been able to orchestrate the events of that evening.

Now she realized that for however long she might know Mast she would never again attain or be able to exercise that kind of control over him. Or herself either.

He would work away at her patiently, wearing her down. It was an infallible psychological technique. Eventually any prisoner, no matter how strong of mind, must crack.

BY FRIDAY—"ONLY twelve more shopping days until Christmas," the TV brayed—she was thinking: Either he's getting crazier or I am.

Already she had a craving to be away from the apartment, to breathe in lungfuls of cold fresh air, to be alone if only for an hour, but Mast, despite his declarations, was obviously uneasy about letting her out of his sight. He himself didn't do much, seemed finally felled by the fatigue that goes with thousands of miles of flying. He catnapped, smoked, drank, took his pills, complained of stomach pains several times.

That morning the photocopier and recording equipment arrived. Mast puttered about testing everything. She called her advisor on campus to say that an unexpected emergency would take her out of town for a week or so and that she would have to miss classes. There was another call, about some party that weekend, hosted by one of her professors.

The Magnavox recorder stood on her desk, its bright red On light glowing. Extension mikes ran to the bedroom and kitchen. "Of course, although I'll be recording certain items of my own, all this is really for you," Mast informed her. "The tapes will be invaluable for your book—oral history, Gritch—essential nowadays to the serious researcher. Also, I might add, irrefutable proof that your 'contribution to knowledge' is not a figment of the female imagination, a sort of phantasmagorical bubble of a febrile academic brain."

Then, abruptly, as though finally conceding to himself that he could not keep a tether on her forever, Mast dispatched her to Columbia, to fetch the books he wanted. "Don't moon about," he warned. "In Treblinka a dawdler's days were numbered."

But she was gone over three hours and had to hire a cab to get the almost twenty volumes he'd requested back to the apartment.

There she found him pacing about the living room.

"It was such a lovely day I took a stroll up Riverside Drive," she said when he interrogated her.

"What're you talking, beautiful?" he grumbled. "Look out the bedroom windows—it's snowing. The TV said twenty-one de-

122

grees." He stared at the proof: Gritch's nose was redtipped, her cheeks pink. "You should have dressed warmer. A person could catch pneumonia. What else did you do?"

"Do you know how long it takes to check the catalog and get Dewey numbers on that many books? Some I had to request on interlibrary," Gritch said. "I stopped for coffee," she added, relishing the moment, small though it was. "And I was tempted. By your offer. To use a phone."

"Ah." He gave her a piercing look. "And?"

She shrugged. "There's no hurry. Why don't you pour yourself a drink? You're as jumpy as a cat. Really."

Thinking to herself: Liar! You were scared shitless.

Then, maliciously: "Did you miss me?"

STILL LATER—IT was almost dark—she was in the bathroom, washing some things in the sink, when Mast came in and thrust a sheet of paper under her nose, smirking and explaining that here was something he had "occupied his mind with" during her absence, a "minor attention-getter."

"What's your opinion? Please. Be nothing but honest. Of course it's rough yet," Mast observed. "Rather clever, don't you agree? I think it *says* something. Of course, I don't wish to offend. Some, you know, are so touchy." She raised one suds-foamed forefinger to poke at the bridge of her spectacles, which had slid down her nose. Mast chattered on, "I'm considering a half-page in *The New York Times* for starters. A way of letting everyone know the old war-horse is back in business. Or, with the copier, we could run off a thousand in no time. How about a direct-mail campaign, starting with the B'nai Brith?"

123

For a second she was ready to blurt out that no ethical publication like the *Times* would ever consider such insanity but then stopped. Wiped instead with the back of a wet hand at her temple, where a damp lock tickled. Gave him a cutting look. "You wrote this to bug me. Admit it."

Mast grinned owlishly, caught. "Nothing ventured, nothing gained, Gritch."

"Nothing ventured, nothing—" She sneered. "I'm living with a deranged simpleton who thinks in sophistic platitudes."

"My dear, platitudes are, up to a point, like an oath of allegiance," he said. "They serve a purpose. What's for dinner?"

"I'm busy. Can't you give me a minute's peace?"

"Don't yell." Then: "A glass tea maybe?"

"Stop *talking* like that. There's nothing worse than a goy trying to imitate a Jew."

"Hot, a slice lemon with cube sugar, what the hell—it's Friday," Mast teased. "Say, how d'you know I'm not an *echt* mockey, eh? You so sure? I bet I could pass easy. A tall glass tea, the cube held between the front teeth—the sweetness stays as you sip, what a truly civilized indulgence, and healthy too for all those fiddler-on-the-roof *shtetl*-shitheads, not to mention cheap."

"Oh, get out of here," she cried. "Leave me alone!"

But that for him seemed an impossibility.


PERCHED ON A bar stool by the hand-over counter separating kitchen and living room, he kept her company while she went about preparing dinner: roast chicken, baked potatoes, hearts of celery marinated in oil, salt, pepper. When she was alone cooking a meal was a casual affair but now she concentrated on the task before her. Anything to keep her hands busy. Never had the fat from a chicken been trimmed with such care, or potatoes scrubbed in cold water with such diligence. Much thought was given to the choice of herbs, oil, and garnishes.

"You know, back in the good old days every German had his pet Jew," Mast was saying. Within easy reach on the counter were his cigarettes, ouzo, ashtray. "I'm beginning to think you were destined to be mine."

"I'm nobody's pet anything," Gritch said. "Keep talking like that, you'll find your geriatric ass out in the snow."

"The pet-Yid idea was Himmler's," Mast went on amiably. "He mentioned it in a private talk to some SS big wheels. Got a hell of a

124

laugh and a big round of applause, Heinie did. The camps were already going full blast."

She worked at the chicken slowly, using a butcher's knife and the heavy cutting board. Carefully she sliced off the pope's nose.

If he *was* Heislinger, at least it lent validity to the book he proposed having her write. What mattered was maintaining objectivity. That wouldn't be easy. Turning to the sink she rinsed the quartered pieces. On the desk in the living room the Magnavox's red eye shone.

"If you're curious about what men in power are like, I can tell you," Mast went on conversationally. Gritch patted each piece dry. "Want to know something Himmler once said to me personally? Afterward, he was so struck by his cleverness he had it made into an official statement. 'Kasper'—in private, you know, it was always Kasper—'we must, all of us, be honest, decent, loyal, and comradely to members of our own blood. But to no one else.' His very words, Gritch. 'What happens to a Russian or a Czech does not interest me in the slightest. What these miserable nations can offer in the way of good blood of the type we need we will take, if necessary, by kidnapping their children and raising them here with us. Whether ten thousand Russian females die from exhaustion digging an antitank ditch for the Third Reich interests me only insofar as the ditch is finished. When someone comes to me, full of pity, and says, "I cannot dig this antitank ditch with women and children, it is inhuman because it will kill them," then I must reply, "You are a murderer of your own blood, because if the antitank ditch is not dug, German soldiers will die, and they are the sons of German mothers. They are our own blood." That's what I'm trying to instill into the SS. These are hard times.'"

She began arranging the chicken pieces in a Corningware tray. Got out olive oil and a small basting brush. "You knew Himmler? Personally?"

"I worked eight years for him, didn't I?" Mast replied. "What a curious mixture. Bright, dedicated, heartless, a semimystic. We called him the Chinless Wonder. Not to his face of course. No sense of humor. Couldn't take a little friendly kidding. Try that and you'd find yourself transferred out of your cushy office with a one-way ticket to the Eastern Front. Awfully brisk up around Smolensk in December, Gritch."

He left the bar stool for a minute to rummage among the stacks of books on her desk while she used garlic cloves and a press to "bless" the chicken. "See for yourself," Mast said, coming into the kitchen and holding out an opened book. She looked. "There was a man who had power, Gritch. The old *Reichführer SS* himself."

The man in the center of the full-page photograph, hands jauntily cocked on hips, was flanked by two officers, apparently of high rank. Their eyes were turned toward him. All three were smiling.

A not especially tall man. Narrow sloping shoulders and a bit of a paunch. Pince-nez spectacles that made him resemble a school-teacher. Or else a mild-mannered bookkeeper. A toothbrush of a mustache, and that weak chin. Except for the elegant SS uniform and visored military cap that had as its insignia a skull and cross-bones, he looked all wrong for the job: a strutting rabbit. The mastermind of the Final Solution.

Mast shut the book, frowned over her shoulder to see how the chicken was coming. "Don't forget tarragon."

He wandered back into the living room, tossed the book onto the couch, returned to the bar counter, but did not sit: "Terrible prude. Disapproved of profanity, boozing, at least among our lads. The feminine side of his nature was almost as strong as the masculine. Worth your life to mention that, though. Homosexuality, latent or overt, a definite no-no. Health addict. Natural foods and all that. Never amounted to much until Adolph spotted him. Nitrogen-fertilizer salesman, later tried farming outside Munich. Married a nurse, older woman. Big Bertha type. She, too, was a health nut. For a while they ran a sort of convalescent rest home, modeled on some of the crazier homeopathic theories. Quack stuff really. Among their medical armamentarium of techniques was the oatmeal enema. It was supposed to revitalize the entire digestive tract." Mast chuckled. "Can you imagine, being *spritzed* with oatmeal? Marve-lously naive man in many ways. Prissy. Couldn't stand smoking. Bad for the lungs. If a junior officer was to have a personal audience with Heinrich and if he was a smoker, like so . . ." Mast held up his tobacco-stained fore- and middle fingers: ". . . well, he was taken to a bathroom first and there he scrubbed his fingers with a brush, pumice, and lemon juice. Heinrich was not above laying a six-month-long *Rauchverbot* on a nicotine fiend. Left me alone, though. Needed me. Just as Adolph needed *him*. 'Got a liddle project for you, Heinrich,' der Führer said."

Here Mast went into a pantomime act: Himmler at rigid attention, Hitler drumming his fingers on a desk, thoughtful, brooding, only this was an act with dialogue: Hitler's a gutteral growl, Himmler's a flutey tenor. As improvisation, the overall effect was successful. Grimacing, gesturing, whirling about to take first one role then the other, Mast created a Chaplinesque burlesque.

126

"'A project?' Heinie says. 'Hey, I'm your man.'
"'I have it in mind to rid Europe of Chewish vermin!'
"'Rid? How rid, *Führer*?'
"'Only thing I can think of is, ve kill 'em.'
"Heinrich, taken aback. 'Hey, *Führer,* you got any idea how many Yiddles ve got running about Europe? I mean, the place is infested mit 'em! Ve got Chews coming outa our ears.'
"'Don't tell me, I know,' Adolph says. 'All I'm asking is, can you do this liddle chob for me?'
"'*Ach, aber bestimmt, du kannst mir glauben, Führer,* why sure, it may take some time, this is no veekend housecleaning you're talking about, but now that you mention it, my poys could really throw themselves into that kind of campaign. After all, ain't you the vun said I got the finest lads Chermany's ever produced? It'll give 'em something to do.'
"'Idle hands,' Adolph agrees. 'If they're on my payroll, they gotta earn their way.'"
"You missed your calling," Gritch told him. "Hollywood could have used someone like you."


MAST PAUSED TO light a Gauloise, inhaled fiercely, exhaled a cloud. "Heinrich adored those boys. And Gritch, would you believe it, SS youngsters *were* as straight as a die. In the *Kasernes* there were no locks whatsoever on footlockers and wall cupboards. Know what was engraved on every SS man's belt buckle? *'My Honor Is My Loyalty.'*"
"Am I supposed to be impressed?" Gritch said. She set the chicken aside and turned to the celery. "They were also murderers and psychopaths. I don't mind trying to assimilate your ravings, Carl, but let's keep things in perspective."
"For you that's not possible," Mast said. "You'd have to have lived through the entire crackpot era. *Every*body was crazy back then. The German soldier stood astride all Western Europe. The SS was the elite of German manhood, and the *Totenkopfers,* the Death's Head boys, were the elite of the SS! Imagine it from the female point of view, Gritch. A girl who wanted to marry into the SS had to pass a physical and psychological exam. No whores or high-yellows need apply. Her genealogy had to be unsullied, unquestionably Teutonic, capable of withstanding an investigation back to the year eighteen hundred, to make sure no mockey was lurking in the background. If she managed to survive all that—love doesn't always conquer— then Himmler himself might personally nominate her to attend the

SS Brides' Academy. How about that? A finishing school for SS brides."

That confounded her. She shook her head. "That's trivia. We were talking about real power."

"Himmler possessed it, and I can attest to that," Mast replied. "As *Reichsführer SS,* his influence was awesome. Combine that with the man's psychological profile and you get something wild. A fanatic imbued with a taint of mysticism. Very dangerous. And that fussiness! Couldn't stand the smell of underarm perspiration—after calisthenics the troopers were kept at a judicious distance from him. Probably just as well. He might have swooned with delight. Yes, the sexual, always. It was he who encouraged the *Sippenbuch*—a sort of quasi-genetic studbook on how well SS men performed, how many infants they fathered, how many tries were needed. 'Marriage in its existing form is the Catholic Church's satanic achievement,' Himmler said. 'The state needs more children.' Aryan kids, naturally. How about the law for the Protection of German Blood and German Honor? God, how the people loved all that Wagnerian *Scheiss.* Heinrich himself condoned the myth which claimed that copulation conducted on the gravestones of one's ancestors endowed any child so conceived with the brave Teutonic spirit of his forefathers. Getting it off on gravestones, Gritch! Hell on those poor girls' backs. But the State wanted kids. If SS men couldn't make it home from the front lines their women were sent to them: 'Assume the position, Irmgard!' There were medals for German moms. Sort of Fallopian Iron Crosses. For five little Hermans and Hildes you got one of bronze. Ten was silver. I think fifteen was gold—Christ, I never received one, so I can't be sure. If you popped *twanzig* you got one of gold, with a diamond in it, I guess, and a free stripping of the veins as well."

"Mass reproduction of humanity. How repulsively degrading!"

The tape deck in the recorder clicked, stopped. Mast got up, went over, dated the cassette, inserted a fresh one, then returned, poured wine for them both. She was still fiddling with the celery hearts, her mind distracted by what he'd been saying. "Actually, no one could fault Himmler for wanting to see the human race improved," he pointed out. "What was so unforgivably stupid, however, was that he believed himself fit to determine what the ideal human being should be."

"But where was everybody's brains in all this?" she objected. "Couldn't the more intelligent people see how utterly insane these so-called leaders were?"

"Ah, piss on intelligence," Mast said. "The populace adored them, partially because of their vulnerabilities. You can worship a god, but

128

to understand him he *must* have human qualities, failings, such as you yourself are heir to. Look at Stalin . . . a monster of such dimensions that even Hitler might be obliged to award him first place. But Josef's propaganda machine made of him the supreme father image to Mother Russia, and, by God, a lot of dumb Ivans believed it heart and soul, despite the untold millions he exiled to the Gulag! Look at Goebbels, that little lame half-pint—incidentally, it was poliomyelitis, not clubfoot. No one, not even Hitler, could squelch the stories about little Joe's satyriasis. Indefatigable, always stuffing it up the nearest hole, laughing and humping away for all he was worth. The man in the street loved him for that, same as Americans admired the Jew Kissinger back in his bachelor days when he'd put on his going-to-meeting clothes and hop on the nearest jet to fly out and say howdy to Marilyn or some other Burbank marzipan. *That's* power. A real hero, little Joe. Intelligent guy despite the perpetual hardon. In my estimation, Goebbels was brilliant. Ph.D. in philosophy, Heidelberg, 1920. Tried playwriting. Dreadful. But a knockout orator. Far more polished than Adolph. Goebbels' tongue was a verbal misericord. Hitler thundered. Joe started out mean, and then eased into nastiness. Especially on the subject of Yids. Minister of Information, controlled all media in Germany: films, radio, photographs, theater, newspapers, the whole ball of wax. When Joe gave a speech there was a little platform for his use, five inches high. Like J. Edgar, who kept a similar aid under his desk. After all, you couldn't have a bigshot like Joe invisible because the top of his head didn't even reach the banks of microphones, eh? Practiced his speeches in front of a full-length mirror. The hand gestures, the calculated pauses, the lifted eyebrow, and curled lip. So too, for that matter, did Churchill . . . and Rosengeld, DeGaulle . . . all men of power, my dear, including that glamorpuss JFK and his Steinway smile. Yes, the neat thing about being a god, Gritch, is that men idolize you. But they must never be allowed to touch. Else they would find out that you exist only in their minds."

MAST PAUSED, AND then, caught up by the memory of that bygone era continued: "You want power? Take Goering. Everybody loved Herman. Our own Fat Boy, full of hell, with his custom-tailored uniforms, and Karinhall, the big estate, and the purloined art collections. But a near-genius. The psychiatrists who tested him at Nuremberg confirmed that. At the Trials he handled most of his own defense and more often than not made the Tribunal's prosecutors look like schmucks. A doomed man but, still, he out-argued all

129

of 'em. He was by far the most popular of the top bunch. A slob, but literally fearless. Leader of von Richthofen's Flying Circus in the first war. In the 1925 *putsch* he was the only one seriously wounded. Took a bullet right in the testicles. Painful, I daresay. Months to recuperate, by then he was addicted to codeine. The obesity by the way was due to a glandular dysfunction, not bulemic face-stuffing."

She concentrated on getting dinner right. If only to show herself that she could. The Corningware tray went into the oven at medium broil. She turned back to the celery. "He was involved with the death of millions."

"But he was a man, Gritch, a *man,*" Mast argued. "That's how you must read him. We cherished him for his foibles. A man who loved the limelight. Once, you know, Hitler tells him to drive down to see Mussolini, this was late '43, I think. Benito sulking. Not getting any attention. So Hermann hops into his custom Mercedes —I mean, kid, today's Mercedes are Datsuns compared to what he had—and he's chauffeured to Rome for tea and spumoni. Car pulls up. Benito's waiting outside his *palacio* in his classiest uniform, with plenty of press cameras lined up . . . he knows Hermann's always a fashion plate. Fatso hops out. Guess what? Over *his* uniform he's wearing a shoulder-to-ground-length sable cape. 'Hey, clock this, Bennie! A little something my furrier whipped up for me. Like it?' Ben most crestfallen. Much one-upped that time. The folks back home went crazy laughing. By then they needed a laugh. The war was already going against 'em."

"Power," Gritch muttered, placing potatoes in the microwave. "You make it sound like kids playing. Like today's hotline telephones and the buttons waiting to be pushed. The biggest video game ever. Were the small-fry just as stupid?"

"Ah, love, far worse," Mast said cheerfully. "I had considerable business at one time with Wolfgang Sievers. SS colonel. Another happy-go-lucky Naziopath. In charge of all SS publications. He was seduced by Teutonic mythology. Talk your bloody ass off about runic symbols, prehistory, the Cimbrian invasion—a real motormouth."

Mast chuckled. "Gritch, you simply cannot imagine that gentleman's delight—enchantment!—when accidentally, one day, he happened to observe that his name began and ended with an S. The runic S is written so:" He drew the symbol ϟ for her on a scratchpad. "From then on, until war's end, that knothead Wolfie Sievers signed every bit of his official correspondence so:"

Mast printed the name in block letters: ϟIEVERϟ .

"Of course, the SS insignia itself was a double runic S, which

130

some mistakenly interpreted as a twin lightning bolt." He drew an ϟϟ.

Gritch tried to smile but it did not come out well. "Adolescent mentalities. One could despise them if they'd just been superefficient psychopaths, but this silliness! It makes me want to throw up."

"All men are children, never forget that," Mast cautioned. "Gods are too, I'm afraid."

HE GAVE HER a dry look. "Let me tell you something else ... you have a terrible habit of bandying certain terms about. 'Psychopath,' 'sadistic,' 'maniacs.' Think a moment. If the ranks of the SS were filled with psychopaths, then why wasn't Germany in the postwar years overrun by hordes of Jack the Rippers and Charlie Mansons? No. The truth, Gritch, is that these were ordinary men who'd been trained to do dreadful work . . . when that work was done they blended back into civilian life effortlessly. All armies commit atrocities. Our SS boys were, for the most part, normal young men. When the war ended, their big adventure was over. Oh, many probably suffered nightmares for years afterward, and I don't doubt that even today there are old-timers who refuse to discuss the nature of their wartime service."

"Let the day stay buried?" she sneered.

"Precisely," Mast agreed. "Such men today are in their sixties and seventies. When hostilities ceased, some were arrested, brought to trial, sentenced to prison, but mostly the sentences were light, or even suspended. Many of these men in fact were absorbed into the postwar Bonn government—that's common knowledge. No, they were normal enough. Today in Germany there are thousands of elderly businessmen, executives, corporation officers, who pursue their careers, decent law-abiding family men, indistinguishable from anyone else. True, in their heyday, they killed but that does not make them psychopaths."

"Says you. Ask those victims."

"You're being sentimental, Gritch. Careful of that, else you'll start sounding like that mewling little Anne Frank brat. A professional noble sufferer."

"Your fucking 'normal' SS butchers killed her too!"

Mast shot her a cold look. "And not a moment too soon! In my opinion, there's far too much scribbling in this world."

"Victims!" she cried. "The point is, they all had *a right to live*."

"*Ach!* You Americans and your *inalienable* rights, to life, liberty and the pursuit of happiness! An 'inalienable' right to life is a patent absurdity! It's one of the most horrendous mendacities ever formulated in human history, and it's been the cause of endless mischief. By being born, one earns an inalienable right to death. That's all. Any other right is something that is created by men, conferred upon each other, and taken away from each other. In the final analysis what matters is conduct. *That* is inalienable: what a person has done and not done. Acts and omissions, Gritch. And never forget that the omissions are as important as the acts. Which may in a way give you a clue to my little Oslo speech."

"Murder is murder," she insisted. "You said yourself."

LATER THAT EVENING she got drunk. Drunker than he, at any rate. The apartment was stifling. Mast had opened the valves of the radiators for maximum warmth. Or perhaps he'd remembered that first dinner and the fact that Gritch, when cozy, liked to shuck off encumbering garments. To spite him she refused to do this and went about barefoot in a pair of hip-hugging shorts and a faded blue workshirt, knotted at the waist. Folded against her forehead and tied at the back of her head was a bright red bandanna.

She was irritable. Mostly with him, but a lot of the anger had to do with her. Oddly, their arguing had gotten her inward-turned, moodily introspective, almost sexual, but in a hostile fashion. Anger was such a strange emotion. It churned up the body, left her ill at ease with herself. She thought derisively: Beaver fever! She needed a man's body. It had been a while.

She glanced at him and in spite of herself experienced a faint stirring. Thought: It's like wanting to do it right after a godawful fight. Why is it always the hottest then?

Mast, although he too had a buzz on, was alert to her mood. He said, "Often when the mind can't cope with an overload, it turns to the emotions. They serve as a cerebral release mechanism."

"Go to hell."

He ignored this. "Perhaps I've pushed you too hard. We all require relaxation at times."

**133**

She looked at him. "I thought we'd agreed that sex wasn't going to get in the way of all this terribly important *work* we have to do."

"True, but there are moments when the libido can be used to provide a shortcut, a breakthrough—a sort of quantum leap, from X to Y."

She didn't understand this but said, "I'm not in the mood."

"My dear, at this moment you don't know *what* your mood is," he pointed out. "Women rarely know what they want. That's why they are often amazed to find themselves entranced by something that five minutes earlier would have passed unnoticed."

Gritch thought: God, another lecture. And this one from the tabernacle of male chauvinism! "I'm glad to see you hold women in such high esteem . . . wouldn't want you to step out of character."

"I grant women the esteem they deserve," Mast said. "I like women. Always have."

"Horseshit!" She drank off what was left in her glass—one of his fancy "vintages," she wasn't sure which one, not that it mattered. "I know your type. Behind the smooth talk, a woman is a convenience, nothing more."

"Well, that's one way of making her feel wanted, isn't it?" Mast said. "Hmn. All work, no play. Couldn't we do something about that?"

"You put me down and then expect me to be foxy?" she demanded, as much astonished as angry. "Anything in particular? No. Don't tell me. I'll bet I can guess."

He smiled. "They say fellatio's fun." She looked at him. "A heady experience, in more ways than one," Mast cajoled, weaseling at her. "An acquired taste, like okra, I suppose. Woman's great weakness. The root of maleness. A bona fide form of worship."

"Am I supposed to be your pet Jew again?" she snapped. "Is that what you're after?"

He shrugged. "You're female. That's what matters. Jewesses have gratefully gone down on their knees throughout the ages. But so have all women, no? It's merely a time-honored way of expressing appreciation. And isn't it a fine thing to display gratitude and at the same time enjoy it so immensely?"

He had come over to the couch where she was sitting, and now he began touching her, his fingers gentle, removing the red bandanna from her head, arranging the sweat-dampened curls.

"I don't feel like it," she said grumpily, while he reached with his free hand inside the velvet smoking jacket to unfasten the zipper of his slacks and take out his member. She stared for a moment while he stood there like that in front of her, and then she wanted it—

134

wanted desperately the solace it would provide. Gazing down at her he said, as though speaking to a child, "Yes. Now then. On your knees. Do as I say. That's better. A true art form, oral sex. Imbued with something of the magic of a Bach sonata."

Mast talked on as, crouched before him, with her heels tucked under her, she took the smooth helmet into her mouth and slowly began to fellate it. "Homage. The best kind of lip service, to the lingam," he murmured. "My dear girl. What a virtuoso flautist. An artist. Yes, that way. Don't stop. *Andante con moderato.*"

He had her pause for a moment while he rearranged their situation, seating himself on the couch. She knelt between his knees and began again, while he regarded her with a bemused expression: a complete sensualist who nevertheless maintained objectivity. Giving in to her needs she grasped the shaft firmly with both hands, her head moving up and down as, gently, she nursed. Mast sighed. "You see? This is instructive for you, Gritch."

"Don't come in my mouth," she warned.

"Why?"

"I don't like it." This was true. She'd done that on professional dates. The experience always made her nauseous.

"But that's the most precious gift a man can give a woman," he objected as she began again. "Humility and honor. That's nice, don't stop, yes, a shade quicker." He adjusted his position slightly. "Ah, if the folks back home could see us now, wouldn't they be impressed. Well, at least we have it on tape."

Gritch stopped, confounded, to peer up at him over the tops of the black-framed spectacles, which had slid halfway down the bridge of her nose. She'd forgotten: he'd been inserting cassettes all evening. "Damn you!" She glanced at the Magnavox. It's single red light seemed to wink knowingly at her.

She was indignant, outraged—understood that this was a *mise en scène* planned by him, one more device with which he could probe and hurt her.

"A Proper Young Lady and Her Old German Prof," Mast said amiably. "Apt title for this cassette. No, no . . . I'm joking, have you no sense of humor? The tape is yours to do with as you wish. Erase it, destroy it, who cares? Now, where were we? Please continue. I thought I was levitating . . ." He rambled on, half to himself, as she began again: "I want this to be educational for you, Gritch. You imagine that by mouthing my penis you are giving me a blowjob, but it's more than that. What difference does it make that you're Jewish and that I once persecuted your people? None at all. And I can prove it to you."

Without warning the old man suddenly broke into song, humming at first, then taking up the actual lyrics. But such a song, she thought. Who but a Jew could ever know a song like that?

This one was unfamiliar but as a child she'd heard similar melodies. Scratched old bakelite 78's. Her father, in the kitchen of their rundown Passaic home, sitting with his cronies, joking, telling stories, gossiping—hour after hour. Then they would play the records and sing, clapping their hands joyfully. She'd felt so unwanted, so left out—a shy little girl in dirty sneakers and a summer frock, peeking through the kitchen doorway at these big boisterous singing men.

It was like she was in a time warp now. Living the past and the present simultaneously. *Had her father loved her?*

*Did Mast love her?*

A long-locked area of her mind seemed to open; she knew that the answer to both questions was "yes." A memory she never thought about anymore surfaced. Her father had loved her. And she had loved him so much that she had done then what she was doing now. The memory was almost a dream it was so vague—who knows, maybe it *had* been a dream!—of her frightened one night by a storm. Her mother dead, what—two years? Gritch had crawled into his bed. For solace. They had slept in each other's arms. And later, much later, they had awakened, and she was doing it. They had never spoken of it afterward.

IT WAS AN old Yiddish ditty. About someone named Yankele. God only knew how far back it dated.

Mast, smiling and gazing down at her, sang the lines, first in English, then in guttural, vigorous Yiddish:

> Oi, how the rabbi will smack me!
> My little ear curls he'll tear out altogether.
> And it was morning, and it was evening the first day ...
> *Oy—Vet mikh der rebbe shyaysn!*
> *Mayne payelekh vet er fin mir oysraysn!*
> *Vay'hi erev, vay'hi voyker—yom ekhod.*

She stopped once more to stare up at her tormentor, her expression a mixture of fascination and horror.

How did he do it? The pronunciation, the inflection. Flawless.

"Carl," she cried, "*stop* it!"

"You don't like my song?" He laughed. "If the neighbors complain, tell 'em they should stuff ten fingers in their ears. Here.

136

Now!" With that he gripped each side of her head in his hands—they had surprising strength—and coaxed it downward. "Find out what life's really about!"

> *Montik vel ikh nisht fergesn.*
> Monday—I won't forget.
> *S'iz nisht geven in shtib vos tsu esn.*
> There wasn't a bit of food in the house.
> *Di mame hot gegosn mit trern.*
> My mother was crying her eyes out.
> Please, faster now. Let it never be said that force was
> used. What you believe in your own mind . . . is one thing.
> But between the two of us, let it be understood:
> *no coercion was used!*

With that he removed his hands. His frame trembled. Beating time in the air with his hands, he sang:

> *Ober shtil, der tate zol nisht hern* . . . quicker!
> But silently, so my father shouldn't hear. That's the
> spirit, Gritch. You're getting the idea now!
> *Der tate shrayt vi a meshigine Yid!*
> My father shouts like a crazy Jew!

She shuddered, and swallowed.

> *UN IKH ZING HIKH YANKELE'S LIED!*
> AND I SANG YANKELE'S SONG TO MYSELF!

SHE LAY ON the couch, face down, silently. He got himself a drink, lit a cigarette, came over to her, tossed down the finished cassette. "Here is life. Not your high-class whore's dates, Gritch. No books either. This is a different classroom. It may seem strange at first, but you'll grow accustomed to it."

She couldn't speak. Had no words. Could not even weep.

He said in a more kindly tone, "In fairness I should reciprocate. Give you pleasure in return. Or at least relief. What is it they say: Cast thy bread upon the waters and it shall be returned tenfold? Sorry. Tide's out. I think I can sleep now. But perhaps in the morning."

# part three

What Slaughters there were in the Forum and the Circus Maximus and open Temples.

—*Bolton*, Flores

AS HE HAD pointed out, Mast did know many important people in New York City, and one of them was a man named Mac Dobkin, a senior producer in the CBS hierarchy. Actually, Dobkin was a prime mover in the network's Special Projects Department.

The executive and the humanitarian had become friendly several years earlier—at any rate they'd gotten on a first-name basis—when they'd put together a ninety-minute documentary that had earned Dobkin his third Emmy.

This was "The Face of Starvation," considered by many in the business a hallmark achievement in television reportage. Dobkin had developed a considerable affection and respect for the old man. These feelings, as far as he could tell, were mutual; Mast, a pro himself, seemed to appreciate professionalism.

"THE POINT I'M stressing is that we have an hour-long exclusive," Dobkin told his boss, Fred Monson, on Tuesday morning, the day after the Oslo speech. "But we can't have any waffling. If it's to be done, we need a decision quickly."

Monson had come down to Dobkin's twenty-sixth-floor office at the latter's urgent request. He brought with him Harry Senutovitch of programming.

Dobkin had caught Mast's speech while watching the early-morning news at his home in Plandome, Long Island. While one side of him registered shock the other, entrepreneurial side was already

141

busy weighing what could be made of the event. Soon enough he had all but the minor details worked out. The late-morning meeting being held now, over coffee and croissants, would either pull the project together or else scrap it. The office itself was pleasant, with an excellent north view. Through the picture windows the three men regarded a besmogged and haze-dimmed vista, the skyscrapers and lesser splendors of Manhattan: black tar-papered roofs, for the most part hidden beneath snow, mazes of TV antennas, cisterns, grimy penthouses, and, over toward Lexington, a warmly dressed speck of a figure flying pigeons, waving a long pennanted baton to direct the orchestrated flock that rose and dipped.

"How quickly, Mac?" Monson asked.

"A week at most," Dobkin said. "Actually I favor Sunday evening. Preempting the movie."

Harry Senutovitch frowned. "Why so fast? I mean, that's awfully short notice." The question was mostly rhetorical. A special could take years to put together, or, when timeliness was a factor, it could be aired within days of its inception. Advertisers, promos, and pre-airtime publicity: these were problems but not insurmountable ones.

"I can knock the treatment together today," Dobkin told them. "Research can supply a work-group, 'round the clock if necessary. By Thursday we can start editing and at the same time launch thirty-second spots. *TV Guide*'s already gone to bed but we can buy local space."

"Skip the minutiae, Mac," Fred Monson said with a small wave of his hand. "Give us the overview."

"We've already got footage on Oslo. More will be coming in," Dobkin explained. "And we've got enough canned stuff on the Holocaust to choke an elephant. Plus the 'Starvation' show. That's the hooker. What I'm seeing is an enigma-type show that invites the viewer to do some thinking. Something with emotional wallop. Not bravura. Certainly not shrill. Deliberately calm but at the same time provocative. Let the viewer provide gut feelings. At this time of year everybody's emotions are keyed up." Dobkin paused. "The thing is, with Mast we have a charismatic personality. Remember 'Starvation'?"

"It had impact," Monson said. He meant it. But that show had been broadcast three years ago, and a great deal had happened since. Mac Dobkin was only too happy to refresh his memory.

MALNUTRITION IN AFRICA. South America. Accompanied by its two deadly handmaidens: drought and disease. Multitudes perishing under the blazing tropic sun. Children with bloated bellies and fly-encrusted eyelids.

Unpleasant stuff for an audience more accustomed to worrying about losing weight than putting it on.

Mast had served as principal coordinator between CBS, WHO, UNESCO, UNICEF, and a host of other organizations. He had the statistics. He knew the right people to approach. Best of all, he had known precisely where to lay his hands on the necessary film footage, most of it never aired before.

As documentaries went, "Starvation" had cost next to nothing. The footage was loaned free of charge. The music was canned. Part of the voice-over narration was provided by a famous Hollywood actress whose off-camera hobby was blatant altruism.

No, there had been nothing high-rent about "Starvation," which perhaps was why it achieved top-of-the-chart ratings. Just those raw, brutal scenes of people dying in far-off places. Dobkin had campaigned—much as he was doing now with his new project—to have the show broadcast one week before a holiday, Thanksgiving. His intuitions about scheduling proved on track.

Carl Mast himself—admittedly after some "waffling" on the part of decisionmakers—had been enlisted to narrate the final twenty-minute segment: a tour of portions of the Sudan, Chad, and Ethiopia. "A gamble," Mac Dobkin admitted later.

The producer had been impressed by Mast's voice and speaking style. That sonorous roupy baritone. The rolling rhetorical sentences. Except for the German accent, they were positively Churchillian. The phrases issuing from those aged lips were of such constructional elegance that they seemed contrived or, at the very least, rehearsed, but they were not. The old man for the most part spoke extempore, with a minimal referral to the script. A ham, "an absolute natural!" So crowed Dobkin to his colleagues later.

A good many of the thousands of letters that poured in during ensuing weeks doted on the touching performance of that "wonderful old doctor."

THE EARLIEST PROMOS for Dobkin's new special were aired on Thursday. It was mere chance that Mast and Gritch missed catching at least one that night or the following day. Mast, when he wasn't fighting with her, liked to have a TV on, especially during newscasts.

At a little after one on Saturday afternoon, however, they did see a

143

spot: *8:00 P.M., Sunday, EST. CBS will present* "Demon or Demi-god," *a profile of Nobel prizewinner, Carl Mast,* along with the teaser: *Parental guidance is advised due to subject matter . . .*

Mast was enchanted. "Let's have a TV party! Too bad we can't ask the neighbors in."

LATER SHE SHOPPED for groceries and after they were delivered went back to the campus for more books. By now the living room resembled a library, and still Mast's list of necessary reading material grew. He browsed here and there, bracketing a paragraph or inserting reference slips, at the same time jotting down questions:

"Who was in command during the Bailystok Massacre, 1942?"

"See what you can dig out on Julius Streicher, the pornographer-propagandist who published Hitler's rag."

"I want the actual names of the two Munich chemical firms that manufactured the cyanide Zyklon-B crystals for the gassing rooms. How many kilograms per month per camp were supplied? What sort of container? What was the cost per kilogram? How delivered? Also the name of the firm that supplied the ovens and iron trolleys for the cadavers."

"Why do you need all this?" Gritch wanted to know. "You've got most of it in your head." This was true. Mast was capable of forgetting what they'd had for breakfast, but like many elderly people he had a good retention of what had happened half a century ago.

Mast, seated on the long couch, surrounded by books and with his Supp-Hosed feet comfortably propped on the cocktail table, smiled. At hand was an enormous ashtray filled with ground-out butts—some menthol, some French—and his favorite Colombard, which he drank when not on ouzo.

She had formed the impression that he lived on liquor, cigarettes, and pills. Outside, the night sky was clear. On the TV the Mormon Tabernacle Choir, in Utahian splendor, belted out Christmas carols. Their harmonious bonhomie did nothing to lessen her unease, the feeling of being torn asunder by this old wretch who'd peremptorily taken over her life. And, damn it, she still wasn't convinced that he was Heislinger. Lighting one of her cigarettes she said moodily, "I was planning on taking a vacation over Christmas break."

"When this is finished you'll be able to afford a year-long spree if you like," Mast said without rancor. "Katmandu, Saint Moritz, Grossingers, Disneyland, take your pick, what's for dinner?"

"I don't feel like cooking," she snapped. "I want to eat out."

144

"Did anybody say anything about you cooking?" Mast murmured. "I'll whip up a little something later. I do a wonderful steak au poivre."

"Yuck!"

"Tsk, tsk. What's happened to little Mary Sunshine?"

"Ah, fuck off, will you?"

THAT NIGHT, SHE satisfied her curiosity by ransacking his suitcases, attaché case, and wallet while he snored in bed. Something was hurting him again; he had doubled up on the pain pills, and they had knocked him out.

She found nothing of informational value. Two thousand dollars in the wallet, along with credit and ID cards. In the attaché case: eleven thousand more, passport, old airline tickets. Also two safe-deposit keys and a signature card made out to someone named Breitmeister. The bank was on Fifth. The suitcases were empty, save for a pair of shoes, handkerchiefs, and two sweaters; his suits, coat, ties were hung neatly in her closet. She rifled pockets, found nothing. Atop her bureau he had left loose change, a key ring, pills, several packs of Gauloises, and—God only knew where he'd come across it—a coupon book entitling under-twelve-year-olds to discount goodies at McDonald's. There was also a stack of Rx's.

She put everything back as she'd found it, then glanced at the man in her bed. Mast snored softly, head flung back against the pillow, the hawklike nose angled ceilingward.

A shiver of apprehension went through her. It was almost as though she was as helpless against him when he slept as when he came at her awake.

She'd wanted to know about fame and power, and now here it was: right in her bed, noisily cutting lumber. This was the man who'd been in *Time* magazine and to whom the *New York Post* had given a headline: NOBEL NAZI IN NY? PD ISSUES APB AS CITYWIDE MANHUNT SPREADS.

Looking down at him Gritch thought: Christ, what a mess!

IN ONE OF the books Mast had requested, concerned with the capture of Eichmann, she'd read about a touching moment when the crack Israeli intelligence team that had been sent over to kidnap him had first confirmed that it was *he*. In the dusk that evening, at the house on Garibaldi Street, in that tacky suburb of Buenos Aires, Eichmann had ambled out to take down some garments from the clothesline. A helpful spouse, no longer young, balding.

And the Jewish agents—hard professionals—had stared upon this disciple of Satan. The enormity of it! This was the expert on the so-called "Jewish question." He'd operated the trains.

Overwhelmed by emotion the watching Israelis felt their knees turn to water. There *he* was. After all the years of searching.

One agent, certainly no coward but unable to face the awfulness of what he was looking at, simply turned tail and ran as though his life depended on it.

Gritch understood that with her heart and soul.

Later, at the capture itself, when Eichmann was walking up from the bus stop—how *ordinary*, Gritch thought, that he would have fallen back on city transport—they threw themselves upon him, wrestling him to the ground.

Crouched over his spreadeagled unresisting figure, they glared down at him. Trembling, one Israeli bent closer, hissing: *"Wie heissen Sie?"*

What is your name?

And he, aware of who it was who had come for him, knowing that after all these years it was finally done with, had said simply, *"Ich bin Eichmann."*

The voice a frightened tremolo.

Unmanned and stricken, they had stared down at him. Stared, seemingly, straight into the face of Evil.

*Ich bin Heislinger.* The awful thing was that *that* name kept cropping up in the books that littered the living room. It was most often mentioned in one volume of *The Trial of the Major War Criminals: Proceedings & Documents in Evidence,* Nuremberg 1947–49, H.M.S.O., London. There was more about Heislinger in the eight-volume U.S. Government Printing Office's *Nazi Conspiracy and Aggression,* which included extracted testimony given at the notorious "Doctors' Trial."

As research projects went, it was not that difficult, Gritch thought. The endless mass of documentation and cross-referencing was like rooting about in a field of potatoes. One poked here and there and very shortly came up with something.

In her own estimation she was a rotten excuse for a Jewess. No temple, no holidays—Gritch said of herself that the only Jewish thing about her was a distaste for ham, which she'd never been able to overcome. She wasn't merely lapsed, she was indifferent. Like many modern Jews, she'd "drifted." For her the Talmud was a historical and literary curiosity, most interesting, yes, but that was all.

Yet there still must have been something Jewish to what and who she was—how else to explain the mounting horror she experienced when Mast talked and when she herself looked into his books? In just a few days, under his tutelage, she had begun to form an accurate picture of what the Third Reich was.

It was like a vast mosaic, but, appalled now, she saw that all the pieces held together perfectly, that they meshed.

And at the same time she saw clearly how and where the Jews had fitted in.

The scholarly research helped, and Mast's vituperative ramblings added to the picture but, oddly, it was the "CBS Special" at eight the next night that exerted a peculiarly strong influence on her imagination.

"I WONDER IF they'll have Cronkite?" Mast said as they made themselves comfortable on the couch. "Be great if they can get him. And David Susskind, to hand 'round the Tab and lox."

It was almost eight. At hand were cashews, litchi nuts, bel paese, hard Italian salami, wine. "In the U.S., you know, God comes first," Mast went on happily, "but standing right behind him is good old Walter, telling him when to smile."

But following the station break the personable face of Dan Rather loomed on the screen, and Mast harrumphed, "Hell! They've got the kid."

His mood brightened however as the credits appeared. "Mac Dobkin's doing it. Excellent. We're in safe hands."

The anchorman was saying:

RATHER: Tonight CBS will examine the background of the most recent Nobel Peace Prize winner, Dr. Carl Mast.

   (CUTS: ARCHIVE FOOTAGE OF PREVIOUS WINNERS AT THE OSLO CEREMONY. SHOTS OF MARSHALL, KISSINGER. RATHER CONTINUES, VOICE OVER)

   Peace Prize winners have been the center of controversy before. General George C. Marshall won the Prize in 1952 for developing the Marshall Plan, but his critics argued that he had been the leader of the largest army the world had ever seen. Moreover, he supervised those who created the atom bomb. In the seventies, Henry Kissinger was awarded the medal, but in Oslo there were street demonstrations when the news was announced: Kissinger had been chief advisor to Nixon during the intensified bombing of North Vietnam.

(CUTS: SHOTS OF HAMMARSKJÖLD, AT UNITED NATIONS AND IN AFRICA. AS *RATHER* CONTINUES)

Another winner, Dag Hammarskjöld, was widely regarded as a man of good intentions—but critics claimed that the policies he helped inaugurate proved a disaster for much of the Congo, where thousands perished because of UN intervention.

"I thought this show was supposed to be about me," Mast said. "Be still for a minute!" Gritch muttered.

*RATHER:*  Last Monday in Oslo, Dr. Mast, at the conclusion of his

(CUTS, CLIPS OF *MAST* IN OSLO, AS *RATHER* CONTINUES)

acceptance speech, stated that he was a former Nazi official, Kasper Heislinger, wanted by Israel, Germany, France, and Poland for atrocities committed during World War II.

"Do you know how much it cost me to rent that monkey suit?" Mast said, obviously pleased by the figure he cut in white tie and tails. "Seventy-five, American. Little shop, downtown Oslo. Bit tight in the shoulders, wouldn't you say?"

*RATHER:*  Following the speech, Dr. Mast fled to New York. His present whereabouts are unknown.

"I didn't *flee,* damn it!" Mast growled. "I merely attended to some personal matters in Geneva . . . nobody detained me."
"Hush," she said. "How can I listen if—"

*RATHER:*  Tonight we'll review portions of Dr. Mast's career as a world-renowned humanitarian, as well as aspects of his reputed "earlier" career. That career began in Nazi Germany and ended in 1945, an era of hate, oppression, and persecution.

(CUTS: ARCHIVE CLIPS. HITLER, HIMMLER, GOEBBELS, GIVING SPEECHES. MASS MEETINGS OF NAZIS. ALL DONE RAPID-FIRE, AS OF A KODAK CLICKING)

148

Horror tales of racial defilement and lurid descriptions of the perils confronting Aryan womanhood were broadcast. Hitler himself set the tone in *Mein Kampf.*

"What's Dobkin going to do, stuff us with ancient history?" Mast caroled. "What's the world coming to? *Oy, oy,* such a favor, God, I'll never forget!" He stared at Gritch. "I was hoping that at least we might get something exegetical about my speech. Who'd they say was sponsoring this cartoon? Jurassic Electronics?"

(CUT: CU OF *MEIN KAMPF.* CUT: HITLER ON PODIUM, IN A TIRADE. FADE SOUND AS VOICE-OVER TRANSLATION COMES IN)

*TRANSLATOR:*
(Voice Over)
With Satanic joy the black-haired Jewish youth lurks in wait for the unsuspecting girl whom he defiles with his blood thus stealing her from her people . . .

(FADE SOUND, MIXING GERMAN AND ENGLISH. SECOND TRANSLATOR'S VOICE UP)

*SECOND TRANSLATOR:*
(Voice Up)
*Wer kennt den Jude, kennt den Teufel!* Who knows the Jew knows the Devil!

(CUTS: BROWNSHIRTS MARCHING, ARMS SWINGING, GOOSE STEPPING. SOBER-EYED THRONGS WATCHING. FLAG WITH STAR OF DAVID UNDERFOOT. BROWNSHIRTS LAUGHING. BYSTANDERS CHEERING)

*RATHER:*
(Voice Over)
Anti-Semitism had been in Germany since the first Jewish settlements. Popular opinion had it that the loss of World War I was the fault of Jewish "big-business interests."

(CUTS: PICTURE-POSTCARD VIEWS OF COBBLED STREETS IN BAVARIAN VILLAGES, SHOPS, GERMANS ENGAGED IN DAILY LIFE. *RATHER* CONTINUES)

It made no difference that the Jew the average German knew was the humblest of shopkeepers, a worker of long hours, a law-abiding citizen who probably was as proud of his Germanness as he was of his Talmudic heritage. The official word went out that "decent" Germans had clasped a snake to their bosoms.

(CUTS: CUs OF GOEBBELS ON PLATFORM, SHAKING HIS FIST. VOICE-OVER TRANSLATES)

**TRANSLATOR:** The Jews will be our undoing!
(Voice Over)

(CUTS: AUDIENCE RISING TO ITS FEET, APPLAUDING. CUT TO: GOEBBELS)

German Aryans are the rightful bearers of human cultural development.
Back to the Middle Ages, Jews have been known as carriers of filth and disease, death and destruction. Plague-spreaders . . . poisoners of wells.

**RATHER:** And of course it was also recognized that Jews caused
(Voice Over) syphillis.

(CUT & PAN: PLEASANT GERMAN GRADE-SCHOOL CLASSROOM)

Schoolchildren were taught that Marxism was a systematic plan to hand the world over to the Jews. The Nazis quoted Martin Luther:

(CUTS: CHURCH SERVICE, MINISTER ORATING, VOICE-OVER TRANSLATES)

**TRANSLATOR:** Next to the Devil there is no enemy more cruel, more
(Voice Over) venomous and violent than a true Jew.

**RATHER:** There were the book-burnings.
(Voice Over)

(CUT: BOOK BONFIRES. FADE TO *KRISTALLNACHT*)

And *Kristallnacht,* a countrywide and state-approved demonstration against Jewish small-business enterprise, in which over four million dollars' worth of plate-glass windows belonging to Jewish merchants was smashed . . . in a single night.

(CUTS: JEWS BEING ARRESTED. ROUGH HANDLING. ELDERS' BEARDS BEING SNIPPED, WIGS TORN OFF WOMEN. *RATHER* CONTINUES)

Jews from all walks of life—the high and the low—were summarily arrested and sent to Dachau or other camps, for one "antisocial" offense or another, including parking tickets. That is, they were taken into "protective custody" for the "good of the State."

(CUT: HITLER, GIVING SPEECH, VOICE-OVER TRANS-
LATES)

*TRANSLATOR:* War is life. Germany requires *Lebensraum* . . . living
(Voice Over)     space.

(*RATHER* CONTINUES)

*RATHER:*     The step-by-step segregation of the Jews continued.

(CUTS: APPROPRIATE TO DIALOGUE. FOR THE FIRST
TIME WE SEE THE STAR OF DAVID SEWN ON GAR-
MENTS)

They were barred from holding public offices, including civil-service posts, which encompassed all teaching jobs. Barred from conducting specified business
enterprises. Forbidden to use public transportation.
Forbidden to use public telephone booths. There were
roughneck beatings. Synagogues were plundered. By
law the Star of David was sewn on the outer garments
of every Jew—man, woman, and child. Goebbels said
of the yellow star:

(CUT: GOEBBELS AGAIN, ON THE PODIUM)

*TRANSLATOR:* A most humanitarian measure of hygienic prophy-
(Voice Over)     lactic defense, so to speak, meant to prevent the Jew
from penetrating our community in disguise, in order
to sow disunity among us . . .

(THE VOICE-OVER TRANSLATION CONTINUES,
ALOOF, FLAT, SUPERCILIOUS)

The fact that the Jew still lives among us is not a proof
that he belongs to us; as little as the flea does not
become a domestic animal because he lives in the
house . . .
Jews are parasites! Potato beetles, bacilli!

(*RATHER* CONTINUES)

*RATHER:*     Hitler had unified the country. The economy stabil-
ized. Unemployment was a thing of the past. Re-
armament, for the sake of "protecting Germany's
national interests," flourished.

151

(CUTS & PANS: THE GERMAN BUREAUCRATIC LIFE,
INTERSPERSED WITH CIVILIAN & MILITARY. BANDS
PLAYING IN BKGND. UNIFORMS EVERYWHERE, AS
INDICATED BY DIALOGUE. *RATHER* CONTINUES)

Suddenly it seemed that practically every German
male was in uniform. One had to look hard to find a
civilian! Village postmen in hamlets from Bavaria to
Schleswig-Holstein strutted about their daily rounds
in military tunics, peaked caps, boots, and britches.
Train conductors resembled colonels more than col-
lectors of tickets, and the traveler by rail who looked
out the window of his compartment might be in for a
surprise. Who was that waiting down there by the
tracks, standing so proudly, stiffly? A field marshal?

(CUT: APPROPRIATE SHOT)

No, a second glance verified that it was a common
switchman, perhaps well into his sixties, but nonetheless quite dashing in his regalia. In former days he
would have been merely stooped and elderly. Now he
stood at full attention and raised his rigid arm in the
Nazi salute as the train thundered by. The arm and
the long steel lever he had just thrown were angled in
a double greeting to those passengers who took notice.

(CUT: THE FAMOUS PAINTING OF HITLER OUTFITTED
IN KNIGHT'S ARMOR, HEADPIECE CRADLED IN ONE
ARM, JOUSTING LANCE HELD AT THE READY)

*Der Führer* was depicted as a latter-day Parsifal,
garbed in shining Teutonic armor, the famous fore-
lock plastered over one brow. His talent as a speaker
could not be disputed.

(CUTS: THE BIG TORCH-LIT RALLIES, THOUSANDS
CHEERING)

So there was ceremony appropriate to the corona-
tion of kings, and the splendid uniforms, and the great
rallies where multitudes bellowed *Sieg Heil!* until
their voices cracked, but there was a deadly side to the
business. Not only for German Jews but for, as Hitler
termed them, the "whole lice-ridden Ashkenazic
gang." As well as Poles, Gypsies, and those other

152

polyglot ethnic groups he had labeled "subhuman species." *Lebensraum* was needed. Panicked, some Jews converted, and so became pariahs to both fellow Jew and Aryan.

(CUT: GOEBBELS SNEERING, VOICE-OVER TRANS-LATES)

*TRANSLATOR:*   If worse comes to worst, a splash of baptismal water
(Voice Over)   will save the business and the Jew at the same time.

(*RATHER* CONTINUES)

*RATHER:*   The idea of the *Konzentrationlagers* meant exactly that. A camp for "concentration." In such facilities members of "dangerous" political groups were to be "reeducated," via lectures and reading.

(BEGIN CUTS: THE CAMPS)

Of course a Jew, no matter what his politics, was always dangerous. One of the first *Konzentrationlagers* was a former gunpowder factory only a few kilometers north of a city famous for its friendly beer-drinking ambience—Munich. Dachau served as a working model for the larger extermination centers that came later. Their names are written in the dark-est page of history.

(VERY FAST CUTS: AS *RATHER* INTONES THE NAMES. BKGND. MUSIC SWELLS—WE HEAR FRANZ LISZT'S "TOTENTANZ")

Bergen-Belsen . . . Auschwitz-Birkenau . . . Treblinka . . . Matthausen . . . Büchenwald . . . Flossenburg . . . Lüblin . . . Natzweiler . . . Oranienburg . . . Ravens-brück . . . Sachsenhausen . . . And it is at about this time that historians begin to notice the name Heis-linger.

"Christ, it's about time," Mast said as a commercial break commenced.

THE PROGRAM RESUMED with Rather sketching in additional infor-mation on the extermination camps, the euthanasia programs, and the function of the *Einsatzgrüppen* strike-force groups, which in the

153

early days of the war swept over Poland and spearheaded deep into Russia. Visual effects were provided by archive footage, as before.

RATHER:
(Voice Over)

There were four *Einsatzgrüppen* killer-units, made up of from eight- to twelve hundred carefully selected men. Their modus operandi was simplicity itself.

(CUTS: ACTUAL EXECUTIONS, INDIVIDUAL AND EN MASSE. THE SHOT BEHIND THE EAR. PILES OF DEAD. SHALLOW PITS. CUs OF DEAD)

Huge pits were bulldozed in some secluded area and then, with the help of pistol, rifle, and machine-gun fire, and later carbon-monoxide-rigged trucks, groups of up to several thousand at a time were dispatched. Kasper Heislinger, by then a colonel in the SS, was assigned the task of maintaining morale among executioners.

(CUTS & PANS: THE DEATH TRAINS & UNLOADING YARDS. CROWDS OF HELPLESS JEWS, THEIR FACES MIRRORING FEAR, DESPAIR, RESIGNATION. SS GUARDS STAND BY STOICALLY)

Meanwhile, elsewhere, Eichmann's death trains were rolling, busily transporting other Jews to their new "resettlement areas." At Auschwitz. Heislinger's name is found in death-camp records, too . . .

(CUTS: SNAPSHOT-SHUTTER EFFECT. THREE STILLS OF HEISLINGER)

This is Heislinger, in 1937.

(CUTS: DITTO, OF CARL MAST)

And this is Carl Mast, as he looks today. Are these two men the same person? Hard to imagine. Plastic surgery? One can only speculate.

(CUTS & PANS: GERMAN HOSPITALS, ORPHAN ASYLUMS, MENTAL INSTITUTIONS. *RATHER* CONTINUES)

Testimony indicates that Heislinger was not always a willing participant in what went on. He had a marked tendency to scoff at the goals set forth by Himmler and was censured on a number of occasions for his

154

cynicism concerning some of the Third Reich's most sacrosanct doctrines.

(CUTS: HITLER, HIMMLER, NUMEROUS AIDES. HITLER AT HIS DESK, SMILING AND CHATTING WITH EVERY-ONE AS HE SIGNS DOCUMENTS)

When Hitler authorized the first euthanasia program in the spring of 1939, Heislinger was made chief of an important office.

"Reluctantly, damn you, I fought it tooth and nail," Mast shouted at the TV. "Can't you assholes get anything right?"

RATHER: This was the ... I'll try to get it right ... *die Reichausschuss zur Wissenschaftlichen Erfassung von Erb- und Anlagebedingten Schweren Leiden* ... the Reich Committee for Scientific Research of Hereditary and Severe Constitutional Diseases. The idea behind this program was to dispose of the insane, the deformed, and the mentally deficient.

(CUTS: INSTITUTIONAL SHOTS, MENTALLY RETARDED, ETC.)

In short all handicapped persons who were a burden on the *Reichsökonomie.* From its inception, the program found little favor with the average German, despite its cost-effectiveness.

"You can say that again," Mast informed the screen loudly. "They hated it. The letters I had to answer, you wouldn't believe. All those blubbering *Onkels* and *Grossmutters,* wringing their hands over some useless crip or feeb—I mean, I'm talking *basket* cases— we'd put to sleep for good. Who in hell ever told this kid he could speak German?"

(VOICE OVER AS CUTS AND PANS OF ABOVE CONTINUED)

RATHER: The "patients" were sent to "observation centers" for
(Voice Over) evaluation and then on to the actual mercy-killing facilities at Bernburg, Brandenburg, Graffenneck, Hadamar, Hartheim, and Sonnenstein.

155

(CUT: LAB-ROOM SHOTS. HYPODERMICS, JARS OF FLUID, RUBBER-GLOVED HANDS AT WORK)

Death was by injection. Raw phenol, 22 cc's, intravenously. The patients usually died in an immediate total convulsion during the actual injection. But aside from initial violent spasms there was, as one physician testified, "No indication that the subjects suffered undue pain."

(CUT & PAN: PHYSICIAN, DOING WARD ROUNDS)

The doctors assigned to this task exhibited a notable diligence.

(CUT: *RATHER.* CU, INDICATING WRY DISTASTE)

A certain Dr. Pfannmueller... may posterity note his name . . . personally "disposed" of 2,058 "handicapped" cases in just eighteen days.

(CUTS: HITLER TALKING TO GROUP OF ATTENTIVE MEN, AS *VOICE-OVER* TRANSLATES)

*TRANSLATOR:* Persons who, according to human judgment, are in-
(Voice Over) curable can, upon a most careful diagnosis of their condition of sickness, be accorded a mercy death.

(*RATHER* CONTINUES)

*RATHER:* Because of public opinion, euthanasia of adults was abandoned in the fall of 1941, but retarded children continued to be mercy-killed until Germany's defeat. Somewhere between eighty and one-hundred thousand died. But we are not done with it yet.

(CUTS: LARGE CROCKERY JARS ON SHELVES)

The brains of the victims were purchased by the General Patient Transport Company, in lots of one hundred fifty to two hundred. As a certain Dr. Hallervorden put it:

(LAB SHOTS CONTINUE AS VOICE-OVER TRANSLATES FROM GERMAN)

*TRANSLATOR:* There was wonderful material among those brains,
(VOICE OVER) beautiful mental defectives, malformations, and early infantile diseases. I accepted those brains, of course.

Where they came from and how they came to me were
really none of my business . . .

(CUTS: NUREMBERG TRIALS, DEFENDANTS TESTIFY-
ING, *RATHER* CONTINUES)

RATHER:　　　Those were also the freewheeling years of medical
experimentation, which Dr. Heislinger, declared "totally unscientific . . . and a waste of time." One of
every three hundred physicians in Germany was
involved. In Nuremberg a doctor later explained his
stance:

(CU: DEFENDANT IN THE DOCK, VOICE-OVER TRANS-
LATES)

TRANSLATOR:　It was a wholly new experience for us all to be offered
(Voice Over)　persons to experiment on. I had to get used to the idea.

(CUT: TO CONCENTRATION CAMP MEDICAL WARDS,
AS *RATHER* CONTINUES)

RATHER:　　　There were the Polish women who were nicknamed
the "Rabbit Girls"—they were given gas-gangrene
infections so that the effects of sulfa and penicillin
drugs could be studied. Mass sterilizations. Involuntary exposure to mustard and phosgene gases. At
Ravensbrück, active cultures of staphylococci and
streptococci were plastered against wounds or in-
jected into the bloodstream. The idea was to test the
efficacy of sulfanilamide on the resultant inflamma-
tions . . . the German troops on the various fighting
fronts were experiencing heavy casualties from infect-
ed wounds. *SS Sturmbannführer* Dr. Ding, who also
experimented with malaria, reported:

(CUT: DEFENDANT TESTIFYING, VOICE-OVER
TRANSLATES)

TRANSLATOR:　The surest way to produce typhus in humans is the
(Voice-Over)　intravenous injection of 20 cc's of fresh typhus-infected
blood.

(CUT: LAB SHELVES, FILLED WITH SKULLS, AS
*RATHER* CONTINUES)

RATHER:　　　Something called the Institute for Practical Research
in Military Science, working in collaboration with the

157

University of Strasbourg, assembled a collection of human skulls to demonstrate the anthropological inferiority of the more "bestial, subhuman" types. Specimens were obtained from death-camp inmates. Once the lethal needle had been administered, the head was carefully detached. Brains, eyes, and fleshy matter were stripped by several hours' immersion in caustic lye.

(CUTS & PANS: SHOTS OF CAMP INMATES IN FINAL STAGES OF MARASMUS, STARING AT CAMERA, HOL-LOW-EYED, PIPE-STEM-LIMBED)

But by then the living inmates themselves resembled little more than walking scarecrows. Prolonged starvation produces a cachexia that has interesting effects. Diarrhea, neurological aberrations, hunger, edema. The protein content of the blood changes, as does sedimentation rate. During the hottest summer months rectal temperatures as low as ninety-two degrees Fahrenheit were regularly observed. In addition to weakness of body movement there was a general decline of concentration and memory. The males experienced impotence. The females amenorrhoea.

(CONTINUING CUTS & CUs OF ABOVE)

Of particular interest was the outward appearance of these wretches. With their sunken eyes, projecting cheekbones, and skin so thin it seemed to have been painted on with a brush, they looked identical. This anonymity was reinforced by their close-cropped skulls and the rags they wore as garments. They were called *Musselmänner* by their SS guards because they displayed an emaciation that conjured up visions of famine in India. And a part of their world was the man known as Colonel Kasper Heislinger.

"Who was just trying to scrape by, like most hardworking Nazis," Mast observed. "I must say that Dobkin's kept his flunkies damned busy this week—some of this crap is almost accurate. If you want the fleas, get a fine-tooth comb, eh?"

(CUT: PILES OF CAMP DEAD, AS *RATHER* GOES ON)

*RATHER:*     The bright blue Zyklon-B pellets that, when activated,

158

sent their vapors through the air ducts of Auschwitz's "bathing rooms," apparently offended the finer sensibilities of certain Aryan warriors.

(CUT: FORMER SS OFFICER TESTIFYING. VOICE-OVER TRANSLATES)

*TRANSLATOR:* ... though ammunition was expensive, shooting was
(Voice Over)   a much more honorable and soldierly way to do it.

(*RATHER* CONTINUES)

*RATHER:*   In 1943 Heislinger was transferred to the camps. He must have been in direct contact with various *Kommandants* such as Auschwitz's Hoess:

(CUT: HOESS TESTIFYING, VOICE-OVER TRANSLATES)

*TRANSLATOR:* It was a terrible job, but somebody had to do it!
(Voice Over)   Whether this mass extermination of the Jews was necessary or not, was something on which I could not allow myself to form an opinion.

(CUT: CU, HOESS)

I must emphasize here that I have never personally hated the Jews. It is true that I looked upon them as the enemies of our people. But just because of this I saw no difference between them and the other prisoners, and I treated them all in the same way. I never drew distinctions. In any event, the emotion of hatred is quite foreign to my nature.

(CUT: TO *RATHER*)

*RATHER:*   During this time Colonel Heislinger hosted several delegations appointed by the International Red Cross to investigate the treatment of "interned political prisoners."

"What the fuck are you talking about?" Mast thundered. "Burkhardt was president of the Red Cross, and knew what was going on! So, for that matter, did the Pope, Churchill, and Roosevelt. You trying to do a whitewash-job, Dobkin? Get off my back!"

*RATHER:*   The allegations were shelved after the Red Cross twice visited Theresienstadt, the model camp set up by Himmler, which was the only one where Jews were

159

treated humanely. Heislinger participated in these tours.

(CUTS & PANS: JEWS IN MODEL CAMP SETTING, WEARING CLEAN CLOTHES, LOOKING WELL-FED, HAPPY, SMILING FACES, WORKING AT AGRICULTURAL CHORES, WRITING AT DESKS IN CLEAN BARRACKS, ETC.)

To prove that Nazis were treating Jews in the very best possible fashion, the censor's office exhibited many postcards

(CUTS: POSTCARDS)

all written voluntarily, addressed to internees' families in Holland, Luxembourg, France, and elsewhere. The cards bore such messages as "We are well here. Come join us as quickly as possible."

(CUTS: MORE CARDS)

As soon as the Red Cross visitors had departed, the Jews were entrained for Büchenwald, where they were gassed.

(CONTINUING CUTS & PANS: ALLIED TROOPS LIBERATING THE CAMPS, THE INTERNEES CHEERING, WEEPING, ETC., STRETCHER CASES BEING CARRIED OUT, HOSPITAL SHOTS OF THE SURVIVORS. *RATHER,* VOICE OVER)

*RATHER:*
Voice Over)

*Judenrein,* or "Jew-pure," was a term coined by the Third Reich to designate those cities or areas from which all Jews had been "removed." To attain this goal the extermination camps operated right up to war's end. By the time Allied troops captured these installations—the SS personnel either surrendered without a struggle or deserted—quite a bit of cosmetic housework had been done in an attempt to conceal the atrocities. But enough corpses remained. Mute evidence. They could not be denied. There were also thousands of Jewish survivors, mostly suffering from advanced starvation, typhus, and dysentery. More than ninety percent required immediate hospitalization. Of these, more than thirty percent expired less than six weeks after their liberation.

160

(CUTS: CONTEMPORARY SHOTS OF SURVIVORS, NOW
ALL ELDERLY)

The fate of those who were nursed back to something resembling normal life is more difficult to follow. Physically, many would be wrecks for the remainder of their lives. Mentally, however, it was worse. They would experience psychoses, neuroses, and other indications of permanently maimed personalities. They felt anger, fear, frustration, horror, and above all, guilt. How could *they* have survived when so many had perished? How does a father who has watched his wife and children walk into the gas chambers go about building a new life for himself? How does one go on living after sustaining such damage?

(CUTS: SURVIVORS VISITING THE CAMPS TODAY, STARING AROUND: AUSCHWITZ, BERGEN-BELSEN, ETC., INTERSPERSED WITH STROBE-FLASH CUT-BACKS TO THE OLD DAYS: THE UNLOADING YARDS, THE CREMATORIA)

How does one forgive? How does one forget? The answers are simple.

(CUT: CONTEMPORARY WOMAN SURVIVOR BREAK-ING DOWN, WEEPING)

One does not forgive. And those who went through the camps will never forget.

(CUT: BACK TO *RATHER*)

Kasper Heislinger vanished before war's end. Although convicted in absentia of war crimes, he was never imprisoned. His name was forgotten. Until last Monday, when it was recalled. In a moment we will review portions of the career of Peace Prize winner, Dr. Carl Mast. But a final word on the mentality of the Third Reich.

(CUT: THERESIENSTADT POSTCARDS AGAIN, AS VOICE-OVER TRANSLATES)

*TRANSLATOR:* We are well here. Come join us as quickly as possible.
(Voice Over)

(*RATHER*, VOICE-OVER SEGUES IN)

161

RATHER:             The final word—if it can be called that—on euthana-
(Voice Over)        sia was provided by one doctor who was determined to
                    convince the judges at Nuremberg that there was a
                    valid basis for what happened:

                    (CUT: THE TRIALS, A DEFENDANT IN EARNEST TES-
                    TIMONY, VOICE-OVER TRANSLATES)

TRANSLATOR:         The underlying motive was the desire to help indi-
(Voice Over)        viduals who could not help themselves. Such consid-
                    eration cannot be regarded as inhuman. Nor did I ever
                    feel it to be in any degree unethical or immoral. I am
                    convinced that if Hippocrates were alive, he would
                    change the wording of his Oath. I do not feel myself to
                    blame. I have a perfectly clear conscience.

                    (FADE: TO THERESIENSTADT POSTCARD LYING ON A
                    TRASH HEAP, AS VOICE-OVER TRANSLATES. MUSIC
                    UP)

                    Come join us, as quickly as possible.

                    (MUSIC CRESCENDOS, CUT TO COMMERCIAL)

THE REMAINDER OF the program was given over to an account of
Mast's achievements.

Two berobed diplomats, one from Upper Volta, the other from
neighboring Ghana, said bluntly that Dr. Mast was a hero in their
homelands for his triumphs over onchocerciasis, or "oncho," more
commonly known as "river blindness," a particularly painful and
debilitating disease.

That Mast was idolized in such capitals as Ouagadougou seemed
no exaggeration. There were film clips of the warm greetings
accorded him—broad smiles and forthright handshakes—and one
especially effective sequence. It could not have lasted more than a
minute. Apparently it had been shot as Mast was preparing to
depart some town or rural village.

Groups of schoolchildren had been organized to bid him farewell.
They gathered along the dusty main street and at the dirt airstrip,
clutching small handfuls of flowers, and singing songs of love.

The scenario was the stuff a public relations man's dreams were
made of.

The Black world meeting the White. The hand of brotherhood
extended.

                    (CUTS, PANS, & FADES: LITTLE KIDS, FLASHING

BROAD GRINS—WHITE TEETH—ALL SPIFFED UP IN
THEIR GOING-TO-SCHOOL CLOTHES, HAIR BRAIDED
INTO CORN ROWS. CU: ESPECIALLY CUTE LITTLE
GIRL, MISSING FRONT TEETH, PINK RIBBONS IN HER
HAIR, SMILING, STANDING BETWEEN HER HAPPY
PARENTS. PANNING SHOTS: CARL MAST, SMILING,
PAUSING AMONG THE THRONG TO SHAKE HANDS
WITH ADULTS, EMBRACING CHILDREN)

Schmaltz? Perhaps. Undeniable, however, was the love that
shone in these people's faces. The old, the halt, and the lame stopped
to kiss his outstretched hand, and some got down on their knees to
kiss his feet, too. Some wept, some cheered. There were chanted
choruses:

(PAN THRONG. DUBBED TRANSLATION)

*TRANSLATOR:* Come back, come back, come back . . .
(DUBBED)

(CUT: CU, *RATHER*)

*RATHER:* To these people, as one ecumenical writer has observed, Mast is a kind of "parthogenetic savior,
sprung fully blown and complete." But they themselves have a better name for him, one that is known
in many places around the world. To them he is
simply . . . Doctor Carl.

"That Dobkin," Mast growled. "The son of a bitch owes me. And
this is what he does." With that he lapsed into a bitter silence.
Oddly, Gritch was made more uncomfortable by his suppressed
anger than by his earlier outbursts.

(CUT: THE CLOSING MINUTES OF "FACE OF STARVA-
TION")

*RATHER:* And this is the world Carl Mast has worked in for
(Voice Over) decades . . . not from behind a desk . . . not in air-
conditioned comfort . . . he went among the people.
Here is Life . . . and Death, of the sort few Americans
ever witness. See for yourself.

(CUT: PANORAMIC PANS. THE BURNING FURNACE OF
THE SUN, HAMMERING ITS BLISTERING HEAT DOWN
FROM THE BRASSY INVERTED BOWL IN THE SKY

163

OVERHEAD. CUT: LOW FOOTHILLS IN THE DISTANCE,
BURNT, TREELESS, GRASSLESS. PAN: DESOLATION IN
ALL DIRECTIONS. THIS IS AFRICA—MAYBE ETHIOPIA,
MAYBE BIAFRA. *RATHER* CONTINUES)

This is where a handful of millet spells the difference
between life and death. But the soil is too barren for
crops.

(CUTS: THE EARTH CRACKED, SCORCHED, BONE-DRY
CLAY, FILMED OVER BY ALKALI DUST)

Yet people exist here.

(CUTS: A CLUSTER OF SQUATTERS' HUTS FASHIONED
OF TWIGS, SCRAPS OF TAR PAPER, TIN. PAN: THE
NATIVES THEMSELVES. ALL DYING. STUNNED, LIT-
ERALLY STUPIFIED BY HEAT AND STARVATION. PULL
IN FOR CUs OF THEIR FACES, STARING VACANTLY
INTO THE CAMERA. *RATHER* CONTINUES)

The people whose faces you are looking at are dead.
No one in this particular village survived. It was only
one of scores of villages.

(CUTS & PANS: THE FACES OF THE CHILDREN. UN-
COMPREHENDING, BEWILDERED, EMACIATED. CUT:
DR. CARL MAST. SHOULDERS STOOPED—HE IS OBVI-
OUSLY EXHAUSTED. KNEE SOCKS, SUNGLASSES. A
TOPEE OF SOLAR PITH. PULL IN, AS HE SPEAKS)

*MAST:*     Now you have seen what it really is.

(MUSIC UNDER: "TOTENTANZ" AGAIN, FUNEREAL,
HORRIFYING—IT CONTINUES FOR REMAINDER OF
CLOSING SHOTS, BUILDING IN VOLUME. CUT: TWO-
SHOT, AS DR. MAST TURNS SLIGHTLY AWAY FROM
CAMERA, BENDS OVER, HIS ATTENTION RIVETED ON
A CHILD NEAR DEATH. THE DISTENDED DRUM-TIGHT
STOMACH. THE SMALL BLACK FACE, A SHOCKING
TRAVESTY OF WHAT A CHILD'S FACE SHOULD BE.
MARASMUS AT ITS GHASTLIEST. THE SERE PARCH-
MENTLIKE SKIN STRETCHED OVER THE INFANTILE
CHEEKS AND CHIN. *MAST* CONTINUES, IN A WEARY
VOICE)

This boy is not alone. Around the world there are

164

millions of other children who need help. For him there is no help. A matter of too little too late. Before sunset he will be dead. No one will grieve his passing. Nobody knows who he is. No name. Just a dying little boy.

(CUT: TIGHT CU, THE CHILD'S FACE, THE EYES, BIG AS SAUCERS, THE CHIN POINTED, FOREHEAD BULG-ING, FLIES CLUSTER AT THE EYELIDS, SEEKING MOISTURE, THE MOUTH IS SLACK, THE LIPS CRACKED, BLISTERED, ULCEROUS, OOZING SORES. A FLY PERCHES. THE CHILD IS TOO NEAR DEATH TO BRUSH IT AWAY. *MAST* CONTINUES)

Yes. Look hard. Do not forget this face. It's worth remembering.

(CUT: TWO SHOT, AS DR. MAST TAKES THE CHILD'S HAND IN HIS. PULL IN: VERY TIGHT CU. THE TWO HANDS. THE CHILD'S IS SO TINY. THE SKIN, WRINKLED AND BLACK. IT LOOKS LIKE A MONKEY'S PAW, LYING LIMPLY IN THE DOCTOR'S SEEMINGLY HUGE HAND. THE CHILD'S FINGERS ARE CURLED. THERE IS PRACTICALLY NOTHING TO THE WRIST, THE FOREARM A MERE TWIG. HOLD, FOR A LONG BEAT, AS MUSIC SWELLS. *MAST*, VOICE OVER)

You have seen the face of starvation. This is its hand. Will you reach out and take it?

(MUSIC UP. HOLD FRAME FOR A LONG BEAT & FREEZE. ZOOM IN: ON DR. MAST'S AND THE CHILD'S HANDS. END "STARVATION" SEGMENT. CUT: DAN RATHER FOR CLOSING COMMENTS & WRAP)

"They can't slough me off like that! I've put too damned much on the line," Mast said. "Making me out to be a two-headed calf in a carnival sideshow. Who listens to what a freak has to say? But they won't shut me up. I should have gone down there and written the goddamn script myself!"

Exactly why he was so furious, she couldn't fathom.

SHE BROWSED IN the drugstore's magazine rack while the pharmacist made up the prescriptions Mast had given her. Outside it was overcast and blustery, with sharp frigid gusts that hurried Broadway's pedestrians along.

The drugstore was a large and busy place. Many of its customers looked like students, which is what she herself had been less than a week ago—or was it a year? She shuffled the magazines, looking for one that could hold her interest. Around her was noise—conversation, the chatter of registers in the check-out lines, the Muzak system playing carols—but Gritch felt cut off, isolated, an island of silence.

She thought: You're worn out. Want to know something? You haven't smiled since he came. Except cynically or angrily. What's he call you? His little sunshine girl? Don't be *kvetch*, he says. The only trouble is, there's nothing to smile about.

Gritch had never been one to indulge in casual levity, which is not to say that she was without humor or the ability to enjoy happiness. She was, by any measure, a quite serious young woman, but when life was right—when she was feeling really good—joy was not an impossibility.

The pharmacist, an outrageous flirt, had said it would take half an hour to fill the prescriptions. He was most apologetic about this.

Seemed inclined to ask her out for a cocktail, were it not for the fact that he was so busy.

THE THREE PHONE booths were beside the magazines; two were occupied. She slid into the third, rolled the door shut, lifted the receiver to her ear, but did not insert a coin. In here some of the noise was shut out. She tried to think.

Put an end to it, she told herself. One call. The FBI. They'll know what to do. Then go to a movie. By the time she returned to the apartment, it would be all over. Except for the questions.

And how will you answer them? she wondered. Tell the truth. To hell with him and all of them. Give the facts and let *them* figure it out. How best to put it? I mean when they arrest and interrogate me?

Q: How did the suspect come to take up residence in your apartment?

A: He proved to me that my father never loved me.

Q: Huh? You let him stay because of that?

A: No, sir. He said he'd teach me about a lot of things I'd never learn in grad school. "Life," he called it. That was the very word he used.

Q: Precisely what did he mean by that? In your words, please.

A: Well, sir, let's see now. Mainly, I think he taught me how to feel like a piece of shit.

A woman bearing gift packages came up to the booth and stared at her. Gritch made believe she was listening to a voice at the other end: nodded or shook her head. Finally the booth alongside was vacated; the woman squeezed into it.

At that moment it occurred to Gritch that it made absolutely no difference whether Mast was or wasn't Heislinger. Not as far as she was concerned. Her only immediate reality was a curmudgeonly old man, waiting for her.

She thought: What am I going to do, hand him over to the authorities and then return to classes as though nothing's happened?

She shook her head and then spoke aloud into the mouthpiece: "You're tired. Not thinking straight. I'll be able to do something tomorrow. Or whenever he lets me out of the apartment again."

She left the booth and walked slowly to the rear of the store where the pharmacy was. As she waited in line with other customers, she reviewed her list of errands. The library. The liquor store. Gauloises —she had by now developed a dislike for their odor. Newspapers— he was still enraged about the TV show—why she couldn't tell— and wanted to see reviews.

When her turn came she paid for the prescription with her MasterCard, smiling absentmindedly at the overattentive pharmacist. Then she left. It was Monday afternoon.

MORDECAI GERBER WAS disgusted. Days had passed. Nothing had turned up. There had been a dozen tips that led nowhere, a few leads that proved false. By now the team had hundreds of feelers out in the city. A regular network. To all appearances a haystack, but where in hell was the needle?

He stared morosely at a clipping from the *Christian Science Monitor*. A piece of claptrap written by some hardworking hysterical etymologist—was *this* the best information the team could unearth? The writer of the article went to great pains to point out that "mast" was an ancient word. It referred to the fruit, especially acorns, chestnuts, beechnuts, and the like, of certain forest trees, that was ordinarily left as forage for free-roaming swine but which in times of famine was consumed by humans. The term "a mast year" meant a time of starvation and so, by stretching the notion to the limit of its elasticity, Dr. Carl Mast himself could be said to have provided *mast* for those suffering deprivation. The author seemed enchanted by this little gem.

Such nonsense offended Mordecai, a practical young man, to the point of nausea. His head cold had gotten better, but not his mood. Also he had not been able to get out with his camera bag. He had hoped to shoot a few rolls along Fifth, very picturesque at this time of year with its festoons of colored lights, not to mention the ice rink at Rockefeller Plaza, and its lovely young girls.

He turned to his friend Abarbanel and said for the seventh or eighth time, "You'd think we'd hit on something."

"He may not be in the city," Abarbanel said. How many times since last Thursday had Mordecai heard that? A possibility. Of course. But then why did his and Abarbanel's instincts say otherwise?

The two of them were sorting through a sheaf of material detailing the team's various activities around town. This was the never-ending, pick-and-shovel work of investigation. By now even the cab companies had been contacted. An additional five thousand prints of Mast were being distributed. If he came out in public, someone would recognize him.

Suddenly Abarbanel paused, frowning at a worksheet that was near the bottom of the pile—the "overnight mailbag," as it was called. "Oh my God! Who the hell put this in with the regular stuff?"

He looked at the entry date. "Yesterday evening. It's sat here since yesterday. Son of a bitch."

"What is it?"

Abarbanel handed the sheet over to Mordecai, who scanned it. Then, for the first time since leaving Tel Aviv, the young agent grinned.

A tertiary tip. The consulate had phoned it in to the agent on duty. The proctologists, Meyer and White, had phoned the consulate. It seemed that an uptown pharmacist had phoned the good doctors. To double-check on the dosage of a morphia Rx, a sizable supply, really. Fifty milligram tabs, Doctor Meyer? A controlled substance after all. Yes, quite all right. The patient, a C. Mast, is experiencing sporadic severe abdominal pain, and what pharmacy did you say you worked at? Rexall? And which one? Ah, thank you.

"One hundred and tenth and Broadway," Abarbanel noted. He was grinning too. The pharmacist's name was Jerry Porkorney. "Do you want to check it, or shall we go together?"

Mordecai was already striding to the closet for their coats and hats.

It had come so easily.

MR. PORKORNEY WAS most cooperative; even better, he had an eagle eye for women. Fortyish and dapper, closely shaven and talced, with wavy blond hair done in a mod cut, and a tailored white nylon tunic with a left-breast placket that buttoned to the neck. A veritable Pfizer fashion plate.

No, the patient himself had not come in. It was his niece. So she said. Such a knockout. No, he hadn't asked her for ID but he knew her. She'd been in before. Several times, with Rx's for vaginal suppositories—probably some g-y-n inflammation, or maybe a yeast thing, young girls these days, you know what they are. Yes, yes, we know what they are.

A student was Porkorney's calculated guess. Lots of students in this neighborhood. You know how students are these days. Yes, that's all they seem to have on their minds, isn't it? Classy-looking young gash, special, you know? We do indeed. Later, before filing the Rx, Porkorney had decided to check with the docs. Just to make sure.

Smiling and nodding, Abarbanel said with all the casualness he could muster, a diffident, supremely bored examiner, "A name? Do you by any chance recall a name? An address? Anything?"

Jewish—Nussbaum, Nebelmann, begins with an N, absolutely sure of that, Nederlarian, no that was the Armenian blister with the silicone knockers, listen, awfully rushed right now, must have thirty-five prescriptions, everybody's got the flu or the crud, but I'm due for a coffee break in half an hour, could look it up in the Atari, no trouble, can't tell you the amount of time we save since we got the Atari, cross-references everything, these Japs are damnably clever, aren't they? Nesselberg, Needlinger.

"Take your time," Abarbanel said. "No hurry at all. We'll wait. I could use a coffee. Let us know when you have a minute. Really appreciate it." He was still holding in his right hand the leatherette folder containing the FBI badge and ID card.

"OF COURSE THE trouble with TV is that it peddles generalities under the aegis of disseminating information," Mast said. "Give a viewer a few shots of the camps and mention Zyklon-B, right away he's a Holocaust historian, an *expert* on the era, pardon me, I should live so long! But what the hell does he really know about potassium cyanide, which, by the way, was what that thanatomaniac Jones used on his gullible nitwits down in Guyana. Intriguing chemical, cyanide. A small dose has the effect, within minutes, of depriving the circulatory system of its ability to carry oxygen. In effect, the subject suffocates even though his lungs are going sixty to the minute. A marvelously painless death. When he was captured, you know, Himmler was carrying a cap of it in a bogus tooth filling. One crunch. Twelve minutes later he was pronounced dead. Despite the frantic ministrations of the physician in attendance. That was up in the British zone, '45."

"I'll keep that in mind the next time I do a quiche for you," Gritch said, not much interested.

They were in the West End, a large, rambling bar and restaurant on Broadway that was a favorite hangout for students, largely because it was the closest place to campus where they could tie one on.

The two had gone for a walk, Mast himself finally deciding that more than a week of being cooped up in the apartment was enough. It was Thursday, the twentieth. Tomorrow was the last day of classes before Christmas break. The risk of discovery apparently hadn't outweighed Mast's sudden restlessness: "If I don't get some fresh air, I'm going to asphyxiate."

And so they had strolled. Gritch had dressed inconspicuously: jeans, a heavy sweater, a pea jacket, boots, and a red, knit-wool cap that sported a large pompon. A young and lovely female student perhaps entertaining an elderly out-of-town *Onkel* who, clad in fur-collared chesterfield and black Borcelino and mufflered to the jowls against the icy blasts that blew up Broadway, might have come for a firsthand look at what his *Liebchen* was up to.

171

It was late afternoon. Dusk not far off. Their leisurely constitutional took them toward Morningside, where Mast pointed out the faculty club. There, he remarked, nearly twenty-five years ago, a luncheon had been given for him following the receipt of an honorary Ph.D. Below Morningside's narrow strip of park lay the ominous ghetto of Harlem, not a safe place to venture. Eventually, they reached Broadway and had stopped to warm themselves in the West End.

The place was fairly crowded with students. In another day or two it would be deserted except for those few scholars who would remain on campus over vacation, to study, make out, get drunk, and smoke grass. Someone at a table of grad students recognized Gritch and waved an enthusiastic hello. She waved back but did not join them. Mast chose a quiet booth and she fetched a carafe of wine.

For a while they sat there talking in low voices, smoking, sipping. He had promised to take her to dinner later. "Not at all fancy but, I can assure you, the best food in Manhattan. You'll like it."

Anyplace, she thought, was fine by her, as long as it was away from the apartment. Odd that something as trivial as dining out could lift her spirits. In the background a juke played reggae. Getting out had improved his spirits too. His discontent with CBS seemed shelved for the time being.

That morning he'd had an attack of some sort. For almost an hour he'd lain in bed, sallow and sweating, doubled up in pain. It seemed to her that the pills were a long time in taking effect.

Now, in her heart she felt a tug of sympathy despite his barbaric treatment of her. This old man sitting opposite her in the booth would never see another Christmas; he'd never even see next summer. That kind of knowledge, she supposed, could fill a person with despair. To know that the clock had almost run out. It was a marvel he could manage a semblance of good cheer, but here he was—could a winter walk be that therapeutic?—apparently recovered, ready to flash that cynical humor, as courtly and gracious toward her as he'd been on their first night. With the white mustache and that brooding hawklike expression he was very much the elder statesman type, dignified but obviously tickled to have as a companion a female openly coveted by younger males—he basked in their envious looks but at the same time kept a baleful eye on her to make sure *her* glance did not stray.

"Yes, how *does* someone punish a person in my position?" Mast said, giving her a sharp glance. "Life plus ninety-nine? The rope? Ha, they'd better hurry. My illness has already handed down a verdict—no clemency, no chance of appeal. Torture? All they'd have to do is remove my medications."

"Carl!" She shot him an exasperated look. "This is suppposed to be an evening out."

"A much better alternative would be to keep such a person alive," he continued chattily, "by every device known to science, eh? Let him *think*. Tubes running in and out of the body, oxygen assistance to combat the growing nitrogen content of the failing blood supply. A similar problem arose when I was working for that screwball *Anherbst* group of so-called scientists, back, I guess, in '37. Goering himself dreamed up the idea. He wanted to know what the ultimate punishment was, ergo the ultimate deterrent. By then, you see, the Third Reich was supposed to be the perfect society. And in a perfect social system you're not supposed to have crime anymore, or political dissension either, right? But of course we had both. So how, crazy Hermann asks, do we scare these mavericks into line? Some of the politicals—especially the Communists—were tough. Execution? They loved it. Chance to be a martyr. Abuse? But a few—so I heard—stood up to the worst anybody could think of, including castration. Well, that was formidable, I guess. I mean, some of the really hardcore SS 'experts' weren't above clamping a man's testicles in a machinist's vise and screwing the jaws shut—by then the man was unconscious. Rape for the women? There were instances when the female expired after being entrained by two or three hundred. It was said that on the Eastern Front, where there was later to be so much guerrilla activity, the SS interrogated stubborn Slavic lady partisan fighters by tying them spread-eagled and then inserting an electric soldering iron into the vagina. Most unpleasant."

"Carl, for God's sake, enough."

"That still didn't do it, though," Mast said reflectively. He drank off his wine and refilled their glasses. "Trouble was, they always died. Dead, you can't punish someone. Hermann much mystified: why would anyone in his right mind want to resist the Third Reich? We never did find the ultimate deterrent. The answer to that and other problems, of course, was as plain as day, and an echo of it can be found in American democracy: the ultimate society that must seek such ultimate answers is ultimately flawed. So it goes." He shrugged. "Drink, and we'll go. This wine and the fresh air. I could eat a little something. If you're a good girl maybe I'll tell you how Heislinger took a powder out of Germany."

"I don't care anymore," she said. But she knew that if he started on that, she'd listen.

Presently they rose. He helped her on with her jacket, mufflered and hatted himself, and they walked out, with her right, gloved hand riding in the crook of his elbow.

THE GLANCES OF several male students followed them as they left, admiring her beauty. Lucky old bastard to have a gorgeous fish like that on his arm.

Some five or six tables from the booth in which they had been sitting, a tall lanky student rose and left too. Cupped in one arm were several books covered with the white-and-blue Columbia University dust jacket. He had sat alone, one of the books propped open before him, a cup of tea at hand, absorbed by what he was reading. A grad student perhaps, his expression serious.

This was Gerber, who had come in person to see what he could see. Bespectacled, handsome in his black overcoat and maroon scarf, plus homburg.

Several young women took note of his departure, perhaps wondering where he had been keeping himself all semester. Probably a yeshiva-freak, from Jewish Theological up the street.

HARVEY'S ON NINETY-FIFTH and Broadway.

Gritch was at first disappointed. As Mast had stressed, there was nothing fancy about it.

A scrupulously clean well-lighted place, unquestionably kosher, with electronic dinner music playing softly. The evening was still early; fewer than a dozen tables were occupied.

Though not ostentatious, the bill of fare was appealing. As host Mast ordered, in the regal manner: two cheeses and thin-sliced smoked salmon for appetizers, a salad, and for a main course skewered turkey breast, with oregano, red and green peppers and onions: *chiboot me hoodoo*. Lastly, wine—white. When the food came he toasted Gritch: *"L'chayim!"* Long life and good health! She raised her glass. "The same to you."

"Me?" Mast chuckled. "Not this *molodyetz*." She frowned, not recognizing the word, and Mast explained: "A lover of the good life. A scamp who is tolerated and even forgiven for violating the stricter Jewish conventions." He began eating with gusto. "The Jews, you know, dine sensibly—don't put a lot of swill into their stomachs. The cloven hoof. Animals that do not chew their cud. *Trichinella spiralis* definitely a hazard in ancient sweltering Egypt—the larvae encysts in the muscular tissue. But then why have so many Jews stomach problems? Stress I suspect. It produces an excess of hydrocholoric acid. Perhaps a consequence of living in a Christian world.

174

All Jews need Tums, Gritch. Little alcoholism, even less suicide. Except, of course, when we cleaned 'em out of Poland. There they self-destructed like moths against a candle flame. The *Judenrat*— the councils of elders appointed by the SS in every city and village— couldn't do a thing about it. 'Be patient, it'll get better,' the elders told 'em. The people wouldn't listen. Worse than Masada or York. At the height of the Warsaw Uprising, when our lads finally went in with flamethrowers, Jews jumped from roofs and windows by the scores, five and six stories up, rather than surrender—definitely a high-risk area because of falling objects." Mast chuckled. "Their own damned fault in a way. The shtetel and ghetto were as much cherished by the Ashkenazim as by the Christians. The Chosen wanted to isolate themselves, so as to remain undefiled by gentile blood. The Sanhedrin demanded it—apartheid even then—but still, in many ways, they were a sensible and orderly people, cleanly too. Different sets of utensils, one for dairy products, the other for meat, that's hygiene! The rite of circumcision, now almost universal in this country, saved God knows how many Jewish males from cancer of the penis, which, take my word for it, Gritch, is no fun. Back in *den alten heym,* it was customary for the circumsizer, once the foreskin had been snipped, to take the child's tiny *schwanz* in his mouth and suck it free of blood. Sort of a good-luck freebie, but how wonderfully practical! Saliva, you know, providing the oral cavity is free of infection, can serve as a coagulant and a healing agent. Those old-time kikes weren't so dumb."

Appetite gone, she gave him a hard look. "Ghoul."

"You find it distasteful?" he asked, and then chuckled again at the dreadfulness of his own pun. "I'll bet you never knew that in the last century physicians would hold a urine specimen up to the light, and sometimes they even tasted it."

"What in God's name for?" she said, making a lemon mouth.

"Well, they could diagnose diabetes if the urine tasted sweet. And when it was cloudy and didn't clear when heated—urinary infection. Normally, heat clears urine, you see, but not when infection's present."

"You just sneer at everything. Circumcisions. Saliva. Old-time kikes."

"Every ethnic group has its own peculiar customs, some useful, some not," he said. "In the Congo, female infanticide—especially with twin girls—is still practiced by the banks of rivers, which makes the crocs grin: a rudimentary but efficient form of population control. In the remoter mountain areas of Afghanistan—what a miserable country!—proud poppas still believe that they alone are

175

the rightful candidates to introduce pubescent daughters to the mysteries of sex. Dad teaches his *Bübchen*. Sigmund would laugh, I think, because there is no evidence that Afghan teenyboppers aren't sexually better adjusted than most American kumquats. Which, come to think of it, isn't saying much."

He rambled on.

At a table near the door, beside the cash register, a tall young man set down the book he was reading, rose, and made his way past their table to the rear, where the washrooms were located. Too much tea, here and at the West End. As he passed them his glance rested momentarily on Mast, and then on Gritch.

Quite by accident, and just as momentarily, her glance happened to meet his, and she felt in herself a brief but nonetheless pleasant sensation. As if a sort of emotional flashbulb had gone off in the pit of her stomach, or perhaps a little lower.

Such a feeling was not entirely unknown to Gritch, and it was heightened by the fact that the person who had triggered it had experienced something similar, for she noticed, as he passed by, that his cheeks suddenly colored. How sweet to be able to blush like that, she thought.

Wide, bony shoulders, slim-nipped. A catlike walk. Really quite lithe. Half listening to Mast she glanced idly, casually, introspectively after the young man as he made his way between the tables, and thought: Hmn.

In a low voice she said, "You promised to tell me how you got away."

Mast looked around; the nearest diners were three tables off. Conversation, he seemed to conclude, was not impossible. He tasted his wine and then cut into the breast of turkey, in no rush. The young man returned to his table, paid his bill, and walked out into the freezing night, offstage for the moment, so to speak, which is not to say he had vanished from Gritch's thoughts.

INTIMACY, AS SHE would have been the first to admit, was not always available to an industrious young woman with complicated ambitions. As a whore she remembered some clients with a great deal more affection than others, but affection is not necessarily related to intimacy. Gritch was too intelligent to confuse the two, which is to say that on occasion she needed and sought the latter.

The thing was that intimacy, despite its inherent risks, had about it a particular charm of its own, which not even the most calculating heart could reject. Caught up by it, if only for a brief time, the soul warmed its most glacial wastelands, as one warms one's chilled

176

hands before the glow of a friendly hearth. It was, without doubt, a very good feeling, perhaps containing an echo of *neshoma yeseroh,* that splendid expansiveness of one's soul and spirit that can be felt on the Sabbath.

Not knowing any other way, Gritch approached the problem of intimacy in the practical manner peculiar to most contemporary women. That is to say, beneath the smooth and alert veneer of the call girl she was singularly human and, moreover, vulnerable. But not too vulnerable. It was a question of the "right" moment; her mood had to be just so. A delicate combination, but when things went well the ember buried in the hot private core of her kindled and caught; it was then that sequential or, to put it another way, ongoing orgasms might occur.

She had not lied to Mast about there being no young man secreted away in her life. Love, to date, had not entered Gritch's life, not "real love," although she suspected and hoped that she was capable of someday being caught up in a warm long-term relationship. But not for the moment. Thanks, but no thanks.

The various friends she'd made among fellow students and faculty members would have been astonished to learn that this marvelously bright and lovely girl was underwriting her living expenses via the second oldest profession. Actually, no one had ever inquired about how she got by, though some may have wondered. Gritch could, on occasion, exhibit a coolness that did not encourage the prying question. She was friendly enough but at the same time reserved, a private person. On campus she tended to business, presenting to the academic world the epitome of scholarly devotion, a slender bespectacled young lady who dressed sensibly and saw to it that her average hovered around 3.8.

In the area of intimacy, perhaps three or four times a year, when this or that grad student or junior prof broadcast signals of an undeniably sexual nature, it could be said that Gritch was guilty of relaxing her code of behavior.

That is, she dallied.

Not for very long certainly. Long enough, though. Was she not, after all, human? What a splendid thing intimacy could be! One literally forgot the meaning of loneliness, such was its seductive power.

At such times she abandoned herself to play, entering into the spirit of the game with the same dedication she customarily reserved for studies. It wasn't anything like "falling in love," but it was an enjoyable approximation. When Gritch lapsed into a loving and erotic mood, with all her sexuality, so to speak, turned on and purring like a finely tuned Porsche engine, she was something else, as certain carefully selected young men could attest. When she elected to take a little time off so that she could devote her attention to a man who had triggered her interest, she had a marked tendency to fuck 'round the clock. Hot romance was all she had on her mind then. The more the better, until the swain pro tem begged for a respite, a breather for Pete's sake, a ten-minute nap at least.

Gritch in the throes of estrus: as one orgasm after another thundered and reverberated through her she moaned and shuddered amid sweat-soaked sheets, gushed and dripped, bucked, bleated sheepily, and, mere minutes later, was ready for another go at it, those incredible emerald green eyes flashing fire.

Out of such occasional "items" had come invitations to make of the situation an ongoing thing, and a couple of marriage proposals as well. All of which Gritch regarded as tributes to her foxy style. Again, however: thanks, but no thanks. As easily as she had slipped these bedazzled now-detumescent Galahads in through, as it were, her front door, she slipped them out, still loving and affectionate but unshakable in her conviction that it was time to get back to her books, her thesis, her 3.8.

In such fashion did she run her life. Selfishly, yes. But it was a fairly honest sort of selfishness. Gritch would have been the first to confess that she kept a sharp eye on what was best for Ms. Nadelmann.

True, the intimacy thing was at times a problem. And it *had* been a while. Not a long while. But how long does long have to be? When this awful mess with Mast was at last done with, it might be time to enjoy life a little.

What, she wondered again, could make such a tall drink of water blush like a fourteen-year-old? Why such shyness? Somehow it didn't fit with that slinky walk. The mouth was beautiful. Made to be kissed. Yes, one could get very intimate indeed, in and around and on a mouth like that.

Would they run into each other again? Such a coincidence seemed unlikely, but certain things had a way of simply happening to her. Almost gratuitously it seemed.

Recollecting her thoughts she sliced off a flake of smoked salmon and placed it delicately between her teeth. Then looked up, giving full attention to what the old man opposite her was saying:

178

"THE GORILLA, YOU know, is a great masticator, so the supraorbital ridge serves as a buttress for the massive jaw muscles that are anchored to the top of the skull ridge," Mast said chattily.

"What are you talking about?"

He tapped a forefinger against the side of one eyebrow. "Here—all this had to be built up. In man the supraorbital ridge has almost disappeared. His diet has made it superfluous." Mast stroked his impressive beak. "Heislinger had what is known as a button nose, so considerable anaplastic remodeling was involved. You go up through the nostrils with slender scalpels and pry or cut away—actually break loose—the nasal septum and remove it, replacing it with new material shaped to one's wishes. Your eyes are open of course, and you're aware of sawing and breaking. Afterward you look like you've been in a fist-fight—magnificent shiners. You breathe through the mouth since the olfactory passages are packed with cotton, but even so you swallow lots of blood. The mouth, too, was changed. Not so much is required to change the shape of a mouth. Tucks were taken in the mastoidal area behind the ears, a gathering-up of loose flesh. Heislinger had the start of a double chin. As for the chin itself, well, I had never exactly been delighted by it. Not such a great chin, as chins go." Mast paused for a moment to light a Gauloise and sip at his wine.

"This was in '44?" Gritch asked. He nodded. She frowned. "No. You make it sound too simple. I don't believe you."

179

"It was not simple, it was very complicated," Mast pointed out. "My surgeon, even by today's standards, was a remarkably competent man. A Jew, by the way. Cosmetic alteration is not something you do over a free weekend, Gritch. Considerable time—in my case over three months—is required. Post-op periods are necessary after each session on the table. One must evaluate the work in progress. This can't be done until the swelling has subsided. There is always the risk that the reconstructed nose or chin will not 'take.' Slippage or sagging is possible—a severe landslide of the face. Tsk, tsk." He grinned. "People might notice."

Sitting there, she stared at his face as though seeing it for the first time. She said, "Prove it."

"There are, among other things in my safety-deposit box, Heislinger's fingerprints, on two SS identity documents. Also some very interesting before-and-after photographs. I brought them from Geneva. Nothing has been tampered with. Ink, paper content—the papers are quite old and so have to be handled with care, but they will stand up under microscopic examination and chemical analysis."

"They could be forgeries," she said.

"But they are not," Mast replied. "Please take my word for it."

"Heislinger would have gotten rid of such incriminating evidence!"

"Yes," Mast said. "That would have been the sensible thing to do. But men aren't always sensible." He considered this, then shrugged. "Years ago I intended destroying everything. But then I decided not to. It's useful sometimes to know not only who you are but who you once were."

He reached across the table and gave her his hand, palm up, fingers extended. She examined it, feeling a trifle foolish. They might have been a fortune-teller and her client.

Mast said quietly, "At war's end I contemplated removing my fingerprints. It's not so difficult. All one needs is Novocain, a hypodermic, and a saucer of sulphuric acid. Enough of the pad must be removed so that after healing there is only scar tissue. If derma removal is too shallow the prints reappear. It's best to work on no more than two or three fingers at a time. Of course, the same results can be achieved with a scarificating scalpel."

She winced. He went on, "There's no pain, with the Novocain. Afterward, that's a different story—extreme discomfort—the pads are filled with sensitive ganglia . . . the better to feel you with, my dear. Again, I decided not to. But not because of the pain. It's true that prints establish a man's identity. Conversely, a man possessing

180

no prints is likely, someday, to be asked why. The authorities, I suspected, might be curious about such a person."

Mast removed his hand and used it to raise his glass of wine. "After much thought I decided to take a calculated risk." He drank. "The risk paid off. It is interesting that in over forty years there has never been any occasion for me to submit to the undignified process of being fingerprinted. Carl Mast. A most respectable and law-abiding gentleman."

"A Jewish surgeon helped you? Impossible."

"He had to," Mast said, refilling their glasses. The deeply set eyes were malicious. "He was in my power, you understand."

"CHIEMSEE IS A lovely lakeside resort south of Munich, not far from the Swiss border," Mast continued. "Very quiet, picture-postcard setting—at least in '44. Nowadays it's a vacation getaway for well-heeled Munich businessmen and their beefy *Frauen*. I visited the old place a few years ago—the criminal must return? Nonsense. Anyway, now the lakeshore is lined with fast-food eateries and discos. Back then it was serene. The lederhosen ambience. Cows mooing. It was safe, secluded. My surgical acquaintance—he was getting on in years—owned a small villa on the shore, gingerbread portico, rustic, very Bavarian. He had made his fortune reconstructing the faces of wealthy front-line officers who had been mutilated in the first war. Of course, with the Nazis, he lived under a Damoclean sword, but somehow he avoided arrest. In the evenings we played chess together, with my face and head wrapped in gauze, and listened to Mendelssohn on the phonograph. We had by then become friends. Fellow physicians. He trusted me completely. As I did him."

"Chess?" she objected. "A Nazi and a Jew? Trust?"

"Why not?" Mast said. "We needed each other. It was as simple as that. I'd arranged his family's deportation from Germany. Yes, I was able to do this. The wife and three daughters spent the remainder of the war in a camp in Austria, not far from Linz, a special camp for wealthy Jews. They were treated well."

"But no one just disappears like that," Gritch said. "What about your friends? Didn't they look for you?"

"I had no Nazi confidants, no intimates," Mast said. "Superiors, subordinates, yes, but no one close. And, yes, there was a search underway, long before the surgery was done with. The SS was baffled, no doubt. Heislinger started off for his office one morning and then dropped from sight. By the time he was missed, he was in Chiemsee. My Jewish friend—how wonderful it is that Jews have always helped me in time of need—knew I'd rejected Nazism and that I was determined to leave Germany. His family was safe. An honorable man, he held up his end of it. We were like two horse traders."

"Very chancy," she said.

"It's *all* chance," Mast said. He extinguished his cigarette. "In '47, I wrote a letter of inquiry to my friend's office, in Munich. He'd died. March '45. One of the very last bombing raids. The mission was more in the nature of a gesture, really. The city had been neutralized back in the days of large-scale saturation bombings. A mere dozen or so planes passed overhead. As I said, an aerial flexing of the muscle, to let everyone know the Allies meant business. A five-hundred-pounder scored a direct hit on my friend's office. He was there. The widow wrote me this. I was sorry. But at the same time relieved. The last lead, gone."

"It still sounds too easy," she objected.

"And I say it wasn't," Mast insisted. "The documentation of Carl Mast, including a Swiss passport—to which, by the way, a photograph could not be affixed until the surgery was completed—took a year's work on my part." He smiled. "You were insisting that the Heislinger papers were forgeries, but the truth is that Carl Mast's old ID's are the ones that won't stand up under careful scrutiny. No." He shook his head. "Not easy at all. Funds had to be transferred. And there were personality changes. Don't think for a moment that a traumatic shock isn't involved the first time you look at yourself in a mirror and see a stranger. And later? I spent a year and a half living very quietly in one village or another. A serious illness. By then the war was over. There was enough money. But a man can't spend his life that way. Gradually I ventured into the cities—Basel, Zurich. I was still very fearful that someone, somewhere, might be reminded of a certain SS colonel. By then the surgery had 'taken.' Also, a natural tendency toward baldness had grown more pronounced. And there was this." Mast smiled again, stroking the mustache. "My Swiss medical peers never suspected. Why should they have? Here, after all, was a still-young doctor, not yet in his middle forties, who'd never practiced in his native country. Educated in Austria and Germany, as indeed some of them had been. Eventually there was the involvement with WHO, and the rest of it."

"I still say you would have avoided the limelight like the plague," Gritch argued.

Mast nodded. "I did. You forget, Gritch, I told you that I never actively sought attention. That's true. However, once it had found me I saw that it mightn't be such a bad thing after all. To be a

182

nobody . . . well, people can get curious about a nobody. But if you are important? Then they accept you for what they know you to be, eh?"

She stared. "If this is true, Carl, then you have a defense. Don't you see?"

He chuckled. "Because I got out? No, my dear. It won't fly, although undoubtedly the big shots at the Trials would have sold their souls to have an alibi one-tenth as good. Yes, I'd come to loathe the Nazi mentality, and so I got away from it. But that doesn't excuse the acts for which I was indicted. You must understand that very clearly." He was staring at her as intently as she was regarding him. "If you are accused of a crime, and if you committed the offense in question, then, quite rightly, you are guilty. No, at Nuremberg they had plenty of defense arguments. None stood up. Including the ex post facto. You know that one?"

"'After the fact,'" she said. "A sort of retroactive legal action. A criminal or penal statute that imposes a punishment for an act not punishable when the act itself was committed."

"Very good. Didn't I *tell* you you were smart?" Mast said delightedly. "The judges threw that one right out the window, along with the argument that the defendants were only following orders from someone higher up. Ha! If the Tribunal had admitted *that*, not a soul in Germany would have been guilty of anything, except Hitler, and he was dead, a double suicide in that Reichstag bunker. I don't mean he killed himself twice, he and that flea-brained Eva did it together."

"YOU'RE ABSOLUTELY SURE?" the voice in the earpiece said.

This was Colonel Armon, speaking from Tel Aviv. Late at night in New York, early morning there.

"I personally made the visual identification," Gerber replied. He was feeling fine, and not merely because his sniffles were abating. Abarbanel and another agent, grinning and nodding, though not participating in the conversation, were listening on extension phones. From a back bedroom of the East Eightieth Street apartment a TV blared. Mordecai frowned. Snapped his fingers angrily at someone, motioning toward the noise. The TV was silenced.

"Where?" Armon asked.

"A kind of student hangout near the campus. Later a restaurant."

"We must be positive."

"We are," Mordecai said. "A stupid move, sending the girl. The druggist remembered her. She'd done business there before. Abarbanel and I got a lecture about how careful one must be with controlled drugs. The girl, by the way, is attractive."

"So? He's living with her?"

183

"Yes. A student, apparently. Abarbanel and I took turns following them."

"What else?"

"We got the garbage. There's no doubt, sir."

Mordecai elaborated. A twenty-four-hour watch was in effect. The team member on duty in a doorway halfway down the block had spotted the super setting out refuse cans. These cans had been emptied, but not by the sanitation department. The contents of the plastic sacks and soggy paper bags were now spread about the living-room floor of the team's apartment.

Much can be learned from the stuff people throw away. Abarbanel and several other agents had approached their task with the dedication of professional anthropologists unearthing a prehistoric midden. Griselda Nadelmann's refuse was quickly identified and then pored over with care. There was junk mail; some of it addressed not to "Tenant" but to her: a catalogue from a Vermont antiques firm; a flyer advertising the pending sale of some expensive condos downtown; a letter from a company specializing in gold and other precious-metal investments. There were also bottles that had contained ouzo and various wines, and an astonishing number of Gauloise- and menthol-flavored cigarette butts, as well as vegetable parings and scraps, bones of a piscatorial and mammalian origin, several magazines and newspapers, a number of facial tissues, some bearing the lipsticked imprint of a girl's mouth, and, wrapped carefully in toilet paper, a nether signature: two bloodied sanitary napkins, supers.

The Greek liqueur and French cigarettes provided the clincher. About Heislinger a good deal was known but a lot was also known about Carl Mast, including his alcohol and tobacco preferences.

Colonel Armon said now, "Has anyone in the building been contacted?"

"No."

"Good. Don't." Armon thought. "What's the place like?"

"Three stories, five apartments," Mordecai said. "She's 1-A. Ground floor, rear. Bit of a garden. There's a wall, about ten feet high, for privacy. Impossible to climb without a ladder. He'll use the front door as long as he's not alarmed."

"Phone tap?"

"Not as yet. The vestibule door's easy, but the basement door's got a padlock on it. Combination type. That'll take a little time."

"Circumspection, Gerber. Go carefully."

"We are, sir."

"These Americans. Touchy."

"True."

184

"Diplomatic relations. It wouldn't pay to offend."

"I understand."

"When we got Eichmann, what an uproar there was," Armon said. "Kidnapping, violating international law."

"Yes, sir."

There was another pause. "Who'd have thought it!"

"Thought what?"

"That he has a mistress."

"That hasn't been confirmed, sir."

"On the sly!"

"Pardon me, sir, but aren't you jumping to conclusions?"

"At his age."

Mordecai abandoned his line of argument. "Yes. Remarkable, I'd say."

"Security people looking everywhere for him," Armon went on admiringly. "Every contact he's had in years, covered, for a week and a half. And all this time he's been shacked up. An eighty-year-old man."

"Yes, sir."

"Who is she? A Jewess you say?"

"Yes, sir."

"I'll be damned."

"Indeed, sir. As you say, who'd have thought it. We'll start work on her end of it first thing in the morning."

"A whore probably," Armon said.

Mordecai frowned. He disliked snap judgments. "That wasn't my initial impression."

"They come in all shapes and sizes, Gerber."

"I'm sure they do."

"You say she's pretty?"

"That's putting it mildly, sir." Across the room Abarbanel bunched his fingers into a bouquet, kissed them loudly, and rolled his eyes heavenward.

"Probably a whore."

"We'll see what we can dig up," Mordecai said respectfully. "Any further orders?"

"No. By the way, congratulations. Good work," Armon said. "Maintain surveillance. Don't get any closer. Let him enjoy himself for another day or so. But if he makes the slightest move, stay on him. If he does one more disappearing act, I'll have yours and Abarbanel's asses."

"Yes, sir."

There was a pause and then Armon said, half to himself, "A chippie he can warm his toes against at night. At his age!"

185

CHRISTMAS DAWNED IN sepulchral gloom with tattoos of wind-whipped ice crystals beating against the bedroom windowpanes, and in the backyard two toms fought loudly and flounderingly atop the drifts. Mast and the girl, wakened by the noise, lay beside each other in the half dark, smoking, not saying much. Presently one or both of the cats capitulated. Outside it was silent again except for an occasional icy blast.

Gritch rose at half-past eight, slopped around for a while, yawning and puffy-eyed, in an old robe and flannel slippers, made coffee, then visited the bathroom twice, not feeling at all well, troubled by sharp menstrual pains.

"My periods are usually no trouble," she complained to Mast, who had padded out to join her at the kitchen table. He too did not look well. The morning attacks were by now a regular occurrence.

At the kitchen sink he swallowed the first assortment of his daily quota of pills, with the help of a glass of water, then sat at the table for coffee, more cigarettes.

They had been together just over two weeks.

LATER, BY MUTUAL agreement, they decided this would be a day of truce. The books stacked everywhere were not to be opened, the dust covers on the IBM and the duplicator would remain where they were. No Holocaust, no tape recorder.

Gritch, awake now, made toast and poached eggs, but neither she nor Mast had much appetite, and they picked at their food.

˙Christmas, it would seem, is not always a time of cheer.

By noon they'd had a few glasses of wine. His mood had improved, but hers had not. "Bloody damned curse," she groused. She was still dressed in robe and nightgown but had brushed the glossy black hair and washed her face.

"This happens frequently?" Mast inquired.

"Maybe once a year," she told him. "It's nerves. It's *you.* Everything. The same thing happened last spring. I was working on a term paper. Staying up all night, too much coffee, cigarettes. Stress, worry. The blahs."

"I'd dash out and buy you something if I knew what you liked," he said.

"Very funny," she replied. "Don't be such a smart ass. I feel lousy."

"The blahs?" He nodded, suddenly serious. "Umn. Yes." Leaving her curled up on the couch Mast went into the bathroom. Returning, he gave her a scored yellow tablet. One of the assortment that made up his pain cocktails. "Take this."

"What is it?"

"Percodan. An analgesic, a derivative of opium."

"No thanks."

"Go on. One won't addict you. It relaxes."

She regarded the pill in her palm. "How many of these do you take a day?"

"As many as I need, Gritch."

"But then you must be hooked."

"Oh, I'd certainly say so."

"That doesn't worry you?"

"Not particularly. With me, addiction is more of an academic question than a social problem. There are things far worse than a narcotic habit."

Reluctantly, she swallowed the pill. Its therapeutic effect, helped along by a glass of wine, was undeniable. Less than twenty minutes later she was feeling fine, or at least lots better than she'd felt earlier. Rather lazy, laid back, very relaxed indeed.

He sat with her on the couch. She curled up on her side in a fetal position and rested her head in his lap. Before joining her he had checked the television. There was nothing on except Christmas abominations: masses, chorales, high church services. Switching the set off Mast placed a stack of records on the stereo turntable: Buxtehude, Satie, Debussy, Mozart horn concerti. Finally he went into the bedroom and got the satin quilt from the bed, spread it over the lower part of her body, fussily tucking the edges under her feet.

188

Although the apartment was warm she seemed to appreciate the added security of this covering.

Now, looking down at her, he said, "Better?" Cigarettes, glasses, and a freshly opened bottle of wine were within reach, on the end table.

"Much." She sighed. "Thanks."

"Good."

She settled herself more comfortably, again making of his lap a pillow. "Rotten period."

"I'm sorry to be such a problem."

"You're a handful, that's for sure." She raised her head. "Could I have a sip?" He gave her his glass and she drank off half the wine. He said, "Would you like me to light a cigarette for you?"

"No. I smoke way too much as it is." She settled back into her former position.

Quite gently Mast began stroking her hair and the side of her neck and temple, here and there, under the lobe of the ear, behind it. The contact was asexual. Merely the touching of that large, wrinkled hand, broad, peasantlike, the fingers spatulate.

Presently she spoke: "When I was small I used to wonder why Jews didn't celebrate Christmas like everyone else. I was very young. Not more than six or seven, I suppose. I always wondered why we didn't have one of those lovely big decorated trees. We'd see them in the living-room windows of the homes. The porches would be hung with strings of colored lights. I said to my dad, 'Why can't we have a tree in our house too?' His answer was simple. 'Because, honey, we are not Christians.' I went and looked at myself in the bathroom mirror. 'You're not a Christian, Griselda.' I couldn't hook it up. I didn't look or *feel* any different from the kids whose folks had trees."

He continued stroking her hair and temple. "Your shock of recognition came early. A sort of reverse *trayf*, I'd say, meaning ritually unfit, unclean, defiled. For Jews anything gentile or not properly blessed is *trayf*, eh? But for a little Jewish girl who wanted a pretty Christmas tree? That was not allowed. A variety of Christian *trayf*."

She wept a little, and he continued to comfort her, murmuring, "Now, now. It's all right."

"Oh, hell."

"Ah."

"Shit."

"Poor girl. No need to cry, there now."

"Don't leave me."

"Of course not. What a foolish thought."

189

Presently she stopped weeping. Blew her nose into a tissue she had in her bathrobe pocket. Settled down again. "What's it like for a Christian, Carl?"

"What's what like?"

"Christmas."

"It never meant very much to me, I'm afraid."

She insisted. "What Christmas do you remember best?"

He chuckled, then tasted his wine. "Out of all those I've experienced? Oh, it's difficult to say."

"There must be one you remember."

"Well, yes. I suppose so," he replied.

She thought he would pull a story out of his long-vanished childhood, a memory of a happier and younger Carl Mast, but the old man's mind was elsewhere. "An SS man's Christmas."

"*They* celebrated it?"

"After a fashion," Mast replied. "Such a holiday, you see, was in a gray area. Himmler's official line was anti-Catholic—anti-Protestant, for that matter. Anti-everything. He espoused atheism. But he had powerful Jesuitic leanings. A leftover from his youth. He'd have made a perfect mystic. Yes, he was pulled in different directions. Religion was anathema, yet it appealed." Mast paused to reflect. "To believe in God must be a comfort. To believe halfway is misery."

"But weren't the troops raised in a religious fashion?" she asked.

"You've hit the nail on the head," Mast agreed. "It was in the lower echelons—your fighting men, if you will—that the incompatability, or schism, between Church and Party was most apparent. Except for the hard-line SS indoctrination, they were ordinary young fellows. Upright, handsome kids from places like Bavaria, Thuringia, Schleswig-Holstein, Prussia. As children they'd seen their families indulge in the entire Christian spectacle, the tree, church, the hymns, the big feast, maybe a fine Westphalian ham or a stuffed goose. But in the SS all that was viewed as antiquated, sentimental. The Church had no role in the Third Reich. So said Hitler himself. There it was. They wanted to be good SS men, but there were memories. They were troubled. Was it really so dreadful to celebrate an old-fashioned holiday? They never said this outright. But they wondered. Unquestioning obedience. They were sworn to that."

Mast paused, sipped wine, rolled it on his tongue, continued: "On Christmas Day of '41 I was with an *Einsatzgrüppen* headquarter's company. It was part of a group that was operational at that time in the northernmost salient of the Eastern Front. The offensive had

190

long since ground to a halt because of weather. We were at a village near Vilnius. I no longer remember the name, but I recall that it was a frightfully bad time for us. Winter had caught the SS unprepared, as it had the rest of the Wehrmacht. Inadequate clothing, no fuel, no food. Our men did the best they could. They'd dug in and made a sort of home out of this small hamlet. It was situated in a heavy forest. The front itself was only thirty kilometers to the east."

"Were they frightened?" Gritch asked.

"Yes. It was unbelievably cold," Mast said. "The alienness of the country. We were so far from home. These young men were like soldiers anywhere who have to fight and die in a strange land. Yes, they were quite simply very young and very frightened and they did not want to die. I would have to say that I felt sorry for them in their situation. I knew that many would be dead before the following summer."

He sighed, shrugged as if the notion was of no importance. "At any rate a *Weihnachtsfest* got started somehow. A Christmas celebration. The commanding officer made no move to discourage it. He too was bitter to be in a place like that. He was still in his twenties. Perhaps like me he knew that although it was bad for his men then, it would soon be much worse. So, a great deal of beer and schnapps and liberated vodka was drunk, along with Russian wines, which are uniformly atrocious. And there was as much food as could be scraped together, including horse meat, which is quite tasty. Someone had even put up a small tree in the mess hall. That's where we all gathered. There were no ornaments naturally. The tree was decorated with, of all things, photographs. Snapshots of wives, sweethearts, mothers, families. They were hung on the branches very carefully with bits of thread. Later the men put them back into their wallets. There was singing. The old carols—*'Heilige Nacht,'* *'Adeste Fideles,'* oh, there were many. Some men wept unashamedly. They sang with their arms about one another. Dirty, unshaven, their lips cracked and split by frostbite. Happy for a little while, the war forgotten. All those brave young boys." He sighed.

"I'd think they would have deserted if it was that bad," Gritch said.

"Absolutely impossible," Mast said, shaking his head. "An SS man was trained to obey."

"What happened then?"

"Oh, we had a fine time. Everybody got a little drunk, and some got extremely drunk," Mast said. "Then an orderly came into the mess hall and made hushing gestures. 'Do you hear them?' he asked us. The hall grew silent as everyone listened."

"Russians?"

"Yes. Maybe regulars, maybe guerrillas. There was no knowing. In the deep forest. Just beyond our perimeter. No more than a few hundred meters off. They were singing too. Orthodox hymns. By then most of us had left the mess hall and gathered in the snow outside. It was night. The Russian voices, raised in chorus, came strongly to us from the black woods. For a moment I thought to myself, 'Good! There is still a trace of humanity left in us, both Germans and Russians.' I was, I fear, feeling a little sentimental myself. The schnapps and vodka—I was never bashful in the presence of free drinks. But then a strange thing happened." He looked down at her. "Do you know Russian choral music?"

"A little. Very moving." She was almost asleep in his lap.

"Wonderfully powerful, yes. All those shrill tenors keening, and the big booming basses thundering out the counterpoint. Lovely. A symphony of jubilant, dominant males joined in song. So beautiful, to hear something like that coming from the dark woods. But yet, on this Christmas night, the singing was ominous. It was terrifying. Then it stopped. There was silence."

Gritch yawned, adjusted her position. "Go on. I'm listening."

"Finally a few of the men I was standing with began singing back," Mast said. "One at a time the rest of our group joined in. A carol of some sort, I don't remember. Quite touching. Very German."

He was silent for a moment and then went on, "When it was over, the singers in the forest began again. And again the effect was terrifying. It was Russia singing to us. We had invaded their motherland, and they were telling us that this was not a time for humanity or mercy or decency. The strength and power in those voices were overwhelming. We stood in the frozen snow and stared at one another in the faint light cast by the open door of the mess hall. And we were frightened. Frightened of being in that bitterly cold country. Frightened of what lay out there in the deep forests. *They* were at home here. As well they should have been."

Mast paused again, reminiscently. "Finally, the commanding officer had enough. He sensed the demoralizing effect. In the First World War, in the trenches, the troops on either side always sang carols to one another at Christmas. But not now. He gave a curt order. Several magnesium flares were shot skyward. Suddenly everything was illuminated in a sickly white glare. Then several of our machine gunners out on the perimeter opened up, laying a traversing cross fire into the woods. The singing stopped. But they were still out there, waiting. We knew they were there. Yes, I'd say that was a Christmas I'll remember for a long time."

192

He looked down again. She was sound asleep. Mouth slightly open, the lips parted, childlike. The breathing deep and steady. One hand cupped beneath her chin in that classic infantile position—the four fingers clenched tightly over the thumb. A sign of insecurity. Odd to see in an adult woman.

CARL MAST'S EXPRESSION, as he gazed down at her, was mixed: thoughtful, protective, almost benign.

With infinite gentleness he pried the fingers open so that the thumb was at last freed. "Poor child," he said aloud. "Perhaps what life has given you is not so much after all."

She shifted, swallowed, went on sleeping.

He began speaking again, though there was no one to hear, the gutteral voice audible above the stereo's music. "If I were younger. Ah! Even sixty. Yes, that would be young enough. I would show you, my dear, what it is like when an older man appreciates a woman. You would be dazzled. The younger ones don't know how to appreciate. They take instead of giving. If you were mine, I would set as my main task one thing. To make you happy. What a delightful project that would be!"

Mast sat silently. The records on the stereo completed their cycle; the arm swung over and, with a leisurely curtsy, settled into its resting place. There was a single click, and the machine went dead.

Finally, he could bear the weight of her head no longer. His right thigh was asleep. Also the pain was starting again. With great care he disengaged himself, groaning softly as he stood erect, and made for the bathroom, there to relieve his bladder and uncap several prescription bottles. Then he returned to the couch to stare down at her. The deep-sunk eyes were expressionless, guarded. Leaning over, he gently tugged the quilt up over her shoulders.

His solicitousness went unnoticed. Gritch, enfolded in the arms of Morpheus, was out like a light.

In the kitchen he quietly got out a tray of cubes, a fresh glass, and his ouzo. Placing these on a tray along with a fresh package of cigarettes, he went into the bedroom and lay down.

Outside the wind howled softly. Dusk came quickly, and then night. A honeyed gibbous moon sailed through skies trailing ripped shreds of angry clouds. From a dark alleyway a cat screeched once; then, silence. Presently he too slept.

ABARBANEL AND MORDECAI were in the team's new apartment.

They had been fortunate in finding a furnished place for rent at 430 West 101st, across and diagonally up the street from the Nadelmann woman's address. It had been necessary to sign a year's lease,

193

which vexed Abarbanel, who was accountable for operating expenses, but at least the team was done with waiting in parked cars or watching from doorways, both of which activities were conducive to rousing the suspicions of New York's finest.

The second-floor apartment had two bedrooms in the rear and a living room that looked out on the street. This room was kept darkened, the drapes drawn except for a crack along the sill of a bay window.

At the window, seated in an armchair, one agent or another maintained a vigil; binoculars, VHF transceiver, coffee, sandwiches at hand. Someone was always in that chair, watching. If he had to answer a call of nature another man took over. As far as the super and the other tenants were concerned they were all graduate students at Columbia. Two or three extra team members were always present so that in the event Heislinger and the girl left the apartment, they could be followed. Piled in one corner of the living room were several boxes of electronic equipment—the tape deck, transmitters, and telephone tapping gear. Heller was the agent who knew all about electronics. He thought a tap could be done fairly quickly once Colonel Armon gave the go-ahead. "Telephones," Abarbanel had said irritably, "are more damned trouble than they're worth."

Now, sitting in the kitchen with Mordecai, Abarbanel was unhappy about something else. "Three and a half days since either of them's stuck their noses out the door. What in hell are they up to?"

"Isn't it always hurry-up-and-wait?" Mordecai said.

The team chief frowned. "You know what's in the back of my mind?"

Mordecai nodded. "That he might run?" The risk here was the back door that led to the small garden. It would take an athlete to climb the wall enclosing it, and even then there were other walls and fences to get over before any sort of alleyway leading to a street could be reached, but, still . . . The perfect stakeout didn't exist, in Mordecai's opinion. Abarbanel knew better than to post a rooftop lookout for very long. A man with binoculars on a roof very quickly attracted the wrong kind of attention.

"Yes," Abarbanel said. "But in this situation there's still another factor."

Mordecai glanced at him. "Suicide?"

His friend nodded.

"I think we can ignore that, Sy. He won't take the easy way out. Sure, he's on his last legs, but he's tough, too. If we backed him into a corner, yes . . . but we aren't going to do that."

194

"You can't tell me he hasn't thought of it. If I were terminal, I'd damned well consider pulling the plug."

"I think he'll fight right up to the last," Mordecai insisted.

"If only we had an inkling," Abarbanel argued. "I mean, if he ran all the way back here with the idea of asking for asylum, why hasn't he done it? Americans will give anybody asylum. What's he *doing* over there?"

Mordecai shrugged.

"Personally, I'd just as soon go in and ice him," Abarbanel said.

"Sy, we want him alive."

"Balls. Just *do* it. A small action," Abarbanel said. Mordecai realized that his friend was feeling the strain. "No judges, no lawyers . . . it's all a waste of time. I'd do it myself, with one man as backup. Be in and out of there in forty-five seconds."

"And Israel'd take the blame."

"Who gives a shit? They'll accuse us anyway."

"And the girl? Would you just get rid of her too?"

"A two-bit slut? Why not?"

"Cut it out, Sy. We haven't got anything on her, and you know it."

This was true. The Columbia bursar's office had verified that she was a graduate student in good standing, but not much else had come to light.

Such a lovely young woman. From that risky garbage pickup they had learned her culinary preferences along with a host of minor trivia: her tastes in cosmetics were definitely expensive—the empty jars of Germaine Monteil creams indicated that she was into taking care of her skin and body. They knew that she was not pregnant and that she and the old man were heavy drinkers and smokers, but that was all.

"Student or not, she's in the life," Abarbanel insisted.

"I certainly didn't get that impression."

"He's paying her, I'll lay odds."

"A possibility," Mordecai admitted. "But until we learn otherwise, I'm keeping an open mind. Maybe he's gaming her."

"Turn 'em upside down, they all look alike," Abarbanel said. "While we sit on our asses he's over there living like a damned sultan, the best of food, booze, and a bit of fancy pussy to keep him company. I'd like to get him alone in a cell for an hour."

"I'll bet you would."

Suddenly Abarbanel smacked the flat of his hand on the kitchen table that separated them. "We ought to give him a nudge. Supposing we were to phone him—'Hey, old man, you haven't got much time, why don't we sit down and have a nice talk together?' No threats. Pleasant, y'know? 'Just wanted to let you know that *we*

195

know, you can't get away, too late for that.' Talk to him intelligently. The reasonable approach. He'd crap his pants. For that matter, I'd just as soon send someone over in person. Knock on the bitch's door. A bit of a social call. 'Evening, folks.'"

Mordecai grinned. "If suicide's on his mind, that's all he'd need!"

"Armon wants him alive and kicking, but Armon doesn't always get what he wants, and you know it. If we wait much longer we'll end up with a corpse on our hands anyway. So, okay, it's a risk. But if somebody talked to Heislinger . . . Damn it, Mordecai, I'm right."

To a degree, he was. In the long run threats and violence counted for little. Money could be important, but talk was the best.

"I'm going to discuss it with Armon when we phone tonight," Abarbanel said.

"I don't think he'll go for it, Sy."

"Don't be too sure," Abarbanel said. "The medical reports scared him. He's fidgety. Heislinger's got to be made to move. And damned quickly."

THE OLD MAN, however, without prompting, made a move of his own on Thursday, and once again he was a major news item.

She'd watched him brooding for days. A part of her was grateful that his anger was focused elsewhere. He was almost a pleasure to have around. The humiliating verbal assaults seemed done with. There were still flashes of irascibility, especially in the mornings when one of his attacks troubled him: then it was best to keep one's distance. Gradually he'd snap out of the sulks, and then there would be a return of the cutting humor. Having him, she decided, was very much like taking care of a willful child who was endearing one moment and capable of smashing every toy in sight the next.

But then, without warning, he picked up the phone.

"MAC, MY DEAR fellow, I would have to tell you that I wasn't at all pleased with your little broadcast," Mast said, after the first effusive barrage of greetings had been exchanged.

Dobkin, sensing trouble, parried. "As a matter of fact, Carl, neither were we. Where in hell *are* you?"

"Here in New York. What d'you mean, you weren't pleased? Did the show bomb?"

"I wouldn't say that," Mac Dobkin said. By which he meant the impact wasn't what the network expected. He explained: "True, we did have hopes that viewer response . . ."

"Serves you right for gluing together a lot of antiquated footage

197

and trying to pass it off on the public as a hot new item," Mast chided. "People are interested in what's happening today. In your business, you're supposed to *know* that, Mac."

"The fundamental concept was sound," Dobkin argued. "We think—"

"Enough already," Mast interrupted. "My time is valuable. So is yours. I want to discuss something with you. Specifically, how would CBS like to give me air time? Live. To make a statement. Listen, Mac, people want to know why I made my speech in Oslo. What d'you say?"

"Live? Now?"

"As soon as possible."

"How much time?"

"How much have you got?" Mast asked bluntly. "I have something to say. You people obviously didn't."

"Carl, I'd have to take it upstairs."

"I'm going to say my piece with or without you," Mast told him. "If you aren't interested, I'll take my business elsewhere. Don't beat around the bush with me, Mac. My health is lousy. I'm a sick man. The authorities want me. I'm forced to hide out. Do you see how it is? Can you do something for me? Or can't you? Will CBS maintain absolute confidentiality if I work with you? I want protection, Mac. Autograph hounds are pests. Give me your word on confidentiality, and I'll come down and talk with you and your colleagues."

They argued back and forth. Dobkin knew he had an exclusive. Handled properly, that could be gold. Mast kept harping on timeliness and confidentiality but gave in when Dobkin demanded the privilege of releasing at least preliminary news of CBS's contact with the Nobel prizewinner that evening.

A meeting was arranged for the following day. "Strictly private, Carl," Dobkin stressed. "You have my word." The time: 3:00 P.M.

The news item itself was handled by wry-smiling Rather that evening and was listened to with fascination by Mordecai and Sy Abarbanel. The item, neatly sandwiched between severe flooding in the Houston-Galveston area and something to do with the still-deposed Yasser Arafat's periwinkle high jinks, was scarcely over before Abarbanel dashed for the telephone.

When Colonel Armon came on the line—he'd been sleeping—the team chief filled him in. Heislinger had contacted the network. He wanted to make a statement. CBS was taking the matter under consideration. Abarbanel said, "What do you want us to do? Shall we go ahead with the plan we discussed? Or should we put it on hold?"

There was a long silence at the other end—the better part of a minute. Finally Armon said, "Let's go for it. Damn it, it's *us* he should be making statements to! He's sucking after free publicity. We have to get to him first. Put Gerber on the line."

Mordecai took the receiver, listened, nodded. "When?"

"This evening."

"All right."

"Can you do it, Gerber?"

"I'll do my best, sir."

THE EXCITEMENT THE Israelis were feeling was the antithesis of the mood in the Nadelmann household.

There, madness had reigned for a while, and even now, in the evening, the atmosphere was seemingly charged with the heat lightning ordinarily encountered in a black, summer thunderstorm.

Gritch, that outwardly demure young girl, so lovely and engagingly feminine—what was it Mast had called her, a true Jewish princess?—was capable of being aroused in ways other than sexual.

That is, not very often, but on occasion, she displayed what can only be described as a vicious, in fact venomous, temper. Then the charming sweetness vanished, to be replaced by something appropriate to a virago straight out of some fiery hellpit. That lilting musical soprano, so capable of captivating the male ear, rose to its uppermost registers and took on a piercing quality intense enough to shatter crystalware.

After Carl Mast hung up the telephone, she sat across from him. Finally she spoke, and what she had to say was to the point:

"YOU NO-GOOD, low-life, conniving, sneaky, two-faced, hypocritical, bald old prick with ears!"

"Eh?" Mast murmured. "What on e—"

"'Gritch, you alone shall have ex*clu*sive rights!' 'We'll research it together.' 'It'll be fun.' 'Such a book.' 'The inside story on Carl Mast.' You slimy son of a bitch. At last, it comes out!"

Mast beat a hasty retreat to the kitchen, apparently in urgent need of ice for his drink. Gritch slithered after him, green eyes ablaze, trembling, hissing, while Mast vigorously smashed trays against the sink's porcelain lip. She stalked closer, catlike. "*This* is why you came back to New York. You had it planned all along. Bastard! You used me."

"My dear girl, there's absolutely no n—" Mast started to say, but then got huffy himself. "I hope you didn't think I flew halfway 'round the world for the express purpose of sitting around with the

199

likes of *you!*" Most of the cubes went into a plastic bowl; a few skittered across the linoleum floor.

"Where do I fit in? That's all *I* want to know."

"You'll get your book."

"Sure! After you're done with CBS and whatever other fartbrain outfit you can get to listen to your bullshit! How about the *Times,* the *Washington Post,* the *National Inquirer,* while you're at it? *I* don't mind being last in line. I've been there my whole sonuvabitching *life.*"

"I should think you'd regard such possibilities as advance publicity for your own project, dear," Mast said.

"You've sold me down the river."

"That happened to *schwartzers,* not Jews, Gritchken."

She went on, bright eyes snapping with fury: "Mister, I . . . don't . . .*trust* . . . *you!*"

"Not so loud, you want the neighbors to hear?"

"Screw the goddamned neighbors," she yelled. "When those two fistfucking faggots upstairs get into a hairpulling contest it's worse than a female glee club! Listen! I've had it. Get out. Now! *Vamoose. Pronto!*"

"Has anyone ever told you that you're even lovelier when you're angry?" Mast said. "Heightens your color wonderfully." He tried another tack. "Believe me, everything'll turn out peachy-keen."

"I hope they string you up by your hairy old balls!"

"Nonsense," he insisted. "No one's interested in harming me. I'm being cooperative, aren't I? A step like this can lead to diplomatic asylum. And you'll still get everything I promised you."

"You're gaming me. Fucking hustler!"

He said calmly, "The safe-deposit box. The contents are yours, if you want. Over two hundred thousand. Plus the documents. Would you like that? Plus the tapes we've recorded already. A signed letter from me, Gritchken. Authorizing a one-time entry to that vault. I checked with the bank official. They allow a one-time visit. The letter needn't be notarized—all that's necessary is that the signature match the one on the master registry. Whatever's in the box after I'm gone could be yours, darling. Eh?"

"You're trying to run that *Kapo* shit on me again," she cried. "'Cooperate, and it'll be better.' They had to, else they died! Screw you!"

"Idiot, we're *all* under a sentence of death," he shouted back, the gays upstairs forgotten. "Silly bitch! What's the matter, you think you're special or something because you're young and beautiful and intelligent and a fucking *Jewess* to boot? Well, you ain't so hot and you ain't so special, *Schatzi.* I thought you had some chutzpah."

200

"You can take your chutzpah and sit on it."

"I'm offering you a real opportunity," he argued. "And don't hand me a lot of damned *Schweinscheiss* about your ritzy-cunt graduate degrees in economics or history. Go down to Morgan Guaranty or Chase Manhattan or the Department of Commerce, they're up to their bungholes in your kind of Ph.D.s, nothing but a lot of glorified pencil pushers wearing lousy two-hundred-buck, off-the-rack suits. Your rotten doctorate and a subway token will get you a ride, right down to Wall Street where, if you're lucky, the boss'll finger your slit while you're making him coffee."

"You tricked me," she insisted. "All this research we've been doing . . . you're going to hand it right over to CBS."

"No," Mast said, shaking his head. "They did all that in their dumb Special. Why can't you listen to reason just once?"

But that was precisely what she was not prepared to do. Her anger persisted and even increased after she burned the lamb chops he'd asked her to make for dinner. Supper was gotten through, but not pleasantly.

CAME A KNOCK at the door, a measured triple tap.

At quarter-past nine that same evening.

Gritch nearly jumped out of her skin, or more correctly the underpants and T-shirt she was wearing at the moment. In the two-and-a-half weeks Mast had been with her no one had come to that door except delivery boys from the supermarket and liquor store.

Wild eyed, she looked to Mast, who in turn was staring at the door, his expression unruffled. Dressed in the frogged, green-velvet smoking jacket and slacks, a silk Charvet scarf folded about his throat, and with his stockinged feet propped on the cocktail table, he sat there stonily.

Then he turned to regard her, saying, with a grave dip of his head, "*I know that knock.*"

"Wha'?" Her heart was pounding.

"Answer it," he said, then noting her attire: "Put something on."

"How did they get *in?*" she whispered. "They didn't ring out in the vestibule." Hurriedly she scuttled into the bedroom, returning with a pair of Calvin Kleins, got them on, tugging mightily to get them over her hips, sucking in her stomach to practically nothing to get the zipper closed.

Made of her taloned fingers two busy combs which, distractedly, she raked through those raven locks, whispering to herself. "What are we going to *do?*" At last, a Jewess gone mad, tearing at her hair.

"For God's sake, girl, see who it is," Mast told her.

201

"Bastard. I should have thrown your ass out days ago!" She tiptoed to the peephole, applied her eye to it. The visitor was standing much too close. All she could make out was an expanse of dark overcoat, a tie, and what seemed to be a beard.

She turned to Mast and silently mouthed in exaggerated lipreader's fashion: "It's a *man!*"

"You were expecting maybe the Queen Mother?" Mast said waspishly. "Damn you, open the door."

Turning back, Gritch touched the palm and fingers of one hand to the door as though it were a living presence, and finally, sweetly, clearly, but with nervousness, sang out, "Who is it?"

From the far side, muffled, came a reply: "If it wouldn't be too much of an intrusion . . . a word perhaps, with you and Doctor Mast?"

She wilted. *Doctor Mast.* To say it just like that!

Again she glanced toward the couch. Mast scowled and made vigorous door-opening motions, and she obeyed, slowly, rotating the three deadbolts first, and then the main latch, but leaving the bronze security chain in place, applying her left eye finally to the inch-wide crack, to squint up at their late-evening visitor. The hallway's light was behind him. She saw mostly a tall silhouette. She said again, but now in a faint whisper, "Yes? Who is it?" Saw too that the stranger was bearded, mustached, bespectacled, and that he held a gray homburg in both hands, chest-high, the fingers somewhat nervously rotating this piece of headgear by its curled brim.

"My name is Gerber, Miss Nadelmann. I'm sorry for the lateness of the hour. A moment only, please. There's absolutely nothing to fear. I have a message, possibly of importance to you and the doctor."

She undid the guard chain, opened the door wider. Then, with a blink, her eyes went wide as she recognized him. "You!" she exclaimed. "That restaurant . . . the other night?"

"Yes," Mordecai said, and reddened slightly.

Though alarmed Gritch was no longer horrified. She had a fleeting memory of the impression this visitor had made on her, and, with that, her composure began to return. "You scared the living sh— wits—out of me. Your name is Gerber?"

"Mordecai Gerber, yes," Mordecai replied edgily, fiddling with his hat and trying not to stare at Gritch's T-shirted chest. "The news. The CBS thing, you know. My superior. I've been on the phone. He saw no reason to . . ."

"Won't you come in?" Gritch said, opening her door still wider.

202

Mordecai stepped through it and into the living room, by no means at ease, his glance moving quickly, taking in everything. Gritch peered down the hallway to see if anyone else was lurking out there and then closed the door, snapping the deadbolts into place.

The old man, sprawled lazily on the couch, regarded him.

Mordecai said, "Doctor, my instructions are to inform you that the government of Israel knows who you are and that it is interested in discussing certain matters with you. Further, it is willing to provide you with protection until the legal and diplomatic aspects of your situation can be clarified."

Carl Mast, calmly regarding his visitor, said, "Israel?"

"Yes."

"Israel's protection I need like a goddamned hole in the head. How long have you known my whereabouts, young man?"

"Almost ten days."

"Gritch, please be good enough to take this gentleman's coat and hat," Mast ordered. Suddenly he was very much master of the house, cracking out orders. "Bring the ouzo. Open one of those bottles of Dom Pérignon in the fridge. This is a celebration. Get that Stilton and some crackers too."

Gritch was still standing beside the door she'd locked. He glanced at her sharply, then clapped his hands in the manner of a hypnotist rousing his subject from a trance. "Move, girl! And get that drooling adolescent expression off your face!"

Mast's sudden air of geniality—whether genuine or specious— had relaxed the tension. He gazed up at their tall visitor, as though weighing the significance of his presence here in this room, and then said with a grave smile, half to himself, "I have, it seems, delivered myself into the hands of my redeemer."

# part four

I have my own laws and my court to judge me, and I address myself to them more than to anyone else.
　　　　　　—Montaigne, *The Essays*

"NOW THEN, GERBER, make yourself comfortable," Mast was saying.

Mordecai weighed this invitation for a moment, then slipped his topcoat off and gave it and his hat to Gritch. He took an armchair facing his host across the cocktail table. Mast blathered cheerfully as Gritch brought a tray from the kitchen bearing snacks, more wine: "Try the Dom, quite good really—Gritch, fetch that Montrachet. Or would you prefer something else?" He pried corks from bottles, filled three goblets.

Mordecai raised a hand. "Thanks, no. I'm on duty."

"Nonsense. Will a taste make a drunkard of you?" The agent reluctantly accepted a goblet. Mast was already quaffing: "*Zum wohl*! Ah, excellent. Was it difficult finding me?"

"You had us guessing for a while," Mordecai said, sipping too.

"What tipped you off?"

"The Rx's. The pharmacist knew Miss Nadelmann."

"As simple as that?" Mast glanced at Gritch. She was seated in the second armchair. "I told you to go where you weren't known."

"In this weather? What did you want me to do, cab all the way to Mount Kisco?" She lit one of her long brown mentholated cigarettes, tasted her drink, sat back to watch and listen.

"No matter. What's done is done." Mast shot Mordecai an oblique look. "In a way I'm glad you found me. Now if I want to, I can go out. You know how it is. The minute you can't do something, that's what you want most. I've been feeling cooped up."

Mordecai said, "I'd recommend you don't start wandering around town. It could be dangerous."

"Oh? Wouldn't your Israeli crowd be at my heels?"

"Of course. However, we don't believe in taking unnecessary chances."

"I see." Mast drank again. "Gerber, are you armed?"

Mordecai considered this. Then, finally: "No."

"Good. Personally I like a peaceful Yid."

"My instructions are merely to speak with you."

Mast nodded. "How many of you are there?"

"Enough."

"Must be boring work."

"It has its moments, Doctor."

"And this is one of them?" Mast chuckled. "Well, then. Here we are. You talk of cooperation, Gerber. Frankly, I don't know what the hell you mean."

GRITCH GLANCED QUICKLY from one to the other—it was like taking in a verbal tennis match—outwardly sedate but inwardly caught up by a whirlwind of impressions, lips parted, her expression imperturbable. The memory of that initial rush of fear lingered. For the first time she understood the meaning of total panic—the knock on the door had unleashed a perfect blast of terror in her . . . she'd actually felt her scalp horripilate.

And now these two. Talking. They could almost have been *grand-père* and *grandfils* enjoying a sociable chat.

The younger one fascinated her. He was almost as uptight as she. In control, but very alert to what was taking place, as far as Mast was concerned anyway. With her there was that shyness. She mused: He's more at ease dealing with men than with women.

She sensed something else about him. He was different from other men she'd known—except of course for Mast, who was a case unto himself. The others had been important or wealthy, or else students, academicians. The former were protected by money or position; the latter were shielded by a scholarly cocoon, as she called it.

Gerber lived in neither world. That came through strongly. Who could tell what he'd been involved with? Danger? What else? He was flustered by her and avoided letting their glances meet, but she caught a hint of coolness and strength. With Mast he was brisk, businesslike.

Something irritated her. The way these two related. Each seemed somehow to gauge, understand, respect the other. It was as if they'd met in former times, former lives.

208

And Mast? As unbearably sure of himself as ever. Other men would have gone yellow with terror at that knock on the door. Their bowels would have quaked and turned to water. She thought: Is he totally without fear?

He acted as though this were a perfectly ordinary manner in which to spend an evening.

In a way he was admirable, for his élan if nothing else. It *had* to be an act. No one could be that much in control. His temerity astonished her. Gerber might be cool. But of Mast she thought now: Christ, he really *is* tough.

And herself? Neither of these men cared about her. She was sure of that. Each was interested in the other. She was a pawn.

MORDECAI SAID, "WE can arrange to have you in Israel in forty-eight hours."

"A lamb led to the slaughter?" Mast observed. "No thanks. I've other plans for the weekend."

"It's either that or you'll go in chains. An international arrest warrant's already been filed with the State Department here."

"For whom? Mast? Heislinger?"

"Does it matter? I should think Mast. They don't tell me everything."

"One of the rank and file, are you?" Mast conjectured. Mordecai nodded. "You see, Gritch? Here's another who's merely obeying orders. Heard that before? This man's nothing more than a toadying flunky who does dirty work in a trade where nobody is above suspicion."

"We only want to see things done properly, Doctor."

"If you mean that, leave me the hell alone."

"Impossible. It's all over. You must see that. Our proposal is generous. You'll be treated well and made comfortable. Total medical care. Also legal counsel. A public trial."

"What's the big hurry?"

"Time's a problem. We have a report from your physicians."

"I've got good conditions here. Do I look uncomfortable?"

"We think you'll change your mind. It's the sensible thing to do."

"Why?"

Mordecai stared at him. "Because Israel is your last resource."

"You're kidding."

"No. There's been speculation in Tel Aviv about your speech," Mordecai explained. "Obviously you're not deranged. The psychiatric view is that guilt's involved. Subconsciously, you want to be brought to trial. And the best—the only—place for such a trial is Israel."

209

"In the midst of the enemy camp?"

"Precisely," Mordecai agreed. "Jews must pass judgment on you. In their own country, on their terms. Not the U.S., or Switzerland. I'm not a psychiatrist but I must say I see the logic of it. It's what you really want. That's what drives you on. In Israel, the final judgment. And, for you, the final absolution."

"You think absolution has ever been provided by a rope?"

"A fair trial, Doctor. You can't ask for more than that. This business with CBS. Whatever you wish to say can be more effectively said in Israel."

"Yes, but CBS won't execute me," Mast said, smiling. "Also, on such a network I might conceivably be addressing a somewhat freer audience rather than a nation of arrogant circumsized assholes who're in bondage to an ethnic superiority complex. More wine?"

"I have enough. Let me ask something. Was all this premeditated on your part? We've wondered about that. The speech, the flight from Oslo?"

"Ha! I expected to be detained the minute I stepped down from the podium! You can imagine my astonishment. By God, Gerber, I felt almost slighted. To go to all that trouble, and then be virtually *ignored?*" Mast chuckled. "Where was I to go? Gritch—Miss Nadelmann. The very embodiment of hospitality. Bless her."

"The word is protection, Doctor. That's why we feel it's best for you to stay here with her until arrangements can be made for your departure. There are people in this city who want to get their hands on you. Radicals. Fanatics."

"Mockeys, too?"

"We can't screen every person in New York to see if he's bitter about the death camps. Yes, there are Jews who want you dead and who'd go out of their way to execute you. As for fanatics ... those types can swing in any direction. They might make a hero out of you. Then again they might assassinate you and blame it on us. Israel has enemies."

Gritch said, "Oh God."

Mordecai turned to her. "You're in no danger. For the time being anyway. In trouble, yes. But if you stay here you're safe."

"And I'm in no danger either," Mast snapped. "You and your protection. I've got a couple of diplomatic buddies down at the United Nations who're only two generations removed from the jungle. They think a lot of what I've done for their countries. I can get on the phone and in an hour they'll have bodyguards up here who'll make your gang of Jewcutthroats look like Boy Scouts."

"You're bluffing," Mordecai said. "If you'd wanted sanctuary with some Third World country, you wouldn't have bothered with the Oslo statement in the first place. No, don't start trouble, Doctor. As far as we know, we're the only ones who've penetrated your cover. Leave it at that. Remember, if we'd wanted to, we could have taken you out of here days ago, under sedation if necessary. You'd be in Israel right now. Think. We've come to you. There's no escape."

"Incredible!" Mast crowed. "You're inviting me to assist in my own abduction. Voluntary kidnapping. It's like old times! Back in the SS all deportations, relocations, resettlings, were 'voluntary.' *Freiwillige* was Eichmann's pet word—you saw it all the time on the train manifests. Free will! All the way to the gassing rooms. Philosophers love that term, free will! Gerber, what do you want from me? Can't you leave a dying old man alone?"

"There's an opinion that you may be able to shed light on certain aspects of the Holocaust."

"And what in Christ's name would that accomplish? The Holocaust can go suck, for all I care. I'm sick of it. The future is what counts."

"What will be accomplished if you stay here in New York?" Mordecai insisted. "Was the Oslo speech bravado? I doubt that, Doctor. I really do. No, it was planned. You have our offer."

"And you can kiss my ass. In Oslo I said I, too, believed strongly in the human responsibility to choose. No, Gerber. I won't go willingly. Never."

"You're afraid!"

"Of what?" Mast demanded. "All that interests me is that I have work to accomplish. And I don't want to be interfered with. Afraid, the man says! God! If there's one thing I can't stand, it's a blithe kike."

Gritch, listening to all this, stared at Mordecai and thought: Your cloak-and-dagger bunch ought to have nailed him right there in Oslo. You fumbled the ball.

SHE KNEW THAT she was in danger.

Now was the time to make a move if ever she was going to. One way or the other. Either go on with Mast or side with the Israelis. If it were the latter, just blurt out the whole business: she'd been coerced, threatened, virtually held a prisoner. The whoring would come to light, but so what? There were worse things.

Strangely, such a move was beyond her. She feared Mast, but in a way Gerber frightened her more—the former was at least familiar.

Playing the middle of the road was safest, up to a point. Beyond that it was the worst place in the world to be. Traffic had a habit of coming from both directions. But all she could think of was: Be careful . . . stay neutral.

Had an explanation for her strange inability to act been demanded of her later Gritch would have said, lamely but accurately enough: "I felt like I was caught between a rock and a hard place."

MORDECAI SAID, "MAY I ask something, Miss Nadelmann? You don't have to respond unless you want to."

"I never respond unless I wish to," Gritch said.

"How'd you get involved in this?"

"Doctor Mast and I met some time ago. A mutual acquaintance."

"Who?"

"The name isn't important."

"Let me be the judge of that."

She ignored this. Mordecai blinked as though accepting a mild rebuff. "When Doctor Mast returned from Oslo he was exhausted. He called to ask if I'd put him up for a few days. I was happy to."

"Two and a half weeks are not a few days."

"He's not well. You know that. He asked if he could stay on."

"Very gracious of you."

"My schedule was relatively free." She got up from the armchair, went to the desk, returned with the disc of gold, which had been doing duty as a paperweight, handed it to Mordecai: "It's an honor to have a Nobel laureate in my home."

"I see." He hefted the disc, then set it down. "I assume you've heard the Heislinger name?"

"Doctor Mast has mentioned it."

"It's also been mentioned on TV and in the papers."

"I don't always keep abreast of current events."

Mast, as though sensing she was moving toward his camp, chimed in, "Such a bookworm!"

Mordecai let this pass. "An unusual situation, Miss Nadelmann."

"Is it?"

"Please, no game playing," he said with a frown. "You've been aiding and abetting a criminal. You know this."

"I know no such thing," she replied. "There's controversy about Doctor Mast's identity, yes. That's his affair, not mine. He asked me to help him with some research. That's why his stay here has lasted so long."

"What you're saying is nonsense," Mordecai interrupted, "but it's also informative. It tells me whose side you're on."

"I'm on nobody's side."

"Is he paying you?"

"Yes. Food. Incidentals."

212

"You realize your situation is delicate?"

"Why? Because I've shown hospitality to a distinguished man? Who also happens to be controversial? Is that a threat, Mr. Gerber?" Gritch gave him a cool smile. "Really!"

Gerber was guessing. Probing in the dark. She knew it, and with this knowledge found herself staring introspectively at their handsome guest who, though he might be many things, was also a man, and moreover one not especially skillful at handling women. She thought: Score, thirty love, advantage Nadelmann.

At that moment Mordecai glanced briefly at her, as though wondering what was on her mind. Their eyes met. He colored slightly. Then he turned back to Mast.

"SHE DOESN'T THINK it's unusual. Do you, Doctor?"

"Guess it depends on how you look at it."

"An old man and a young woman?"

"Please. Not old. 'Post middle age,' *Modern Maturity* would say."

"Half a century's difference in the ages?" Mordecai asked.

"Lucky me. Two scholars can always find something of mutual interest to discuss," Mast replied. "She's doing a book on contemporary German history. I've been consulting with her."

"I'm sure you remember a great deal."

"Singular opportunity for her, don't you agree?" Mast said. "You know how the elderly are, Gerber . . . Mordecai, did you say? Always mulling over their past exploits."

"I'd have thought you'd avoid talking about yours," Mordecai said. She saw that he was irritated by the act Mast was putting on. Suddenly he made as if to rise. "It's late. I'd better go."

With that Gritch realized that she wanted him to stay. The idea of Mast and herself alone again . . . anything was better than that. "Don't leave yet," she said earnestly.

Was he confused for just a second or was she imagining it? Unleashing a devastating smile, she added, "We're night people."

Mast glanced sharply from Mordecai to her, his expression malicious, amused. A touch of jealousy perhaps, but he was also enjoying himself.

Mordecai again made as if to rise. Mast scowled and then, still with that cynical expression, imperiously snapped forefinger and thumb at her and made refilling gestures.

She looked at him affectionately and thought: You snap your fucking fingers at me one more time . . .

NONETHELESS SHE GOT up and advanced toward Mordecai, Dom Pérignon in hand. He set down the goblet and placed both palms

213

over it, shaking his head, but then, after reflection, surrendered as Gritch leaned over him to fill the glass, at the same time treating him to a heartwrenching close-up of those T-shirted breasts that, bent over as she was, swung slightly, enchantingly, mere inches from his admiring eyes. Girl cyclists, hunched doggedly over their handlebars, have a similar effect, sometimes causing serious traffic accidents. She was close enough for his nostrils to detect her scent: faint, feminine. The refilling accomplished, Gritch turned and treated him to a posterior view of her snugly held Calvin-Kleined bottom. The posterior following hard on, so to speak, the anterior was in the nature of a superfluous coup de grace. Mordecai took notice. Gritch had, so she'd been told, a highly provocative way of moving her hips when she walked, quite remarkable. And then she paused to bend once more, refilling Mast's glass, again displaying the front of her chest to advantage, such a symphony of pendulous curves and slopes and rounds, the nipples clearly, all too clearly, visible through the fragile fabric, sixty percent polyester, forty percent pure cotton, machine-wash, tumble dry.

Her duties as hostess fulfilled, Gritch sat down primly in the armchair. Glanced at Mast. He was taking it all in. Had that glint of jealousy brightened? She didn't want that. The old fiend was appalling enough to put up with. She thought: Eschew wounded male vanity, please. No offense meant. She remembered a wonderful proverb a visiting Algerian dignitary out for a wild non-Islamic time had taught her, a Tuareg saying: *The wise man kisses the hand he cannot sever.* Down to earth folks, those Tuaregs. Calmly she remarked to Mordecai, "I dislike superlatives but I'd say that Doctor Mast is the most unusual man I've ever met. By the way, my name is Griselda." She paused. "But all my friends call me Gritch."

"Procrustean is what she says of me when we're alone," Mast said benevolently. "You know Procrustes? The Greek brigand who mutilated or stretched his mistresses to make them fit the length of his bed? But we shan't do that to Gritch, eh? No. She *is* a scold, though."

"She takes good care of you," Mordecai remarked. "Israel, too, wants you in good health."

"You make me sound like some sort of historical artifact." Suddenly he frowned, and glanced at their guest. "How old are you?"

"Thirty," Mordecai replied, surprised.

"Married?"

The Israeli shook his head.

Mast said, "No sweetsie-pie? A plump little *zaftig* pigeon back home? Tsk, tsk. A nice boychik like you? Bet you got 'em eating out of your hand."

214

"I really should go," Mordecai said, setting down his glass. "I'll report this conversation to my superior. A lot of it was a waste of your time and mine. But we've made a start. You'll be hearing from me."

Reluctantly Gritch fetched his coat and homburg. As Mordecai donned the former, Mast said, "By the way, have you put a tap on the phone? Is this apartment bugged?"

"No, Doctor."

"You aren't trying to pull my leg, are you?"

"I might be, but I'm not. Establishing tonight's contact is sufficient for the present. Cooperation, Doctor. Think it over."

Mast gave him a look, as if questioning whether or not electronic devices were monitoring every word spoken. Apparently he was either satisfied with Mordecai's statement or too disinterested to pursue the matter. Abruptly he dropped the subject. "If you're not on duty, come over for lunch tomorrow. Twelve-thirty?"

Gritch stared at him with amazement. Mordecai, too, seemed uncertain whether it was a joke. Mast smiled: "The girl here is hot stuff in the kitchen. She knows the way to a man's heart."

"I'm not sure what my schedule will be," Mordecai said.

"Check with your boss. Bet you a hundred he gives you the go-ahead. Sure. You do that little thing. Make it twelve-forty-five. In the morning I'll be tied up."

Gritch accompanied their visitor to the door, unsnapped the deadbolts, opened it wide, then paused in a girlish pose beside it, hands clasped behind her back, smiling, head tilted up, the better to gaze into Mordecai's face. "Is there," she inquired, "anything special you like to eat?"

"Whatever you have," Mordecai said. "so long as it's kosher." With that he tipped his hat and was gone.

"SURE. I'LL MEET with the man," Fred Monson said the following morning. He was talking with Mac Dobkin and Kyle Benedict, who was in Legal. Monson, tall, lean, handsomely hawkfaced, in his early sixties, dapper in a pearl gray three-piece job, a nonsmoker and nondrinker, sat behind his desk, which was long, modern, teak; on the wall behind him hung a framed and signed photograph of Monson and a recent U.S. president golfing on the Palm Springs links. On that day Monson had won; the former chief executive, as with foreign policy during his tenure, had consistently chipped to the right. Monson said now, "I'm not sure we can work up anything—in fact, Mac, after that special of yours I'd have to say I'm in a definitely negative proprioceptive mood about Doctor Mast—but it won't hurt to talk. My appointment book's jammed, but we'll squeeze him in. Maybe something'll trigger. Do you agree, Kyle?"

The man from Legal did. "I'm still checking on confidentiality. We want to be absolutely sure we're in the clear, Fred."

"That's your job, Kyle," Monson agreed. "Mac, you know what I'm thinking? If we do elect to work with your man? Something along the lines of *The Confessions of a Nazi War Criminal.*"

"Nice," Mac Dobkin said.

"I like it," Monson said. "It *says* something to me. American viewers are mesmerized by death. To actually see, right there live on the screen, looking you in the eye, a man who's personally helped snuff how many? Understand, I'm not saying yes, Mac. But I'm not saying no, either."

"Fine," Dobkin agreed. "I'll line up a conference room."

"We'll meet here," Monson told him. "I want to treat him properly. Respect, right? He's got the Nobel. You say he's a character?"

"Definite maverick."

"Interesting," Monson said thoughtfully. "Mavericks can have pulling power. They can also be aggravating. Want the impossible. But let's go with the meeting. A brief chat, that's all. I won't over-fringe, Mac. He's your baby." The executive smiled. "In a way all I want is to say hello. I mean, I've never actually shaken the hand of someone who's put a couple million through the smoker."

"DO YOU KNOW about the teredo?" the voice, a cultured English-accented basso, inquired as the lecture drew to a close.

A sepia-hued forefinger and thumb were held up, indicating a size of not much more than a quarter of an inch. "The teredo... well, you see, he is a *very* small beast."

The speaker looked around and then smiled before continuing. But what an odd smile—at once friendly and at the same time hostile. It was a smile that was empty of love, and in the burning eyes there was no humor at all.

The voice, even with its sonorous timbre, had a lilting quality, seductively musical. The speaker was Winfield Parkinson, a tall and handsome Negro in his early forties. He hailed from the Caribbean's islands in the sun but had knocked about for years in other places—Central and South American mainly—before coming to rest like a storm-driven petrel on Central Park West.

Win, as he was known to his followers, fluent in English and able to scrape by pretty well in Spanish, Portuguese, and French, was the leader of a small organization known as the Pan-American Liberation Society, or *La Sociedad de Pan-Americano Liberación*. The thirty-plus members who made up the New York chapter came mostly from the lower walks of life, and were malcontents, some psychopathic, of the Black or Hispanic variety. This parent cell's activities were known to the CIA and FBI, but for the time being the Society's existence was viewed by federal agencies as potentially, rather than overtly, dangerous.

217

Certain men seem born with a craving for violence and upheaval. If trouble does not come to them, they seek it. They seem to exist perpetually under a dark, roiling cloud, and are no strangers to crime and destructiveness.

Such adventurous spirits often make ideal revolutionaries of the sort that can be found sulking and planning great deeds along mosquito-infested tropical shores, where life in the best of times is counted as *nada,* meaning not much. Many souls come and go with depressing regularity in the tropic of Cancer. People live, then die, often violently. The prevailing attitude is fatalistic. There is always a new supply of human beings to replace what has been taken away. An entire coastal village disappears in a *hurracán,* a prime minister is dynamited, a child dies of dysentery: no matter. In the northern latitudes much money and attention are devoted to preventing such events but in the simmering tropics there is a shrug followed by a casual *vaya con dios.*

Out of these climates there occasionally comes the irrefutably deadly personality who, given half a chance, will turn the world upside down—for money, for glory, for power, or for the joy of it.

To him the death of thousands counts for nothing. What matters is the accomplishment itself. The means as an end. *Trouble:* there is a positively delicious sound to the word. The end may never be achieved but who cares? It is the struggle that matters. And why not? For such people, who have lived out a life in economic and psychological bondage, there is little to lose. One must not die silent. A true man will fight to be remembered, to leave his thumbprint on a page of history. Perón, Batista, Guevara, Zamora, Castro. To paraphrase Marx: Cast off thy chains and you may end up idolized. People may loathe or cherish your memory—but they will not forget you.

Win Parkinson was such a man. He was intelligent, alert, alive with intensity, a descendant of Afric sugar-cane transportees. He had a consuming hatred for all the white world. In the eighteenth century he would have been pegged as an incorrigible agitator and been quickly hanged or flogged to death. Today he lived as free as a bird, with a counterfeit Jamaican passport, in Manhattan. As good a place as any in which to ruminate and refine his vision of a new social order in which Caribbean Man, long humble, was a power to be reckoned with.

HE CONTINUED: "NOW let us imagine that an elegant yacht pulls into, say, Port-au-Prince or Saint Johns or Kingstown. Aboard are *los ricos americanos,* out for the good time, oh my, yes, the suntans, the coco-locos, the souvenirs, 'Hey, mon, come take-alook by my stall, best prices anywhere on this island.'

"Mister Teredo finds for himself along the underside of the hull a little place, and there he hangs on tight," Parkinson said. "Most tenacious." He smiled, displaying magnificent teeth. "Ol' teredo begins boring into that wooden hull. He is, you know, only a soft little worm, except for one interesting characteristic. On top of his head there are two tiny . . . like clamshells." Parkinson made a pincering movement with finger and thumb. "That is because the teredo is a kind of mollusk. Once under the surface of a plank he eats a tunnel along the length of the grain. The little clamshells scrape at the wood. In such fashion does this curious animal make his way in the world, digesting, growing. The tail of this voracious beast remains at the original entrance hole." Parkinson smiled again. "His *ah'ss,* so to speak, is at anchor. The wood scrapings are processed by the tube of the body and then excreted out the tail.

"Would you believe it, I have seen worms over eight feet long and more than an inch thick that have been removed from a ship's planking, which from the outside, looked as strong as the day it was bent to the frames."

Win looked 'round and chuckled. "What you think happens? Pretty soon that big yacht springs some leaks. Presently, she goes down. Like a rock. That lovely ship and all its whites are soon covered by the waters of the ocean!"

He paused and then said with relish, one hand flattened against his breast, "We are brother to the teredo. Start small. Grow big and strong!"

THE LECTURE WAS being held in the living room of the Central Park West apartment the group rented. Regularly, various members who happened to be in New York met there to lay plans against capitalistic and imperialistic oppression and to verbalize their credo of discontent.

The CIA evaluation, periodically updated, contained remarks that were valid enough:

An ultra left-wing organization. Membership: under 250, here and abroad. Members predominantly of African descent, intermixed with Hispanic. Headquarters: New York City. Sympathetic political contacts in Cuba, Haiti, Jamaica, San Salvador, Nicaragua, Costa Rica, and most of the Leeward islands south to Brazil.

*Geopolitical Overview:* The 1500-mile-long archipelago comprising the Leewards represents a natural defense perimeter guarding the southeastern approaches to the U.S., from Florida to the Mexican border. At present these approaches are used by oil-tanker fleets on the South Atlantic run from Capetown. Any threat to this vital supply link would trigger immediate and serious effects on U.S. economy.

*Political:* The Pan-American Liberation Society has a documented history of violent activism plus a categorical affinity to side with any anti-U.S./antiwhite faction. Its role in the Grenadan revolution is still being evaluated. There are unconfirmed reports that it helped organize and launch anti-American demonstrations in Jamaica in 1976, which resulted in over forty deaths.

THE DEBACLE IN Grenada had been all but forgotten. Life in the Caribbean had been serene for some time. Which is not to say that Parkinson was silent. Via lecture and mimeographed newsletter he sent forth the word. His rhetoric, though lacking polish, was straight from the shoulder:

Again and again the U.S. will support any oppressive dictatorship: in Haiti, San Salvador, Honduras, Nicaragua. Why is this? Because such a regime is the best device by which vested American interests in foreign lands can be *insured.*

Americans wonder why they are despised. The reason is obvious: oppressors themselves, Americans eagerly support oppression— hail Poppa Doc, hail Iran's Shah, and all those who controlled what amounted to little more than slave populations. Were I an American, out of shame I would conceal the fact.

Our primary goal is to free the entire Caribbean sphere of capitalistic influence. The day of the white overlord has passed.

The U.S. claims that this area must be kept free of "subversive infiltration," by which is meant only that their supply of Middle East crude will be guaranteed. How can we *infiltrate* areas where we have worked the land and lived and died for over three hundred years? We have an equity in the Caribbean and we will not be denied! We ask but one thing: autonomy! But America, which swaggers and at the same time talks softly, cannot allow this. The "invasion" of Grenada must stand as the most unequal contest ever conceived. Grenada's downfall would have been a different story if they'd had more nuclear weapons and fewer bananas.

No despot ever voluntarily gives an oppressed people its freedom. Those who labor under the yoke gain independence in two ways. The despot "cedes" it to them because he knows he can no longer control them; or they take it. The price of freedom is blood.

220

Never look to the U.S., with its long history of slavery, for a generous spirit. Capitalism itself is a form of slavery.

All this was either hard truth or, as one cynical CIA analyst said, "Merely a lot of recycled Franz Fanon, Third World gibberish set to marimba music." What matters is that Parkinson believed his utterances. So did his followers, many of them outcasts from the islands in question.

Win Parkinson, with his chilling smile, had started from Bridgetown, Barbados, where as a youngster he'd worked as a stevedore and slain his first man in some long forgotten dispute. He was twenty-two then, quick to anger and quicker with a knife; since then he had learned to control the temper, and with a bodyguard he no longer needed to go armed. Working on the docks for ten hours a day under a tropical sun had given him the physique women and bodybuilders gawk at; he was forty-three now, and weighed 230. Six-feet six. No fat.

Funding for the group was catch-as-catch-can. Most members worked at various jobs, including one who pimped a string of white girls on Fourteenth. Occasionally, marijuana and heroin changed hands among certain people, along with the breakfast of champions, coke. From time to time Parkinson wandered down to Miami—he was simply a wonderful man to talk to because he knew so many ways to move people and boats from one place to another in the Caribbean. He was even seen in San Jose, Costa Rica, the unofficial spa of international professional mercenaries and other condottiere-entrepreneurs.

Win, with the patience of the teredo, was willing to bide his time. But not for the rest of his life. The truth was that he'd had no luck at all with his dream of driving white influence from the Caribbean. Money, among other things, was needed. All he wanted was one real opportunity he could clutch at. Meanwhile, he went about his daily affairs. A black dreamer. Entertaining visions of a rainbow coalition of his own in the Leewards, from Havana all the way to the Brazilian coast.

He desired a brotherhood, with himself at the helm. Win Parkinson. Lecturing, writing, and dreaming on Central Park West, made glum by so much snow and cold. In spare moments he refined the anthem he'd already composed for his Leeward Federation. It began:

Onward we march, hand in hand
Toward a greater glory for all.
Ablaze, brighter than the noonday sun,
We are the Leeward Creation . . .

221

He'd even designed his army's uniform. A practical light-tan twill. Sam Browne belts. A jaunty cap and red epaulets. For the officers, a braided gold fourragère at the left shoulder.

In creating a new society, attention must be paid to every detail. It's the little things that count.

WIN PARKINSON WAS not crazy. Fidel himself had whirlpooled into a self-generated and inward-turned hysteria years ago when he was skulking like a brigand in the fever foothills near Havana, living on cigars and vitamin pills, while he tried to keep his ragtag gang of criminal-guerrillas, numbering not even a thousand, from melting away into the jungle. Fidelito, not a bad amateur baseball player, had served out his exile in New York, too, in the Bronx.

Batista had brayed like a jackass at this scornful invasion by a crowd of ideologically loony Cuban exiles. Not many weeks later his formerly invincible regime lay in shards about him as Fidel was screamed by hysterial throngs into the capital city.

Effort. That was what was required. The force of will. Perseverence. Like the teredo.

WHEN THE LECTURE was over there was discussion time. Strong coffee, stronger drink for those who wished. Rich Havana leaf. Friends commingling. A common purpose.

Carl Mast's name arose. Leaning back in an armchair, rum-and-lime in hand, Parkinson mused, "I'd like to get my hands on him. Indeed."

"Why?" This was Maximillian Guzman, known as Max. Win's bodyguard. They'd knocked about the world together for over ten years. Not a large man at all, compared to the personage he guarded. Max Guzman had an incredible complexion—a pale apricot yellow, that reflected his Honduran heritage: Spanish, Indio, Negro, and a tinge of Austrian blood.

With Max it was not easy to differentiate between history and legend. It was not even certain where he and Win had gotten together, let alone why they'd stayed on with one another. One rumor had it that Max, in seeking a sensible outlet for his homicidal leanings, had once served as a professional soldier in the Congo and Basutoland. He said of this period in his life that it had been a "happy time." Africa seemed as likely a place as any for him and Win to meet. Max had an eighth-degree black belt and was a member of the World Shorin-Ryu Karate-Do Confederation. Win Parkinson might be intellectually dangerous but his acolyte was perilous on another level.

Parkinson said now, "If he killed as many as they claim he did, I'd sit down and talk with him, listen to what he has to say." He smiled at Guzman and the others. The British inflection was royal. "And you know? After that, I'd sell him. To Israel. A million. Two million, maybe three. They'd pay. What couldn't we do with money like that?"

Guzman scowled. "Ransom, yes, that makes sense. But talk?" He looked at the handsome man across from him. "You think he might teach you something, Win?"

Parkinson thought: How does one learn to control the destiny of millions?

To be godlike, all-powerful. The need for it burned in his brain like fire. To be obeyed, feared, adored. Even momentarily.

Because for a fact: he could do no wrong.

If destiny guided him, that was where his future lay. He would raise up his people. Despite themselves. As had kings and popes and emperors down through history.

"Yes," he said, "I think I could learn a good deal from a man like him. It pays to keep an open mind."

With that the cruel smile broadened, displaying healthy pink gums and the white teeth. Then he raised one dark hand in a kind of oddly casual blessing gesture.

The palm a paler pink, the life line short. "Learn. Take."

"A CAPRICE YOU say?" Carl Mast grinned. "A sudden whim? No, there's always a motive behind a rapid change of mind. Let's just say that, having invited this superficially appealing young clod to lunch, I intend seeing to it that the repast is properly presented. As host, I have an obligation."

It was the following morning and they were giving the apartment a tidying-up.

"You don't even know if he'll show," Gritch said.

"Ha! Is a pig's ass pork? He'll be here. Wild horses, my love. On time, that is to say, punctual. Spiffed in his Shabbes best, and plucking that goofy homburg to pieces."

"What the hell are you, some kind of collector? Every-German-and-his-pet-Jew . . . now all of a sudden you need two? You've got something ticking away in that crazy brain of yours, Carl, I know it."

"Sure, maybe I'll collect him and his whole team of nosy Yids while I'm at it," the old man said. "He's too smug, *Liebchen,* too clever. That kind of Jew will build you a new asshole just to keep in practice. I wouldn't mind shaking him up."

Mast had evidently been carried away by the idea of lunch and had decided to make of it a Very Big Thing. Harvey's, the restaurant he had taken her to a week earlier, served as *deux ex machina.* By telephone Mast arranged to have a first-rate catered lunch delivered: *felafel, kaved, avocado im dvasch, dag afuye, off sum sum,* and, for dessert, *shtrudel peyrot*. "No later than 12:15," he told the manager. "Yes, we have an oven to reheat food. What d'you think we cook on around here, peat fires? By the way, throw in a few dozen extra *latkes*—our guest may have an appetite." *Latkes* were fried potato cakes which, along with pita bread, formed a sort of basic ballast for heartier Jewish gourmands.

It was after the order had been placed that Gritch accused him of having indulged in a sudden caprice.

Dressed in a gray-flannel jogging suit she was working on the living room. A diligent vacuuming of the rug had helped lift the nap. Books, periodicals, and papers were still stacked everywhere, and from out back there was the sound of feline combat, the more easily heard because the bedroom windows had been opened to air out the stench left by cigarettes.

Earlier Mast had experienced severe discomfort, but his pills and a little wine had brought back some kind of ebullience. Now, perched on a bar stool at the hand-over counter, he drank black coffee, smoked, and studied her as she worked. "You rather like that big beanpole, don't you?"

"I don't even know him," she said, down on both knees, applying lemon oil to the cocktail table. "Rings. Can't you ever use a coaster?"

"But you'd like to know him better?" Her reply was an indifferent shrug as she scrubbed at a cigarette burn with the oiled rag. Mast smiled. "Come, my dear. I'm not blind."

Sitting back on her haunches she wiped one wrist across her brow and looked up at him. "Why don't you get off your dead ass and make yourself useful for a change? I *hate* housework! Do I have to do everything around this dump? And I'll tell you something else. In addition to being a collector you get your jollies fucking people's minds over. Well, don't try it with me."

"I did the dishes, didn't I?"

"Umn, and you only managed to break two glasses this time."

"I'd be glad to help but you're doing such a splendid job that I'd only be in the way," Mast said without rancor. "Listen, there's nothing wrong with your being attracted to a man who, let's face it, is half a century closer to your age than an old has-been like me. I think he's handsome, don't you? Rather dashing. Sensual mouth, what you can see of it under that foliage. Gentle manners, but I suspect there's some real steel in his backbone, and perhaps elsewhere as well. He'd be a nice boy for you to know, Gritch. I mean, know better."

"Bug off." She moved over to one of the end tables and began again with the lemon oil. "Is fucking all you think about?"

226

"No," he said. "I merely assign sex its proper niche, which is to say I think about it a good deal. Remember the argument between Freud and Jung? About how frequently a man thinks of sex? 'At least once every three seconds,' Jung said. Freud reflected on this and then observed, 'Three seconds? That would apply to a subject who's just orgasmed and who is satiated.'"

"Listen, I've been too uptight to feel horny ever since you barged in here. That's the effect you have on *me.*"

"Thank you."

"Be my guest."

"I thought I was."

She stopped rubbing and gave him a fishy look. "Why the matchmaker crap, Carl? I'm perfectly capable of working out my own arrangements."

"I want to see my little girl happy," Mast said. And then, casually: "Why don't you seduce him? You have my permission. I shan't be angry."

"I have your *what?*" The bright emerald eyes burned.

He said reflectively, oblivious to her anger, "Really, Gritch. Are you telling me the idea hasn't occurred to you? My observational skills must be failing." He gave her his best smile. "My dearest girl, you must understand, I've really become terribly fond of you. Please believe that. The old must make way for the young. I won't be jealous . . . well, a little bit perhaps. These past weeks with you . . . they have been new and different for me, too, you know. I've treated you harshly, yes. Knowing this, my better side urges amends." He paused. "You see, I *like* you, Gritch."

She listened to this speech with interest, still down on the floor, legs crossed and tucked yoga fashion, head cocked a little to one side. When he was done, she chuckled. "Know what I think, Carl? You want me to take this dude to bed so that I can maybe learn something, the idea being if I know, *you'll* know." She sighed and then poked at the bridge of her spectacles. "Games! Don't you ever quit?"

Mast shrugged. "He's guarded about what he lets slip. A mild curiosity on my part, okay? Such an investigation might be lot of fun for you."

"It would also tag me as being on your side."

"They already believe that."

"You fucking shit."

"They'll try to woo you away if they get a chance. But you won't betray me, I think."

"Damned sure of yourself, aren't you?"

He got up from the bar stool, stretching creakily. "Why not put it to the test? Let's see what happens, shall we?" He went to the stove and refilled his coffee cup. "I'll be leaving here, say around two-thirty. After a delightful lunch with two handsome and enjoyable young people. You will then be free to work out your own 'arrangements,' as you call them. Try to use finesse. Your young man, I suspect, has a certain refinement. Don't come on like some simpering, sweating schoolgirl in estrus. I should be gone until, when? Sixish? Let's make it four hours. Is that sufficient time for youthful romance to bloom? Yes, I daresay it should be. Two or three times even. With the proper watering and attention."

She stared up at him, amazed. "I've got a stark, staring madman on my hands. You're going out? After what he said last night. Knowing how many crazies may be looking for you?"

"Nonsense," Mast said. "In Manhattan who pays attention to an old man? The elderly are everywhere in this town. No one will notice a quiet, unobtrusive sort like me." He considered this. "Besides, unless you have some time to yourselves, how else will you be able to ascertain whether horniness—what an atrocious term—is possible? Weren't you just saying that you scarcely know the lout. So, Gritchken? I make you a present. Out of the goodness of my heart. An entire afternoon. Exceedingly generous, if you ask me. Do whatever it is young people do these days in order to become friends. What *do* they do?"

"You're disgusting." She threw down the oily rag and stood up. Even so she sensed his possessiveness.

"Talk. Play chess, sit, hold hands," Mast said. "Let him help wash the dishes, maybe he'll be less *clumsy* than old butterfingers-me, or if all else fails, you can regale him with the poignant tale of your revolting Jewish-American childhood in, where was that incestuous shithole, Passaic? Is that an Indian name? Remind me never to go there. He will, a little birdie tells me, be enchanted. You see, Gritchkela, he too likes you." He paused, scowling. "Christ, is your period over? Yes, thank God, a *schmendrik* like Gerber would probably pass out at the sight of an ensanguined wick! In any event I shall be curious, even anxious, to hear a full disclosure of what, if anything, has transpired or developed or occurred between you two youngsters. From Mast you'll get nothing less than an attentive ear."

"You won't hear anything from me."

"I'll hear what I'll hear, maybe the Dow-Jones closing average, maybe a tale of frustrated love and lust, Jesus, I'm glad I'm not young anymore."

228

She thought: Liar. God, being old must be hell. I hope it never happens to me.

AS HE HELPED her set the table—though careless in many ways Mast had a peculiarly sharp eye for certain niceties, napkins folded just so, flatware precisely aligned—she glanced at him and said, "Carl? What did you mean last night?"

"Hell and damnation, we should have ordered flowers. This table looks bald."

"When you said, 'I know that knock.'"

"When all this is over, Gritchken, remind me to take you down to Tiffany's." Mast regarded the table. "I spotted some silver there a year or so ago that was *you*. Czech, a design of orchids, very slim in the hand. Consider it a bonus. Any girl eventually craves a husband. Even a trollop like you. When that time comes every strategy must be brought into play, to help her set up shop. What did I mean? *Nacht und Nebel*, of course. The most terrifying action the Nazis invented."

"What could be more awful than the camps?"

"The ultimate stroke of a creative totalitarian imagination. Give the Germans their due." He thought for a moment. "*Nacht und Nebel* was, how shall we say it? Kafkaesque? Yes. Everything shrouded in a dark mystery. That was Night and Fog. Imagine. You've been singled out. Why? Who knows? No reason was ever given." Mast paused and then motioned toward the front door of the apartment. "In the night comes a knock, authoritative. You and your family waken. You stare at one another. Another sharp rapping. Already you are terrorized. But you answer. Standing in the doorway, four SSers. One speaks. '*Sie sind Gritch Nadelmann?*' '*Ja, was wunschen Sie, Herr Ober?*' '*Kommen.*' That's all. You ask again: What do you want? No response. Why are you here? Silence. I must assure you, sir, I have done nothing, absolutely nothing illegal. Finally: Get dressed and come with us. No arrest warrant, no charges. You dress and go with them to the *Braünhaus*. That, you understand, was the nickname given to every SS building anywhere in Europe. If you went to the *Braünhaus* you were as good as dead." Mast paused. "From the *Braünhaus* you were taken elsewhere. Where? No one ever knew. Totally random executions. Was there a trial? Never. What happened to you? No one found out. You had simply vanished. Into the Night and Fog. Maybe an unmarked grave, but who knew where? Weeks, months later, family or friends might timidly visit the *Braünhaus* to inquire: 'If you don't mind, sir,

229

we don't wish to bother, but this young woman, daughter, sister, wife, lover, coreligionist, yes, Nadelmann was her name, a lovely girl and with such bright prospects . . .' The SS *Oberscharführer* checks his logbooks. Awfully sorry. You must be mistaken. We've no information on such a person. Have a good day." Mast paused again, sighed. "That was last night's knock on the door. It happened thousands of times. Always in the night. Not one grave of those who were taken was ever found. Can you think of anything more intimidating? Gritch! To be here? And then, *not* be here?"

She shuddered. The beautiful table he'd laid was suddenly ugly. She groped for good sense, reason: "What I can't understand, Carl, is your obsession with the era. From everything you've said, it's the last thing in the world you want to interest CBS in." She gestured toward the stacks of books. "Yet, all this? Why?"

"Originally I had the idea that certain material should be reviewed. For my own defense, you know, if it came to a trial. It's true, I'm vain about my memory, but memory plays tricks. What one remembers is always different from what actually happened." He frowned. "But it will never come to a trial. I know that now. I've beaten them, Gritch. D'you understand? I'll never stand in the dock. A Pyrrhic victory. One wins but at the same time loses."

"Yet you persisted. All the notes. The tapes."

"No harm done," he said. "I've heard so much about Carl Mast it did me good to think about Heislinger again. Also, our labors helped provide ingress to your mind. Poor child. What's the expression . . . I had to *get* to you? I shall have to do the same with Gerber. He will be difficult. He's already far down the road to total brainwashing. His mental computer automatically de-tunes anything except approved messages."

"You always have to control everybody."

"Not at all, my love," he replied. "It's merely that I happen to be extremely discriminating about who's trying to control *me*." His voice had the old arrogance. "Remember what I said in Oslo about free choice? The big problem is raising consciousness to the level where the individual can grasp that something resembling a choice actually *exists*. Most prefer living in oblivion, Plato's Cave. American democracy being a case in point. You people bray about being able to elect whom you please! How utterly absurd. American idealism is based on naiveté and gullability."

"It's a hell of a lot better than the Soviet electoral process," she argued.

"*Any*thing's better than what Ivan has."

"Listen, do you need the bathroom?"

230

"Not at the moment. Why?"

"I think I'll run a tub."

"Oh, oh. I know you once you're in there. Better let me make sure."

HE PISSED NOISILY and leisurely into the middle of the bowl, standing spraddlelegged, his flaccid member's aim assisted by thumb and gently cupped fingers, the door wide open as she busied herself about him, laying out an oversized towel and fresh underwear, Gucci's sexiest.

She thought: Why do men pee in so many different ways?

A modest type—Mordecai?—zeroed in on the side of the bowl, seeking not to offend. The more brazen strove to imitate Niagara Falls or, at least, an apprentice fireman thrilled with his first aquatic instrument. When done, some cracked the whip, sending the penultimate driplet flying with a sharp fillip, while others milked out the last trace of moisture with a vigor that was probably as much pleasure-oriented as sanitary. And damn it, they always left the seat up. If the seat was up, you knew a man had been around. How many times had she squatted in a rush only to leap up with a muttered "Yack!" Only one man had not. He, a sweet humanities prof but a sort of sexual oxymoron, one of the most energetic lovers she'd known, had invariably hunkered in the female way to micturate. Why, she'd asked? "Never know when you might have to shit," he'd told her. "Saves time."

Her bath—a luxurious hour-and-fifteen-minute soak—was fine. She came out refreshed, glowing, pink—dodged an automatic bottom patting from Mast, and retired to the bedroom, there to do finger- and toenails, curl and coif her still-damp raven hair, apply makeup, and dress.

A simple outfit. Her best tweed skirt, high-heeled, dark brown pumps, a pale tea silk blouse, the diamond pendant glittering at her throat, a slim eighteenth-century silver bracelet on her left wrist, a bit of scent here, a bit there. A final toss and touch-up of the hair. Lip gloss blotted. Mascara and eyeliner just so. The hemline straightened before the full-length bedroom mirror. A small wrinkle in the panty hose attended to.

Scarcely two hours had passed.

THE DOORBELL RANG twice that afternoon. Once at 12:15. This was the delivery boy, a Jewish gentleman in his seventies, with the meal from Harvey's.

Mast ladled the courses out of their cartons into various serving bowls and dishes; what needed to be placed in the oven went in. He wore a charcoal gray business suit, black oxfords, a maroon Sulka tie, vest.

The second ring came at 12:46. Gritch, though she was perfectly aware of her appearance, nevertheless asked, "Pass inspection?"

Mast gave her the drollest of looks. "I daresay you'll do."

She went to the door, released the various locking devices, opened it, and stared up into Gerber's eyes. Clutched in his right hand was the homburg; in his left, a dozen American Beauty roses wrapped in tissue. The conversation began as most conversations do: "Good afternoon. I hope I'm not late."

"Oh, hi. Come on in."

Mordecai did, tripping slightly on the metal weatherstripping of the sill. Regaining both balance and composure he extended the bouquet toward her and murmured, "For you."

"You lovely man," Gritch said, accepting the floral tribute. "My favorite flower." It wasn't. "How did you know?"

"I didn't," Mordecai said. "Good afternoon, Doctor."

"How very nice of you to come," Mast said with a smile. "Ah, let me have your hat, coat. Gritch, a vase, quickly. They'll look splendid. Yes. I was just saying."

233

Wine was poured, three tall goblets, her best Swedish crystal raised in toast. *"Zum wohl und l'Chayim!"* Mast intoned, tasting. "No difficulty in getting time off, Gerber? I mean Mordecai."

"No."

"By the way, call me Carl. I thought there wouldn't be." Gritch, after sampling her wine, got up and went into the kitchen to don an impractical but rather incredible little apron of Chantilly lace. "Miss Nadelmann had been looking forward to our get-together."

"So have I," Mordecai said.

"Would you believe it, she's been slaving in the kitchen since eight this morning? Such an old-fashioned girl, you'd never think it to look at her, eh? For an old man like me, a crust of bread smeared with chicken fat is enough. Imagine my astonishment? A chef nonpareil." Mordecai listened to this with interest. Mast went on, "You're going to *like* it!"

Gritch, from behind the pass-over counter, and behind Mordecai's back too, glared at Mast and gave him a raised middle-finger salute. "The food itself is kosher," Mast continued, "but I'm afraid the dishes and cutlery are not."

"You shouldn't have gone to so much trouble," Mordecai said, setting down his glass on the lemon-oiled cocktail table. He turned to glance at Gritch over his shoulder. "A delivery van from the Harvey's establishment was here awhile ago with an order. Of course, it could have gone to any of this building's tenants." He turned back to Mast. "Are you having fun with me?"

"Okay, a small joke." Mast shrugged, smiling. "I was wondering how sharp you are. So now I know. The meal will be just as good. Forgive?"

"You ask too much," Mordecai said. "Cooperation, Doctor. That'd satisfy me."

"And your boss as well?" Mordecai nodded. Mast was watching him closely. "You can't bring yourself to call me Carl? Or Kasper?"

"I have too much respect for either or both of you, sir."

Mast grinned. "The trouble with your type is, you don't know how to relax. Why don't you get a little enjoyment out of life, son? That's what it's all about."

Mordecai stared at Mast as though he was slightly daft. Then he said, "Would you excuse me? I'd like to wash my hands."

In the bathroom he quickly washed his hands, dried them, inspected the medicine chest, combed his hair and beard, and stroked his mustache to make sure it was not lopsided. Finally, satisfied that he was presentable, he adjusted the lapels of his jacket and double-checked the miniature battery-powered transmitter in

234

his left breast pocket—the mike itself was concealed in a tiny gold Star of David emblem worn in the buttonhole—bared his incisors for a last-minute cosmetic check, and opened the door to join his host and hostess.

MAST HOLDING FORTH as usual, dapper, garrulous, the reigning autocrat of whatever table he happened to be sitting at, in this case the long low cocktail table about which the three of them were now seated and upon which were arranged vintages he deemed appropriate for preprandial enjoyment—two Château d'Y'quems, a Chardonnay-Maçon and a couple of Alsatian Rieslings. "These madcap Americans with their fast-food mentality! Always in a rush. They've forgotten how to talk, enjoy. Ah, I remember afternoons on the Disengoff! You know the Disengoff, Mordecai?"

"Everybody in Tel Aviv knows Disengoff," Gerber said as Mast corkscrewed, sniffed, poured.

Mast explained to Gritch: "A broad avenue, a tacky Tel Aviv equivalent of the Champs, only lots more fun. Stores, shops, restaurants, sidewalk cafés where people gather, in no hurry, to sip coffee or yoghurt or spoon glazed ices, and talk, watch the world saunter by. The Disengoff's the finest place in the Middle East for birdwatching—you'd knock 'em dead, Gritch. Interesting place, Israel. Smaller than Massachusetts. Why is it always these pissant countries that cause so much trouble?"

Mordecai objected. "We don't want trouble. But autonomy is difficult to achieve, let alone sustain."

"Lord, let the scales fall from their eyes," Mast said. "I've been watching this world for a long time. The emotional climate today, of which Israel is a contributing factor, is a lot closer to what it was in '39 than you think."

Gritch leaned back, listening, goblet delicately held. "That's about the first thing you've ever said that I agree with."

"Doctor, I'm not here to discuss world affairs," Mordecai interrupted. "I want to ask you a few questions." In the apartment across the street, Heller, the electronics specialist, would be crouched over the Ampex, monitoring the audio level, recording everything as the big reels slowly rotated. Abarbanel would be there, too, absorbed in what was coming in over the earphones.

Evidence. The pieces interlocking. Anything Mast said was of interest. Or Heislinger, rather.

GRITCH SAT IN an armchair, the meal-to-come forgotten. Mordecai's rapid-fire interrogatory style may have lacked subtlety but it certainly was forceful. He went after Mast like a badger harassing a prey that sooner or later must succumb. At first both men were calm: Mast droll, blasé, bemused, replying forthrightly, while the young agent fired off question after question. But soon their voices grew heated:

"Exactly how did you first become involved with the SS?"

"Probably in the way one drifts into any career-type job."

"A career? The SS?" She couldn't tell whether Mordecai was incredulous or sneering.

"Certainly. In the middle thirties they were looking for a few specialists in public health. I was interviewed several times. They found a place for me. Himmler—at that time he wasn't so important—learned of my longtime interest in psychology. Later he was to make use of it."

"You were not coerced, then. You participated voluntarily."

"Yes, I took part."

"You made no attempt to leave Germany?"

"In a totalitarian state one simply doesn't stand up and say 'I resign.' Liable to find yourself on indefinite vacation in dear old Dachau."

"How exactly did Himmler make use of you?"

"There were always morale problems in the SS, though we tried to keep them hidden."

"Can you be more specific?"

"Look at it this way, Gerber. We had thousands of young fellows. I'm talking about the early forties now. They'd been raised decently, see? They thought their country was great, which is what they'd think if they were Americans or Swahilis or Israelis, which is as it should be because kids sure don't know from *scheiss* about any *other* goddamned country. So, right away, you dress 'em up in a classy uniform and tell 'em what a grand job they're doing defending this country of theirs, and when they go on furlough back home everybody's proud as hell and all the pretty young girls can hardly keep from groping these splendid heroes. I mean, Mordy, if a chick likes you *that* much, to the point where she can't wait to hop out of her pants, you gotta be doing something right, eh?"

"Must you ramble, Doctor?"

Mast grinned. "Okay. Let's say you give one of these boys a nice shiny Schmeisser submachine gun, wonderful weapon, very high rate of fire, and you bring him out to this big ditch where maybe a thousand Hebes or Iranians or Vietnamese—it doesn't matter at all who these people *are,* see?—have been assembled, and you tell the kid, 'Spray 'em.'"

236

"And that is genocide!"

Mast pointed with his right hand, thumb cocked, forefinger extended: "Bang, bang, guess what folks, you're dead, just like in the movies, only it's not quite like the movies, and your parents aren't standing there applauding, or the girlfriend either, and in a way you're damned glad they aren't because by now you're starting to get a very bad taste in your mouth."

"You're saying these executioners suffered psychological damage," Mordecai snapped. "They deserved to."

"Not 'damage,' but massive trauma, hysteria, disintegration of emotional stability, nightmares, nervous breakdowns, suicides," Mast said. "Nine out of ten enlisted men in the killer units were alcoholic. It wasn't any easier for those who operated the extermination centers. Quite simply, they saw too much death. Not like on a battlefield, where you deal with hundreds, maybe thousands of cadavers. For the SS there was *no end of death.*"

"All right, so you helped toughen them up."

"I never made 'em tough," Mast objected. "I merely kept 'em from falling apart. I bet I wrote ten thousand Rx's. Sleeping potions, you name it. No, we had others with real talent, whose specialty was turning raw troopers into efficient killers. Listen, I once saw how it was done. Would you like me to tell you a little story?"

"I want to hear what *you* did."

"We were in eastern Poland," Mast went on. "This was '41. A time of savage cruelty for the conquered—Poles, Jews, Russians: they were all treated with a severity that cannot really be described. There was an SS major, at one of the advance bivouacs. I forget his name."

"You're—" Mordecai interrupted. Then, with an effort, he stopped and settled back in his chair, scowling, like an impatient traveler facing a long but unavoidable delay.

"What *was* his name?" Mast was saying. "Well. He was lecturing a group of thirty or so replacement troopers on the afternoon I witnessed this. Youngsters who'd completed training but who'd not been blooded. They were gathered in the town meeting hall. A village somewhere, and it was July, hot, you know, and one can doze off during a lecture on such a pleasant afternoon, many a good student has. This man—ah, Huber, yes—was declaiming about the inferiority of the Jews. Those present had heard the same junk a thousand times. Huber not a bad-looking fellow, dark haired, trim, erect, excellent speaking voice. Seated on a sort of raised dais, at an ordinary wooden table, talking away in, I must say, a rather monotonous fashion. Jew Christkillers, Jewslime, Jewfilth, et cetera.

"The trainees listened, but half of them were in a torpor. The windows of the meeting hall were open and they let in the sound of a noncom's shouted commands as he put a squad through close-order drill somewhere. A large fly buzzed about Huber's head. Most of the men watched the fly, more interested in it than in what Huber was saying.

"Finally Huber paused and took his Luger Parabellum out of its holster, worked the toggle-action, and then he remarked with a smile, 'This, gentlemen, is what we use on Jews—it's the only language they understand.' He placed the pistol on the table in front of him and continued with his lecture.

"Several minutes passed. Then he gave a signal to an aide. The aide went out a side door and returned in a moment, leading a young Jewish girl by the arm. She was, I recall, a very pretty child. Perhaps twelve or thirteen. Terrified out of her wits. Doubtlessly someone selected from a nearby processing area.

"Yes, strikingly pretty. She'd been given a bath, and from somewhere a clean summer frock had been found for her, a cotton print, belted at the waist. Brown shoes, white anklets. There was a ribbon binding her black hair, a bit of dark blue velvet.

"In the audience there was a stir of interest. Major Huber, still lecturing, snapped his fingers for the aide to bring a chair for the frightened girl. This was done. She sat there beside the wooden table, on the low dais, her hands twisting and working. But gradually, as the lecture went on, she began to calm down, since it appeared that no harm would come to her. I myself believed this. She'd been brought in to serve as a model for Huber's harsh litany against everything Jewish, a living illustration of how insidiously appealing a Jewess animal could be!

"She was, of course, horribly shy. To be made such a spectacle of, in front of all these soldiers. A girl barely into her teens. Can you imagine what she must have felt?"

"All you big, tough, grown-up *men,*" Gritch said bitterly, "sitting around, getting your kicks!"

"She did not utter a sound during all this," Mast continued. "Merely stared down into her lap at her nervously moving fingers. Huber droned on, soporific, the dull phrases mechanically repeated, Jewpigs, Jewhomosexual corrupters, Jewperverts, Jewsyphs . . .

"And how, Major Huber inquired mildly, was Aryan manhood to cope with such degradation? There is no knowing if the child understood any of this, but she well may have—there were plenty of German Jews in that processing area. She sat there dumbly, head lowered, hearing these vilifications piled upon her race and her-

238

self. If ordered to speak, she could not have. You've seen a frightened child? They have no words. They become mute.

"A Jew after all is a fleck of flyshit, Huber explained, a bit of lice, vermin. And what you did with such vermin was crush them beneath the heel. 'That's the only way—like this,' he said, and with that, still speaking calmly, he picked up the Luger and fired a shot into the head of the child sitting beside him, once, behind the ear.

"After the droning of his voice the sound of the pistol was devastating. The girl gasped, leaped up. Reflex action. She was dead before she collapsed to the floor. The amount of blood a shattered human skull will void is astonishing. There were the usual spastic thrashings and contortions, the slim legs kicking and jerking, and then the stench of feces and urine, the involitional small blasts of flatulence being expelled. The human organism does not die easily. She lay there in a bloody pool, face down, the frock driven waist-high by her death spasms. The faces of most of the new replacements had gone quite pale."

And so, in fact, had Gerber's.

Mast concluded: "Huber, rather fantastically, went on with his talk as though nothing had happened, for another half hour, with the cadaver sprawled there. I must say that his audience listened to what he had to say with complete attention."

Mast nodded thoughtfully. "Yes. That's how green cadets were toughened. This, they learned, was what they were *for*." He puffed at his Gauloise, which by now had an inch-long ash. "Huber of course was a degenerate, the sort Himmler disapproved of, and of which the SS had its share. I did some inquiring about our man, the major. I learned later that he'd given that particular lecture a number of times, always with a live model. My inquiry came to nothing. He had an impeccable record. Father of four, Iron Cross Second Class. He was untouchable. The candidate who was chosen always had to be appealing. Huber himself made the choice before the lecture. A beauty contest for young Jewish girls, a judge and jury of one.

"Just that single shot in the silence of the meeting hall." Mast thought for a moment. "I have never, you understand, been opposed to the dramatic touch. My Oslo statement, I think, substantiates this. I witnessed many things during the war, including cannibalism. But I would have to say that I never saw anything that shocked me more than what occurred that afternoon."

"Was he brought to justice?" Mordecai demanded. "Where is he now?"

"Huber died, in '74," Mast said. "In my small way I kept track of the old club. He was on that flight into Orly that took out 350. He had by then, interestingly enough, risen to a position of importance in the principality of Liechtenstein. Perfume manufacturing. Leichtenstein's no more than a wart on the ass of Europe but it's a swell place if you're into perfume, postage stamps, and tax dodges. He'd become quite wealthy, far more wealthy than I, at any rate. The *Wall Street Journal* carried an obit. He willed a sizable part of his fortune to Boy Scouts International. A much-respected man. Strictly legit, as Gritch would say."

She cried, "You just sat there and watched an innocent child murdered? And you call yourself civilized!"

"Shut up, idiot!" Mast snapped. "What do you know? Spoiled shit! Sterling example of American womanhood! How *dare* you suggest that I am uncivilized. I know your sluttish breed. All clitoris and 'independence.' At the same time babbling about wanting a 'genuine' relationship . . . what d'you call it, an *item*? Why, you shallow snip, all you are is a sort of cheap free-lance nun of a more earthly order! *Never* say I'm uncivilized."

"Killer! Fascist! That's all you ever were and that's all you ever will be," she shouted.

"SHUT UP, BOTH of you!" Mordecai broke in. "What is this?"

"Who're you telling to shut up?" Gritch demanded.

"Do the two of you always fight like this?" It was one of the few times in the young agent's experience when he felt not in control of himself *or* the situation. Knowing this was highly unpleasant. A part of him wanted to side with Gritch. Mordecai, in fact, felt a strong urge to do something about this old man—to silence, here and *now,* all those insults, the revolting anti-Semitism! It would be so easy. That scrawny old neck with its turkey dewlap practically begged to be wrung. How delightful that would be. Unfortunately such an overt action would also be a selfish indulgence. At this moment, all that mattered was the Ampex in the team's apartment, recording evidence. With luck, some day Heislinger would stand in the prisoner's dock in an Israeli courtroom and have his very words thrown back in his face. That was justice—*that* was the best revenge! Mordecai was well aware that it was not he alone who was the listener here—with that concealed mike, *he was all Israel.* Every Jew who had ever suffered, who had ever died unjustly, was here in this room, listening to the Devil confessing! Mordecai felt weighed down by a great responsibility, but also by a considerable joy: he was adjurer here, a sort of trigger by which an informal exorcism was taking place.

"Take care, Mordecai, she hates being told to shut up," Mast cautioned. "It merely spurs her on to more lyrical heights."

"In my own house I can't open my mouth?" Gritch wanted to know, frowning.

"I could remark on that, but I think I'll let it pass," Mast said.

"May *I* say something?" Mordecai asked.

"Go right ahead," Gritch said. "God forbid we should have a Jewish Gary Cooper. Around this dump, everybody gets in his two cents' worth."

"She's right," Mordecai said to his host. "You were a Fascist and a killer, as an accessory if not in actual fact."

"True, okay, undeniable, I accept it, so what d'you want already, I should genuflect?" Mast snapped; and to Gritch: "Bitch, just don't come on with me like some fancy-assed, grad-school know-it-all. You're not running this show."

"This is my place. You don't like it, leave. Now!"

"You'll regret that!"

"Says who? Bastard! Creep."

Mordecai got in again: "But you *stayed,* Doctor. That's what matters."

"Damned right, and so what?" Mast cried, glaring at the young agent. "By the way, sir, d'you have this apartment wired? I'd like to know at least that much from a guest at my table."

"*My* table," Gritch snapped.

"Your miserable Jew-pissant table then, but it's my food. We sweep the latter into the sink, if you like. Gerber! I asked you a question!"

"The house isn't wired. And wasn't your staying the essence?"

"Ah, kiss my bagel. Are *you* wired?"

Mordecai uncoiled his rangy frame from the armchair, rose, approached Mast, arms akimbo. "Examine me, if you wish."

"Get away. Your skinny body doesn't interest me," Mast said. "Nadelmann! Search him. Who knows, you might find such a task fascinating."

Mordecai towered above him. "Wasn't your staying the essence of it?"

"*Yes,* damn it," the old man answered. "There! Is that what you want? Good or bad, I was what I was! A mature man, almost forty. An M.D., a lifelong devotee of philosophy, psychology. Heislinger was no green kid. He was there, sonny, he knew what was going *on.*"

"Then you're a war criminal, just as the others were."

"You dumb Yid, I only hope your own miserable circumsized life rides down iron rails that're so level," Mast growled. His entire consciousness focused malevolently on Gerber. "I gotta sit here and listen to a shitprissy yarmulkehead like you, you're worse'n la madonna Nadelmann here. You are from nothing, believe me. Don't bust my balls, I'm wise to your sort. Seen 'em by the trainloads. Right up to the moment of truth!"

He grinned. "The trains grinding to a halt in the unloading yards. And them singing '*Shema Yisrael Adonoi Elohenu Adonoi Echad* . . .' As they marched to the shower baths. 'Excuse me, sir. I'm ahead of you in this line. We'll all have our turn and, ah, what an odd-looking doorway, let me give you a hand, brother, sister, wife, mother, don't stumble now, looks airtight, doesn't it. These Germans. Give 'em credit, they build well, and let's show 'em that we Jews can cooperate, get along, get by, it'll be better, and *who* shut that door so suddenly with such a clank and turn of locks, and *what* is that eye staring in that inch-thick peephole, ha-ha-ha-ha, y'know what we always called that? A *Judasfenster,* a Judas window, are they playing some trick on us, is this a new damned joke or prank they're pulling on the Chosen, and what *is* that coming down through those vents, hey, just a minute, really, this ain't funny, in all seriousness now, getting a bit stuffy in here, and why're there no *windows,* will somebody let in some air, a bit short of breath, well, all I can tell you is that if this *isn't* a joke I most assuredly intend filing a formal protest, yes, I have my rights, a letter, to my rabbi, my Gauleiter, my Bürgomeister, the *Judenrat,* will somebody lend me a stamp? *Halloooo?* Anybody out there? *Will someone please give me pen and paper?*'"

Mast threw back his head and laughed—the rasping snarl of an old rogue male wolf who has survived.

242

RAGE AND INDIGNATION—there was a sweetness to such emotions, and Mordecai felt it now as he glared down at Mast. "You can make a joke out of genocide if you want to, but you're still guilty. By your own admission!"

"For Christ's sake, man, guilty of *what?*" Mast tromboned up at him. "Of trying to behave intelligently? Of doing what little I could to lessen the insanity once I understood how bad it had gotten? I should have tried harder maybe? *How* harder? So tell, Mister Expert!" He drank the contents of his wineglass and rambled on, "Gerber, I *supervised* many of those docs who later stood trial at Nuremberg. They did crazy things. I'm a physician myself, I know. The problem was simple: you got maybe three million Hebes for slave labor. Jews from one end of Europe to the other who've been grabbed by the back of the neck and flung into the cattle cars that would transport them to the camps and factories. Yids up the gazoo, right? Money in the bank because you don't have to pay the fuckers a goddamned pfennig for the work they turn out.

"But how d'you keep 'em from cohabitating? Eh? I mean, Gerber-boy, people fuck all the time. They're addicted to it. And it's a well-known fact that kikes are insatiable, you'd think they invented humping, put a Jew male and female together it's worse'n gerbils. Y'don't keep an eye on 'em, in a few years you're stuck with a goddamned *town*ful of simpering gefiltefish addicts."

Mordecai said nothing but his expression told it all: the brow drawn into a scowl, the eyes glaring furiously. His breathing was forced, as though he had run a distance; yet he did not speak.

"Poor Himmler much vexed. Defense industries needed workers. How to keep 'em from gerbilizing? The SS docs worked overtime solving the problem.

"Vasectomy, outright castration, tubal ligation, *ech*, too *slow*! Squirting twenty cc's of caustic lye into the mouth of the cervix was quick. Cheap too. Can be done in a moment by any g-y-n once he's got the girl in the stirrups, spread open. But it was still a one-at-a-time shot. Gotta get the show on the road, right? So we were very into mass sterilization.

"They built some x-ray machines. Not the sort you get your tooth x-rayed with. Hundred-thousand watters, Gerber. Placed 'em behind ordinary plywood counters and desktops. The candidates were marched in and ordered to fill out mock questionnaires. All those Jewkids, bursting with spermatozoa and eggs. It took between two and three minutes, fifty at a time, lined up at the counters. And all the while the machines are humming away down there at crotch level.

"It was marvelous! They never felt a thing. Neutered 'em, straight out. Painless. Of course, in a day or two the burns developed. I mean, you can't fire that many roentgens into someone without second-degree burns."

Mast paused, shook his head, reached for a bottle, refilled his glass. "Imagine. Scorching 'em. Strips of burned, peeling epidermis hanging from the genitalia, male and female. '*Oy, weg, Herr Doktor, bitte*, something awful's happened,' they said. 'Nothing serious. Lotta scabies and impetigo in this camp, come on down to the dispensary, we'll give you a nice aspirin.' The medical aides had to assist the Jewish boys and girls because most of 'em couldn't walk by then."

Mast chuckled mirthlessly. "Know what the topper was? A tribute to SS thoroughness? When they got the boys into the dispensary they put 'em up on a table and castrated 'em, took the balls off neatly, sewed up the roasted scrotum, painted it with iodine, and turned 'em loose. Why? They wanted to make sure the x-rays had taken *effect*. They couldn't know this for sure until the testicles were examined microscopically! Thousands of roasted Jewballs. Those poor kids were taken care of twice. No cost at all, courtesy of the NSDAP, thank you, next in line, step up sir, we just want to make sure that your nuts are dead, burned, and all the while, on the other side of the camp, the people were standing in front of those counters, filling out questionnaires. That's the sort of idiocy I had to

244

contend with, Gerberchik, now that you ask. Okay, you didn't ask. You can have it anyway. A freebie, from Doc Heislinger, your friendly family physician."

Mordecai had regained control of himself. His expression was attentive, intense. "Always the comedian, aren't you, Doctor?"

The old man shrugged. "What I argued for was total separation of the sexes. This would have triggered widespread institutional homosexuality but it would have been a lesser evil. My superiors laughed at me. Himmler himself asked if I'd lost my nerve, even though he had no taste for killing, y'know. The first time he saw an execution he nearly fainted. Unable to stand the sight of blood, couldn't look at the crematoria with their iron trolleys, the meathooks, the blazing ovens. Heinrich long on theory but a weak sister when it came to the old down-and-dirty. As it turned out, the x-ray technique was abandoned after a year or so."

"Are you implying that your arguments finally had an effect?" Mordecai asked.

"Not at all. It was a matter of cost effectiveness. The equipment was frightfully expensive, you see—and operating it required huge amounts of kilowatt-hours. The German mentality is much like the American, always after something cheaper, faster."

"But, earlier, you were in charge of the euthanasia program," Mordecai put in.

"An academic point," Mast said. "Someone's name had to be on the letterhead. I was involved, but under duress. Check the testimonies given at Nuremberg. I have in my possession documents in which I argued in the strongest terms against the mercy killings of the retarded, the lame, and senile. Very bad press, I told Himmler. Believe me, that took guts. 'These are Germans we're blitzing, not Yids. The families of these patients are unhappy. I mean, Heinrich, if you start injecting syringefuls of industrial-grade ammonia . . . that's what we were using at the time . . . into all these feebs and crips and spastics just to save the cost of the daily oatmeal, that's *very* bad press.'"

Mast suddenly glared at Gritch—as though she, by merely being present, epitomized the American way of life: "The handicapped of this asshole country should just shut up for once, they don't know how lucky they have it. Back in the good old days there was no talk of wheelchair ramps and crip toilets and that crap. Germany had *important* things to do. Instead you got 200 cc's of ammonia straight into a ventricle." He snapped his fingers: "Five seconds, massive trauma and convulsion, it's over, your miserable crip never knew what in hell hit him. The ultimate cure—we made their *day!*"

"AND THAT'S WHEN you decided to bow out? Escape?" Mordecai said.

"Afraid it was an idea that took root slowly," Mast told him, sounding tired. "I knew we'd lost on the day *Barbarossa*—the invasion of Russia—was announced over the radio, by Goebbels himself. The tiny man spoke surpassingly well, as he always did ... 'On this day all forces of the Third Reich have been mobilized ...' Germany had never been able to hold two fronts. We knew of Napoleon at the gates of Moscow, and that's how it worked out again. Hitler, sure of victory. *Götterdämmerung* orders and no winter clothing for the Wehrmacht. It went to seventy below in places.

"The Ivans chipped away at us. Ah, they were cruel. They had a right to be. Hadn't we been cruel to them? I heard a story once. Never found out if it was true. Something like sixteen thousand Wehrmacht POWs lined up in a column of fours, three kilometers long, with only a few Russkies to guard 'em. A hundred-kilometer trek to the nearest POW camp.

"A blizzard struck. Five days of subzero snow. Fewer than two thousand made it. Ivan never fired a shot. A line of men, three kilometers long, singing, so I was told, German songs, until they dropped, one by one.

"The wild dogs ate well along that wintry route. Choice meat for some peasants too, since there was no food anywhere. Just those vast snowy plains. And that serpentine line of figures, black specks against a backdrop of desolation and overcast gray skies, trudging across the tundra. Hunched, shivering. Singing. And then, gradually, the singing stopped."

MAST PAUSED TO light a fresh Gauloise.

Across the street, Sy Abarbanel relaxed too, shook his head, yes, Heislinger was impressive all right. The team chief's respect for Gerber had increased. Actually to sit in the same room with such a man. Abarbanel himself had been shaken by what he'd heard.

He was at a loss about the woman. She'd lashed out at Heislinger but that meant nothing. No ordinary student would have such a person in her home. Suddenly he leaned forward. The old man was speaking again:

"Yes, I decided to get out. Gritch, here, once said that my escape was a legal defense. My personal refutation of the Nazi mentality. However, it could just as easily be argued that because I didn't stay on and do what I could to lessen the senseless slaughter I was all the more guilty. You see, Gerber, it's never clear-cut. The extermination centers were lazar houses but, don't forget, in some areas of Auschwitz there were trees planted along the blocks of barracks,

246

and there were lawns, and a library, and at times movies were shown.

"Of course the *kapos* did the dirty work. After the war the story was broadcast that they were made up of the worst criminal elements in the camps, but this is not true. The men were mostly Jews. Take my word for it. No, in too many ways the descendants of Jacob, David, and Abraham were as guilty as their SS warders."

"What I'm hearing is a cruel and amoral man," Mordecai said forcefully.

"'*Amoral*' is a stupid word. It means everything and nothing. Yes, I was involved in the deaths of many. Among those faceless hordes there may have been a Goethe, a Pasteur, a Schiller, an Einstein.

"But at the same time there may have been another Stalin, another Hitler. By being a participant I may have done mankind a far greater service than it deserves.

"Just as, in the long run, my years of work as Carl Mast may produce disaster. I've saved the lives of millions. That's true. But who knows if among those multitudes there is a latter-day Caligula? One who will this time unlease a nuclear firecracker that will make *my* little Holocaust a two-finger exercise?

"Think, Gerber-boy. World War II took out thirty-five million. Today we can do it to billions. We can denude the planet of life. That's amorality!"

"None of this is germane to your situation. You're hedging!"

"Fool! I'm an autonomous man! Your problem, Mordecai, is that you fall prey to Manichaenism, dichotomizing Good and Evil. Ridiculous. You would make of me a monster or a savior." Mast peered owlishly at the agent. "In your neatly organized world you'd like to reward good, punish evil. How? A youngster in eighteenth-century England who stole a loaf of bread was hanged. A common occurrence. Today the same youthful thief receives job counseling. Which century was more just? Think! At first glance the twentieth century gets the vote. After all, we are more *civilized*, more sophisticated, yes? But this is the era that gave us the extermination camps, the Gulag, millions starving, the oceans already savaged beyond repair, acid rain, mass psychosis in every city, madness everywhere.

"Gerber, you don't understand, it's all over!

"Mankind's long journey. Aborted. Short-circuited. Christ, man, we're on the verge of the ultimate suicide. Lemming genocide, upon ourselves."

The old man seemed to experience an epiphany of his own choosing, his hands weaving in the air. "I got a medal. Is that good? No. I killed people. Is that bad? Who knows? Gerber, can't you understand? I'm neither a moralist nor am I amoral. I am an observer! I merely *survived.*

"You may say, like that Arendt woman, that because of my particular offenses I am the ultimate pariah, abhorrent. She said of Eichmann, ditto yours truly, that he was no longer fit to walk about on this earth or to share it with his fellow men. My own view is that I have as much right as anyone else to pollute the atmosphere with my breathing, although I must admit that an Israeli court might adjudicate a harsher opinion.

"Yes, your trouble is that you want to reward good and punish evil. But how does one do that? How do you punish someone like me? I have twenty-five of my original teeth left. Will pulling them compensate for the millions that were extracted by the camps' workgangs? All you can really say is that the death of so many innocent people was a waste. I detest waste. There is no such thing as justice. It's a mercurial idea that changes from year to year, century to century, and at base we are no better off today than we were when we hung starving children. Christ, Gerber, if this is how the race doth progress, who knows what tomorrow will bring?"

"GRITCH, YOU MUST tell me where you stand in this matter," Mordecai said.

The two of them were sitting on the couch in the living room. He seemed edgy now that they were alone. Gritch was studiedly calm.

A half hour earlier Mast had suddenly risen and, as though bored by his own morbid recollections, announced that he had business downtown. Mordecai had immediately objected: "But, Doctor. You can't go out. Besides, I thought . . . this lunch—"

"You and the princess snack," Mast interrupted. "Save me a plate."

She saw the indecision in Mordecai's eyes. Then he gave a bored shrug. "As you wish."

With that she divined his position. He was here in the apartment. The moment Mast stepped outside, agents would be dispatched to trail him. Mordecai meanwhile would be free to work on the "Nadelmann female." She wondered: Is that how they speak of me? The idea of being alone with him was appealing, but it angered her to think that he, or they, regarded her as a tool.

In response to Mordecai's "As you wish," Mast, who had already gotten his topcoat and hat, smiled. "The well-bred guest never argues with his host, eh? You're okay, boy. Come again. Tomorrow if you like. Next time I promise not to be so inconsiderate. Afraid I monopolized the conversation. A common failing with someone my age."

"I was interested in what you had to say," Mordecai remarked. "I'll just bet you were." To Gritch: "Take care of him. Don't let him sell you a lot of hot air."

"I really don't think you ought to go out," she said. He made a deprecatory gesture. "Wait," she said, and went to the closet. "You forgot your muffler." She arranged it about his neck and tucked the ends into his coat. "Do you have cigarettes? Here are the keys. The brass one's for the front."

He took them and then, quite spontaneously, or so it seemed to her, she kissed him briefly on the left cheek.

She was startled by her action. Then she realized what had prompted it: this would be the first time he'd left the apartment without her. Still surprised, she heard herself say, "Be careful. If you can't make it back by six, telephone." Mast nodded, shook hands with Gerber, and left.

She thought: Men! Mast was such a mixture. Deliberately, he hurt her twenty times a day. It was obvious that he intended using her in any way he could—just like this Mordecai, who was so cool, so smart. In his conceit Mast cared for no one save himself.

If he was a mélange it was because her emotions about him were ambivalent. He infuriated her, but at the same time she was powerfully drawn to him.

Now, for the first time, she understood why.

Around him she could be herself. No need for subterfuge or false facade. From the moment she'd let him into the apartment her two separate personas had merged and become one.

Mast was not just another client to be wheedled or flattered. Yes, he paid her but it wasn't the same. She'd abandoned the pose of the professional date with him . . . the pretty smile, the coquetry, the eternal access to matters sexual.

Instead she could be vituperative or sulky in accordance with her mood. He, rather amazingly, enjoyed her cranky behavior. The angrier she got, the more he grinned.

With him, the little, bespectacled college bookworm let down her hair and unleashed a cascade of blistering remarks that no one who had seen her in a seminar would have imagined she was capable of.

He knew both sides of her. Was neither shocked by the whore nor bored by the academician.

As a matter of fact he knew her better than anyone. In a few short weeks. And he liked what he'd found in her.

He liked *her*. She knew he did, and not merely because he said so. How perfectly lovely, she thought: To be liked for one's self.

250

A whore with a brilliant mind. A true woman.
Contemporary in every way.

SHE SAID TO Mordecai, "I wish I'd never gotten involved. Really."
"Do you know where he's going?"
"CBS, I think."
"That's stupid of him." Mordecai settled back. "What about this research you're doing?"
"A book," Gritch said.
"He'll never live to see it finished."
She looked at him. "His health?"
"Yes."
"That sick?"
"His doctors are amazed he's still on his feet."
"So. It's that bad." She frowned. "How long?"
"They say any time."
"I can't have him dying here. This place—it's not large." She gestured vaguely, her expression distant, troubled. "Would you like to see the rest of it? At night I make up a bed for him here on the couch."
They toured the kitchen, the bathroom, the bedroom. Mordecai mused aloud, the better to implant the apartment's layout in his mind, and on Heller's Ampex too: "Small, but comfortable. Double bed. Lots of books. You *are* the student. Ah, how nice, two windows facing on the rear, and a door." He unlatched the latter, swinging it open to a blast of frigid air. "The garden must be pleasant in summer." The wrought-iron outer door was secured by a heavy chain and padlock. "Very wise. Burglars. A young woman living alone. Good that you have that grillwork on the windows, too. One can't be too careful."
He shut the inner door and locked its deadbolts. They returned to the living room and sat on the couch again. She lit a cigarette, poured wine for both of them, kicked off her pumps, and tucked her feet under her, smoothing the tweed skirt over her knees, moved so that she was sideways on the couch with not much distance separating them, and said, "You're sure he's Heislinger?"
"There's no doubt," Mordecai said, tasting his wine and looking at her. "What he was describing before. No one could make up something like that off the top of his head."
"I know," she said. "Still, I sometimes wonder. The other—Mast—had such a fine career. Then, to throw it away—" she snapped a forefinger against the base of her thumb, "—and now—

he's dying. He'll have to go. I couldn't endure something like that, though I'm sorry for him."

"I'm not," he said, drinking again. "There are limits to compassion. When we tried Eichmann no one felt pity. Jews came from all over the world to look at this man. They said it was like seeing the Devil himself in the courtroom, locked inside a glass cage. The cage was to protect him. Otherwise the people would have torn him to bits. No. I have no pity for Heislinger."

"He fascinates me."

"He's evil. You must get away from him immediately." Mordecai considered this. "Yes, now that I've heard him talk . . . Gritch, he exercises an influence over you. He's cunning. And intelligent."

"I want to know why he did it."

"Did what? The horrors?"

"No. Oslo."

"We want to know too. You could help us. Will you?"

So now at last it came out.

She gave him a tiny smile. "Jews sticking together?"

"Yes, if you want to put it that way. You're close to him. He may reveal things to you he'd never tell us. Even under interrogation. He likes to impress you, Gritch." He paused. "In turn we could help you."

"In what way?"

"Protection. Money. Both."

"I'll think about it," she said. "I do feel sorry for him, though. And you're right—I'm the only one who's close to him. That's sad. We don't even know each other. Not really. To be that old, and alone. No fun."

"No fun for those who rode the death trains," Mordecai pointed out. "He brought it on himself."

"Don't all of us do precisely the same?"

"You miss my point. All of us aren't mass murderers." In the same breath he switched subjects. "How much money does he give you?"

She shrugged. "I told you. Expenses."

"Has he promised more?"

"It was left vague. I'm not doing it for money."

Mordecai weighed this and then said, "In intelligence work, you know, the rule of thumb is to say nothing. And if you do have to speak, say as little as possible. But if you must talk, be careful about lying. It's always the lies."

"Are you saying I'm a liar?"

"I merely asked how much money was involved."

"I really wouldn't mind doing a book on him. There'd be money in that."

"Aren't you frightened?"

"Very." She looked at him. "Not now, though."

"Good. Sooner or later in my work, the time comes when you must take someone on faith. I'm glad you're not frightened of me."

"You have a job to do. The Holocaust. We weren't even born."

"That's no excuse."

"How could such cruelty exist? Not just Hitler. Carl talks of Stalin. Tens of millions down the drain. We can't visualize it."

"Heislinger must account for his actions."

"But how? What's the *point?*"

"He can't escape. He'll stand before the world, and if he can't stand he'll kneel."

"You're going to try him?"

"Who knows? He may not survive the trip to Israel."

"He's tough."

Mordecai shrugged. "The case will still be resolved."

"In what way?" She gave him a cold look. "What do you mean? Are you saying what I think you're saying?"

Mordecai smiled. "Nonsense. What sort of people d'you think we are?" She thought his smile was sweet—pleasanter than his serious, stern side. "It'll be resolved, that's all, properly, legally, expeditiously. Take my word."

She returned the smile with one more charming. "So, we have to trust each other? All right. Let me ask you something?"

"Anything you like."

"Were you telling the truth when you said this place isn't wired?"

"Of course," he said. "Gritch, there's no real point in it. Last night when I showed up . . . that was our way of coming out into the open with him. To place a microphone now . . . why bother?"

"You could be lying."

"Yes."

"I simply take your word?"

"I'm afraid you'll have to," Mordecai replied. "My boss may order a tap. Personally, I'm against it. The possibility of cooperation, Gritch. Having you here is far more important."

"Like having an Israeli living with him?"

"I wouldn't go that far."

"I didn't ask you to," she said smiling again.

They talked on, lunch forgotten. More wine was uncorked, their overall mood eased. In the bottom drawer of the bureau in the bedroom there was a lid of grass, and now she dearly wished for a

253

joint, just one long drag, that would ease her mood, a blessing, yes, but another side of her said that this was not the time for recreation; better to keep her wits sharp. Even so, various emotions tugged at her; despite her unease she felt deliciously feminine: how nice.

SHE WANTED TO reach out and touch his hair. Behind the ear. Where it curled so. At play in the curls of the Lord.

Her own mood was divided. One part on guard, the other giving and receptive. The wine tasted good. Gritch experienced the meaning of the phrase, "she desired him." It could happen so swiftly. The two of them. Alone here in the apartment. And what a long time it had been. Between her thighs she felt warm. A prelude, she knew, to an intolerable ache.

Was it possible, she wondered vaguely, that Mast had "opened" her mind in certain other ways? Her feelings were so jumbled. Or perhaps it was the bizarreness of the past weeks. She seemed different. Moving closer, she said, "Tell me about yourself."

"What's to tell?"

"Who are you?"

"No one important."

"An exciting life?"

"I wouldn't say that."

"Rewarding?"

"At times."

"What turns you on?"

"I like photography," Mordecai said.

"Ah. A man of talent. Are you good?"

"Fair, I suppose. Yes. Competent. I've won prizes. It's something one has to plug away at, you see."

"I'm sure you do."

"In Tel Aviv I'm in a course for advanced professionals."

"Your work must be good."

"It's getting better all the time."

"I'd love to see a sample. Do you have lots of equipment?"

He smiled. "You know what they say about a hobby. Unless it takes half your salary, it's not really satisfying."

"I wouldn't say that," Gritch said, sipping her wine. Her free hand was on the lapel of his jacket. "I wish we'd met under other circumstances." She was at last able to touch those black curling locks. Behind the ear. His color came up slightly. She said, "I can't tell you how wonderful it is to just sit here like this." Gently she touched one of his hands. "So large. But graceful. A pianist should have such fingers."

254

With that she moved closer to give him the benefit of her perfumed fragrance, the essence of her femaleness. Visually she was splendid. The pale complexion seemingly whiter than cream, heightened by that wonderful jet black hair. Her throat and the V of the cleft revealed by the silk blouse's décolletage, white too. Youthful smooth skin. The moist coral-glossed lips, the green eyes and the iridescent multicolored eye makeup. She felt so womanly, utterly willing. Gentle, pliant, ready to be led and taught, the blessed naturalness of it, this commingling of man and woman, each in his or her way caught up with a sigh and a gasp that renews life, and, damn it, was he just going to sit there forever?

He too was shaken, she sensed it. Her parted lips were mere inches from his left ear behind which her forefinger and thumb teased and twiddled a curl. In a whisper: "Do you ever dream? About your ideal woman?"

"That's a bit hard to say," Mordecai said, crossing his legs. "Shouldn't we have lunch?"

"Lunch? You're hungry?" She paused. "I've got it in the oven. It'll stay warm."

He turned as if to address her and then, as if changing his mind, kissed her, gently, on the lips. Her own were parted, slightly sticky with lip gloss and wine, and her tongue, a soft spear, went on an exploration job all its own, darting under the mustache. That mouth of his! She felt dying and dizzy all at once. Her mood urgent yet reserved. The insidiousness of foreplay. It was both heaven and hell. She forced herself to stop; then her lips moved to his ear, the closest one, that is the left. Such a lovely ear, she thought, nurbling the lobe.

"I like you very much," Mordecai murmured, taking a breath.

"Really? Oh, I like you too."

"You are," he began, and then lost it, ending lamely, "—beautiful. I have never. Really." They kissed again, and he added, "Will he be gone all afternoon?"

"What would you like to do?"

He kissed her again. Gritch shut her eyes, experiencing that incredible wilting of strength and resolve, actually went limp as she lay there, half sprawled against him, the tweed skirt hiked above her opened knees. Her lips nuzzled under his chin, and then she returned to his mouth, tasting, "Try . . . thish. Umn . . . yeth . . . nithe," and his hand at the small of her back, pressing her closer, was warm through the thin silk. Again that sensation of vertigo, of falling; his skin, where he'd shaved, smelled and tasted of sweat and after-shave, and by then she was crouchsprawled across his lap, the skirt carelessly higher now but still constricting the freedom of

movement. She wanted to tear off that frustrating, binding garment, to shuck off everything separating skin from skin. Her hips
moved seemingly of their own volition, and she babbled, "I feel like
I'm dying. Mordecai, please." The door leading to the bedroom was
open. In there: a world of privacy.

His hands were touching her body now, and then he kissed her
again and whispered into her ear, "Let me go to the bathroom first."

She shook her head impatiently, urgently. "There's no need. It's
perfectly safe."

"You don't understand," he whispered back, urgent now too. "I
have to wash my *hands*." With that he left her and crutchhobbled
away.

ROUND-EYED WITH DELIGHT Abarbanel stared over the top of the
Ampex at Heller. "D'you hear what I'm hearing?"

The electronics man nodded, smiling too. Both men canted their
earphones forward a bit so they could talk to each other and listen at
the same time. The needles on the signal-input and modulation
meters danced or jumped with what was going on in the Nadelmann
woman's apartment: each spoken word, the clink of goblets being
placed on a table, a fainter rustle, as of fabric rubbing against fabric,
a creaking as a chair was vacated. Abarbanel leaned forward,
frowning. "I wish they'd say something."

"You expect them to talk?" Heller asked happily. "What the hell
good is it if you're talking all the time?"

"That Gerber," the team chief mused. "As smooth as they come.
Five minutes and he'll have her on her back."

"I'd say he has a certain style," Heller agreed.

"He'll do the water trick next. Want to bet? Five bucks."

"He may."

"May, my eye. That's what he meant when he said he had to
wash his hands."

CLAD IN A half-slip that was mostly filigreed lace, and a filmy Gucci
bra, she had just drawn the bedroom drapes and was turning down
the coverlet and sheet when she looked up to see him in the doorway.

He was watching her with what struck Gritch as the oddest
expression, almost one of scientific detachment. As if he were in
sóme way standing back from this moment, apart not only from her
but from himself, as though, somehow, he were a spectator coolly
observing two strangers going about the preliminaries to love-
making.

Whatever shyness she had observed earlier was gone, but the

256

passion she had felt in him not five minutes ago had vanished too, and she thought: We'll have to begin over. That's all right. There's time.

She started to go to him but he came to her instead, put his arms about her, kissed her—yes, the shyness had gone—and stared down into her eyes. She was about to speak but he frowned, shook his head, whispered, "Shhh. Be quiet. I must tell you something."

She waited.

"Earlier," he began softly, "when we talked, you were suspicious of me. That's understandable. But I meant it when I said it's also necessary in this business to trust someone. I'll show you. But don't speak." Smiling, he took her by the hand.

Mystified she allowed him to lead her out of the bedroom. Through the living room toward the bathroom. The door to that inner sanctum was ajar. She heard the sound of running water.

Had he left a faucet turned on? Or was it the gismo in the toilet that sometimes got stuck? Twice the super had been in to look at it, each time with a promise to have it fixed.

Mordecai silently swung open the door for her to see. It was the tub, the cold-water tap turned half on. And near it, by the soap dish was something. A transmitter, rather like a flat metal cigarette case, and the wire leading to the button mike. She had never actually seen such a device but one glance told her exactly what it was.

With that he shut the door softly and led her back to the bedroom. The door to that room was quietly shut too, and then, the appropriate and necessary privacy at hand at last, Mordecai, smiling—the complete master of the situation—turned toward her and began loosening his tie. "We're safe in here," he said, sitting and slipping off his shoes. "That model can pick up a whisper twenty feet away, but all they'll be taping is Niagara Falls." Off came shirt and T-shirt.

"You were lying! When he asked you—"

"I invited him to search me," Mordecai pointed out. She saw that though slender he had a splendidly developed chest and shoulders, with a dense shag of black hair across the breasts; trousers vanished; he stood before her in maroon bikini shorts that seemed insufficient to the task of containing him; the flat muscular stomach was bisected by a strong line of dark hair. "Everything he says is evidence, Gritch," he said, coming to her and enfolding her in his arms; she felt him swelling against her. "But what happens between us is not," he added, tilting her chin up and kissing her with infinite gentleness; it was starting again. "You see, I've got certain quirks. Who doesn't? And one of them is that I like privacy.

Do you know, you're the most beautiful girl I've ever seen in my life? Of course they're onto what's happening—they know it already— that I removed the transmitter. Let them. That's all right. They trust me, Gritch. They have to. After all, I've given them seven years of my life." Leisurely, almost in slow motion, he helped her shed bra and slip; his touching hands were wonderful, and she gave in to them as they arranged her on the bed; she felt his lips as they began kissing her body. "I hadn't any idea this would happen," he said as they found her breasts. "That's why I was hesitant before. Do you see what I mean? About removing the transmitter? It's not just a statement to you, but to them too. It tells them, 'Gerber, yes, he's a devoted son of Israel, but he's not a machine, no, there are moments when his own life is his business.' They'll understand. I'll make them understand. After all, I'm not a slave. I've rights too."

"DIDN'T I TELL you? The old water trick!" Abarbanel grinned.

"How'd you know?"

"I was with him on assignment in Alexandria. He pulled the same stunt," Abarbanel said. "Well—" he sighed and removed the earphones "—we may as well relax for a while. He'll be busy inspiring confidence in the subject. About eight inches' worth, I'd guess. That Mordecai. Something else, isn't he?"

"Why didn't he just turn the transmitter off?"

"How would the woman know if it really was off?" the team chief said. "No, it's much better this way. It's like having a pair of sharp ears trapped in the bathroom. Helpless. While the two of 'em go at it in the bedroom. In secret, y'know? That's what Gerber's laid on her—everybody's got a right to a little privacy once in a while. It works, Heller. In the mood he's got her in, that's what she wants to believe."

RECEPTION DID NOT begin again until shortly after six that evening and then it was badly muffled, as though the sender had perhaps carelessly dropped transmitter and mike into a jacket pocket. A few distinguishable sounds came through that led Heller and Abarbanel to conclude that the pair across the street might be having a leisurely snack: the clink and rattle of glass or bottle, the clatter of dishware, a badly muffled but casual-sounding banter, followed, here and there, by lengthy silences, perhaps appropriate for chewing.

Eventually there were different noises, a drawn-out exchange of undecipherable remarks, whispers, murmurs—a farewell?—followed by the sounds of doors or closets opening and shutting.

Another long silence—by Abarbanel's watch it lasted four minutes—could a kiss go on that long? Then, another door.

Seconds later the man stationed at the bay window called out, "There he is. I think that's him."

It was hard to tell because of the darkness, and it had begun snowing again, but yes. Abarbanel, focusing binoculars, identified Mordecai as he passed beneath the glare of a street light. He was strolling along at an easy pace and so far had made no attempt to cross to the watchers' side of 101st.

"Is something wrong with him?" the lookout asked. "Shall I go down and get him?"

"No," Abarbanel said, squinting through the eyepieces. "I think he'll find his way home."

"What's he doing?" The figure across the street was acting oddly. "Is he drunk?"

"I'm not sure," Abarbanel said, lowering the binoculars, "but I think he's either skipping or playing hopscotch."

# part five

When lovely woman stoops to folly,
And finds too late that men betray,
What charm can soothe her melancholy?
What art can wash her guilt away?
                                        —Goldsmith

Creep into thy narrow bed!
Creep, and let no more be said.
Vain thy onset, all stands fast—
Thou thyself must break at last.
                                        —Matthew Arnold

"GRITCHKELA? HELLO, I'M back," Mast brayed after much fumbling with the locks on the front door. "So? How was?"

Why did he mock her so?

"Hey," she said, "in case nobody's told you, some people can't imitate a Jewish dialect. Among which are Eskimos and Gentiles, namely asshole you."

She was ensconced on the long couch, seated prettily cross-legged, feet tucked under yoga style, in white cotton pj's, not at all glamorous except to the beholder's eye, a fantastic feminine pose, operating with surgical care on long pointed fingernails with a collection of files, clippers, orange sticks and chamois buffers.

Her face had been scrubbed, all traces of what Mast liked to call "whore's makeup" removed. She could have passed for a contented teenager. Her expression was wonderfully pensive, inward-turned. On the cocktail table in front of her, a cup of hot chocolate.

Mast regarded. Then hung up his coat, hat, and muffler. Went to the kitchen. Poured a glass of wine. Came back into the living room. Sat down in an armchair. Untied his shoelaces, kicked oxfords off. Stretched his legs, wiggling all ten toes in dampened socks. "Nice boy, Gerber. I'm so happy for you. Good hump?"

"Fuck off," Gritch muttered, concentrating on a middle-finger dagger. "I *loathe* that Cheshire-cat grin. You jump to conclusions."

"One jumps or tortoises, all that matters is that the conclusion is correct," Mast said, tasting wine. "An enjoyable afternoon?"

"It was okay, I guess."

"Behind his creepiness he has an aura of what—male vigor?" Mast said. "I suspect you noticed it too. Odd how females pick up on something like that. Sixth sense, I suppose."

"You and your dirty mind. Always sex."

"Yes."

"Why?"

Mast Cheshired at her. "Because it always is. Has he finesse? Expertise? Style, dear girl, is everything. Regardless of whether one tootles a fife or wallops the tympani, the virtuoso approach separates the crass from the sublime. Now then. How much did you tell him about me, about us?"

"Are you nuts?" She tasted her chocolate. "I'm an admiring gullible student-acolyte. He thinks you sleep on this couch. If you don't stop acting like an utter shit, you will."

Mast reflected, then glanced around. "From the way you talk, you believe the place isn't wired? Not that I give a damn. Let every Yid in Manhattan tune in."

"No, I think we're okay—for now anyway," she said. "But I'd be careful of what you say in front of him. He's wearing a transmitter of some kind, and a microphone dingus. He showed it to me."

"No! You cultivated his acquaintance—in depth—with an audience?" Mast asked. "Gritch, you're incredible."

"He took it off and left it in the bathroom," she said matter of factly. "He's a touch shy."

"And I assume that later on you confirmed that he had nothing else concealed on his person? No weapon?"

"Nothing of a deadly nature."

"Umn. You do have a way of disarming a fellow."

"Jealous?"

"Yes."

"You have no right. Nobody owns me."

"Jealous is jealous." He shrugged. "I never said I was perfect."

"You set the whole thing up."

"I was only thinking of your happiness."

"Balls." Taking up a buffer she began on a ring finger. "I've been thinking. Odd how I can think when *you're* not around. What about that letter of entry? You promised. What about my book?"

"You've already enough material to write anything you want about me," he said. "And you'll get the letter. For now I won't sign it, of course."

"What the hell good is it to me unsigned?"

"What the hell good is it to me if I sign it and hand it over?" Mast countered. "You could dash out for a perm and in ten hours be in Europe, two hundred thou richer. Come on. I'm playing straight with you."

"If I gave you a ruler you'd draw a French curve. Straight!"

"What else happened?"

"He's observant." She held out her left hand, palm outward, admiring. "I'll bet he memorized fifty titles in those stacks of books. I gave him the impression that you and I are busy at other things besides perverted saturnalias. He thinks a decent girl like me shouldn't be shacked up with the fucking filthy likes of you. Alone, he calls you Heislinger, never Mast. He'd like me to boot your rotten ass out into the street. Then he and his pals could take over."

"Men are so protective about women, aren't they?" Mast sneered. "The way they hover about a vagina, as though it were something fragile. You could fling anvils and granite boulders into such fragility."

She ignored this. "He knows you're dying."

"In the pink, Gritch."

"Bullshit. For Christ's sake, d'you think I'm blind? D'you know how heavily you lean on me when I help you out of bed in the morning? You can hardly walk! You try to wash the blood out of the bowl but, God, you're bleeding to death! And your complexion. Your color's all off."

"Next trip to that drugstore, remind me to have you get a good sphygmomanometer," Mast said. "Academic curiosity, mostly. Blood pressure can tell you a good deal about what the body's up to."

"At night you groan."

"Probably a result of your wretched cooking."

"You're existing on morphine, booze, and cigarettes," she argued. "Why don't you take better care of yourself? I put a plate in the oven on Warm. Chicken, *latkes,* zucchini, other stuff. I don't know why I worry about you. What the hell did you do all afternoon? CBS couldn't have taken that long."

"CBS was a waste," Mast said. "I got to shake hands with a someone named Monson. We could have used his sort in the SS. I was there for less than an hour. We're to meet tomorrow morning. To kick it around, as he said."

"Good. I've asked Mordecai for brunch."

"I also went to my bank to get more money," Mast continued. "Then I walked over to the Algonquin and had several martinis. A highly civilized place in which to relax and reflect. Thirty years ago, for some reason, they charged ninety-three cents for a Martini. A small one, though it packed punch. Monson is a Fascistic mentality.

Luckily he's involved with a commercial endeavor, not government. Then I cabbed home. I didn't like that. The cabbie, a *schwartzer,* kept ogling me in the rearview mirror. Tried to strike up a conversation. What a droll idea! That some colored ignoramus and I should have anything in common to discuss."

"You think he recognized you?"

"I doubt it."

"My God, I hope you had him drop you up on Broadway, not outside."

"What are you talking?" Mast snapped. "I'm wet, I'm cold, my feet are like icicles, you have a hotsy-totsy time with that Tel Aviv cunthound, and you want me to *walk?* You're not getting a crush on him, are you?"

"Don't be ridiculous."

"Umn." He scowled at her. "Well, It's not surprising. Gerber in his naive way is probably a good man. God protect us from good men! He wants to do 'right.' Be careful, girl. You may not have a thing for him, but he has one for you. Which you go to great lengths to encourage. Cunning bitch."

She gave him a cold look. "You're to say absolutely nothing to him about me. Understand? Or us."

Mast smiled. Raised a forefinger to pursed lips. "Word of honor. May I be struck. Relegated to limbo. Mums."

"I've gone through hell having you here."

"Wouldn't have missed it for anything," Mast said. "Great fun. For me at least." He looked at her with real fondness. "Hope it hasn't been too tedious for you, *Liebchen.*"

"Dirty bastard."

SUDDENLY HE HAD that change of mood. It came like a flash. Seemed old, tired, used up. An old man with wet feet who'd been out too long on a winter's day. Bitter, querulous, resigned. Yet oddly not resigned.

Once again he touched her emotions. If he'd snarled and cursed, it would have been easier, but his voice was low, introspective, and in a strange way it wooed her as Gerber's never would.

"I wish I'd met you forty years ago," he said. "My mind is too cluttered by now. Too much of the detritus is foul. I'll tell you something. You're no innocent. But to me, comparatively, you are. There's much about you that's attractive. I'm speaking beyond the you-use-me, I-use-you of it. Yes, I treat you atrociously. I ask forgiveness for my self-centeredness. Behind it there is genuine affection. Believe that."

266

Cigarette held elegantly in one hand—he *did* have an odd way of holding a burning cigarette, as though it were a baton—his wine glass in the other, Mast continued: "You've become far more important to me than you realize." He stared at her, eyes glittering from their deep sockets. "Too late for me. When all's said and done, what does a man crave most? Fame, success? The laurel wreath? To be an elitist, like Plato's philosopher king? No. To hell with that. What a man requires is a woman at his side. The male is incomplete, only partial, without the female. Yes, I'd have been a better man if I'd known someone like you way back when. The truth is, you could have taught me a great deal. And I could have taught you. Each could have learned from the other while enjoying happiness."

Mast chuckled. "How ironic. At his age, Gerber can't comprehend a woman. At mine I do, but the knowledge is wasted. In many ways you're magnificent. I bow to you. Always give respect where it's due." He shook his head unhappily. "I have dire forebodings about this CBS business. I think it will come to nothing."

Suddenly he shot her a rueful smile. "I ought to have my head examined. Such a dummy! That afternoon I telephoned, I should've said, 'Pack a bag, Gritchkela, we're going on vacation!' The two of us could be screwing around on the beach down in Puerta Vallarta right now, drinking Marguaritas and getting a tan instead of freezing our asses off in this stupid town. Someplace, anyplace, where it's warm and we could dunk our toes in the ocean without getting frostbite. Yes, a month in the sun. It'd make a new woman out of you. You'd look fantastic with a tan. You're too damned pale. That comes from being indoors all the time." Mast frowned. "Yes, a bona-fide Jewish princess. All brown and gold. You'd paralyze 'em in their tracks. I'd buy you bikinis like you never saw, the kind you roll up and store in a thimble. And white cocktail dresses. The finest silk sheaths, slit right up to the crest of the ilium, nothing but the best for my precious girl! Spiked heels, and that coloring, the tan, those green eyes, the hair, and maybe a single bougainvillea worn behind the ear. No stupid panty hose, just those incredible naked legs. '*Oy, oy, Herr Doktor! You sure got some cutsie-pie for a granddaughter!*' No Gerber either! Him and his *nudnik* spaniel eyes, like olives floating in warm milk, may all his wet dreams be dry. I *loathe* young love!"

But, like him, she knew it was too late. The cancer was progressing. It wasn't just the weight loss, which left him looking somehow smaller, shrunken, or that he seemed to have aged years in these weeks. There was something else.

An odor. Most apparent in the bathroom after he'd used it. There was a powerful overhead fan that vented toilet smells and steam from a bath into an airshaft. The old man let it run for minutes but still, afterward, the smell lingered. A most offensive odor, as of decaying flesh.

Mordecai had asked about it that afternoon.

"A mouse," she'd lied. "I think a mouse must have gotten into the walls somehow and died. It's happened before."

But it hadn't. The building was relatively free of vermin. And the traces of blood splashes under the toilet lid. Her period had been over for days.

"He's dying," Mordecai had told her. It took no genius to see that. The question was when?

For a moment sadness welled up in her. She had to blink away a stinging at the eyes. But she gave no other sign. Merely kept polishing with the chamois buffer. At the already perfect nail on her left little finger. As though a lifetime of patient effort was not nearly enough to italicize its shining spearlike beauty.

THAT NIGHT IN bed he warned, "Don't fall in love with him."

"You talk like a fool."

"An admirably adamantine attitude." She heard a low rumble of amusement. "But all that really tells me is that a woman has a right to change her mind. Brunch, you said?"

"Tenish. I took out steaks."

"A return engagement so soon?"

"It was his idea," she said. "He wants you to finish what you were talking about this afternoon. But you won't be here?"

"Monson said eleven. I think I'll make it a bit earlier."

"In a way I'd like to go along."

Mast rumbled again. "You can't have CBS and Mister Wonderful too."

"I bet they don't know what in hell to make of you."

"The cavalier approach, Gritch. Useful. Condescension and arrogance are the only way with certain types. Keep it in mind." In the dark he fumbled searchingly for her hand, found it, clutched for a while.

"How're you feeling?"

"Tired, my dear," he said. "Weary. CBS better shake its ass. There isn't much time. I'd go on camera tomorrow. They talk of format." He sighed. "Nothing's simple anymore. It's all format and target appeal and impact. By the way, I'll be leaving some Rx's for you to have refilled. Will you do that?"

"You used what I got last week? How many are you taking?"

"As many as I need, *Liebchen*."

268

THEY RESTED AMONG roiled sheets and blankets, naked, whispering in the nacreous light filtering in from draped windows. Somewhere out in the backyard a cat screeched.

Gritch, lazily propped on one elbow. An odalesque pose: that sweeping curve of hip and thigh, reminiscent of Rodin's Danäid, the buttocks moonily relaxed. In the dim light her eyes smoldered emerald-bright, alive with tenderness: soot black brows and thick furry lashes.

She inspected his body, tracing with the tip of an outstretched forefinger the route taken by her gaze, here, there, everywhere. He was so long-limbed and rangy, at the same time smooth and limber. Like those lovely boys she'd seen on Olympic swim teams, and where there was no hair his skin was as white as a girl's.

She bent now to kiss each nipple in turn, feeling them harden as her wandering fingers searched and found a nether stirring. Her lips moved up, exploring, finding the warm and hairy nest between Adam's apple and chin: the pointed tongue paid homage. Then higher, to an ear, into which she whispered a mesmeric litany, the words repeated endlessly, huskily, so that there was no knowing who was more seduced by them, he or she:

"Lie still. Can you do that? For me? Is that possible? Try to relax. Yes. Like that. Every muscle. As though you were floating. Oh, that's wonderful. Close your eyes. Lie perfectly still."

Her own breathing betrayed her—the heart thumping, as though all of her had been exhausted by what she was urging him to attain: that relaxation, the abandonment of self. She murmured again, a recitation that was part instruction, part confession: "I want to give you pleasure. Let me do as I wish. I'll be gentle. You'll like it. I promise you will. There's no hurry. Yes, gently. I can't help it. Oh, yes. Hush. Don't speak. Don't even think."

She began moving over him, crouched on elbows and knees, not touching at all except for the contact of parted lips, moist tongue flickering, the labored exhalations of her breath a contact too. The whispering continued, "I want to kiss you. Gently. Oh please. Don't move now. Let me. I must. Do you like this? Hush. This way? Oh darling."

Hovering, she kissed shoulders, chest, arms, hands, sucking each fingertip in turn, back to the chest, and then lower, her breathing now ragged as she found the deep hollow of his navel, burying her face in it, moving at last to the hairy thighs, parting them, "Is this good? Or this, yes? You're trembling. I feel you. Yes, lie still. Let me. I want the secret things with you. A woman loves to worship. Is that unbearable? They can't help it, they need to."

Gliding smoothly, her lips moved to the glistening helmet. "How lovely you are. I want to. I'll die if you don't let me. I can't help myself. Like this? Oh darling."

She accepted him into her mouth then, her head moving slowly up and down, then stopping, holding perfectly still, waiting for him to tense so that he hardened momentarily, and now a groan escaped from her. He was close to losing control but she was closer and finally, with a gasp, she came up and mounted him, slowly lowering herself until she was filled. "Don't move. Try not to. Please. Let me." And she did, with infinitesimally small rocking movements, until it was too late, there was a tremendous rush inside her and she spasmed; moments later he did too, and she rode him as he thrashed. Presently they both came to their senses. She dismounted, bent to lick the last wetness. "You see?" she purred. "The secret things." It was the third time in slightly less than two hours. He seemed to need only minutes to recuperate.

Marvelous. Simply marvelous.

AT ABOUT THE same time, downtown, Carl Mast, angry, impassioned, was delivering his final pitch. Present: Fred Monson, Kyle Benedict, Mac Dobkin, and four other gentlemen from Programming and Legal, all seated in armchairs in Monson's office suite. Coffee, tea, snacks were available. Mast, somewhere en route, perhaps to bolster strength and courage, perhaps out of defiant cantankerousness, had picked up a bottle of Pernod, which he was drinking mixed with Perrier. The strong odor of anise hung in the air along with that of French tobacco.

When he had finished, Fred Monson leaned back in his chair, reflecting, making of his fingers a well-manicured arch. Finally he said, "A most interesting concept, Doctor. Let me try and get it in focus. Are you telling us that the reason you made that speech in Oslo was to lend added weight to a lecture you want to give on *childbearing?*"

"Precisely," Mast replied. Those in the room saw that he was not well. The complexion. The labored breathing, the trembling hands.

Kyle Benedict smiled. "A former Nazi on camera, telling the world how to raise kids? Well, if you don't mind my saying so, that's a little like having a child molester lecture about sex education."

"A child molester might have an extremely useful point of view," Mast snapped.

"Chancy," Benedict cautioned. "It might fly. Then again we could be laughed off the air."

"It'll be one of the most significant programs ever broadcast," Mast argued.

270

"Possibly," Benedict said. When Kyle Benedict said possibly, he usually meant no. "Even so, with all due respect, I'd have to point out that a show based on a war criminal's confessions has a certain valid currency your concept lacks. It's really difficult to put across an abstract theory to millions of viewers. They want palatability."

"It's not abstract, you moron, and it's got to be done," Mast said. "D'you think I got up on that podium and threw away my whole life's work in order to be *palatable*? Damn you, I want attention! Who in hell listens to Nobel winners anymore? Look at poor old Linus with his meanderings about ascorbic acid and world peace. Who hears him? Well, maybe a couple of health freaks and aging flower children, but that's about all."

"Let's keep things in perspective," Monson interrupted. "Doctor, I think what stopped me in your presentation was your remarking that most of what you'd like to say isn't even new. Fresh material is a must in TV."

"What're you talking? You organgrinders spiel the same tired bullshit day in and day out, year after year," Mast said. He stood up, the better to claim their attention, a frail old man, though the voice was still authoritative. "So okay. Back to square one. I'll put it in monosyllabics. You've *got* to understand."

He drank off his liqueur and began: "Everyone knows that Evil coexists with Good. My point is that to remove from man the capacity for evil is also to remove from him the capacity for good. Take away the possibility for doing both good and evil and we end up with automatons of the sort described in *1984* or in Koestler's *Darkness at Noon* ... Marxists set out to remove 'error'—which was their version of 'evil'—not only from public life but from the private minds of citizens. The citizen thinks what the party thinks because the party is always right. Ergo, thought and choice are removed from the individual.

"Without getting too deeply into existentialism, let me mention, Sartre wrote that freedom or liberty is the inalienable condition of being human, and the companion of that liberty is dread. Take liberty from the individual and that individual is no longer human. The power to think and choose is what specifically constitutes a human being, and that means a human being has both a capacity for good and a capacity for evil.

"Now! My own view is that progress starts all over again with each human being. Since the capacity for evil can't be eradicated from children if we want them to be human, the challenge is to foster in them the capacity to think and choose for themselves.

"The capacity to choose is like the human capacity for language. We have in us a sort of innate or genetic predisposition to language,

271

but children don't learn language unless they're exposed to it. In the same way, every individual born has an innate capacity for thinking and choosing, but this capacity has to be developed, like muscles, through use and exercise. If it remains undeveloped, the individual will, out of lethargy, do the easiest thing in all cases—he'll follow the leader, or will indulge in Pac-Man or punk rock.

"As an aside, Jews, by the way, are among the best teachers of children. There are many jokes about doting Jewish mommas and poppas, but the fact is, they are incredibly good at parenting.

"To continue. It's obvious to me that conflict can't be eradicated from the human condition. There's been a lot of thought given to why this should be, including theories about the dichotomy between the reptilian brain and the neocortex . . . one of the foremost intellectuals of this century has argued for worldwide chemical tranquilization of the entire race, to keep it from destroying itself. Not a bad idea!

"So what we're faced with is the question of what kind of conflict there will be. Armed conflict, whole populations of people set against one another, represents a capitulation to cheap or easy conflict. Any thinking human being recognizes that the enemy or 'competitor' is necessary—therefore, the competitor is accorded rights and respect, is not killed off. We're going back to Nietzsche here. What we're faced with is fostering in an individual the idea of a conflict in which he strives against himself to be the best and do the best he can, or against another individual, to see who can achieve the greatest advances in medicine, compose the finest music. Granted, a piano sonata is of no interest whatsoever to a starving Ethiopian, but it's the elitist populations that threaten the race's existence—they are the ones who must be reeducated! They have the surplus time, energy, material possessions. I want to address the haves, as opposed to the have-nots of the world. Let them be taught to indulge in conflict of a constructive, not a destructive, nature, gentlemen. A liking for this superior kind of conflict has to be, and can be fostered in the children who will be tomorrow's decision makers."

Kyle Benedict said, "Sounds to me like a mix of evangelical altruism and Mondale's plank for raising taxes. If I remember correctly, he bombed badly with that one. Setting the world right through self-sacrifice. You a Democrat by any chance, Doctor?"

"No, just an old Nazi."

"Well, sir, what you're talking about is a sermon," Benedict said. "It just won't do, I'm afraid. They'll label you a weirdo. Strictly gonzo-round-the-bend. CBS isn't in the business of revamping mankind. We leave that sort of pamphleteering to *Watchtower* messiahs and the Scientologists."

With that the old man lost his temper.

F-3.5, 1/100TH, PANATOMIC-X, ASA 200, window drapes open now to let in that natural light, soft diffuser-screened strobe bounced off the ceiling to fill in darker shadows, Mordecai excitedly clicking away with the Nikon, to which was mounted a versatile 50–135-mm lens. In the bathroom, same as yesterday, button mike and transmitter picking up the sound of gurgling water, but here in the bedroom, spread out on the bureau, were the contents of his camera bag.

Atop the rumpled bed Gritch posed prettily, clad only in her prized teardrop diamond pendant. Head-on, three-quarter, profile shots. She loved having her picture taken but had grave doubts about this. From the living room came the sound of Pablo Casals playing Bach's *Suites for Unaccompanied Cello*. Mordecai arranged her in a demure kneeling position, hands folded in her lap. She said, "I've always thought there was something creepy about guys who like to take pictures of nude women. You into bodypainting too?"

"No one'll see these except me."

"Why don't you come back to bed?"

But his artistic eye had been excited by her beauty. The Nikon's motor drive whirred, advancing frame after frame as he worked. "I'm not sure . . . won't know until these're developed . . . but I think you're one of those naturally photogenic types . . . from any angle. Impossible to take a bad picture of you. God, your face. What bone structure. Open the mouth just a bit, look off to the left . . . yes, that's it. I've never photographed anyone . . . Hollywood . . . ah, perfect!"

"You act like this is the first time you've seen me."

"Never saw you through a viewfinder before."

"You coming back to bed?"

"Let's shoot one more roll."

"We can't do that with you over there."

"I'll only be a minute."

"Not if I can help it."

"Think of something sexy."

"Gorgonzola," she mock-snarled, scowling.

Click, whir.

LATER THEY LAY in each other's arms and talked as lovers will, their expressions inward-turned, contemplative. For her a hiatus much to be desired. Mordecai had for a fact provided something she needed.

An escape, even if temporary, from fear and worry. And a reminder of a former more ordinary life-style. She thought: This is what normal people do. They make love. Try to be kind to each other. Share a little. If things had gone differently ... There'll never be anything for us. Fun to fantasize, though. If we'd met another time, another place. Dreamer. Could you have made a life with him? To hell with the Holocaust and all that. This matters more. A big dumb shutterbug.

She turned to kiss him but found that he was staring at her. "Gritch, I know a way out."

"Oh darling, please? Just for now? Let's not talk about Mast or Israel or any of it. I feel good about myself. About us."

"We must," he said. "There isn't much time. This is important. They want to know everything. No secrets, nothing concealed—that's how it goes. By not using the transmitter, I've put myself in danger too. When I report back, they'll want every detail."

"Wing it."

"Better if you and I were in agreement about certain things," he insisted. "Don't you understand? Gritch, I'm in between. I love Israel and I'd give my life for her, but—all right, I'll say it—I want you too."

She looked at him, wondering: Is he serious? Was it a line? He seemed dead earnest. But that signified nothing. Where did trust stop?

"If I can convince them you're in collusion with me," he said. "Gritch, you've got to make a gesture. Of coming over to our side. Your life depends on it. When this is over, you'll either be admired or despised. In this country and in Israel. You could be a heroine. It's possible. But you must make at least a token gesture. I'm thinking of my own future too." He looked at her. "Or, if you like, ours. We could come out of this clean. It can be done. Would you like to go back to Israel with me? A different life?"

"I can't," she said. "School—"

He frowned, shook his head emphatically. "How can you be so naive? That's over. No matter what happens, that whole part of your life is done. In Israel, a fresh start. With my testimony backing you, they'd set you on a pedestal. The brave Jewish girl who helped capture one of the last war criminals. You'd write your book."

"And what would you get out of it?"

"You," he said simply. He grinned. "Which means I might be able to take lots more pictures." Then he shrugged. "I'm confused too. I've been thinking. I'd like you to stay with me. Who knows? Perhaps I'm looking for a lever to break loose from this kind of life. I'm a

274

selfish man. Intelligence work does queer things to a person—the secrecy, the impossibility of trusting anyone, and there's danger too. Occasionally an agent will last for decades, but that requires a peculiar type of personality. Most of them crack, or just burn out— five, ten years. It happens. Maybe you're the lever I've needed. If a man has no reason to change his life, he won't. But if an alternative is offered . . ."

"I won't take sides," she said, shaking her head.

"I'm not asking you to. Let me handle it," Mordecai said. "Don't double-cross me if I submit evidence that's favorable to you. Just keep quiet. Don't you see? My testimony carries weight. If I say you've been an innocent bystander, well, they won't swallow it completely, but they won't reject it either. Forget Heislinger! The man's as good as dead. Forget me, if you like. Think of yourself. My people are serious. This isn't a game. Someone could be killed very easily. I'm trying to find a way out for both of us. But don't cross me. If I take a chance with you, it's my life too. Play straight. Will you do that?"

She frowned. "Suppose they were to give me some kind of truth serum?"

"If I handle it, it will never come to that," he said. "Don't you see what I'm saying? If I protect you, I'm coming over to *your* side. That's what they'd say, and they'd be right. An Israeli allying himself with a Nazi collaborator? My superior, you know, is convinced you're Heislinger's mistress." He gave her a sharp look. "Are you?"

"Why? You jealous?"

"Of *him*?" Mordecai smiled at her. "That's really funny!"

"Well, the answer is no," she said. "What a gross idea. At his age? Your superior's nuts."

"I may tell him you said that," Mordecai agreed. "He's a good example of what intelligence work can do to a man. Suspicious. All things are possible—you never fully believe, but you never fully disbelieve either."

"And if all this should work out?"

"Up ahead? I don't know. You may never want to set eyes on me again. Then, you might. I'm willing to leave it at that."

"But you'd like to have me with you?"

"I've already said so."

"Because we make great love?"

"Yes," he said simply. "We're awfully good together."

"With enough practice we might get even better," she said. "What a nice thought!"

"Am I good for you?"

"Mordecai, darling, if a woman climaxes three times with a man in one morning, he's got to be good for something."

THE TELEPHONE IN the living room rang. Both of them jumped. "Probably Carl," she said, getting up. "I'll lay odds he wants me to run out for some booze. Oh, *Christ*! His prescriptions! He wanted refills."

Mordecai lay there admiring her nakedness as she padded out. That ballet dancer's walk, slightly duckfooted. Those firm buttocks, and that adorable coccygeal cleft! She was indeed photogenic. From any angle.

But it was not Mast.

Constantine Phraxeteles, cheerful as always, said, "Gritch, my lovely, where in the name of all that's sacred and profane have you been *keep*ing yourself? Not a peep, not a sound out of you since I don't know when. Listen, honey, I've got this perfectly lovely gentleman from Somaliland, not one of your tacky *charges d'affaires,* but a person of real *con*sequence, the big man himself, sky blue cordon bleu right across the chest, loads of sophistication and charm, just got off the phone with him, Gritch, said he was absolutely bored to tears in this dreary old city, will this snow ever stop, he's definitely interested in grinding a little white hide tonight, not his exact words, of course, so I thought right away, give Gritch a jingle—"

"I'm busy."

"Gritch, one evening?" Constantine pleaded. "Is that so much? Not an overnighter, you can be home and tucked safely away in your little truckle bed before the witching hour strikes—"

"I'm busy. Don't call me, I'll call you."

She hung up the phone and stood there for a moment. Took one of her long mentholated cigarettes from the pack on the cocktail table, lit it, and puffed reflectively.

What had Mordecai been babbling about? In Israel they'd set her on a pedestal. A contemporary heroine. We're really awfully good together.

He came out of the bedroom, a sheet florally imprinted with Tahitian themes wrapped about his middle. "Who was it? Heislinger?"

"No." Her voice was glum. "Just someone I know."

"What did he want?"

"Nothing that can't wait," she said.

276

MAST RETURNED BEFORE two in the blackest of rages, ill, literally pale with anger from brooding during the cab ride uptown.

Straight off he stormed into Mordecai who, fully dressed except for tie and jacket, was enjoying his third steak sandwich.

Baleful, dangerous, Mast shouted, "Gerber, get the fuck out of here, scram, take a walk already, go away for a while with your big sheepy eyes, what the hell d'you think I'm running here, some kind of goddamned YMHA for every horny kike on the West Side?"

Mordecai, genuinely startled, whispered to Gritch that it might be best if he left, and did so, tie stuffed into the pocket of his hastily donned jacket, homburg on the back of his head, overcoat clasped in one hand, camera bag in the other. He did not take with him the remains of the sandwich. As he headed down the corridor toward the vestibule, Mast yelled after him from the open door of the apartment, "For somebody who *eats* so much you shouldn't be so eager to bite the hand that feeds you! And tell your crowd of shit-nosed Jew hoodlums to lay off me. Call me tomorrow, next week, next year, maybe I'll have some gossip for you. Until then, don't take any wooden knishes, smartass! We had plenty like you at Bergen-Belsen, WE TAUGHT 'EM SOME MANNERS, YOU BETTER BELIEVE IT!"

The old man slammed the door and flipped the deadbolts. In the kitchen he poured himself a stiff ouzo, stomped into the living room and sat down. "That ballbuster thinks he's so special," he fumed. "I despise smugness, especially in the young, who're rarely, if ever, justified in the fine opinion they have of themselves."

"What in hell's wrong with you?" Gritch asked. She had been listening wide-eyed to his Vesuvian tantrum.

"Nothing's wrong with *me*," he almost snarled. "It's colder than a witch's tit out there, now I know what's happening to the money I'm pouring into this household hand over fist—it costs me *bucks* to keep you and Abie-the-Adonis in style, I'm going broke, practically an outcast in my own home, while he rams it up you 'round the clock! What're you trying to do, make the *Guinness Book of Records*? I'm frozen to the marrow. I feel sick! Did you get my prescriptions?"

"I'll go now," she said.

He glared up at her for a moment and then practically exploded. "Good-for-nothing bitch! Fucking, is that all you can think about? A small errand I ask? A minor chore for an old man in pain! So what happens? Miss Hotsnatch can't be *bothered,* she's too busy gulping *schwanzes.* Got herself a real lover, he can't wait for me to turn my back so he can wave it under your nose! I know his type, turns his shitty drawers inside out on Saturday so's to get another week's wear outa 'em, that *schmuck,* wow, you got some taste in guys, that's all *I* can say. Give me those Rx's. I'll get 'em myself. Lazy cocksucker, I hope you grow warts on your nose with shame. I don't feel good. Do you understand—I AM SICK!"

"Well, I'm *sorry*," Gritch cried. "Christ, what happened down there? What's wrong, Carl?"

"So what's right for a change? Tell." He made a bridge of his joined fingers and knocked his forehead against them. "*Ach, scheiss!*"

GRADUALLY HE CALMED down. Had another ouzo. Was still furious but at least in control. Snapped his fingers: "Dry stockings!"

She brought fresh Supp-Hose, knelt and removed shoes, socks. Toweled the ugly vein splotched feet. "Ah—the suppliant maiden," he muttered.

"Cut the crap. You're shivering. Let me turn up the heat." She helped him off with the chesterfield, hung it, Borcalino, and muffler in the closet. "Why didn't you take your umbrella? You used to brag that every black mugger in town was deadly afraid of it. You get brave all of a sudden?"

"I carry fives and tens secreted about my person," Mast said sourly. "That's the only safe way to go about Manhattan these days. Pay 'em off as they accost you. They should be shot, every one of 'em. Animals. Breeding like flies. Loaded with sex and hatred. Bring the ouzo and a pitcher of water, no ice. Damn CBS to hell and back! They want me to get up on camera and be enter*tain*ing, con*trite,* a sniveling groveler."

Heading into the kitchen for the liqueur she said over her shoulder, "That's the goddamned business they're *in.* That's show business, baby! What the fuck else'd you expect?"

"I demand dignity!" he yelled.

"What dignity? A crazy old dying Nazi Kraut, so he should have dignity all of a sudden? Why?" She filled a pitcher, brought it and the ouzo.

"*Ach,* is there no sympathy here? Do I have to eke out my last days in a Yid house of hate? I didn't get up on that podium for nothing."

"It was *your* career, stupid."

"I didn't just want a little attention, a stinking medal, a pat on the back for the benign old dodderer on his last legs. Piss on 'em all! I wanted to catch the ear of the world. To warn. Too late."

"Too late? Ah, come on! You've been pulling the dying-swan routine on me ever since you finagled your way in here. All this 'research.' For my 'book.' I've listened to you for weeks, Carl, waiting for one positive statement. Instead: 'Everybody's an idiot.' What d'you expect from people? We're *human,* every fucking one of us! Even you."

"Nonetheless, they must be warned," the old man said angrily. "It's every man's responsibility. Heislinger's too."

"What're you saying? As a man of evil you think people will pay more attention to you than as a man of good?"

"Yes! Who gives a royal turd about Lorenzo de Medici, to whom Machiavelli dedicated *Il Principe?*" Mast demanded. "Lorenzo was a great and good man, but it's Machiavelli who's read today. When he was alive they called him an amoral cynic—there's that asinine word again!—the most wicked of men." He gave her that satanic look. "But they forgot his anguished despair of ever seeing *sensibilité* triumph, and his tragic sense of Evil. The truth, Gritchkin, is that the Devil has always been more interesting than God. Why? Empathy! God is too mysterious and wears his sanctity like a cashmere hair shirt, but the Devil is the man next door, because he's just like us. We *know* his every mood. As well we should!"

"You sure as shit can say that again."

SHORTLY AFTER SIX they left the apartment and headed east toward Broadway, walking slowly out of consideration for him. It was no night to be out. Snow blasted up the street from Riverside Drive and blew against their backs.

Mast held onto her arm and listened as she groused. "Damn it, I *said* I'd go. Why do you insist on having your own way?"

"I want to pick out that sphygmomanometer myself," Mast informed her. "Knowing you, you'd bring back an electric hair dryer or vibrator-schlong or some other piece of nonsense American females can't exist without."

"You ought to be in bed," she insisted. "You're killing yourself."

"It couldn't happen to a nicer guy," Mast replied. "I also want to make sure about the Rx's. Gerber—that moosenosed muffdiver—and his gang of rabbinical thugs may have scared the pharmacist. Druggists, you know, aren't supposed to be handing bucketfuls of morphia over the counter to any two-bit hooker with a fluoride smile. If he balks, I'll flash my passport. Some very important pills for a very important person. Who happens to be feeling lousy."

"All he has to do is look at you to see that," she said, gritting her teeth as flurries of snow tore at them. "You also happen to be bombed in case you don't know it." This was true. Mast had finished part of a bottle of ouzo and then, creatively, had switched to Calvados. She added, "Mordecai warned you. Sooner or later, you'll be recognized."

"Recognized? You driveling idiot, what in hell are you talking about?" Mast said testily. "By now I think half of New York knows where I am. We've got the kosher contingent squirreled away in some apartment down the street, enough gun-toting Talmudic scholars to start a fucking kibbutz! At CBS, some hotshot from the legal department, name of McCluskey—a real carrot-top mick smoothie—came right out and said he'd been in contact with a 'private resource' at the State Department about me, to make sure the network doesn't get its fingers burned. Who knows, probably he's been talking to the Department of Justice and the FBI too. Pretty soon on 101st, they'll be coming out of manhole covers or poking periscopes up through gutter gratings every time I stick my nose outside."

This alarmed her. Mordecai, when they had been alone earlier, had voiced a warning: "If the time comes when you need help and if you can't reach me personally, phone the Israeli Consulate. Ask for Specialized Services. Give them my name. They know who I am. With luck they may be able to move fast. I merely mention it."

Now Mast muttered, "Hell, I'm surprised the Guardian Angels haven't been called in to patrol this street and make sure I stay put." He gave a derisive snort. "A quasivirtuous group of self-appointed vigilantes, ostensibly dedicated to maintaining law and order. They gained notoriety in New York, you know, by patrolling subways,

280

making citizens' arrests, and whacking out muggers and other strong-arm types. The members wear berets and, in summer, T-shirts with the sleeves rolled up to show their Angelic biceps." Mast paused, puffing. "Another latent neo-Fascistic group, those Angels —they've never really worked their way through the anal-oral phase. 'If the law will not or cannot protect the honest citizen, *we* will provide that protection.' That remark, darling, in case you don't remember, was made by none other than Hermann Goering in '33, I believe, in reference to his braying brownshirted SA bully-boys. They too began as a sort of unofficial police force, a deterrent to lawlessness. In time the SA became the SS, whose activities you've heard me mention. Once the system breaks down, it breaks all the way."

They walked on, unaware of being followed by an overcoated and hatted stocky figure who had left the Israeli team's building seconds after they had come out of their own.

This was Abarbanel.

From still farther down the street a Yellow cab that had been parked in a loading zone pulled out and cruised after the three.

"MY WORD, TO look at him you'd think he owned the city!" Winfield Parkinson marveled from the back of the taxi. "He's got style, all right. Give him his due. A wanted man with a price on his head, but no different from any respectable citizen. White or not, you've got to respect courage."

"Why's he out on a night like this?" Max Guzman wondered.

Like the *Mossad* team, the Pan-American Liberation Society had mounted a 'round-the-clock vigil, although its members, operating out of necessity from the Yellow cab, had not nearly the comfort available to the former. Parkinson had thought the job so vital that he himself had spent a number of hours in the vehicle, and now at last his patience had been rewarded.

"He come right out of this old hotel down on Forty-fourth," Miguel Delapaz, a Santo Domingan member of the society, explained for the fifth or sixth time. "Get right in this fuckin' cab. An' I know him *al instante*! He look the same like in *los periódicos*."

"Compadre, we are eternally in your debt," Win said. "*Un hombre muy importante y también precioso. En verdad sin precio!*"

"*Pero tacaño!*" Miguel said, shaking his head and making a rubbing motion with thumb and forefinger. "Tip me two dimes."

Some minutes passed. "Look! They're going into that drugstore. Max, you and Miguel drive back to where we were parked. Wait for me. I'm going to check them out."

"I stay with you," Max Guzman objected. "This city ain't safe."

Win chuckled. "You worry too much."

"That's my business."

"An old *viejo* and a girl? They're going to hurt me?"

"For a man with brains you sure act stupid," Max said. "Haven't I always told you that? No thought for protection. That is what I know how to do. You never listen. You never have. Head in the clouds. *Estúpido!*"

"I appreciate your concern," Win said, smiling and patting Max on the knee.

"If something happens, don't come around complaining to me," the apricot-colored man said. "Because *this* person won't listen."

"That man fascinates me, Max. I want to be close to him for just a minute, bask in his radiance. Don't you see? He's one of the true White Beasts. He killed millions of his own kind. Just for the fun of it! *Sabe?* That little old man is Death!"

SO IT WAS that some twenty minutes later Mast and the girl found themselves standing in line at a main checkout counter. The drug purchases had been paid for separately at the pharmacy and now were contained in a large, brown paper sack that had been stapled shut.

Directly behind them: a tall and handsome black gentleman dressed in a vicuña overcoat and snap-brim fedora. There was nothing flashy about him except for the diamond-ornamented middle and ring fingers of his left hand, which held his solitary purchase, a large Mars bar. Win Parkinson intended eating that bar as he followed the two back to their apartment or wherever it was they might be headed.

Over by the magazine counter: a solitary idler of apparently Levantine extraction, who'd come in out of the storm and was casually flipping through an issue of *Rolling Stone*. The doughty Abarbanel; mustached, blue jowled, double chinned, the mild gaze absorbed by an article on Cindy Lauter.

Gerber was out too. At Kennedy International, awaiting the arrival of Colonel Armon from Tel Aviv, via Rome and Paris. The weather was at best marginal. It was hoped that the *Mossad* official's plane would not be routed to Boston.

Win waited politely in line, wondering what the two ahead of him could want with such a strange assortment of purchases. A bag of prescriptions. Two boxes of absorbent cotton. Four pressurized cans of air freshener, lavender, mint, pine-balsam, gardenia. And a narrow box with a label that read *Blood Pressure—the Silent Killer.*

The old man paid for the items with a hundred-dollar bill. He and

282

the girl left. To be followed, seconds later, by the tall powerfully built Negro who had already peeled the plastic wrapping from his Mars bar and was consuming it in small thoughtful bites.

THE STREET, SO silent and empty on such a stormy evening. As many side streets in Manhattan are. Parked cars, their hoods and roofs whitely mounded.

One Hundred and First, lit here and there, well enough but not all that well, by cast-iron streetlights whose small circular arenas of glare were half obscured by swirling billows of snow driven up off the Hudson and Riverside Drive.

Mast and Gritch trudged slowly, heads lowered, collars up. The squally blasts now met them face on, and arm in arm they headed into them, holding tightly to each other.

They were not far from the doorway of 417 when something, or someone, caught up with them, blocking their way, candy bar in hand.

"Good evening. Dreadful night, isn't it?"

The British accent, warmed as it were by the Caribbean sun, was flawless, distinctive. Faintly visible in the gloom, their accoster looked down at them. With a smile that was not a smile. The fine teeth whiter against that ebony skin than the driven snow that gusted beneath the streetlight's glare.

Mast peered up. "Out! Out of my way!" he said curtly. But of necessity, since his route was blocked, he stopped.

The dark specter took a long admiring look at Mast's companion. "My, you certainly are a lovely young lady!"

Gritch said in no uncertain terms, "Beat it! Leave us alone."

"I want to make your acquaintance," Winfield said, and, to Mast, "Yours too, sir."

"Call a cop, Gritch," the old man snapped. "Who needs this shit?"

"I merely want to know you. There's nothing to fear."

"My grandfather's sick," Gritch said waspishly. "Haul ass, mister. Or I'll let out a screech that'll break every window on this block."

"Don't try that, miss. That would be a mistake. Besides, he isn't your grandfather." Again that cold smile. "You wouldn't lie to me, would you?"

She looked up at him, horrified. "*Who are you?*"

"A friend."

Mast meanwhile was fumbling around in his pockets for a five- or ten-dollar bill. "A man can't walk the streets anymore. This is a civilized country?"

"A lot of people are looking for you," Win said.

283

Appalled, she stared at him. That this giant stranger should know. She whispered, "Who sent you?"

"Fate, miss. Destiny. Lady Luck. You name it."

"What," Carl Mast demanded, "is this oversized jungle bunny gibbering about?"

The tall man threw back his head and laughed. "I like that. I *love* it! God, you're good. Fearless. A rare quality. We are brothers, man."

"I'm an only child. *Raus mit dir.*" Mast turned to Gritch. "What's he want? Money? Fearless? What fearless? Fearlessness is for fools!"

"Get lost," Gritch said, desperately, automatically.

"We're going to talk," Win said, suddenly all business. "Your place is a few doors down. I must know how you figure in this, child. How come you take care of him?"

This speculation triggered a sudden inspiration. "My heavens! You're in the life! *That's* it. I feel it in my bones."

"Leave me alone. Fuck off, will you?"

Occasionally she'd been approached by black pimps who'd come on strong, crooning their line of sweet-talk jazz, the kidding around, half in fun but always half serious. She'd been able to handle it. But this. It wasn't that he came on big and threatening. He *knew.* Suddenly the possibility of violence and death seemed not far off. "Hey, *please?* We aren't bothering you."

"I'm with you now," Win said pleasantly. "You're both mine. You may as well understand that." He reached out with one hand and caressed her pale cold cheek. She wanted to run but couldn't. Stood as though rooted to the snowy sidewalk, trembling. Visions of switchblades and deadly straight razors filled her mind.

She thought: He's crazy! To just . . . it'll get worse.

"Now. The three of us are going to your apartment," he said firmly. "We'll talk. Then I'll decide what we'll do next."

OUT OF THE darkness and billowing snow a portly stroller materialized. Sy Abarbanel gently cleared his throat. He was nervous. His voice a tremolo compared to the black man's sonorous bass. "Mister, let them go. Okay? No trouble? I'm asking nicely."

Win turned and stared down, regarding the person who had interrupted him. "Are you talking to me?"

"You're creating a problem," Abarbanel labored on. "I happened to be passing by. If it's money, I have some. Not much, a little. How much? Yes, that'd be best. Let's be reasonable, can't we?"

Win listened to this brief speech at first with astonishment and then a mixture of alarm and growing anger. From the look and sound of him, the speaker was a New Yorker, and a Jew. So. Someone else was on the scene. Jews. Were they after ransom too? That had to be it. Nobody—no New Yorker in his senses anyway—would interfere with what appeared to be an ordinary mugging on an ill-lit and empty street. Winfield peered around. In the snow the visibility was bad, but there seemed to be no accomplices. Even as he did this Winfield knew he had to get the old man and the girl out of here. Throw them into the cab and move them to the Central Park apartment, where they'd be safe and where he'd have time to plan. Yes, move fast.

This decision took mere seconds; then, having decided, Win, frowning sullenly, grunted, "You, *israelito,* I don't need."

With that he reached out brusquely and took the stranger firmly by the shoulder of his overcoat, the clenching not rough but viselike enough. Winfield's hands were broad, black, massively structured, and now he said simply, "My man, you have made yourself a terrible mistake, troubling me and my friends here."

Abarbanel winced and bleated, "Ouch!" Then, rather astonishingly for a person of such unathletic appearance, he twisted free.

Though Gritch was watching closely she never saw how it actually happened. Somewhere, from a sleeve or the interior of his coat, a remarkable instrument materialized in the stranger's right hand.

The gadget, or device, was a two-foot-long, snakeskin-covered whip or blackjack. Reptilian scales shone along its limber length. Such a weapon had been a favorite item of defense, and offense, too, among Odessa gangster-Jews around the turn of this century, who, as usurers and racketeers, had been a formidable criminal element in that seaport. It was less a whip than a flexible club, lead weighted at the business end, something that was capable of smashing heavy planks or skulls. Perhaps—who knows?—a souvenir or remembrance from some venerable Ashkenazic granddad on the lower East Side, south of Houston, where Abarbanel had been birthed and raised, between Avenues C and D, ghetto home of nickel knishes, Tomaschevsky's Yiddish Theatre and balalaika lessons at two bits an hour.

With ballet grace the smaller man smartly rapped this Slavic cosh across the larger's face. The Afric nose, broad, the nostrils wide, disappeared with a crunch. The recipient of this traumatic insult sat down spraddle-legged in the snow, not out, but instead honking like an injured goose, fingers gently probing the spot where a nose had once been. Blood gushed, spattering the white snow blackly.

The gentleman who had materialized out of the storm turned to Gritch and Mast. He frowned, breathing huffily, and when he spoke it was in the voice of an irritated father.

"Didn't Gerber *tell* you to be careful? Now please go home!"

With that he walked away, muttering once, "They never listen."

WHEN HE HAD recovered enough to walk, Win—reeling, slipping in the snow—staggered down to where Max Guzman and Miguel of the Peace waited. They helped him into the back of the taxi. Guzman chattered nervously, an angry bird of prey, "I *told* you. *Madre de mio,* Jesus, they really . . ."

"Get me to a hospital," Parkinson blatted.

"Who did it?"

"I think it was a Jew," Win gasped. His nose was starting to hurt. He blinked back tears. "They know where the old man is!"

"A *judio* did that?"

"Cut-down baseball bat. Something," Win said. "I'll put my hands on that man. Last thing. Oh, shit."

"Don't worry, I'll get him for you," Maximillian Guzman promised as the taxi drove off.

A man of his word. A total pariah, both fearless and dangerous. "They don't know it yet but I've personally declared war. On all of 'em."

"FRANKLY, GERBER, YOU'RE a liability and an asset," Colonel Armon said. "As I think you'd be the first to admit."

He and his protégé, along with Abarbanel, were having a critique of the Heislinger situation as it stood to date.

Four days had passed since the old man and the girl had trudged down 101st. New Year's had come and gone. For three of those days the weather had been sunny and dry. Along Riverside Drive pigeons strutted and young mothers, happy to be able to get their children out of apartments at last, sat bundled on benches ringing the playgrounds. But now the temperature was dropping again as a fresh storm swept toward the city from the Great Lakes.

In the *Mossad* team's apartment everyone waited edgily as the hours slowly passed. On Armon's order, Heller, the electronics expert, had been sent over to 417 dressed in Ma Bell's uniform and equipped with appropriate ID. He'd been let into the basement by the super. There, in less than twenty minutes, a battery-powered minitransmitter had been wired into the Nadelmann line. Armon had finally decided that a tap was necessary, and he summarily dismissed Mordecai's arguments about the questionable value of this sort of eavesdropping. From then on, or for at least the life of the transmitter's batteries, the team would be able to monitor incoming and outgoing calls. The reels of the big Ampex deck were activated when the Nadelmann receiver was lifted off its cradle—otherwise they were motionless.

Unfortunately there were no calls of significance. Two from CBS. Heislinger himself had talked to a Mr. Dobkin, but he'd said only that he was sick and would be in touch. Three calls to Harvey's, asking that meals be delivered; other messages went out to local liquor stores, and an A&P, requesting additional foodstuffs, tobacco, sundries. The Nadelmann woman received several invitations to postholiday grad-school parties, and there was one contact, extremely brief, from someone who identified himself as Constantine. This person had barely spoken his name before being interrupted by Miss Nadelmann, who snapped out something about being extremely busy and that he wasn't to phone again.

Thus the person known as Constantine became an enigma to *Mossad*. Who was he? Taking the cautious view, Colonel Armon assumed that anyone involved, even via the girl, had to be on Heislinger's side. "Constantine" therefore became a top-priority suspect. Ultimately, however, he proved a dead end. He never telephoned again, nor did the Nadelmann woman phone him. He remained a mystery.

Most important, though, was the fact that neither Heislinger nor the girl left the building, nor, so far as the team could tell, did they have callers except for various delivery boys.

This sudden seclusion on the part of Heislinger and the girl troubled Armon. "They've pulled in their horns. That Negro scared them." It was as if the pair had made of their apartment a siege fortress. "Give them a day or two longer," Armon decided. "We can go in and get them anytime."

ON ARMON'S ORDER Mordecai telephoned every day to chat with Gritch. Two lame lovers.

Was everything all right?

Everything was all right.

Was there anything he could do? No.

Why couldn't he come over?

Mast had caught the flu or something, the old fool, running around in this weather. He wasn't at all well. She thanked Mordecai for his solicitousness. No, Mast wasn't in the slightest angry with him. The outburst had merely been a fit of temper. Old people, y'know. Difficult at best.

287

Who was the giant Negro who'd intercepted them? She had no idea. Here Mordecai heard concern and fear in her voice. He'd simply come out of nowhere. A big Caribbean type. His accent. The Bahamas maybe.

A mugger?

Too well dressed for that. Educated man. She'd been paralyzed. What had he wanted?

She couldn't say. He'd started talking. Senseless stuff.

Like what?

Oh, where did they live? What were they doing out on a night like that? Kind of a crazy. Not an addict. Definitely strange, though.

Did she realize he'd followed them from the drugstore? No! Really? But wait! Stupid Mast had cashed a hundred at the counter. Maybe the black had clocked that, was a mugger after all. Yes, she mused, that had to be it.

Mordecai knew she was lying but said nothing. With a sudden inspirational flash he was tempted to ask her flat out if the Negro's name might be Constantine, but did not. To mention that name would reveal that a tap was in operation. He bit his lip, trying to think of ways to probe further, keenly aware of the colonel's increasing suspicions. A black stranger. A mysterious caller named Constantine. Gerber's own role.

Of the customary messages young lovers cooingly exchange, there were few. Mordecai said he missed her terribly. She missed him too. Et cetera.

In the earpiece her voice sounded oddly preoccupied. As though she was off in a brown study. She was coming down with a cold too, she said. From the adnoidal drone of her voice, this was taken to be accurate reportage.

Would they see each other soon?

Yes, soon, she hoped.

Was anything wrong? Nothing was wrong.

Was she angry with him. No. Merely tired.

I miss you.

I miss you.

*Au revoir.* And take care.

*Au revoir.* I will, she said. Click.


"YOU CAN'T ALLOW yourself to become too involved with her."

"I understand."

"I've never liked these emotional entanglements. Necessary at times, I suppose."

"As Abarbanel himself said, things were at a standstill."

"Yes. Seducing her was the sensible thing to do."

"Thank you sir."

Colonel Armon stared at Mordecai. "Do you have a thing for her?" Gerber was silent. Then: "No sir. I wouldn't say that."

"I didn't expect you to," Armon said. "Couldn't blame you. She's a looker, Abarbanel tells me. A charmer, no doubt." He frowned. "We're relying on you."

"I'll do my best sir."

"I'm sure that's what you've been doing." Armon was still frowning. "Wish we knew more about her, that's all. You say you're positive she's not his mistress." The colonel paused. "I thought you were being naive at first, but now I agree. Heislinger's too old, too ill. But what else is there?"

Armon sat back, lit a cigarette, speculated. "Her record at school is impressive. Very highly thought of. The collateral informants indicate she's bright and dedicated. But then who in hell's this Constantine? Just that one call. Who was the Negro? Okay, so she's not Heislinger's whore. Why then does a young graduate student suddenly and for no sane reason take in a criminal half a dozen countries are searching for?"

He glanced from Gerber to Abarbanel. "Know what I think? What we could have here is anti-Semitism of the worst sort. When a Jew hates his own kind, he does it with a vengeance. Whatever the reason, such a hatred can become irrational, psychotic. I've seen examples. So. Let's imagine that this Griselda Nadelmann has some epic resentment against Jewry. Through circumstances, she encounters a man such as Heislinger. To a zany like her, he'd symbolize the hatred eating at her ... she might lay down her life to protect him. And, gentlemen, I must tell you that if this is the case, she's as dangerous as Heislinger."

"I think you're off track, sir," Gerber ventured.

"Understand, I'm not saying this *is* the case," Armon went on. "I merely offer it as a possibility. My point is this: she doesn't fit. Before we're done with her, she's going to have a lot of explaining to do. I'd give a month's pay to pry the whole story loose from her. Strap her down. A little sodium amobarbital. Pump her dry."

Gerber considered this. The room was warm. A faint sheen of sweat filmed his brow but his expression was imperturbable, the voice indifferent: "As you wish. But I think we'd be flogging a dead horse. My point is that she's not important. A minor witness, an unwitting accomplice perhaps." He shrugged. "Personally, I wouldn't take the trouble."

"There's something about this case that hits me wrong."

"You worry too much sir."

"Umn. They're paying you to screw her. And they pay me to worry," Armon said. "If he slips through our fingers again . . ."

Abarbanel interrupted. "We can always terminate him. Just say the word."

"You know I can't," the colonel said sourly. "It's in the Prime Minister's hands now. So? We wait. I understand that Switzerland has already asked for extradition. Germany and France will climb on the bandwagon, but it'll have to start with Switzerland. They've been damned cooperative."

"They've confirmed that Mast is Heislinger?" Abarbanel asked.

Armon nodded. "As of last week there were six Swiss citizens with the name Carl Mast. One died of a coronary as the search was going through the computers, so that leaves five. None with the middle initial W. None a physician. They're thorough. Birth and school records, addresses, occupations, all of it. The man living across the street is a figment, despite being one of their country's foremost citizens. They found nothing on him prior to July '44. The name turned up on the register of some inn or *Gasthaus*. Near Berne. Before that, nothing. Clever. To carry it off that well. Forty years."

"If we can keep him alive, what chance is there for a trial in Israel?" Abarbanel wanted to know.

"None, in my opinion," Armon said. "Which doesn't mean that we won't finish the assignment properly. The Swiss can slap him away for years on illegal entry and forgery, but I think they'll toss him to the Germans. Germany doesn't want him, but she'll take him—she'll have to. They could give him to us, but I don't think they will. If he goes to trial there, the case'll be a farce." The old colonel paused. "Naturally we won't permit that. He won't escape. Not if I have to go over to that apartment myself."

"That won't be necessary," Abarbanel said.

"Personally, I'd enjoy it," Armon replied. He sighed. "That man's capable of anything. I even worry if he's managed to create counterfeit symptoms that would fool all of us, including his doctors. Is that paranoia on my part? They say he's dying. But *is* he?"

"I know what you mean," Mordecai said. "You ought to see him. Drinks enough to put a man half his age under the table. Always a cigarette in one hand, booze in the other. A nonstop gabber. You heard the tapes. The mind, sharp. Quite astonishing."

"And you say you went there unarmed?"

"The situation didn't call for weapons."

"Not even a Matilda?" This was the standard-issue Israeli bulletproof vest, a soft flexible garment that would stop anything from a handarm.

290

"No sir. Sy and I agreed that talk was appropriate enough. Heislinger's nonviolent."

"In his time the violence he perpetrated was stupendous."

"Not now. He's too old and sick," Mordecai argued.

"Another of your assumptions?"

"Yes, now that you mention it."

"In future contacts, I want you armed," the colonel said irritably. "Just because some alluring slut arranges a couple of *Kafeeklatsches,* don't think Heislinger wouldn't love to see you dead. Take protection."

"Of course."

"Ninety percent of intelligence work is being prepared for contingencies," Armon said. "Look at Abarbanel here. He goes out the other night. A cut-and-dried field surveillance. They shop at a drugstore and on the way home get into trouble with some Negro... and I still want to know where *he* fits into this. The girl herself says he didn't act like a mugger. So what the hell's he doing out in a snowstorm, accosting her and Heislinger?" The colonel's frown deepened. "That bitch bothers me. Every time she turns around we pull a blank. Abarbanel, you're sure you didn't catch what they were talking about?"

"No," Abarbanel replied. "The colored guy was following them. After they turned off Broadway I maintained surveillance from the other side of the street. I was sure they were returning home. Then he moved in. It took me twenty or thirty seconds to get to them. That's when I disabled him."

"Good work," Armon said. And, to Gerber: "You see? The moment you think nothing'll happen, something does. You're not on vacation. And I'm still not convinced this girl is as innocent as you say she is."

Mordecai shrugged. "I haven't any reason to think otherwise, Colonel. And that's what'll be in my written report."

MAST WAS DYING.

She understood this, yet a part of her rejected it. The thought that he might be *that* ill didn't jibe with his abrasive personality. He seemed too permanent. He would endure, if necessary out of sheer stubbornness. "The Devil in Residence," she called him, with her usual medley of derision, dislike, frustration. He tested her patience—and sanity—to the limits. The Devil was Mast at his awful best, holding court, his speech mordant, his humor cruel, a glass of something within easy reach. At such moments the old demon gave the impression that he'd be around for another eighty years.

Seeing him monitor his blood pressure emphasized the reality of his illness. That evening, after returning from the drugstore, he'd sat at the kitchen table, right sleeve rolled high, the pressure cuff pumped tight, stethoscope plugged into his ears. The tube of mercury was slowly released. It began beating as the systolic came through, then the diastolic. "One hundred eighty over 110," Mast grumbled. "Higher than I'd like. But not rare in someone my age."

"What can you do about it?"

"Oh, I could take a vasodilator. There are several."

"*Please* see a doctor."

"I am a doctor. The high pressure isn't good but it could be worse. A sudden drop. You watch for that."

"What would that tell you?"

"To set my affairs in order," Mast replied. He did the pressure again. Seemed calm, though Gritch was not—she paced up and down beside the table. He saw how edgy she was. "Trouble sometimes comes looking for you, doesn't it? I've never cared for the Negro population of this country. Whining opportunists for the most part."

"I'm checking the deadbolts," she said. "If the buzzer rings out front, I'm not answering. No more chances. I'm getting a funny feeling. That black guy's got friends. Carl, I'm scared. Holy Toledo! Did you see the way the wimpy one laid him out? Then he just strolled off. Like it was nothing. It's getting worse. I knew it would. God! It's all your rotten fault. This woman's sticking close to home. We've got liquor, food, cigarettes. I'll teach you to play Scrabble."

"Isn't that something from your pusillanimous American South? Hog chitlings and fried mush? And what of Mordecai?"

"That's scrapple, idiot. And they make it in Pennsylvania. The hell with Mordecai."

"Excellent. For once you're thinking with your brain instead of your clitoris. Virility and trustworthiness are not interchangeable. When he calls, he'll ask about the *schwartze.* My suggestion, play dumb. Don't even say that that gorilla knew my identity. But who am I to tell you what to say? With that criminal mind of yours, I'm sure you'll concoct some fable that'll reek of verisimilitude."

LATER THAT EVENING he got drunk. The speech slurred, the alcohol-fumed mind wandering among curious cerebral backwaters that ranged from erudite to ribald. "Okay, college girl, you're so smart, tell me, how d'you get a one-armed Swede out of a tree?" She scowled at him and when he said, "Wave hello at him," the scowl deepened.

At one point—he'd just knocked over a glass of vodka—Mast suggested that the only way to get an accurate blood-pressure reading was via the penis. Would she perhaps be interested in wrapping the pressure cuff about that organ? She declined. "Pump it tight enough, it'll double as a splint," he argued. "In my case a real plus. Old One Eye needs a crutch these days."

"Why don't you go to bed?" she said wearily. "You're exhausted."

"Plutarch, y'know, wrote of the hippopotamus that will, as a matter of habit, kill his father and impregnate his mother," Mast continued, "which, of course, is what we mean when we refer to an Oedipal complex. But, after all, with the prices shrinks charge it wouldn't do at all for them to tell a patient he was suffering from a Hippopotamus complex, would it?" He poured more vodka. "Chinese apothecaries over a thousand years ago used to dry and then

294

grind the eggs of female frogs and dispense the stuff to middle-aged Chinese ladies with hot flashes. And it helped. Or else they merely ground up the entire frog. Know why? Fantastically high estrogen content. Wonderful. Kitchen-counter endocrinology! We think we learn something new, it turns out we haven't."

He rambled on. "What's right and what is wrong? At CBS I used a restroom. Ended up on one of those crip toilets. Damned uncomfortable—the right way to shit is with the anus as close to the ground as possible, otherwise a complete evacuation doesn't occur. Anyway, as I was sitting there, it occurred to me that for the price of that chrome-handled porcelain facility I could keep a whole village in East Africa alive for a year. Not fancy food, but nutritional. Vitamins, and best of all, inoculations. For the price of two of those dumb crappers I could save a thousand lives, Gritch. You know how *little* it takes to keep a human alive? Give me ten cents a day! I'll do it! One plays God."

"No one has a right to play God."

"Nonsense. Every politician does it, and loves it. It's the biggest game of all. Who will live, who'll die? Any doctor does it, every day of the week." He stared drunkenly at her. "You know what playing God is? Really? I'll tell you. Years ago at World Health I had a delightful Italian-American doctor working for me. His name was Olmi. A most decent and caring sort, who loved life and women and his work, a conscientious physician, admirable. He told me a story. It happened to him in 1945 when he was younger, just out of med school. It turned out that he was part of a team on the first relief freighter that went into Athens after hostilities ceased. The ship was mostly laden with powdered milk, and the team was in charge of distributing this lactate lifesaver to thousands of marasmus-stricken children, many of them also suffering from tuberculosis and other diseases. The distribution took place right at dockside, beside the freighter. Word flashed through the city. Thousands of children of all ages streamed toward the port docks to queue up. It was the task of my doctor friend Olmi to decide, then and there, which ones might survive and which were so far gone that the milk would be wasted: *'This one . . . this one, yes . . . no, not you, son . . . sorry, little girl.'* He told me that he had nightmares about it for years afterward. He was, you see, performing the same function as Auschwitz's Mengele, who waited on the unloading platforms. Each meted out life or death. Olmi, a reluctant God. Mengele, joyous in his power. That's the God game, Gritchken. You think a woman is 'justified' in aborting for Down's Syndrome? She's no different from Hitler, who ordered the deaths of thousands of mentally retarded.

'You live, you die.' Playing God is merely acting upon a decision. Understand, I'm for abortion. But call it what it is—you are simply disposing of the helpless when they are unwanted. *Ach!* I'm tired, Gritch." He was indeed nodding off. "So tired, you wouldn't believe."

She put him to bed, tucked him in as he muttered to himself, "In Benvenuto Cellini's Italy wrongdoers were punished by being inserted headfirst into full-length cylindrical holes dug in the ground. The hole then was tamped full of dirt until only their ankles and feet protruded. At the sides of roads it was a common sight to see hundreds of these pairs of upside-down feet. As though a whole population were living in some subterranean world. As if their feet had in effect broken through to our world. Maybe we're all living our lives in similar metaphysical holes, eh?"

THE NEXT MORNING he couldn't get out of bed. Finally, at eleven, she helped him to the bathroom, where he stayed a long time. He managed to emerge on his own, trailing a strong scent of gardenia, made it to the living room for a while, but then expressed a desire to lie down.

Again she had to help him.

The poisonous by-products manufactured by his own body in its futile struggle with the carcinoma were reaching a level of toxicity that would ultimately send him into delirium and coma; that is, if something else didn't go first, like the metastasis eating through until it reached a major artery. This would mean a mercifully quick end, or at least somewhat quicker than the disease usually offered its host.

The medications were no longer providing the succor they once had. When the pain hit, Mast endured it, his complexion yellow, his body sweat-drenched, until the attack passed. The face itself was emaciated, the sagging skin parchmentlike.

Gritch, wildly distraught, begged him to let her call an ambulance. He rejected this idea. The day passed slowly.

That night she slept on the couch. The next day it was the same. Mast dozed frequently. Short catnaps. When awake he was quite lucid.

By now the bedroom smelled strongly of air freshener. She sprayed frequently. But then, soon, the sickly sweet perfume would be tainted by something more pervasive. The same smell was in the bathroom, which he used less and less, and then only with her assistance to and from the bed. Between his buttocks he wore a thick wad of absorbent cotton. He was leaking pure blood. Now he stayed in bed to urinate, into a plastic salad bowl.

He showed her how to use the sphygmomanometer, and she sat there beside him with the stethoscope mounted to her ears, listening for the telltale systolic and diastolic beats. The mercury column's millibar readings went lower. His pressure didn't plunge so much as slowly descend.

On the third day it went still lower.

WHEN THERE WAS no pain he asked for ouzo, cigarettes, and megavitamins. During such times he often talked, lying there in bed, his head propped on pillows. When his hand was too shaky, she held the glass he sipped from.

He dictated and then signed the one-time-entry letter to the bank, using the Breitmeister name. "What I want you to do, when this is over, is rent another box immediately. There are several banks nearby. Don't attempt to bring the box's contents home with you. Poor bitch, I hope the money does you some good. You may need it for lawyers."

"The money's the last of my worries," she said, tight-lipped, dark circles under her eyes.

"Do I detect concern in your voice? For *me?* How touching. But how unlike you. Hand me a Kleenex, I think I may shed a tear."

"You son of a bitch."

"Ah. You're upset. To see me like this. Take heart, my dear. Just think, you're earning wages honestly for a change. Or at least vertically. Later, you'll thank me. You'll be able to finish your education. I like that. I have a hunch about you. I had it the first night we spent together. In this *Glasperlenspiele* we call life there are only two kinds of players: winners and losers. You're a winner." He smiled. "It's never been my custom to hang out with losers. What else should I do with the money? Leave it to some foundation? Nonsense. Charity begins at home."

"CBS called again."

"Was I asleep?"

"Yes. Should I tell them anything?"

"Tell 'em I just signed a two-year contract with the Dallas Cowboys. Wide receiver. Better, bring the phone in here. I'll tell them myself."

"I talked with that Dobkin. He said there's a very good chance they'll do a special your way."

"Too late. Cigarette!" He tried his infuriating forefinger-and-thumb snap but the result was scarcely audible. She lit a Gauloise, puffed at it, and then passed it over.

Mast drew at it; then, suddenly, the pain came. "Oh Jesus," he gasped. "The pills. Quick."

She ran for them. He took two. Gradually the attack passed. She wiped his face with a wet washcloth. "A little wine," he said crankily. "No damned ice. Why do you put so much *ice* in it?"

She got him a drink and when he could talk more easily he said, "What a waste of my time, that Oslo business. Hope is just a carrot God dangles in front of a man's nose. So where do I end up? Me, a prizewinner. Bending the ear of a know-nothing New York Jewess. Damn them."

"Who?"

"The Committee. Three times my name was submitted."

"You'd have done the same if you'd gotten the Prize earlier?"

"Why not? I would've been able to fight 'em longer. How much did I have to lose? Yes, I wanted to show the way. A man of good intention, I thought of myself. And that is a dangerous self-deception." He sighed.

"You know the only real prophet of this century? Hitler. Yes. *Heute Europa, morgen das Welt.* Today Europe, tomorrow the world. He was right.

"The Holocaust is said to be the greatest crime ever executed on innocent people, but it was merely a warm-up, a game of tiddley-winks. Now we can do it to everyone.

"I was at Dachau and the ravine at Babi Yar! All of us who were alive at that time and who are alive today were there. If guilt is what you demand, we're all guilty. You don't expunge mass culpability any more than you can expunge individual guilt or stupidity. If God existed. He'd shake his finger at us and say, 'So, didn't I tell you?'"

"What about me?" she said, close to tears. "Why did you come to me? Surely you could have gone elsewhere. Did you have to ruin my life?"

"You once accused me of capriciousness," the old man said. "Could I have gone elsewhere? Maybe. Yes, perhaps it was a caprice. Maybe what I need most before I die is the forgiveness of one Jew. Is that possible, Gritch? Is it conceivable that one miserable little Jewess out of millions can find it in her heart to forgive? Would that hurt so much? *That* would help persuade me that decency, love, still exist somewhere in this dark twilight of the human soul. How about it. Can you forgive me? Just a bit?"

"No," she said as tears came. But whether they were for herself or for him she couldn't tell.

298

MORDECAI WAS UNEASY. His position, he knew, was insecure.

*Mossad,* though only a minor function of his government, was no different from the government itself, no different from any government anywhere. Allegiance, loyalty, were mandatory. He who straddled a middle line was suspect.

And the individual who for whatever reason put his own interests before those of the State was in danger. Mordecai knew this. His problem was simple:

He believed in Israel with all his heart. All that is, except the part that wanted Gritch.

Did he love her? But love is such an abstract word. Well, perhaps he did. A little. To a degree. But exactly how much is a degree? There are small degrees and large degrees.

Perhaps possessiveness is a better word. He wanted *her.* On his terms, not *Mossad*'s. Conceivably, if he'd asked Colonel Armon diplomatically, the old intelligence chief might have given Gritch to him, as a plaything, a freebie, a reward for Mordecai's good work, but he didn't want this.

To have her as he wished, freedom of choice was necessary. She must come to him voluntarily, as a woman should always come to a man. Anything less would not be a true validation of his worthiness. Mordecai was young. And handsome. Many women had told him this. *They* had given themselves. So why not this one too?

He asked himself why must such a state of mind afflict him now. There seemed to be no answer. A fatalist might say that the time had simply come for Mordecai to experience something like "love." But a more seasoned observer of the human condition might have gotten closer to the truth by noting that Mordecai was not, despite the glacial calm and ruthlessness he brought to an assignment, an unfeeling automaton, an unthinking extension of his government. He was in many respects a quite decent young man, in a profession that scorned all virtues. He might love Israel but he also cherished himself.

Further, he'd gone out on a limb for the girl. Lied to protect her. Or at least stretched his interpretation of the truth. He'd said on that afternoon they'd become lovers, "Israel owes me. I've given her a lot." And now Gritch owed him. Through his intercession she'd end up an insignificant player in this Heislinger business, which was as it should be. Afterward, when everything had calmed down, there would be the two of them.

Strange visions and fantasies troubled him, of a future that, conceivably, he and she might share together. Why not? All men occasionally indulge in such visions. Madness? Most certainly.

Common sense is not always the first order of the day in men's dealings with women.

MAST DIED LATE in the afternoon of the fifth day after he and Gritch had made of the apartment a barricaded sanctuary.

She had never seen anyone die. Her father, Steve, had passed away immediately, in the office shack at the Passaic landfill, of a coronary. Mast's death tore her apart.

She didn't think it could happen so quickly. Mast faded in and out. Was in a coma for a while, then came to, awake and in possession of his senses. He drank a little water, with her supporting his head as he sipped.

"Get the bowl," he whispered, "I'm pissing in your bed." She got it, and saw that the flow was now bright pink. "Christ, funny things are happening inside me," he said, trying to grin at her. "My stomach. Feels like a clothes dryer, with everything tumbling inside a drum. Get the Percodan!"

Astonishingly, he began reciting something from Yom Kippur—the *Unetane Tokef.* ". . . and on the Day of Atonement the decree is sealed, how many shall pass away and how many shall be born; who shall live and who shall die, who at the measure of his days and who before it; who shall perish by fire and who by water; who by the sword and who by wild beasts . . ."

As cancer patients go, he died easily, sinking into longer periods of delirium as his nitrogen-poisoned blood failed. "Hold me. Please? Just a little?"

She did. She could feel the ancient heart pounding frantically as it fought to keep the dying body alive, the lungs wheezing like tired bellows, forcing air in and out.

FOR A WHILE toward the end he came out of his stupor, was alert and apparently in no pain at all. Not everything he said made sense to her. "It's all part of a vast mosaic. The Warsaw Ghetto and this city's South Bronx—everything's connected.

"Not all my work has been accomplished in far-off steaming jungles—that's the picturesque part. Population control's always been my real racket, and I'm not making a joke about extermination camps. I've warned 'em, even in this country. Statistics, endless statistics, but they tell the story. The United States is bankrupt. Half the people alive here today weren't born until after World War II. Much of the remaining half is of retirement age. So you have a nation of kids and geriatrics, with an ever-narrowing middle-class segment that supports them. Social security, Medicare—what a

300

laugh! You're going to end up with a country full of day-care centers and old-age homes. Where does it stop? If you practically erase the infant mortality rate and then find ways to keep everyone alive into their nineties, what the hell are you left with? Who's to pay? We *need* death!"

Again he began reciting something from Yom Kippur. The Confessional: "*We have trespassed. We have robbed, slandered, acted perversely.* Can you say the words, Gritchkela? Can you follow?"

"I don't know them."

"*We have been wicked, presumptuous, violent, deceitful. We have counseled evil and spoken falsely* . . . Say them, Gritch."

"I'm not even a good Jew."

"So? What else is new? I'm no Jew at all."

"I can't!"

"Let me hear you. *We have been stiff of neck, we have acted wickedly, we have committed abominations* . . . *we have erred and have caused others to err* . . . I can't *hear* you, Gritch."

"Don't ask me to do this," she cried.

On and on it went, the endless heaping of self-abuse upon the head of the confessee, a *selihoth* from a dying man.

Mast's whispers were sibilant and faint now. "I tried to become a Jew once. In Geneva. Years ago. Studied for it. Met with a friendly rabbi. Hellman, his name. Then I was finally summoned. To the Beth Din, the high court. There I was most sternly warned that as a Jew I would have to conform to no less than 613 commandments. I told them, if that's what it meant to be a Chosen One, no thanks. Gritch? Are you crying? Why are you crying?"

"I don't know," she said, holding him in her arms.

He tried to raise an arm to put it about her shoulders but was far too weak. Managed instead to find one of her hands. Feebly patted it:

"There . . . there now. You mustn't weep, you know. It's all right. Yes."

SHE WAS SITTING in the living room on the couch, half in the dark. The worklight over the ventilator hood of the kitchen range was all that was on.

Smoking a cigarette. Sipping at a glass of wine. The phone rang.

She let it go off six times and then switched on a nearby lamp, reached over and lifted the receiver.

It was Mordecai, wanting to know if everything was all right.

"All right? What do you mean?"

"What are you doing?"

"I'm just sitting here alone. Having a drink."

"Alone? Where's Heislinger?"

"Mordecai—"

"You sure you're all right?"

"Yes. I'll be all right."

"You sound strange. I better come over."

"Not now, darling."

"I won't stay long."

"I listened to something from Yom Kippur," she said in a girlishly high voice that was close to the edge of hysteria. "I didn't know it would bother me that much. When I was little, we never went to temple."

"I'm coming over."

"Please—" she started to explain.

He'd hung up.

SOMETHING'S WRONG," HE said frowning. He went to the closet, got his overcoat. "I don't like the way she sounded."

"I'd better come with you," Abarbanel said.

"She's upset. I can tell that much. I can handle her."

"Better take a transmitter."

"No. I shouldn't be there more than a few minutes. I want to check the scene. If I have to be any longer, I'll phone." He put on his homburg.

Abarbanel, who had listened to the brief interchange between Mordecai and Gritch via the Ampex's earphones, said, "Hey, take it easy. So she's upset." He frowned, noting the other's unease. "Stay cool."

"Sy, you don't understand. Something's gone all wrong. I can feel it." Gerber said as he went out.

SHE LET THE bell ring for almost a minute. Then finally got up and pressed the buzzer that opened the vestibule door.

In the peephole she saw him striding down the corridor. She released the deadbolts and lifted the security chain to let him in.

"What's the matter?" he said, staring down at her.

"Must look awful, don't I?" she said, raking fingers through her mop of hair. And then, distractedly: "Oh, Mordecai. I'm so tired. Listen, darling, there's something I have to tell you."

Wary, almost felinelike, he looked around, sniffing the air, frowning. "What's that smell?"

"I had to do something about it," she said, in that little girl's voice. "It was starting to make me sick."

"Where is he?"

"Carl?"

302

"Heislinger."
"He went a little while ago."

SUDDENLY HE PUT IT together. Gave her a look of astonishment and horror. "You helped him escape."
"No, that's not true."
"I trusted you!"
"Mordecai, for God's sake, he's—"
Then, from out in the backyard, there was a crash, as of something being knocked over, a can or a flowerpot, and a cat's low yowl. These sounds were quite audible through the open bedroom door, and indicative to Mordecai that the back door to the garden patio was wide open to the night air.

HE MOVED BACK a pace from her, frowning. As though seeing her for what she truly was, for the first time. While she, wild-eyed, anguished, wringing her hands with grief, tried to speak to him. Tears brimmed at the corners of her eyes, as she stammered miserably, "Oh, Mordecai, darling—"
Then, suddenly, she saw his features relax as composure returned.
He was staring over her left shoulder, toward the open bedroom door behind her. His head tilted back just a little.
He smiled, immensely relieved, and then said conversationally:
"Ah . . . Doctor Mast! It's you."

"WHA'?" SHE STARTED to say, whirling, horrified, to glance over her shoulder at an empty doorway, and before she had finished the movement Mordecai, with casual grace, withdrew the Colt .22 Woodsman from inside his jacket and shot her once neatly behind the left ear where the neck met the skull, the so-called medulla oblongata shot. The pistol was a standard CIA-type model, six-inch barrel, with a sleeved silencer that fit over the length of the barrel, a very sensible weapon for indoor use, one that made only a soft *chug* when .22 hollowpoint longs were used.
With a gasp Gritch collapsed to the floor, on hands and knees, dying, entirely unaware of what had happened to her.
She crouched there like that for a moment, supporting herself on stiff-stretched arms, head hanging between her shoulders, the head itself moving back and forth in spastic jerks, as though she were trying to clear a ringing in her ears. Blood began trickling from her nostrils, dripping to the rug, droplets spraying this way and that as she shook her head.
Mordecai calmly and efficiently shot her through the back of the

303

head seven more times, emptying the magazine. By the third shot she was dead.

When he was done he ejected the magazine, reached into a pocket for a fresh clip, inserted it, jacked a round into the chamber. A sweet-pungent smell of smokeless powder hung in the air along with the other, stranger scent.

With the toe of one shoe he flipped Gritch over. One green eye was gone. Another slug had exited through the mouth taking with it an upper incisor and a piece of lower lip.

HOLDING THE WOODSMAN at combat ready he moved into the bedroom and switched on the overhead light. He had heard correctly. The back door to the patio was wide open, as were the windows, letting in frigid air, and a considerable bit of snow, too, the curtains flapping.

But the iron-grilled security gate was still chained and padlocked, and in the spill of bright light that flooded out into the yard there were no footprints at all except those of a cat. Even with the fresh air the odor was stronger in here. Then he saw the shape in the bed, the quilted coverlet pulled up over the head.

Stupified he went over, drew the coverlet down. Stared for a long moment at the dead man. Presently he drew the coverlet up again.

He went back into the living room, functioning more or less automatically now. Knelt for a minute beside the body of the girl, but did not touch it. The shattered head lay in a widening pool of blood.

Then he noticed his hands. They were shaking, moving this way and that in small sudden jerks. It got worse, and then his whole body was doing it, trembling and twitching uncontrollably. Some time passed this way as he fought to regain control. After a while the shaking lessened, and it was then that he heard the telephone ringing. The jarring sound seemed to come from a long way off.

At the other end was Sy: "Is everything all right?"

"Yes. It's over."

"What?"

"He's dead. It's all over. Listen, I'm going for a walk. I need to be alone." Before the team chief could respond, Mordecai hung up.

Distracted, incapable of really thinking, he wandered about the living room, not looking at the figure on the floor. Paused almost absentmindedly at the Magnavox for several minutes, trying various of the cassettes for a few seconds each, to see what was on them. Carl Mast's voice filled the room: fragmented observations on the Nazi era, a commentary on totalitarianism, interspersed with

304

occasional remarks from Gritch. The reproduction was excellent. Both of them seemed actually present. Fast Forward. Pause. Play. One cassette after another.

And then, how odd. Mast singing something. In Yiddish. He had a terrible voice. Hadn't the faintest idea how to carry a tune.

"... that's the spirit, Gritch, You're getting the idea now! *Der tate shrayt vi a meshiginer Yid! IN IKH ZING ZIHK YANKELE'S LID!*"

Strange. What did it signify? That such a man would know a Yiddish song. Frowning, Mordecai hit the reverse. Replayed a few seconds.

It meant nothing. He turned the machine off.

In the kitchen he found a paper bag and put the pistol into it after wiping it clean with a towel.

Carefully, methodically, he switched off the lights in the apartment and left, closing the door silently behind him, as though not wishing to disturb those he was leaving.

Down the corridor and out the vestibule door. At the curb were three refuse cans. He dropped the paper sack into the nearest one and replaced the lid. Then the trembling began again. This time he gave in to it, abandoned himself entirely to the strangest emotion of all: grief.

THE SNOW WAS very heavy now, white billowing swirls, sticking to the cars parked along the deserted street, except for one, a taxi, whose driver, from time to time, cleared the windshield by turning on the wipers.

*. . . who by earthquake and who by plague; who by strangling and who by stoning; who shall have rest and who shall be restless—*

As the man wandered past the cab those inside could hear him sobbing and singing to himself, in Yiddish or some other language, it wasn't easy to tell because of the howling of the wind.

Who but a madman or a Jew would be out on a dreadful night like this?

*. . . who shall be tranquil and who troubled—*

Hatless, half-blinded by the stinging snow. Unbuttoned overcoat flapping wildly. No gloves. Crooning some crazy lament or tune. Wringing his hands, then raising them, fists clenched overhead, as though to strike at the sky, and then, from time to time, beating his breast, as though consumed by anguish or passion or despair, who could tell?

*. . . who at ease and who afflicted; who shall become poor and who shall wax rich—*

This strange apparition wandered westward, a lost soul, toward Riverside Drive, surely a desolate and uninhabited wasteland on such a storm-blasted wintry night. In some places the snow had already drifted shin deep.

307

*. . . who shall be humbled and who exalted—but Prayer, Atonement, and Charity will avert the Evil Decree.*

"THERE GOES ONE of them," Guzman said to his driver and companion, Miguel of the Peace.

"How do you know that?"

"He just came out of 417. He's a Jew. Didn't you hear him carrying on?" The apricot-colored man was speaking softly, almost twittering with excitement. He had cranked down the rear window on his side and was peering in the direction the hatless figure had taken . . . that strange person had walked right past the parked cab. "Come on."

*"Amigo, pero no es absolutamente."*

"*Creo,* I bet he's the one crippled Winnie. I'm going to talk to him."

"Guzman, you are *loco.* You don't even know who that man *is,*" Miguel argued. "What you mean, talk? You got a *cuchillo?* You want to cut him?"

"Talk to him good with my hands."

Delapaz frowned. *"Loco."*

"You coming?"

*"Gracias, no."*

"Winfield won't like that. He don't like a *maricón*-coward, that's for sure." Delapaz sighed unhappily. Guzman said, "I'm going. Come on."

The two got out of the cab and began walking toward Riverside. Presently, some distance ahead of them, they spotted the apparition they were following. Once it fell, then got up, moved on, in the direction of Grant's Tomb.

Twice the lights of a passing car lit up the Drive but it was no night for traffic. By dawn snowplows would be out, but now chains were needed. Here and there in the windows of the tall old-fashioned apartment buildings that faced on the Hudson, seen only dimly in the heavy snow, were Christmas wreaths, framed brightly by colored lights. From somewhere far out on the river, hidden in the mists, came the forlorn wail of a vessel's foghorn, an invisible traveler in the night, whether inbound or outbound, no way to tell. It was cold and miserable. The two quickened their pace, their footsteps silent.

They were less than a dozen paces away, and still the apparition moved on, a snow-*golem,* crooning brokenly and pausing now and again to make vague despairing gestures, head bowed, then flung heavenward, to mutter something unintelligible, and then the lament or melody would recommence.

308

"He going to walk all the way to Yonkers?" the taxi driver complained softly. "What you going to do, Guzman? Kill him?"

"Wait'll we get out of range of this streetlight."

Ahead, the wide ghostly pale granite steps of Grant's Tomb loomed out of the storm. The final resting place of America's Gaius Marius, renowned as a soldier but a disaster as a politician. This imposing edifice, built to last for centuries, had very nearly collapsed a few decades earlier. The architect had neglected to stipulate that wire screening be installed in the roof's louvers, with the result that, for half a century, generations of pigeons had deposited an accumulation of droppings on the floor of the upper ceiling, a veritable guano bonanza, which in places had reached a depth of over seven feet.

"Listen to the noise he makes," the taxi driver whispered, marveling at the sounds coming from the person up ahead. "Do all Jews carry on like that? Tearing his hair. *Pocito loco*, for sure."

"*Loco*, like you say," Guzman replied softly. He quickened his stride. "Ain't none of 'em happy unless they feel like they got the whole world's problems riding on their backs. That's the truth, man."